HONEYCOMB

ALSO BY JOANNE HARRIS

The Chocolat Series
Chocolat
The Girl with No Shadow
Peaches for Father Francis
The Strawberry Thief

Blackberry Wine
Five Quarters of the Orange
Coastliners
Holy Fools
Gentlemen & Players
Jigs & Reels
Different Class
Blueeyedboy
A Cat, A Hat, and a Piece of String
A Pocketful of Crows
The Blue Salt Road
Orfeia

Cookery Books
The Little Book of Chocolat
The French Market
The French Kitchen

Writing as Joanne M. Harris
The Gospel of Loki
The Testament of Loki
Runemarks
Runelight

JOANNE M.
HARRIS

HONEYCOMB

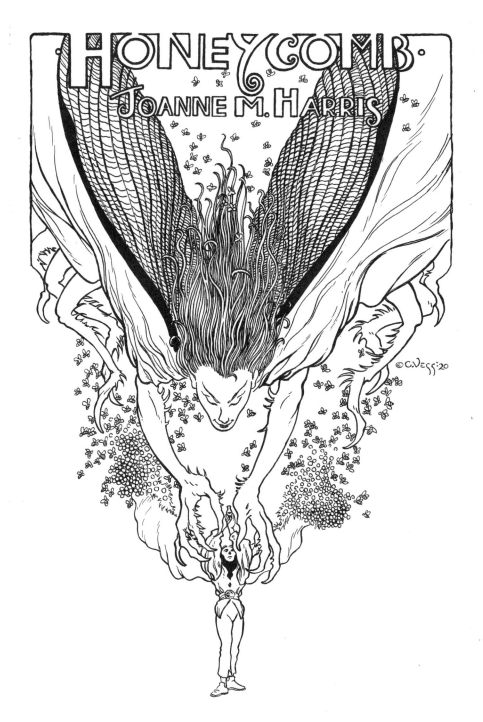

ILLUSTRATED BY CHARLES VESS

First published in Great Britain in 2021 by Gollancz
an imprint of The Orion Publishing Group Ltd
Carmelite House, 50 Victoria Embankment
London EC4Y 0DZ

An Hachette UK Company

1 3 5 7 9 10 8 6 4 2

A CIP catalogue record for this book is
available from the British Library.

ISBN (Hardback) 978 1 473 21399 9
ISBN (Export Trade Paperback) 978 1 473 21400 2
ISBN (eBook) 978 1 473 21402 6

Typeset by Born Group
Printed in Italy by Elcograph S.p.A

MIX
Paper from
responsible sources
FSC
www.fsc.org
FSC® C115118

www.joanne-harris.co.uk
www.gollancz.co.uk

To all the little bluebirds . . .

Book One
Long Ago

There is a story the bees used to tell,
which makes it hard to disbelieve.

TABLE OF CONTENTS: BOOK ONE

1	Nectar	5
2	The Midwife	8
3	The Lacewing King	12
4	The Lacewing King and the Spider Queen	16
5	The Teacher	25
6	The Moth Mother	28
7	The Parrots and the Nightingale	32
8	The Lacewing King and the Harlequin	35
9	The Puppeteer	42
10	The Craftsman	45
11	The Wolves and the Dogs	48
12	The Girl Who Loved the Silken Folk	50
13	The Lacewing King and the Silkworm Princess	57
14	The Traveller	62
15	Clockwork	64
16	The Bookworm Princess	67
17	The Troublesome Piglet	71
18	The Wasp Prince	74
19	Death and the Artist	80
20	Revenge of the Spider Queen	84
21	The Clockwork Princess	89
22	The Watcher and the Glass	95
23	The Courtship of the Lacewing King	98

24 The Bull and the Snail 103
25 The Cat Who Was King 105
26 The Return of the Wasp Prince 107
27 The Old Woman and the Rocking-Horse 116
28 The Poor King 120
29 The Blue Sash 123
30 The Honeycomb Child 127
31 Penance of the Lacewing King 136
32 The Barefoot Princess 144
33 The Sand Rider Who Dreamed of the Ocean 147
34 The Persuasive Parrot 151
35 Five Princes In Search of Their Heart's Desire 154
36 Travels of the Lacewing King 157
37 The Silent Songbird 162
38 The Singing Frog 165
39 The Gardener 168
40 The Arrogant Baker 171
41 The Moon Queen of the Undersea
and the Moon King of the Sky 173
42 The Barefoot Princess and the Spider Queen 177
43 The Return of the King 182
44 The Peacock 186
45 The Girl Who Never Smiled 189
46 The Cockroach Queen 191
47 The Spider Queen Sails West 196
48 Truth or Dare? 200
49 The Queen Below the Water 204
50 Trial of the Lacewing King 212

1

NECTAR

When the Nine Worlds were still very young, there were no stories. There was only Dream, the river that runs through all the Worlds, reflecting the hearts and desires of the Folk on its journey towards Pandaemonium.

But by the side of that river, there grew a flower with no name. It grew only there, on the shore of Dream, between the dusty plains of Death and the dark cliffs of Damnation. Its petals were pale as young love; its leaves were like the starry sky; its roots were drenched with the dreams of the Folk; and its scent was like honey and heartbreak.

But no one saw the dreamflower, or caught its scent on the rapturous air. No living creature had ever seen the colour of its petals or touched even one of its shining leaves. Until, one day, a swarm of bees found its way into World Below. They settled on the flower and fed; took nectar from its scented heart. And when at last they returned to their hive, they made honey from the nectar, and fed it to their young Queen as she grew in her cradle of honeycomb.

The honey was dark, and scented, and sweet. The Queen, in her golden citadel, fed well on the nectar of dreams. And she grew in wisdom and beauty until at last, she became the Honeycomb

Queen, the very first of the Silken Folk, whom some call the Faërie, and some the First, and some the Keepers of Stories.

Through this cross-pollination, the Queen was born into the Aspect of the people from whose dreams she had sprung. She could pass between their Worlds. She could see into their hearts. She could use what she saw to spin glamours of the most marvellous kind; glamours that built worlds in the air; that opened every secret door; every chamber of the heart. And these were the very first stories.

But, from across the river Dream, the Hallowe'en Queen, half-woman, half-corpse, ruler of the kingdom of Death, was watching the Honeycomb Queen from afar. From her dead eye she could see into the darkest dreams of the Folk; from her living eye, she could see everything in the Nine Worlds. The touch of her living hand was a gift that no man had ever known; the touch of her withered hand brought Death. Her kingdom was desert on every side. Nothing grew; nothing changed; and the only stories she ever heard were those that ended in death for everyone concerned. And as time passed, she grew jealous of the Honeycomb Queen and her stories; and she began to make plans to steal the lovely dreamflower for herself.

And so she crossed the river one night, and went in search of the dreamflower. For a time she stood watching it, breathing in its rapturous scent. Nothing was scented in her realm; nothing was soft or beautiful. A terrible loneliness welled up in her heart, and a single tear trickled down the living side of her ruined face. She stretched out a hand to pick the bloom—but in her haste, the Queen forgot to use her living hand, and touched the beautiful dreamflower with her dead and withered fingers.

At once, the dreamflower wilted and died. Its like has never been seen again. But its nectar remained with the Honeycomb Queen, and with the good, industrious bees, passing from flower to flower; taking pollen back to the hive; and telling their tales wherever they went—for they, too, had fed from the nectar, and they were part of the river, now; the River than runs through Nine Worlds, taking with it the dreams of the Folk and spinning them into stories.

Some of those tales have stings attached. But then, of course, that's bees for you.

2

THE MIDWIFE

Once, there was a midwife, renowned for her skill. One winter's night, a man came knocking on her door to ask her to deliver a breech-birth child. It was late; it was dark; there was the scent of a storm on the way, but the man—who was a foreigner—promised the midwife rich rewards if she could save his wife and child.

And so the midwife went with him, riding in his pony-trap to a village she did not recognize, and to a cottage, poor but clean, in which a woman in labour lay, fevered and delirious. The midwife ordered the man to leave. He seemed reluctant to do so. When the midwife insisted, he said:

"I'll leave on one condition. When the baby is born, dab this medicine into his eyes. It's a remedy our people use whenever a child comes into the world." And he handed the midwife a tiny vial, no bigger than the ball of her thumb, filled with something that looked to her like honey, dark and clear and just out of the comb.

"But whatever you do," said the man, "do not allow the medicine anywhere near your own eyes. Although it is harmless to our kind, it would be dangerous to you."

The midwife agreed, and delivered the child—a healthy boy—without difficulty. She took the vial of medicine and anointed his eyes with her fingertip, as the father had instructed, before turning her attention to the mother. The mother's condition was serious, and it took all of the midwife's skill to save her life. And when she had finished, the midwife wiped the damp hair from her eyes, and a tiny smear of the medicine with which she had anointed the child went into her left eye, making it sting and water.

For a moment the midwife was afraid that the medicine had made her blind. But as the mist cleared from her eye, she found that, far from having lost her sight, she could see all kinds of new things. Closing her unaffected eye, she looked around at the cottage and the woman whose baby she had birthed.

But it was no longer a cottage. Instead she found herself standing in a fine bedchamber, with marble pillars and mosaic floors and a four-poster bed, all hung in white silk, in which lay the most beautiful woman she'd ever seen; a woman with lidless, honey-dark eyes. The baby, too, looked different; it was plump and golden-skinned, with its mother's troubling eyes.

Some instinct made the midwife hide her new-found vision. She simply swaddled the baby, put him back into his crib (which her left eye now saw as a silver swan all draped in moon-blue muslin), then went to fetch the baby's father, who was waiting outside the door.

Here, too, the midwife had to hide her surprise at what she saw. Instead of the humble living-room which she had seen some hours before, she now saw, with her left eye, a hall, with a double staircase and a floor of chequered marble. The small stove at the back of the room had become an enormous fireplace, upon which roasted a whole ox, turned by a couple of turnspits. A pair of armoured guards stood by, all in black, and gleaming; and the stranger who had come for her help was sitting there on a gilded throne, a golden band around his hair—hair the shade of a moth's wing. For a moment he looked at her. One eye was a curious butterfly-blue; the other, as dark as honeycomb.

Then he said with impatience: "*Well?*"

The midwife kept her face very still. She knew that if the stranger guessed that she had disobeyed his orders, she would never leave that place, or see her village, ever again. For the midwife had realized that she was among the Silken Folk; weavers of glamours, spinners of tales, most dangerous of the Faërie.

"Mother and child are well," she said. "Now remember, you promised to pay me."

He nodded and gave her a handful of coins. From her right eye they looked like gold, but with her new-found vision she saw nothing but a handful of golden autumn leaves. The midwife said nothing, however. She put the leaves in her pocket, and silently she followed the man outside to a courtyard in which a silver coach awaited, drawn by four grey horses. (This was what the midwife had seen as a pony and trap only hours before.) She climbed aboard without a word, ignoring the marvels around her, and the stranger drove her home through forests and fields until they reached her village and her little house, just as the sun was rising.

It was over. Or so she thought. But in the weeks that followed, the midwife found herself unable to forget the strange things she had seen that night. The crowned man and the beautiful woman; the newborn child in the silver crib. The palace that had seemed to her just like an ordinary cottage beneath its veil of glamours. And now, with her new-found vision, she could see all kinds of things that no one—no one *human*—could see: little grey men under the hill; a dark man in a spotted coat of black-and-scarlet velvet; a woman riding the evening sky on a horse of rags and air; a pretty girl, dressed all in white, in the birch tree in the yard. All of them invisible to any but the midwife; all of them silently watching her with their strange and lidless eyes. But the midwife never looked back or gave any sign that she'd seen them. And little by little, the Silken Folk returned to their daily business.

The midwife longed to tell someone about her strange adventure. But she knew that no one would believe her. They might even think she was mad, or worse; possessed by some evil spirit. She learnt to ignore her unwanted gift, until, one day, five years later, as she was at the market, she saw the man with the troubling eyes and the golden band around his hair, moving among the market-stalls unseen by anyone but her.

The midwife flinched.

He looked at her. Understanding filled his eyes. And then, in a movement so sharp and precise that she did not even feel it, he snatched out the midwife's left eye with his long, pale fingers.

The midwife lived to a ripe old age. But she never saw the man again, or any of his people.

3

THE LACEWING KING

And that was the birth of the Lacewing King, the last King of the Silken Folk, who live in the shadows and cast none themselves. What happened to the old King—who vanished without warning one day, taking with him the crystal vial containing the last of the nectar of dreams—is a tale for another time, but the boy ascended the throne when he was only five years old, and—perhaps because he had entered the world at the hands of a human midwife—was fascinated from the start by what he called the Sightless Folk—or as we call them, Humankind.

At the beginning, his duties were few, and he was given into the care of the Glow-Worm Chancellor until the time of his coming-of-age. Thus the young King learnt the ways of his people; the kind and industrious Honeybees; the fierce and warlike Cockroaches; the voracious Greenfly; the dutiful Ants; the Beetles, Earwigs, and Centipedes; the many Butterflies and Moths. He also learnt the ways of the court; the etiquette and the ritual; the history of the Silken Folk.

A King must be accomplished; and so he learnt to hunt and ride; to shoot a bow and fight with a sword; to read maps and charts of the night sky; to write poetry and compose music. He was an

able student, but he was wilful and trouble-some, and from his palace underground, lined with silk and moths' wings, protected by glamours and conceits and buried in the heart of the woods, he would watch the world above and its folk; their little dramas; their fears, their dreams, their adventures; their seemingly endless quest for love.

As he grew older and more adventurous, he would often evade his teachers and the

duties set out for him and go out into World Above; and sometimes he would take human form and walk among the Folk in the
guise of one of their children. The young King had soon realized
that children go unnoticed, even where strangers are viewed with
mistrust, and he would often amuse himself at the expense of the
Sightless Folk, playing tricks to alarm them.

Thus the milkmaid would find that the milk had turned, not
to butter in the churn, but to a quart of earwigs, spilling forth
in loathsome exuberance; or the baker, cutting one of his loaves,
would find that it was empty inside except for a single fat mag-
got. The boy (for he *was* still a boy, in spite of his royal status)
would watch them from the top of a tree, or from the roots of
a thorn-bush, or from a foxhole underground, and laugh at their
fear and confusion. Sometimes he would show himself, but only
to a child of his own age—always a solitary child with no other
friends, a dreamer—and he would befriend them, play with them,
show them the ways of the woods and the trees, then, tiring of the
game at last, would vanish without warning, leaving them to wonder whether he'd been real at all, or whether they'd imagined him.

Anxious parents, hearing the tale, would warn their children
against him, telling them not to go into the woods, and to guard
against imaginary friends. But the young King always found someone reckless—or lonely—enough to disobey the warnings.

No one stopped him. No one dared criticize his actions. The
Glow-Worm Chancellor lived in a state of perpetual anxiety for his
royal charge but was unable to find the words to express his concern
for the young King, or to forbid him his cruel games. Because they
were cruel—but the young King never really considered that, any
more than a human child would consider the feelings of an ant, or
hesitate to pull off the wings of a fly, or step on a spider. No one
taught him otherwise; no one ever challenged him.

His gentle mother, the Honeycomb Queen, had not been
allowed to stay with him. Custom decreed that a new King or
Queen always stands or falls on their own. Cruelty and intelligence

would serve him better than kindness and love; and so as he grew, the Lacewing King became increasingly ruthless. He also grew to be handsome: tall and straight as a sapling, with hair the shade of a moth's wing and eyes as dark as honey. And because the midwife had given him the nectar of the dreamflower—the nectar that allowed him to see things as they really were, and not just as they *seemed* to be—he could walk between the Worlds and look between the shadows.

What he found there is a tale that only bees know how to tell. And the bees still tell it to this day; taking the story from flower to flower; adding other tales to it; whispering it to the winds; making it into nectar. For thus it has always been with the bees, wisest of the Silken Folk; the spinners of stories; builders of Worlds; the living heart of the Honeycomb.

4

THE LACEWING KING
AND THE SPIDER QUEEN

When the Lacewing King was a boy, he liked to escape into the woods. There, he would swim in the quiet streams, or swing in the canopy of the trees, or run for miles with the forest deer, far away from his underground realm and from his royal duties.

One day, when he was still only half-grown, he came to a wall, deep in the woods. The wall was brick and very high, overgrown with vivid moss that fell in great, green, velvety swags all along the perimeter.

The Lacewing King was curious. He followed the wall through the undergrowth, and soon uncovered a wrought-iron gate, almost as high as the wall itself, faded rust-red with the years, its scrolls and florets of metal grown as fine and brittle as autumn leaves.

The young King tried the gate, which was locked. But through the bars he found himself looking into a garden—or at least, what was left of one—now grown monstrous with the years, with peonies and hollyhocks and roses tall as houses, with thick and thorny branches and heads like those of shaggy sea monsters rising from the greenery.

This was the lair of the Spider Queen, who lived with her three daughters in the heart of the forest. She was old—and cunning—

and her home was a silken pavilion under a canopy of leaves, shrouded with gossamer curtains and guarded by legions of spider guards. The Spider Queen never left her lair, and yet she knew everything that went on in the forest. Through the skeins of her web, she could sense the approach of a greenfly over half a mile away; her coronet of a thousand eyes could see in all directions at once. And now she saw the young King looking through the rust-red gate, and felt her heart beat faster. She knew exactly who he was, and for years she had watched him from afar, coveting his youth and strength, and longing for him to come closer.

It had been a long, long time since a son had been born to the Silken Folk. Most of the royal children were Queens, powerful in their own right, but a new King was rare and exceptional. All the Queens deferred to him—and the one he chose to be *his* Queen would stand alongside him in glory. And so the Spider Queen called her three daughters to her, and ordered them to prepare themselves for a royal visit.

Then she dressed in her finest clothes, her train of silver spider-gauze and her cloak of dewdrops, and gathered up her retinue, and came to meet the young King in a carriage made from a silken cocoon, drawn by a dozen white spiders with ruby eyes and legs of spun glass.

The young King watched through the bars of the gate. He'd heard about the Spider Queen; her secrecy; her appetites. He knew that she was as dangerous as she was clever and powerful. But he was not at all afraid. In fact, he had a plan of his own. He climbed up onto the rust-red gate and jumped down into the garden.

The Queen stepped down from her carriage and curtseyed deeply to the King. "What an honour this is," she said, "to receive a visit from Your young Majesty. I am only a poor widow, but please, I beg of you—allow me to extend what little hospitality I can."

The young King smiled. "Of course," he said, and stepped into her carriage. It took him back to the Spider Queen's lair, where a lavish banquet awaited. Pomegranates and persimmons; dragonfly candies and cockroach claws; and wines of every colour, from lemon-yellow to berry-black. The young King sat on cushions of silk in a hammock of spider-gauze, and ate, and drank, while choruses of captive cicadas sang to him in voices sweet as honeycomb.

"And now for something special," said the Spider Queen in her whispery voice. And, raising her hand, she summoned her three daughters, now clad in their most diaphanous silks, and ordered them to display their skills for their guest's entertainment.

The three princesses were all beautiful, graceful, and accomplished. Their dancing was exquisite; so was their embroidery. One spun the King a handkerchief of such an intricate design that a seamstress of the Folk might have spent her whole life making just the border. Another sewed him a moths'-wing cloak so delicate that it could hardly be seen, but that kept off even the hardest rain, gleaming with fugitive raindrops. The third made him a pair of gloves as fine as dragonfly leather, but as strong as steel and as flexible as his own, unblemished skin.

Next, the princesses danced for him on cords of twisted spider-silk, then made their curtsey to the King, eyes lowered; hands outstretched.

The Spider Queen watched intently. She felt sure that such beauty and grace would not fail to seduce the young King. And yet, he acknowledged the three princesses with no more than common courtesy, turning back to the Spider Queen as soon as etiquette allowed. The Queen, who was vain in spite of her years, felt absurdly flattered. She smiled and offered the King more wine.

"And what do you think of my daughters?" she said.

"My compliments," he told her. "I can see where they took their charm."

The Spider Queen hid her surprise. "What a flatterer you are. I'm old enough to be your mother." (In fact, she was old enough to be his *great*-grandmother, but saw no need to tell him *that*.) "A poor widow like myself must learn to put vanity aside and leave that kind of thing to the young."

The Lacewing King gave a little smile. "I much prefer the elegance of experience," he said. "Shall we dance, my lady?"

The Queen took a cockroach cluster and ate it, slowly and reflectively. She wasn't hungry, but pretending to eat gave her time to sit and think. Could it be that the boy admired her? Of course, she had intended his throne for one of her three daughters, but could it be that her seasoned charm was more attractive to the King than mere youth and freshness?

Perhaps it was, she told herself. Perhaps she had misread the signs. And so she dismissed her daughters and most of her spider retinue, and set to seducing the young King herself. She danced for him on a silken rope; she spun him elaborate tapestries. She fed him fruits and candies and played to him on a spider-glass harp all hung with shining dewdrops. For three whole days, she wooed him; changing her outfits ten times a day; displaying every charm, every skill with clever, counterfeit modesty.

At night, the King slept in a hammock of silk and arose to the song of cicadas, while tiny, multicoloured spiders stitched him into his day clothes. Throughout the day, the Spider Queen worked hard to ensnare him, feeling increasingly certain that he would soon succumb to her charms.

But the Lacewing King was no fool. He knew the Queen's history very well. He knew her ambition; her vanity. He knew she'd been widowed sixteen times due to her ancient custom of eating her new husband on the night of the wedding. This was how the Spider Queen had gained much of her power; and this was why the Lacewing King had come to her lair in search of her. His arrival at her gate had not quite been an accident; he had heard tell of her powers and longed to know more about them.

Over three days he had noticed that, although she often changed her clothes, the Spider Queen never took off her coronet of a thousand eyes. It gleamed upon her ice-white hair; blinking in all directions. This was the source of her magic, he knew. This was how she had seen him approach; how she had watched him from afar. A plan began to form in his mind. It was a very wicked plan, as well as being cruel and dangerous; which, of course, to the Lacewing King, made it all the more amusing.

And so on the night of the third day, the young King asked for the Spider Queen's hand. The Queen accepted graciously, but warned him to be cautious.

"You are still young, Your Majesty," she said with a look of tender concern. "Your Chancellor will try to advise you against making a rash decision."

The Lacewing King took her hand. "We can marry in secret," he said. "Then no one will interfere."

The Spider Queen was very pleased. She stood in front of her mirror and combed her long white hair and smiled, and thought of how much more power she would have when she devoured the young King on the night of their wedding. She decided that the ceremony would take place in nine days and nine nights. That would give her time to prepare herself and her folk for the happy event.

Over those nine days, the King went back to his underground citadel. He told no one of his plans, but read his books and rode his horse and went about his duties in such a good, obedient way that the Glow-Worm Chancellor was moved to comment that His young Majesty should be away from home more often, and that his travels had sobered him.

Meanwhile, the Lacewing King had no intention of marrying. His plan was to steal the Spider Queen's crown, which gave her the power to know and see everything in the kingdom. All he needed to do was wait until the Queen took off the crown—and then to hide his crime until he had managed to make his escape.

First, he went to his mother, the Honeycomb Queen, who lived among her beehives in the heart of the forest. He asked her for a swarm of bees, which she granted him willingly. The Honeycomb Queen knew her son and suspected he was up to some mischief; but she knew the bees would keep him safe and allow her to watch over him. And so the King went back to his court wearing a coat of golden bees; bees that would do his bidding and were sworn to his protection.

Eight days had passed since his return. On the eve of the ninth day, which was the eve of his wedding, the young King returned to the Spider Queen, wearing his coat of living bees. The Spider Queen welcomed him with delight, already tasting his flesh with her eyes.

That night, he said to the bees, "Tonight, fly to the lair of the Spider Queen and find her crown of a thousand eyes. When she is sleeping, take out those eyes and quickly bring them here to me. But for every eye you have stolen, take care to leave a bee in its place, so that the Queen does not notice that her crown has been plundered. Now, be careful—and be quick—the Queen only sleeps a few hours a night, and even then, not deeply."

And so the bees flew out to do the bidding of the Lacewing King. They flew to the Spider Queen's chamber, where she slept under a canopy of silk. Swarming over her coronet, they brought a hundred eyes to the King, and left a hundred bees in their place, winking, silent and alert.

The Spider Queen shifted in her sleep. She opened twelve eyes and looked around. But the missing eyes in her coronet had been filled with winking bees, and she did not notice the trickery. Meanwhile, the bees in her coronet began to hum a little song:

"Long ago, and far away,
Far away and long ago.
The Worlds are honeycomb, you know;
The Worlds are honeycomb."

The song of the bees was so comforting that the Spider Queen fell asleep again. While she was sleeping, the bees returned, and took another hundred eyes, leaving a hundred bees in their place. Once more, the Queen stirred in her sleep; once more, the bees sang her to sleep.

"Long ago, and far away,
Far away and long ago.
The Worlds are honeycomb, you know;
The Worlds are honeycomb."

Throughout the night, the swarm of bees worked to plunder the Spider Queen's crown, and the Lacewing King stayed watchful as they stitched the eyes into his coat with skeins of silk and beeswax. By dawn, he had nine hundred eyes winking from his coat of bees, and only a hundred eyes remained before the King could make his escape.

In the Spider Queen's chamber, a hundred bees prepared to take flight with the last of their plunder. In the ransacked coronet, a thousand honeybees nestled and winked. But, just at that moment, the Spider Queen stirred. One eye fluttered open, and she saw a bee crawling over her pillow. Once more, the bees began their song:

"Long ago, and far away,
Far away and long ago—"

But it was too late. The Queen was awake. She reached for her coronet of eyes and saw that it was filled with bees. "What is this?" said the Spider Queen. "Treachery, treason, thievery, *theft!*"

The bees in the coronet winked at her, then started to rise into the air. The sound of their wings was a murmur at first, then a hissing, then a roar. The Queen put on her coronet and tried to see beyond her lair. But her vision was darkened and blurred, and she knew that she was blind.

Seizing the delicate threads of her web, she sought the thief in the heart of her realm—and blindly, through her fingers, she sensed the young King in his hammock of silk, wearing a coat of nine hundred eyes.

The Queen gave a howl of outrage. The honeybees rose like a column of smoke. The young King saw the column and knew that his ruse had been discovered. Jumping from his hammock, he threw on his thistledown moths'-wing cloak and fled through the overgrown garden towards the wall and the rust-red gate.

The Queen ran into the heart of her web, hoping to cut off the young King's escape; but without her crown of a thousand eyes, she was unable to see her prey. She ordered her spider retinue to take the King and bind him—but with his new-found vision, the King could see the danger approaching; and reaching the gate of the Spider Queen's lair, he quickly climbed to safety and escaped with his stolen treasure.

The Spider Queen sensed his escape through her web. She looked out of her window. Below, in the courtyard of her lair, the preparations were underway for a wedding she now knew would never take place. Nine days of preparations; of kitchens filled with roasted caterpillars stuffed with ants; of damselfly comfits and greenfly jellies and woodlice fried in their jackets. Nine days it had taken her daughters to make the wedding dress with its jewelled train, so long that ten thousand spiders had had to be stitched into the hem, to ensure its elegant drape and to keep the delicate lace from touching the ground. The veil was spun from moonlight and air; the petticoat from blue butterflies' wings; the gown from finest thistledown gauze, stitched with living lacewings.

The Spider Queen, in her nightgown, stood in front of her mirror and looked at her reflection. Her face was very pale beneath the eyeless, empty coronet—and yet, at that moment she seemed to see more clearly than she had in days.

She summoned her three daughters and ordered them to clear her lair of every servant, every cook, every courtier and cleaner and squab. "I want to be alone," she said.

And then she put on her wedding dress and once more looked at herself in the mirror, and saw how foolish she had been, and how the King had duped her. Now she could see him in her mind's eye, sitting in his library, wearing his golden coat of bees. And stitched all over that coat were the eyes from the Spider Queen's coronet; a thousand eyes, bright and alert, gleaming in the lamplight.

And right there, she promised herself that one day, she would have her revenge on him. She would make him pay in full for all that he had done to her. She would see him humiliated and broken into pieces. She would find what was precious to him and take it away, whatever it was.

Then she lay on her marriage bed under her canopy of silk and started to spin herself a cocoon. She used her train and wedding veil, stitching their folds around her. Before long, there was nothing left of her but a bundle of jewelled gauze, and moths'-wing fur, and thistledown.

And when it was finished she went to sleep, and dreamed dark dreams of vengeance.

5

THE TEACHER

There is a story the bees used to tell, which makes it hard to disbelieve—except for a teacher of some renown, who disbelieved them every one. He lived in a village by a bluebell wood, not far from the Lacewing King's domain, and his greatest joy was to sit and watch the children at play and mock them.

"Don't you realize," he would say, "that all your games are just make-believe? You there, with the wooden sword; you're not really a knight," he said. "And you, with the sheet around your head; you're not really a princess."

Sometimes the children ignored the man. But he was difficult to ignore.

"Why do you waste your time," he would say, "with games and fairy stories, when Science and Reality have so much more to offer? Admittedly," he went on magnanimously, "there is virtue in the fairy tale, for the young, in that it teaches Critical Thinking. But Lies are Lies, and the Truth is the Truth, and the Silken Folk are no more real than dreams that come to us at night."

Now it happened that the Lacewing King overheard the man's comments one day. With his coat of a thousand eyes, he could see almost anywhere, and he often ventured forth from his under-

ground citadel and came to watch the children at play by the edge of the bluebell wood. Most of the children could see him, being too young to have learnt to be blind. But of course, the teacher saw nothing—except for bees and butterflies.

That day, the Lacewing King was abroad, regal in his coat of bees and crown of living centipedes. He heard the words of the teacher and came to sit beside him. The children stopped their games and watched. But of course, the man saw nothing.

The man said, "What are you staring at?"

But the children were so used to being scolded and ridiculed for seeing the things that he could not that they did not dare tell him what they saw. And so they watched as the Lacewing King walked up to the man who did not believe, and put his hands over his eyes.

And when he removed them, the teacher found that he could see the Silken Folk, watching him from every branch, every leaf of every tree. Golden-eyed and silken-winged, and cluster-clawed, they watched him; the Cockroaches, in their black armour; the sleepy, furry-footed Moths; the Butterflies, with their rainbow wings; the Wasps, in their yellow livery.

The man began to scream, then to run.

He ran right out of the bluebell glade, and through the village, and into the woods. He ran right to the end of that World and into the cities of the Folk, in the hope that concrete, and plastic, and glass would keep the terrible visions at bay.

But the world of the Silken Folk, once seen, is not so easy to ignore. The man now saw them everywhere; in the streets; in his bed at night; even in the mirror. Moth men; Butterfly women, dressed all in leather and dragonfly lace; Woodlice in their armour; Flies in their sable jackets, and Ants in titanium helmets; all watching him with their lidless eyes and mocking his discomfort.

But the man was stubborn and refused to admit that they were real. Instead, he said, "I am going insane."

And many people agreed with him.

6

THE MOTH MOTHER

Not far away, there lived a boy, who was convinced that his mother was not his mother. She certainly *looked* like his mother; she had the same hair, the same expressions; she sang the same little songs to herself. She had the same friends; she wore the same clothes; she spoke to him in just the same way. And yet the boy remained convinced that she was not his mother.

Why did the boy feel this way? Not even he knew for certain. He had no father, no siblings. His mother was his only kin. They lived in a cottage in the woods, and they were very seldom apart. When the boy went to school, she was there, walking him to the school-gates. When he went to church, she was there, making sure he said his prayers. When he was feverish, she was there; sitting at his bedside, feeding him broth from a china bowl and singing softly to herself.

"There once was a citadel under a dome
Long ago, long ago,
All lined with silk and honeycomb,
Believe me child, believe me."

And she was the perfect mother. She always cooked his favourites. She kissed him every morning, as he woke up. She tucked him into bed every night. But sometimes, the boy would wake up and see his mother watching him, silently, from the shadows by his bed, and her face was different then: blank, wide-eyed, and frightening.

He tried to tell his teachers. Nobody believed him. He told the village doctor, who put him on a diet of bitter greens and valerian tea. He tried pretending to go to sleep, and lying awake in secret. But on those nights, she never came, and the boy was none the wiser.

His mother noticed how pale he looked. "What is it?" she said. "What ails my boy?"

But the boy would not tell. Instead he went to the library, where the old librarian lived among his towers and turrets of books. The old librarian often told stories of the Silken Folk, and how they sometimes managed to steal into a person's body, eating their soul from the inside out, so that nothing was left of them but skin that moved and smiled and spoke—although there was nothing left inside but the Silken Folk in their clusters and swarms.

"But that's just a story," said the boy. "No one can *really* steal your soul. The Silken Folk aren't real—are they?"

Each time he said this, the old man shrugged. "The Silken Folk are everywhere. In the air you breathe, in the walls, in your bed, in the food you eat, even under your skin. And when you die, they'll be there still, feeding on you in the dark."

This, too, was only a story, of course. But as time passed, the boy became more and more convinced that not only were the Silken Folk real, but they were in his mother.

He started to watch her more carefully. He noticed how she never undressed in front of him, and how sometimes she seemed to go for minutes at a time without blinking. Most of all, he noticed how she never killed a wasp or a fly, or even stood on a cockroach.

He asked the old librarian, "How would you know if the Silken Folk had made their home in someone you knew?"

The old man said, "There's one way to tell. Put camphor under their pillow. There's nothing the Silken Folk hate more."

And so the boy saved up to buy a box of camphor. The scent of it was so pungent that he was almost overcome; but he wrapped it tightly, took it home, then, when his mother was making dinner, crept into her bedroom and slipped it under her pillow.

Night came. As always, the boy's mother came in to kiss him goodnight. The boy waited. His skin crawled with terror and anticipation. The dreadful scent of camphor seemed to be in everything, but his mother seemed not to notice, and went to bed without a word.

The boy waited. The night wore on. The scent of camphor intensified. In the next room, he could hear his mother, tossing and turning in her sleep. Surely, soon, he would know the truth. The mother's secret would be exposed—

Then, he heard an ominous sound that seemed to come from everywhere; a low, metallic buzzing noise, like termites in the wood-

work. The crawling in his skin had become a terrible, loathsome itching. The boy got out of bed and looked down at his naked body. In the moonlight, he saw himself covered in living goosebumps. As he watched, he saw that each one was a tiny, translucent moth, hatching out from under his skin, with dusty feelers and velvety wings. The terrified boy began to scream.

He looked up and saw his mother standing in the doorway.

She said to him, "What have you done?"

But the boy could not reply. He opened his mouth, and a cloud of moths flew out into the warm air. The scent of camphor grew stronger. The itching under his skin grew worse. Now the insects were hatching out of every part of his body; crawling from under his fingernails; swarming out of him in waves; streaming from his nose and eyes; rising into the moonlight that shone through the open window.

The mother ran to his side, but too late. Nothing human was left of him. The boy had melted into the air, leaving nothing behind him but a cloud of tiny moths. No one ever saw him again. But sometimes, the old librarian would think of him and shake his head, and tell himself:

"The boy was right. That woman *wasn't* his mother."

7

THE PARROTS
AND THE NIGHTINGALE

An emperor of the Southern Isles kept a nightingale in a cage. A visiting prince had brought it with him, many, many years ago, and its song was so sweet that visitors came from afar to hear it.

Now the king of a neighbouring country heard the song of the nightingale and was consumed with envy. He went to the keeper of the royal aviaries to discover how he could obtain a bird of his own.

The keeper of the aviaries shook his head regretfully. "These birds are very rare," he said. "They live only in the deepest part of a dangerous forest. They cannot be bred in captivity, and catching them takes tremendous skill. I know of only one man who can do it."

"Then summon him," demanded the King. "Whatever his price, I'll pay it."

The keeper of the aviaries bowed his head respectfully and promised to deliver the bird as soon as he was able. The King went back to his own country and waited. He waited three months, after which the keeper of the aviaries arrived, looking thin and exhausted and carrying a bamboo cage in which sat a small brown bird.

"Here is your nightingale," he said. "It took me three months to trap it and to bring it to Your Majesty. Now for my fee." And he named a sum that made the King draw breath very sharply.

Three long months had already passed since the King had heard the nightingale's song. His desire to compete with the emperor; his envy; his sense of wonderment; all these things had faded with time, to be replaced by a deep resentment of the price to which he had agreed. He looked at the little brown bird in its cage.

"How do I even know it sings?"

The keeper of the aviaries whistled a few notes of a tune. Immediately, the nightingale started to sing; a melody that made the tears stand in the eyes of anyone who heard it—anyone but the King, that is, who set his teeth and scowled, and said:

"What kind of fool do you take me for? This isn't even the same kind of bird."

The keeper of the aviaries assured him that it was.

But the King refused to believe him. "Even if it were," he said, "the woods are filled with birds like this. Their singing is free for everyone. Why should I pay you anything for something that should be free?"

The keeper of the aviaries shrugged his shoulders. "So be it. Let it be free," he said, and he opened the door of the bamboo cage, releasing the little bird into the air. As it flew, the nightingale opened its beak and sang a fragment of song so sublime that the King's heart was close to breaking, and he knew that he had made an error of judgement. But pride forbade him to say so.

He called for his servants and told them, "In my woods, there are parrots with colourful plumage and rousing song. Let them be brought to my palace at once, in cages of gold and silver. Let them be placed in every room, and let their song delight us."

And so the King's servants obeyed his command. Soon every room in the palace was filled with parrots in gold and silver cages. Their cries were loud and raucous, but the King, having praised them so highly, was now unable to have them removed. He suffered terrible headaches, as did the members of his court, but no one dared say what everyone thought. Instead they praised the King's judgement and pretended to admire his birds. They made such a good job of doing this that word spread to the Emperor's court that the king of the neighbouring country had birds superior to his own. Soon, everyone was whispering. The Emperor felt ridiculous, with his single little brown bird.

One morning he went in secret to the keeper of his aviaries. "One nightingale is no longer enough," he said. "I must have parrots. Parrots, like that foreign king's, but in far greater number."

The keeper of the aviaries wisely kept his thoughts to himself and promised the Emperor that he would have as many parrots as he wanted. The parrots were brought into his palace, and everyone admired them. People came from far and wide to see the collection of colourful birds, and no one dared point out the fact that not a single one could sing. The nightingale in its golden cage was forgotten in the excitement, and eventually, the keeper of the aviaries took it into the imperial gardens and quietly set it free.

The King of the neighbouring country heard about the Emperor's collection of parrots and was most put out at having been upstaged.

But the Emperor took to spending time outside in his gardens whenever he could, where, at dusk, the song of the nightingale could still be heard from far away.

8

THE LACEWING KING
AND THE HARLEQUIN

Word of how the Lacewing King had stolen the crown of the Spider Queen travelled fast through the Nine Worlds. Though he was still very young, the tale had earned him the respect of his people, and one by one, the rulers of the many tribes of the Silken Folk paid him homage and bowed their heads, acknowledging his leadership.

Only one tribe remained hostile. The Sightless Folk call them *ladybirds* and view them with affection, but to the Silken Folk they are among the fiercest of predators. Even the wasps and the fire-ants feared their insatiable appetites, which ran not only to aphids, but also to the eggs and grubs of any creature they could find, even to the larvae of bees in their cradles of honeycomb.

The ladybirds had no King or Queen. Their ruler was the Harlequin, an ancient creature of indeterminate gender and habits, with whom no ruler had ever established a treaty. The Harlequin could change its shape, becoming male or female at will, sometimes ate its own kind, and sometimes wore black spots on red, or red on black, or brown on gold. No one knew its hunting-grounds, or in what form it would strike next; but spotted, striped or dappled, it was always deadly.

"Beware the Harlequin, Your Majesty," warned the Glow-Worm Chancellor. "It hunts in pied splendour, and it kills without mercy. It has no allegiance; no honour; no heart. Therein lies its power."

But the Lacewing King was still too young to be afraid of bug-bears. "Am I not the King?" he said to the Glow-Worm Chancellor. "Am I not the ruler of World Above and World Below? Do my folk not fill the Nine Worlds, even to the shores of Dream? I shall seek out this Harlequin, and make it bow to me."

The Chancellor shook his bright head. "Oh, Your Majesty," he said. "If ever you see the Harlequin, run for your life. Summon your guards. Lock yourself in your fortress. Above all, *do not look at its eyes.*"

"Why?" inquired the Lacewing King.

"Because," said the Glow-Worm Chancellor, "the Harlequin's eyes are mirrors that reflect the gateways to all the Worlds. Even a glance can drive you insane. They say, long ago, the Spider King once tried to tame the Harlequin. He looked into its eyes and fell through the gap between the Worlds, where he still wanders, lost and mad, forever, in the darkness."

But the Lacewing King was too arrogant to take these warnings seriously. Instead, he became determined to do what his predecessor had not; and he longed for a glimpse of the Harlequin, and dreamed of breaking its power.

Time passed, and at last the King came across the Harlequin hunting in the forest. That day it had chosen a female form; tall and dark and languorous, with a corset of scarlet and black and a cloak of translucent silk. The young King approached. He was handsome; regal in the moths'-wing cloak that covered his coat of living bees, and he stood before the Harlequin—wary, perhaps, but unafraid.

The Harlequin watched as he approached, and felt a little curious. It was used to seeing prey run at the first glimpse of its colours. But the Lacewing King was no common prey. It knew him by reputation. From its lair it had heard the tale of how he had stolen the Spider Queen's crown, and it knew him to be clever, if maybe more reckless than was good for him.

Not that it cared for those things, no. The Harlequin cared only for prey. Living, helpless, delicious prey; the younger and sweeter, the better. And the young King smelt of privilege, and honey, and damselfly comfits, and mealworm candies, and summer nights, and that subtle, fleeting scent of youth that clung to him like a perfume.

The Harlequin ran its honey tongue over its scarlet lips and beckoned to the Lacewing King. It was wearing long, black leather gloves that sheathed its claws and hid them from sight. Beneath the gloves, the elegance of its long-fingered hands was hypnotic.

The young King took a step forward. Remembering his Chancellor's words, he did not face the creature directly, but averted his gaze just enough to avoid looking into its jet-black eyes.

"You must be the Lacewing King," said the Harlequin, with a curtsey.

"And you must be the Harlequin," said the King, with a gracious bow.

"That's what your people call me," said the Harlequin, coming closer (though still not *quite* close enough to be sure of catching him if it made a move). "But I was once a ruler myself, with a kingdom far greater than yours."

"Really?" said the Lacewing King. "What happened to your kingdom?"

The Harlequin gave a smile that was at the same time tragic and predatory. "Come a little closer," it said, "and I'll tell you my story."

Of course, the Harlequin had no desire to confide in the Lacewing King. But by luring him closer, it hoped to make him look into its languorous eyes, after which it intended to drink his young and privileged life. If it had to tell a tale to gain satisfaction, so be it. The Harlequin was a collector of tales, and it had many tales to tell.

The Lacewing King took a single step, but kept his gaze averted.

"Just a little closer, please," purred the Harlequin, flexing its claws in the long gloves.

The Lacewing King smiled. "Later, perhaps. For now, let me hear your tale."

The Harlequin gave another smile. Behind the scarlet of its lips, its mandibles worked silently. It hungered for the young King; his youth; his freshness; his promise. But it also knew how to be patient; besides, it was rather enjoying the hunt. If the King ran, it would catch him. What harm was there in telling a tale to a man about to die?

The Harlequin sat down on a stump. "Sit beside me, Your Majesty."

The Lacewing King also sat—on a fallen tree some distance away. Beneath his cloak, his coat of bees winked and blinked in anxiety.

Don't look! Don't look! hummed the bees under the cloak.

"Look at me," said the Harlequin.

"I listen better this way," said the King, drawing a fold of his moths'-wing cloak over his eyes to shield them. "But, pray, tell me your tale. How did you become the Harlequin?"

The creature flexed its jaws again and began its tale.

"I was the Hallowe'en Queen," it said. "I lived between the World of Men and the banks of the River Dream, which runs through all Worlds, to the Land of the Dead. My name was known, in those long-ago days. I fed well on the souls of the dead. Kings—and even gods—were my prey. Now I have no name; no crown; only a boundless appetite that can never be satisfied."

The Lacewing King smiled from behind the silken folds of his moths'-wing cloak.

"Come closer," said the Harlequin.

The Lacewing King moved closer, though not quite enough to be caught. "How did you lose your kingdom?" he said.

"I lost it," said the Harlequin, "to a very handsome young man—though perhaps not quite as handsome as *you*—who came to me from World Above. His mission, he told me, was to plead for the return of a soul that Death had delivered to me. She was his wife; his one true love; the mother of his infant son, and he would rather die, he said, than live a day without her."

The Harlequin paused. "Come closer," it said.

Once more, the King came closer, though still not quite enough to be caught. Under his cloak, his coat of bees hummed and buzzed with anxiety.

"And so I gave the man his wish," went on the Harlequin softly. "I told him I would release his wife, as long as he swore to take her place."

"And did he?" said the Lacewing King.

The Harlequin gave a wistful smile, revealing those restless mandibles. "He did," it said. "I freed his wife and led him to his place by my side. But as I was about to take the life that he had promised me—" It paused to glance at the Lacewing King, still just a *little* too far out of reach. "He pulled something out of his pocket, and showed it to me in his hand. It was a vial of cut glass. He said:

"'This nectar comes from the Honeycomb Queen, long ago; far away. This is what you hungered for, when you touched the flower that grew on the banks of the River Dream. A single taste will unlock your mind; a single droplet on your tongue holds the key to a million stories.'

"I looked at the man. I was curious. More than that; I was hungry. 'Why do you tell me this?' I said.

"'Because you know only Nine Worlds,' he said. 'But there are so many worlds out there; a world for every story. Stories wield enormous power; greater even than yours, my Queen. A story can change the course of Time; a story can even raise the dead. A story can take you anywhere; into any world you choose. And the Honeycomb Queen sees into them all, as *you* will see, when I give you this.'"

And at that, he held up the tiny cut-glass vial to my face, and I saw myself reflected there in all its mirrored facets. And as it shone into my eyes, that reflect the gates to all Worlds, all Time, I fell from my throne in the Kingdom of Death and into the world of the living."

The Lacewing King was curious. "Could you not return?" he said.

The Harlequin raised its claws, deadly in their long black gloves, and took a single step closer. "The ruler of Death never leaves their realm," it said. "The young man had already taken my place. You see, he had sworn an oath to me, and his word was binding. And so he rules the Land of the Dead, never to return to this world, and his son is the King of the Silken Folk, and now—" The Harlequin

sprang forward and seized the King in its terrible claws, and said: "And now, *for my revenge—*"

The Lacewing King struggled, averted his eyes, but could not break free of the Harlequin. It held him fast between its claws, its mandibles working hungrily, slashing at his shoulders and arms and digging its knives into his back, and as it spoke, it forced him to look into its black and merciless eyes. . . .

But the bees had not been idle. During the struggle, they had crept over the eyes of the Lacewing King, so that when the Harlequin came close and gazed into its victim's face, it saw only the eyes of the bees, and its own eyes, mirrored in the abyss—

The creature gave a cry of rage and released the Lacewing King. Too late. It had already looked too long, and now the abyss was calling. The Harlequin broke into a cloud of red-and-scarlet ladybirds—thousands—*tens* of thousands of them—rising into the air like smoke. For a moment, the sound of their wings was like the sound of an avalanche. And then they were gone—every one of them—into the space between the Worlds, through the honeycomb of Time, never to be seen again in the realm of the Silken Folk.

The Lacewing King returned that night, bleeding and torn from the creature's claws, but told no one of his encounter. He summoned a team of leafcutter ants to stitch up his wounds, and nurse bees to anoint him in honey and bandage him in silk. Of course, the Glow-Worm Chancellor saw the scars on his master's skin, but if he guessed what had happened, he wisely kept his thoughts to himself.

As for the bees, they did not reveal what happened to the Harlequin. Perhaps they never knew for sure. But the Lacewing King never forgot the tale of his mother and father, and he gave orders that, henceforth, he would tolerate no ladybird of any kind anywhere in his kingdom; and that none of his people should ever wear its livery of scarlet and black, so that if the Harlequin ever returned, he would know it immediately. For he knew that its tale was not over, nor its appetite for vengeance slaked; and that one day they would meet again; in this world, or another.

9

THE PUPPETEER

Once, there was an artist, whose genius lay in the making of puppets. He could make them from anything: rags; ceramic; gloves; socks; feathers; clockwork; leather. He used them to act out his stories, for he was a storyteller, and all the children loved his tales, and followed him wherever he went.

But as time passed, and his fame and wealth grew, he found that stories no longer satisfied him. He was unhappy and did not know why. He had no friends and did not know why. He began to believe that everyone was thinking ill of him all the time; envying his wealth and fame, criticizing his handiwork.

And so he began to make puppets to use to spy on the people he feared most. And into each beautifully made figurine, he put a little piece of his soul, so that their eyes would be his eyes, their ears his ears, their words his words. He hid these elaborate puppets in the homes of those he suspected. In this way, he could overhear what other people said about him. And he became very bitter. He learnt that he was not generally liked. People thought him contemptuous; unkind; people did not trust him.

The maker of puppets grew angry (and secretly, still more afraid). He abandoned his storytelling to devote himself entirely to

the making of puppets. And into each of the puppets, he put yet another piece of his soul. And at night, the puppets would whisper to him, telling him everything they had seen and everything they had overheard, and he grew increasingly angry.

Very soon, even those who had once been his friends began to avoid him. They saw an emptiness in his eyes that made them very uneasy. They heard an emptiness in his words that made them shiver and turn away. And this made the maker of puppets feel ever more bitter and angry. And so he began to make figurines to spy upon his closest friends and family. And into each and every one he put a little part of his soul. But still he was not satisfied.

Until one sunny day, he found that he had finally lost his soul. He no longer cast a shadow, and his eyes were like old pennies. Even among strangers, he could no longer pass as a human being. And so he went into the woods and made his home under the bridge that went across the river. And all the children avoided the bridge, knowing a monster lived there.

But sometimes, during the winter nights, the puppets he had hidden away in the homes of his neighbours and friends would open their eyes—and whisper.

10

THE CRAFTSMAN

There once was a craftsman who worked in wood, whose skill was unequalled throughout the land. But he was no businessman. He had no head for money, and therefore no means of selling his work. And so he went to the city, where the owner of a shop agreed to take his work and sell it for a commission. This arrangement worked well, for a while. The wood-carver's work was popular, and the shopkeeper made money. The craftsman grew to consider the owner of the shop a friend, and was very grateful to her for having offered him a chance.

But he was an artist, and curious to find new ways of developing his craft. And so one day, he tried working in glass. He worked in secret, fearing, perhaps, that his work in glass would not equal the beauty of his work in wood. But when he had finished, he looked at his work and felt a joy in what he had done. And so he took his work to his friend, and asked her what she thought of it.

The shopkeeper praised the craftsman's work. And yet, she was uneasy. She had a reputation for selling beautiful things made out of wood. She owed her fame in part to him. But, in spite of its quality, she had no desire to start selling glass. On the other hand, she had no wish for the craftsman to take his work elsewhere. Finally, she told the man:

"I will buy all your glassware and sell it for you in my shop."

The craftsman was delighted. He continued to work in both wood and glass. But while his pieces in wood sold well, and his reputation grew, his work in glass remained unknown, and he began to grow suspicious. One day, he went in secret to his friend's shop in the city. He saw his work in wood on display, though none of his glass was anywhere to be seen. But, looking in the cellar, he found all his beautiful pieces of glass hidden away in the darkness, their cases unopened; gathering dust.

He went to his friend and asked her why.

"I'm sorry," she said. "There does not seem to be a market for glassware."

The craftsman was disappointed. But he still loved working with glass. And so, while he continued to carve wood for his friend, he also continued to work in glass, and tried to sell his work elsewhere. He went to a local merchant, who, knowing the craftsman's work in wood, promised to make him equally renowned for his wonderful work in glass.

But the city friend was displeased. She had hoped to sell *all* the man's work herself, and to reap all the benefit. And so she grew cold towards him, and lost her enthusiasm for his work. The glassware remained in the basement, gathering dust. No one saw it, and even when folk came to ask whether the merchant sold glassware, she refused to sell it, or even to admit it was there.

One day, the craftsman decided to ask for the return of his glassware. "It's doing nothing but taking up space," he said. "My glass-merchant friend can sell it for us."

But the city shopkeeper refused, saying: "You may *buy* it back, if you wish."

The truth was, she was angry at him for changing his medium, and for affecting her business. And she named a price that was so high that neither the craftsman nor the glass-merchant could afford to pay a tithe of it.

The craftsman tried to change her mind, but still she refused to give it back. "I gave you a chance to sell your work," she said to the craftsman. "It's hardly my fault that you failed to repay the money that I invested in you."

Once more, the craftsman tried to reason with his shopkeeper friend. But as time passed, his friend became increasingly cold and distant. His letters remained unanswered; his pleas for a meeting were ignored. Finally, one day, as he was passing the city flea market, he saw his glasswork on sale there. Some of it was broken, all of it was dusty, and it was priced so cheaply that the man was amazed and angry.

"What is this glassware on sale here?" he asked the market-stall holder.

The market-stall holder shrugged. "It's just some scrap that a merchant in town couldn't manage to get rid of."

And now, at last, the craftsman understood that the shopkeeper had never been his friend, and that she cared nothing for his work. And so he went back to his village, and to the things he understood, and continued to work in wood, and in glass—and sometimes in stone, or clay, or bronze—whenever the fancy took him.

The shopkeeper and the merchant of glass were both disappointed to see him go. But as they knew from experience, artists were temperamental, and unaccustomed to business.

11

THE WOLVES AND THE DOGS

In a time of famine and drought, the animals of a certain farm were badly in need of strong leadership. The pastures were almost exhausted; the river almost dry; and from the forests and out of the wilderness, wolves were coming to feed on the sheep. Something had to be done, and fast.

"Let us elect a leader to protect us," said the Sheep.

The Dogs, traditionally herders of sheep, agreed with this, and made their case most eloquently. "If you elect a Dog," they said, "we will keep you safe from the Wolves. And we will divide the pastures fairly so that no one has to starve."

But some of the other animals objected. "We don't want to eat grass," said the Hens. "We want corn and barley."

The Pigs agreed. "Bread, and cornmeal!"

"Hay," said the Horses. "Oats and hay."

Some of the younger Dogs chimed in, saying, "What good is hay or corn to us? We are Dogs. We need fresh meat!"

At this, one of the Wolves, who had crept closer to listen to the debate, spoke up. "Choose a Wolf to lead you," he said, "and I promise you food in abundance."

This sounded attractive to the younger Dogs, although the

Sheep were less convinced. "But won't you eat us all?" they said. The Wolf smiled broadly at the Sheep and said, "We must all make sacrifices, but we can survive together. And, unlike the Dogs, I can protect you all against the other predators."

The Sheep debated among themselves. Some of them were still afraid. But the Wolf was very persuasive, and some of the young Dogs were on his side, lured by the promise of food for all. "The old Dogs are weak and toothless," they said. "Better vote for the Wolf instead. The Wolf will bring prosperity."

"That makes sense," said the Sheep. "And besides, if even the Dogs believe that a Wolf could do a better job, then who are we to disagree?"

And so the Sheep, who were in the majority, voted the Wolf as their leader. The Wolf brought in some of his friends to help, and soon they were settled in happily.

"What happened?" said the older Dogs. "How could we have lost the vote?"

The Wolves sneered. "Losers," they said, tucking into the carcass of a freshly slaughtered Sheep. "We have ended the famine."

"Er, not really," said a Sheep, who happened to have overheard.

But the older Dogs had been greatly moved. "*That's* where we went wrong," they said. "That's how we lost the confidence of our younger pack members. If only we had been more like the Wolves, then we might be in charge by now!"

And so all the Dogs applied themselves to becoming as wolf-like as possible. They started to run around in packs, terrifying the other animals. They slaughtered sheep and cattle. They spread terror in their wake, and found that by doing so, they had solved both their own leadership problem and that of the meat supply.

A few of the Sheep protested. But they were only Sheep, of course, and no one really cared what they thought.

12

THE GIRL WHO LOVED
THE SILKEN FOLK

Once, there was a little girl who was always asking questions. One day, she said to her old nurse, "Tell me how you lost your eye."

The nurse, who had a porcelain eye as blue and white as a china plate, said, "I don't remember. Maybe I left it lying around, and one of the Silken Folk stole it away."

"The Silken Folk?" repeated the girl.

"There are as many tribes of them as there are people in our world. They're everywhere; in the food you eat; in the fruit you pick from the tree; on the path; in the air you breathe; in your house and in your bed; and when you die, the Silken Folk will be there still, feeding on what's left of you."

"That's horrible!" exclaimed the girl.

"That's life, my dear," said the nurse. "Life is filled with horrors. But never hurt an insect, child—not a bee, or a wasp, or a moth—or the Lacewing King will get you, for sure, and then you'll be in trouble."

The girl said, "Who's the Lacewing King?"

"Some call him Lord of the Flies," said the nurse. "Some call him King of the Faërie. He lives under the forest floor, and underneath the mountains, and in stagnant water, and in the trees, and his people have always been in the world, even before First Man and First Woman."

And she sang a little song to the girl; a song that the honeybees used to sing:

"He has a coat of a thousand eyes,
Far away, far away,
His people fill the summer skies,
Believe me, child, believe me."

"Have you seen him?" said the girl. "Have you seen the Lacewing King?"

"No one sees him," said the nurse. "Not unless he wants to be seen. But you'd know him, if you did. And you'd live to regret it, too."

"What does he look like?" said the girl.

"Sometimes he looks like a man," said the nurse. "Tall, with hair like a moth's wing. But sometimes he is a swarm of bees, or a cloud of dancing butterflies. Sometimes he comes to visit us, stepping between the cracks in the Worlds, and sometimes he walks in the light, although he casts no shadow."

"Can I see him?" said the girl.

"No," said the nurse. "But he sees *you*. With his coat of a thousand eyes, no one can ever hide from him."

And so the girl began to learn all about the Silken Folk. She learnt how ants can carry loads a dozen times heavier than themselves; how butterflies spend one life as a grub and then grow wings for a life in the air; how bees make honey; how wasps fight, gnats bite and even the cheery ladybird is a predator fiercer than a wolf, biting the heads off greenflies as it travels up the flower stems. She watched how the mantis dines on her mate, wringing her hands in silent prayer; and how the termites shape their nests into great pale cathedrals. She watched them all attentively, but she never saw the Lacewing King.

"Well, of course not," said the nurse, when the girl complained to her. "The Silken Folk walk in disguise. They never cast a shadow. No one sees them, except in dreams. They're far too clever and quick to be seen—and besides, they only move when they know people can't see them."

"How?" said the girl quickly, having already decided that *she* was going to see them, however long it took her.

"They move when we close our eyes," said the nurse. "The Silken Folk have no eyelids. And every time we blink, they move, faster than a dragonfly's wing. That's how they can hide away, even when they're among us."

After that, the young girl watched more curiously than ever. But this time, she watched from the tail of her eye; spending hours in the woods, or by the bank of the river, staring, trying not to blink. Once or twice she even thought she saw a flicker of movement—and often, there were clouds of gnats, or tiny brown-winged butterflies, or summer swarms of golden bees that circled in the sleepy air.

Time passed, and the nurse became anxious. "It isn't good for you," she said, "to be spending so much of your time in those woods. Why do you *want* to see the Silken Folk? They're dangerous and cruel, and the Lacewing King is the worst of them all. Best to leave them well alone."

But the girl didn't listen. She wanted to see the Lacewing King. She already saw him in her dreams, with his coat of bees and his honey-dark eyes. Sometimes, as she was waking up, she even thought she'd seen him there, watching her from the foot of the bed, but she could never be quite sure.

And then, one day, years later, she came across a stranger in the woods; a man with hair like a moth's wing and eyes the colour of honey. In the dappled light, she saw that he cast no shadow. But she was not afraid; instead, she came to sit beside him, and they talked all afternoon in the scent of the hawthorn-trees.

"Can I see you again?" said the girl.

The stranger nodded. "I'll be here. But if you tell anyone, you'll never see me again."

So the girl came to the woods every day, and every day met the stranger. He told her stories, taught her songs, and they kissed in the shade of the hawthorn trees. The girl was so happy, she barely knew how to hide her excitement, and yet she did not speak of it to anyone in the village.

But her nurse soon grew suspicious. She saw the roses in the girl's cheeks, and the sparkle in her eyes, and knew that her charge had fallen in love. For a time, she hoped it was with one of the boys in the village, but knowing the girl as she did, she sensed a different danger. One day she followed the girl to the woods, and saw her, sitting on the ground, talking to someone who wasn't there. She knew at once what was happening, and leaped out from her hiding place—

The man without a shadow turned. For a moment the girl saw him change; watched his body twist like a curl of smoke as he fell to his knees on the forest floor. She cried out in alarm; but he did not seem to hear her. A blanket of bees seemed to cover him like the folds of a living suit, so that soon it seemed to the girl that there was no man lying there at all, just a multitude of bees, streaming away into the air, leaving only his discarded clothes and the distant sound of humming.

The old nurse said to the girl, "Well, that's the last you'll see of *him.*"

She was right. The girl went back to the glade, but her lover was never there. Sometimes she almost saw him, fleetingly, briefly from the tail of her eye, or when she awoke from deep sleep, but although she begged him to give her a sign, he never showed himself again.

"It's for the best," said the old nurse. "You'll get over him, you'll see. The Silken Folk are dangerous, and you had no business running after them, nor wanting to see things that shouldn't be seen."

But the girl didn't get over him. Weeks passed. Months passed, and still the girl did not forget. She lost her bloom, which had once been so bright, and her rosy cheeks grew pale and wan. People began to call her mad, because she was always talking to herself, and because she so seldom blinked. And she often sang to herself, the songs of the Silken People—

"Long ago, and far away,
Far away and long ago—"

The nurse grew increasingly worried. "What are you trying to do?" she said.

"I *have* to see him again," said the girl.

"Silly, stubborn child," said the nurse. "You don't even know who he is. He never told you his name, did he? Why do you think that was, eh?"

The girl looked at her wearily, with eyes that were red from not blinking. "Why?"

"The Silken People have no names, just as they have no eyelids. Just as they have no shadows, and, some might say, they have no souls. That young man you met in the woods? That was the Lacewing King, for sure, the cruellest and most terrible of all the Silken People. Didn't I warn you when you were small to beware them and their sweet talk? They feed you honey, but they sting. Never forget that, child. They sting."

Well, the girl had been stung, all right. Now the poison ran deep in her veins. Nothing the nurse could say or do made any difference to that, or changed the way she went every day to the little glade in the wood, and sat there, tearless, unblinking, waiting for her lover's return.

And then one day she did not come home. She went to the glade as usual, but when night fell, and she still had not returned, the old nurse went to look for her. By the time the old woman reached the glade, the moon had risen above the trees, and its light

filtered down through the branches onto the figure of a girl, sitting on a fallen tree. The tears were running down her face, and as the old woman came closer, she saw that they were tears of blood.

The girl had cut off her eyelids.

The nurse fell to her knees in shock, as her heart gave way at that instant. No one saw her alive again, and no one watched, as, shadowless, the girl stood in the moonlight, looking down at the old nurse with her huge, unblinking eyes.

"I will see him now," she said, and walked away into the night.

No one ever saw her again. No one human, anyway.

13

THE LACEWING KING
AND THE SILKWORM PRINCESS

After that, the Lacewing King went back to his court in World Below. It wasn't that he was sorry for the unhappiness he'd caused—in fact, he didn't even know what had become of the girl who had loved him, or the nurse with the porcelain eye. But a kingdom needs a ruler; and in his absence things were becoming dangerously unstable.

The Glow-Worm Chancellor had managed things as well as he could while the King was away. But a Chancellor is not a King, and there were those among the Silken Folk who were eager to hazard a chance at the throne.

But the Termite Prince was penniless, barely able to afford a bannerman, let alone an army. The Spider Queen had gone mad, so they said, refusing to stir from her silken bed or leave her beloved embroidery. The Dragonfly Queen was engaged in a war with the Red Ants, while the Queen of the Black Ants was occupied in waging war with the Centipedes. The Cockroach Queen was at war with them both, as well as with the Hornets. That left only the Honeycomb Queen, who would never harm her son; the Harlequin, who was still missing; and a handful of minor Princes and Queens who offered little threat to the King. However, the Glow-

Worm Chancellor feared that these minor warlords might raise an army together. The King had been absent for much too long, and there was unrest in his kingdom.

The Lacewing King saw the wisdom in this. With his coat of a thousand eyes, he could watch his enemies without ever leaving his throne room, and he had an army of Cockroaches, sworn to his service, with a whole armoury of weapons and war machines of all kinds at their disposal. And so he watched from his termite throne, and sent his spies into the kingdom to find the source of the unrest, and to put an end to rebellion.

"If only you had a son, my lord," said the Glow-Worm Chancellor, "then these rumours could be dismissed. But a King without an heir—and especially a young and reckless King who likes to travel abroad without an escort—is always a liability. Perhaps, if you were to seek a Queen and settle down to family life, then you could put an end to this unrest."

The Glow-Worm Chancellor went on to inform His Majesty that he had already made a list of prospective consorts, and proposed to invite to the court whichever of the suitable candidates the King was inclined to favour.

The Lacewing King sat on his throne and thought about this for a long time. He was not a stranger to dalliance, but marriage had never occurred to him. To give up his travels among the Folk, his lovers and his concubines, seemed to him not only unfair but also unnecessary. His travels among the Sightless Folk had taught him this much about love: it was a weakness. If he married, he told himself, his marriage must be one of convenience, in which neither partner would complain if the other were not attentive, and which would provide the kingdom with the heir it so badly needed.

And so the Lacewing King took the list that the Glow-Worm Chancellor had made for him, and from his termite throne he observed the suitable ladies from afar, a goblet of honey wine in one hand and a dish of candied earwigs in the other. With his coat of a thousand eyes, he watched them in secret as they bathed; watched them in their gardens; observed their personal habits and their interactions with others.

Thus, he found out that the Grasshopper Queen had hairy legs; the Fishfly Princess, an annoying laugh; and the Mayfly Princess, though beautiful, was frivolous and demanding. He learnt that the Damselfly Princess would only make love in water; the Mealworm Princess was muffin-faced; and the (widowed) Scorpion Queen was addicted to eating her spouses.

One by one, the Lacewing King crossed off the names from his Chancellor's list until there was only one candidate left: the Silkworm Princess, who was beautiful, modest, virtuous, and good; and who lived in the sunlit Eastern Isles on the far side of the One Sea.

The Lacewing King watched the Princess through his coat of eyes for a month before he made his decision. Then, he issued his commands to the Glow-Worm Chancellor.

"Send word to the Silkworm Princess," he said. "Tell her of my deep regard, and of my plans to marry her."

Six weeks passed, which was how long it took for the message (borne by a cloud of golden fireflies) to reach the realm of the Silkworm Princess, and for the Princess to reply. She did so politely, but cautiously, and through the intermediary of her royal translator.

> *The Silkworm Princess of the Eastern Isles thanks His Majesty the King for his most flattering offer. She feels, however, that such a union should be based on mutual acquaintance and regard. She suggests, with the greatest humility, that she and her entourage should pay a state visit to His Majesty's court, to determine whether a suitable compatibility might exist between them.*

The Lacewing King agreed, though impatiently. Messages took so long to arrive to and from the Eastern Isles that he feared the year would be out before the royal wedding could take place. After that, who knew when his Queen would provide him with an heir?

While he was waiting, he used the time to clear up a minor rebellion among the Long-Nosed Weevils, then to end a minor war against the Queen of the Hoverflies.

Time passed. The Silkworm Princess set out with her royal retinue. Meanwhile, the Lacewing King toured his kingdom with an escort of his most fearsome warriors. He visited the Leaf-Cutter Bees, and resolved their long-standing dispute with the Red-Tailed Bumblebees. He dealt severely with an assassination attempt by the Prince of the Red Ants, and made several useful alliances. By the time he returned to his court, whatever unrest had existed in his kingdom was at an end, but there was still no sign of the Silkworm Princess. The Lacewing King began to question whether he needed to marry at all.

Finally, the royal party from the Eastern Isles arrived. The Silkworm Princess, with her entourage of five dozen handmaidens; her Chancellor; her translator, and her cook. She was as lovely as the King had observed through his coat of a thousand eyes: with jet-black hair that touched the ground, and a gown of a hundred layers under a cloak of yellow silk.

The King greeted the Princess (who spoke only her own language) through her official translator, an ancient silkworm with a hearing problem and a habit of sitting between them to discourage inappropriate contact. Nevertheless, the Silkworm Princess was delighted with the Lacewing King, and was amazed that he seemed to know so much about her habits and tastes.

For instance, he knew, without having asked, that her favourite food was honey-roast ants, cooked in a sauce of nine spices and served on a bed of saffron rice. He knew that she liked music, and so he summoned a quartet of millipedes to play on their harps of a thousand strings. He knew that she slept under yellow silk sheets, with lavender on her pillow. He knew that she bathed in rainwater that had been filtered through rush baskets of jasmine flowers, and, knowing she liked calligraphy, had made sure to provide her with a generous supply of rice-paper sheets, butterfly scrolls, and brushes made of moon-moth antennae.

"Her Royal Highness would have you know her delight," said the silkworm translator. "And she would have me ask how you came to know so much about her tastes and customs."

The King indicated his coat of eyes and gave a modest little bow.

For a moment, the silkworm translator stared. At last, he said, "Forgive me. But I fear I may have foolishly misunderstood Your Royal Majesty's meaning."

The Lacewing King obligingly explained the many practical uses of a coat of a thousand eyes. There followed a long discussion between the lady and her translator, in which the lady seemed to become more than a little agitated.

Finally, the silkworm translator stood and addressed the Lacewing King. "My lady is unwell," he said. "She craves your forgiveness, but must retire."

The Lacewing King, whose research had shown that the Silkworm Princess was sometimes prey to abdominal cramps, and who had gone to the trouble of providing various remedies to deal with this, offered the services of his royal apothecary.

The elderly translator conveyed the message to the Princess. But if anything, the Princess seemed more agitated than ever. She left a few days later, having kept to her chamber for the remainder of her stay. Not even a gift of her favourite mealworm candies were enough to tempt her from confinement, and she left in the night, without saying goodbye, in a covered carriage drawn by a team of dragonflies.

And so the Lacewing King gave up his plan for an alliance. Women, he thought, even Princesses, were not at all reliable, and prone to peculiar fits and starts that, surely, no reasonable man could endure.

Besides, as he told the Chancellor, when that gentleman dared enquire after His Majesty's plans; the incident had taught him a number of valuable lessons in life; the foremost of which was that there was *no such thing* as a marriage of convenience.

14

THE TRAVELLER

There once was a man whose ambition was to see a certain, fabled mountain. One day, he set out to travel there, taking with him his pack, his tent, his bedroll, and food for the journey.

On the first day, he walked through a forest of trees in which every leaf was a butterfly. On the second day, he passed a blue lake dancing with golden mosquitoes. On the third day, at sunset, he made camp on a river of molten bronze. On the fourth day, a beautiful woman spoke to him from the heart of a willow-tree. On the fifth day, he passed by a market, where goblin men sold strange wares. On the sixth, he found true love, and told it to wait till he came by again. On the seventh day, he slept on the outskirts of a city of glass. On the eighth, he walked across a floating kingdom of water-lilies, governed by a Damselfly Queen with wings like silver shadow.

Nine days he walked, through wind and rain, through sunshine and starlight and rainbow, until at last, he came to the foot of the fabled mountain.

But to his disappointment, he found that the mountain was obscured by cloud, and all he could see was the skirt of scree that surrounded it, half-hidden in a feathery mist that seemed to mock his efforts.

And so he turned back and headed for home; through sunshine and starlight and rainbow. And when he reached his village after nine weary days of travelling, his friends, who dreamed of adventure, but who had never dared to go much further than the neighbouring village, all came running to greet him and to shake his hand, and say to him:

"What was it like? What did you see?"

And the man said, "I saw *nothing*."

15

CLOCKWORK

There was a man who married for love but lived to repent at leisure. He was a toymaker by trade, and his passion for precision work was known across the Nine Worlds. It was said that he'd made a mechanical bird that sang as sweetly as a lark, and great battalions of clockwork Hussars with sabres at the ready. His dolls looked as if they might draw breath; his engines blew real steam from their stacks and were fed with tiny coals by mechanical stokers wielding tiny mechanical shovels. His dolls' houses were marvels in miniature; with tiny gilt mirrors on bedroom walls reflecting tiny four-poster beds and tiny children playing with baby dolls no bigger than a grain of rice. Everything was perfect in the toymaker's world; down to the smallest detail. Well—

Everything but one thing. His wife.

Of course, they'd been in love, they said. But now, some years later, he began to see that his wife was no great credit to him. She was no beauty; her judgement was weak; her housekeeping was slovenly. She loved her husband, to be sure, and he loved her too—in his way. But was it enough, he asked himself? Didn't he owe himself more than this?

One day the toymaker noticed that his wife's hair was going grey. It displeased him to see it; and so he made her a new head of hair, spun from skeins of gleaming gold, and stitched it into place on her scalp, as he had done so often when he was making dolls. The wife said nothing, but looked at herself in her dressing-room mirror and touched the bright, stiff strands of her hair, and remembered a time when he had thought she was perfect in every way.

For a while, the toymaker was pleased. But then he started to notice that his wife often spoke out of turn, or said things that he found unnecessary or even downright stupid. And so, as she slept, he cut out her tongue and replaced it with a mechanical one, sleek as a silverfish, crisp as a clock. After that, the toymaker's wife was always perfectly precise in her speech, and never said anything stupid, or dull, or bored him with her chatter.

All was well for a time, until the toymaker noticed that his wife often looked at him with reproach, and sometimes wept for no reason. It made him uneasy, and so he made her a new pair of blown-glass eyes that were bright and approving, and never shed tears, or seemed to express anything but contentment. He was very proud of his handiwork, and for a time, he was content.

But soon he noticed his wife's hands; hands that were often clumsy and slow, and so he made some mechanical hands and fixed them into place instead. His wife's new hands were as white as milk, and as clever as any automaton's, and so he made a pair of feet, and then a pair of perfect breasts, so that little by little, over time, he had replaced every flawed and worn-out part with clockwork and gleaming porcelain.

"At last, she is perfect," he told himself, looking at his beautiful wife.

But still, there was something missing. Still, she wasn't quite as he'd hoped. And so the toymaker opened her up to see what part of her inner workings he might have neglected to tune or correct. He found everything in place—except for one thing he had overlooked. One small, insignificant thing, so deeply embedded in the intricacies of clockwork and circuitry that he hadn't noticed it. It was her heart—it was broken.

"I wonder how *that* could have happened?" he said, fully intending to make her a new heart to replace the worn-out, broken one.

But then he looked at his beautiful wife, lying so still and so pale on the bench; quiet and lovely in every way; every part shiny and gleaming.

"Why, you don't need a heart at all, do you, my darling?" he told her.

And so he took the broken heart and threw it onto the rubbish heap. And then he turned back to his wife and kissed her lovely silverfish mouth, looked into her shining blown-glass eyes and said:

"At last. You're perfect."

16

THE BOOKWORM PRINCESS

It so happened that the princes of two neighbouring lands both fell in love with the same princess. One was the pallid Termite Prince; clever and industrious. The second was the Cockroach Prince; warlike in his armour. Both were handsome; both were rich; both were young and ambitious. Both were desperate to have the girl—who was known as the Bookworm Princess—the first because she would make him a beautiful Queen when his father died; the second, because his rival wanted her. Both swore their devotion by special royal envoy, and sent deliveries of gifts—jewelry and silver and lace; scents and silks and chocolates.

But the Princess was blessed with more sense than most and was unimpressed by Princes. Princes, in her experience, were often selfish and arrogant, viewing girls as territories to be won, or trophies to be collected, rather than people with feelings and dreams. She sent the royal envoys away, declaring that she preferred her books, and would rather have actions than empty words.

The Princes sensed a challenge. They decided to prove their worth. The Cockroach Prince immediately declared war on a far-off land and sailed off in a fleet of ships, promising a victory that would prove to her his undying love. The Termite Prince called his stonemasons and commissioned a wonderful palace for her, with walls of pink marble and towers of glass, surrounded by gardens and orchards and lakes. Each Prince believed that *his* magnificent gesture would win the heart of the Bookworm Princess—and each kept his rival under close supervision via a secret network of spies, to make sure that neither was cheating.

The Bookworm Princess was disappointed. Since her sixteenth birthday there had been a long procession of suitors—barons and princes and warlords and kings; rich men and wise men and businessmen; astronomers and silk-merchants and slavers from the Outlands—

all competing for her hand. Now she was twenty-four, and still no one had ever touched her heart.

And so she sat on a gatepost at the edge of her garden and read a book, as the Cockroach Prince directed ships to sail his armies to the battlefield and the Termite Prince directed his workmen to build the grandest palace ever built. Both were absorbed in their chosen task; neither noticed the Princess.

Then one day a young man came along. He wasn't a prince, and he had no idea who the girl on the gatepost was. He only saw that her eyes were sad; and so he bent down and picked her a flower from the many that grew by the side of the road, and gave it to the Bookworm Princess, and said:

"What's that you're reading?"

The Bookworm Princess was very surprised. In all her years of talking with men, no one had ever asked her anything about herself. She said, "It's a book of stories."

"I make up stories," said the young man.

The Bookworm Princess stared at him. "People really do that?" she said.

"Of course," said the young man, and smiled. "Come with me and I'll show you exactly how it's done."

So the Bookworm Princess jumped off the gate and followed him, right there, right then—without stopping to collect her belongings, or her pony, or her shoes, or her jewelry, or even to tell anyone that she was leaving.

As for the two Princes, the Cockroach Prince waged war for ten years and returned a famous General, missing an eye, but having wiped out the enemy and razed his cities to the ground; and the Termite Prince, having spent ten years overseeing the construction of his palace, was now a famous Architect, creator of the most exquisite piece of craftsmanship in Nine Worlds.

Both felt that their achievements deserved to win them the Bookworm Princess. But when they learnt that she had been gone ten years, while they built and fought and struggled, the two Princes were outraged.

"How dare she!" said the famous General.

"After all we've done for her!" wailed the famous Architect.

And so, because the General's long campaign had left him virtually penniless, and the Architect's quest for rare marble had brought his country to the brink of economic collapse, they decided to pool their resources and live together in the pink palace, abandoning the pursuit of love for more manly pleasures.

As for the Bookworm Princess, no one knows for sure where she went with her young man. Some say he was the Lacewing King, and that he took her away to his underground lair. Some say that she went off alone and had countless adventures. Some said she learnt to write stories herself, and told them to folk all over the Worlds. Some even said they'd read them.

17

THE TROUBLESOME PIGLET

In a piggery not far away, there lived a troublesome piglet. The smallest of a litter of twelve, it was also the noisiest; always loudest at feeding-time; always complaining about something. Its mother was at wits' end; for a squealing, discontented pig was most likely to end up on a roasting-dish, and as such, the mother sow was at pains to keep her young family as quiet as possible.

But the troublesome piglet didn't care. "I will not be silenced," it boasted to the other animals. "What this farm needs is a spokespig who isn't afraid to speak its mind."

Consequently, the troublesome piglet spoke its mind about everything. It was neither clever nor well-informed, but that didn't stop it having (and voicing) shrill and angry opinions on every topic imaginable.

If a dog trotted past the sty, the piglet would say, "I hate dogs. They're so woofy. Woof, woof, woof, that's all they can say. That's why they're so *stupid*."

The farm-dogs, who were both rather old and used to hearing nonsense, ignored the troublesome piglet, which made it all the more determined to attract their attention.

If a fox crossed the yard at night, the piglet would hurl invective. "Foxes!" it would say. "They're such cowards. Always chasing hens and ducks. Why don't they pick on someone their own size? Because they're *afraid*, that's why!"

The fox rarely deigned to comment, being largely preoccupied by the hunt, which didn't stop the piglet from hurling abuse in his silent wake.

If a duck went past the sty, the troublesome piglet would shout out, "Ducks are so stupid. All beaky and waddly. Why do we have ducks, anyway? They're just a pointless waste of time."

The ducks rarely responded, having far better things to do, but the other piglets listened in envy and awe, and gradually the troublesome piglet gained a reputation for fearlessness and plain-speaking.

Even the old mother sow felt proud that she had given birth to a piglet who wasn't afraid of *anything*. Cats, dogs, geese, cows— not even other pigs were exempt from the piglet's contempt and scorn. It mocked the other pigs for being fat; ridiculed the donkeys; called the cows all sorts of names; and even baited the toothless old guard-dog asleep in the sun. After a while, the other animals grew to expect the piglet to misbehave, and even encouraged its silliness. They were only farm animals, after all, and they had precious little else to entertain them.

One day, the farmer's wife came round with a basket of scraps for the piggery. The old sow hid her piglets, knowing that the farmer was partial to roast pork, and that this might be a ploy to catch a sucking-pig for dinner.

But the troublesome piglet would not hide. Instead it squealed at the top of its voice, "Look at the farmer's wife with her scraps! What a ridiculous woman she is! Well, if she thinks we're going to come running every time she tips a handful of potato peelings into the sty, then she has another think coming!"

"Quiet! Shh!" said the mother sow. "Have some sense and stop squealing!"

This only angered the piglet more. "How dare you try to silence me!" it squeaked. "How dare you deny me freedom of speech?" (It had learnt this phrase quite recently from a visiting weasel and was keen to use it as often as possible.)

The mother sow tried very hard to calm the troublesome piglet. But this only encouraged it to squeal even louder—so loudly, in fact, that the farmer's wife was reminded how long ago it had been since she and her husband had enjoyed a nice bit of bacon. She reached into the pigsty and grabbed hold of the piglet.

"Help!" it squealed. "This is oppression! This is censorship! This is an attack on free speech!"

The farmer's wife paid no attention, but carried off the piglet, which duly found its way onto her plate in the form of a very nice Sunday lunch.

The other pigs lamented the loss of their youngest relative. Some even staged a protest, although their indignation was short-lived. For a while, the farmyard bemoaned the lack of entertainment; and then a nest of weasels moved in under the old henhouse, providing all the excitement they craved. The troublesome piglet and its ideas were very quickly forgotten. After all, as the old sow said, in matters of sense or censorship, whichever way you sliced it, it was only bacon.

18

THE WASP PRINCE

In a village of orchards and fields, a woman desperately wanted a child. Since she and her husband had first been wed, this had been her dearest wish; but time had passed and no child had come, and now the couple were old.

The husband was a farmer, and like most of the men of his village, spent his time in his orchard, tending his peach and almond-trees. *They* were his children now, he said, and he cared for them with love, but the woman had nothing. And so, one night, she left her husband sleeping, and crept through the village in secret to find the court of the Lacewing King, who, it was said, could grant any wish—if you were fool enough to ask.

By then the Lacewing King had earned himself a reputation. Many, many years had passed since his theft of the Spider Queen's coronet and his wooing of the Silkworm Princess, and he was known both for his cruelty and for never selling his services short. But the woman was desperate. She told her tale to the Lacewing King, who listened in silence from his termite throne, occasionally popping a candied cockroach into his mouth and watching her with his amber eyes.

"I'll grant your wish," he said at last, when the woman fell silent.

"And your price?" she asked him.

The Lacewing King said nothing at first. It had been a long time since he had entertained the thought of becoming a father. Now his desire for a son returned, and he looked at the woman with a smile.

"All I ask of you," he said, "is that neither you nor the child should ever harm one of my folk. Not a wasp, or an ant, or a green-fly. Do you understand?"

The woman (who had been half-expecting a demand for her soul) gratefully nodded agreement. And then she went back home, to bed, and in the morning could not quite recall if she had seen the Lacewing King, or whether she had dreamed it all. But in her bedroom that morning, she found a dozen yellow wasps crawling on the window-ledge, a gift from her strange benefactor.

Her husband wanted to kill them. But his wife, although she hated wasps, would not allow him to touch them. "Even a wasp can serve," she said. "Go to work, and let them be."

The next day, there were more wasps crawling on the window-ledge. And by the end of the week, there were so many that the windows were garlanded with clumps of yellow-black blossom. And yet they never stung anyone, but simply waited patiently. And every morning, there were more.

By now the man had realized that something unnatural was happening. He questioned his wife, but she refused to tell him anything about her visit to the Lacewing King, or the promise she'd made him. And so that night, the man stayed awake to watch his wife as she slept.

At first, nothing happened. The woman slept, breathing softly by his side.

Then, she murmured in her sleep, and he knew she was dreaming. And, as she dreamed, a wasp crawled from the woman's half-open mouth. It crawled across her cheek, black in the moonlight, then dropped onto the bedroom floor.

Then, another wasp crawled out of the dreaming woman's mouth. And another. Silently, and in horror, the man watched as wasps continued to drool out of the woman's open mouth, dropping onto the coverlet. By morning there were so many that heavy swags of black and gold hung at the windows like curtains.

By now the man had guessed the truth; but he said nothing. He simply moved out. In the village, the gossips' tongues began to murmur and speculate. But the woman paid no attention. Instead she stayed home and observed the wasps, which grew more numerous every night. She fed them with peaches and sang to them the lullabies of the Silken Folk. And every day their numbers increased, so that soon they covered the whole of the house in black-and-yellow blossom.

Meanwhile, in the village, the gossips still talked. The husband, who was a fool for drink, let slip a careless word or two. Soon, everyone in the village knew that the woman had given herself to the Lacewing King. The priest denounced her. The neighbours moved out. But the woman didn't care. She just sat among the wasps, singing and dreaming to herself, crowned and gloved in black and gold, waiting for something to happen.

And then, one night, she woke up cold. Her coverlet of wasps had gone. In fact, every wasp in the house had gone, and in their place, on the window-ledge, she found a baby boy, asleep. The Lacewing King had granted her wish.

The lonely woman was overjoyed. Her son was perfect in every way; dark-haired, golden-eyed, with skin as soft as a ripe peach. She fed him, and rocked him, and sang to him, then wrapped him in a blanket and took him into the village. But the villagers turned away in horror as she approached. Parents called their children inside; women spat on the ground as she passed; and the grocer shut his door in her face and said:

"That's the spawn of the Lacewing King. You and your brat will get nothing from me."

And so the woman went back home, and never went into the village again. She built a fence around her house and raised her son there alone. She grew vegetables in her garden, kept hens for their eggs, and never spoke to anyone but the boy, who grew to be strong and handsome. She called him "My Prince" and "My Golden One," and made his shirts from her wedding dress, which had been fine once, years ago, with a train of white silk and twelve petticoats of the most delicate gauze. The villagers kept away from the house and allowed the path that led to it to become neglected and overgrown. As the years passed, they almost forgot that anyone lived there at all.

The boy and his mother were happy at first. No one dared to trouble them. Their garden was always luxuriant; their crops were never plagued by pests. The boy could see the Silken Folk; and they often came to him while his mother was at work; golden-eyed and cluster-clawed, bearing gifts of honeycomb. From afar, the Lace-wing King watched through his coat of a thousand eyes, and over the years, he came to feel a kind of affection for the boy, and little by little, he grew immersed in pleasant dreams of fatherhood.

And then, when the boy was nearly grown, a plague of wasps came to the village. It devastated the fruit trees from which most of the folk made their living. Great swarms of the insects came on the wind, finding their way into walls and thatch, building great nests in the dry ground. A baby was stung to death as it lay in its crib by a window, and at last, the villagers remembered the birth of another child, years before, and the woman who had called him into the world.

"This is *her* doing," they whispered. "The witch and her brat must be dealt with."

And so, one night, after some of them had drunk themselves into bravery, the villagers went to the old woman's house, bearing torches and cudgels and knives. They broke down the fence and pounded the door, demanding that she put an end to the plague.

The woman was confused and afraid, weakened by poverty and solitude. She knew nothing of the plague of wasps—wasps had never troubled her, and never attacked her garden—and she spoke angrily to the villagers, refusing to let them into her house.

But the drunken, frightened villagers had come too far to be sent away. They broke down the door of the woman's house and ran wild inside, smashing jars from the kitchen shelves, tearing down the curtains, toppling the dresser with its load of painted plates. The old woman tried to stop them, but they grabbed her and tied her to her chair, while the rest of the mob went after her son.

They found his room; but the boy had gone. His bed was empty; the window ajar. The villagers said that the boy must have changed himself into a cloud of wasps and flown away into the night, as the Lacewing King was rumoured to do when enemies came looking for him. (In fact, there was an apple tree just outside the window, large enough for a boy to climb down; but no one thought that likely.)

And so, in rage, the villagers set fire to the little house, with the woman still inside. And, waving their torches, howling mad, they laughed and danced as they watched it burn, knowing that the only sure way to get rid of a wasp's nest is by fire, while, from the shelter of the nearby wood, the boy watched the scene in silence, flames reflected in his eyes and streaming down his golden cheeks.

The following day, the villagers were very quiet and subdued. No one spoke of what had happened. No one admitted to having been there. Days passed, and folk could almost believe that nothing had really happened, and that the fire had been an accident. The plague of wasps was over. The villagers made preserves from what was left of their peaches. A few went looking for the boy, but they never found him. He stayed in the woods, in hiding, alone, grieving for his mother. The swarms of wasps had followed him; they were his only companions, filling the air with an angry sound that matched the turmoil in his heart.

Sitting on his termite throne, the Lacewing King, with his coat of eyes, saw the smoke from the house fire and understood what had happened. He saw the boy hiding in the woods; and the swarms of wasps that surrounded him. He put on his armour and picked up his bow and his quiver of hornet-tipped arrows. Then he went in search of the boy.

He found him in a clearing. The air was thunderous with wasps. The Lacewing King raised a hand, and the wasps settled gently onto the ground, into the leaves of the nearby trees, onto the shoulders of the boy like a royal mantle.

The Lacewing King looked at the boy. For a moment, neither spoke.

Then the King said, "Son, it's time."

And both of them took terrible wing and flew towards the village.

19

DEATH AND THE ARTIST

There once was an artist of great renown, but his work was not immortal. His portraits were life-like; but they had no spark. His still-lifes were real in every way, except that they were not alive. His landscapes were almost perfect, and yet the sun never shone there, nor did they make the heart quicken. And although he had made his fortune from painting, the man was unhappy and unfulfilled, and longed for something greater.

One day, in despair, he consulted Death. Alone, in his bone-white citadel, the ruler of the Land of the Dead had seen generations come and go. If there was a secret to capturing Life, then surely he would know it.

Death listened to the artist's plea. His living eye, blue as a butterfly's wing, gleamed with secret knowledge. His dead eye, dark as honeycomb, was filled with grim amusement.

"Can you help me?" said the man.

"Yes," said Death. "I can help you. There is a word, which will bring to life everything you capture. Every flower, every fruit, every human figure. But we must beware how we use the word—for there are always consequences."

The famous artist was overjoyed. "Tell me the word," he begged.

Death smiled and whispered the word in the artist's ear. "When you have spoken it," he said, "the secret to capturing Life will be yours. But again, beware—once spoken, the word can never be unspoken."

The artist fled home from the Land of the Dead and ran straight to his studio. There was an apple there, in a bowl. Taking up his palette, he chose a clean scrap of canvas, and started to paint the apple. Then he uttered the secret word given to him by the Lord of Death.

At first, nothing happened. But as he painted, the artist began to realize that there was something different about his work. The apple gleamed with ripeness. Its skin was taut and shiny. Even its scent seemed to overwhelm the scents of oils and turpentine. And as he worked, the artist saw the apple in the fruit-bowl wizen, and wither, and finally rot, so that by the time he had finished, all its life had been captured in his perfect canvas.

The artist was greatly excited. At last, he had managed to capture Life. He tried a vase of flowers next, with the same pleasing degree of success—although the flowers themselves lost their bloom as soon as his brush touched the canvas.

"These must be the consequences against which my Lord Death warned me," he thought. "But what is such a sacrifice compared to the pursuit of Art?"

Soon, the artist's renown had spread far across the country. His paintings of fruit and flowers were admired by kings and emperors. A portrait of the Empress's lapdog earned him yet more money and fame—still more, because the animal died so shortly after the work was complete. And yet he was not satisfied. He wanted to be immortal.

And so the artist cast his eye over the streets of his city. He saw beggars and street-urchins, gypsies and whores: people whose lives would not be missed, he thought, in the noble pursuit of Art. And so he painted them—perfectly. He immortalized them in paint. His fame grew throughout the Nine Worlds; no man was considered his equal. Royal princesses came to him to have their wedding portraits painted. And if they died soon afterwards, then surely it was a warning to other royal houses to have their children immortalized before the Reaper took them, too.

No one suspected the artist for the wave of deaths that occurred all across the country. People were even grateful to him for keeping their vanished loved ones alive. Kings and queens showered him with gifts, honours, and titles. And still the artist was not convinced that he was an immortal.

Finally, seeing old age approach, once more he consulted Death. Death was waiting, a hint of a smile in his half-living features.

"You want to be immortal?" he said. "There is only one way to be sure." And, beckoning the man closer, he whispered the secret into his ear.

The artist went back to his studio, filled with triumph and certainty. He pulled up a great gilded mirror alongside his easel and started to paint a self-portrait. And when his servants came the next day to bring him his morning coffee, they found him lying dead on the ground in front of a marvellous canvas from which their master's eyes seemed to shine with a terrible understanding—

They gave him a lavish funeral, with all the honours of the state. The King himself laid flowers at the grave in the city cathedral. And everyone marvelled at the detail of that last self-portrait—although they never understood why the famous artist had chosen to paint himself with such a look upon his face; almost as if Lord Death himself had come to carry him, screaming, away.

20

REVENGE OF THE SPIDER QUEEN

After that, the Wasp Prince, as the Folk now called him, vanished for a long time. Even the Lacewing King could not see where the boy had gone. He assumed that his son was grieving for the death of his mother, and did not attempt to track him down, thinking that once he was ready, the boy would come to join him.

Time passed. But the Wasp Prince showed no sign of returning. Occasionally, the King would hear rumours from his many spies, and sometimes he caught a fleeting glimpse of his son from his coat of a thousand eyes, but most of the time, he saw nothing, and life went on as always.

Meanwhile, the Wasp Prince was troubled by the recent events in the village. His mother had been a gentle soul and had taught him to respect all life. But now she was gone, and for the first time, the young man had a new path to tread. His mother had never told her son the circumstances of his birth, but he had heard tales of the Lacewing King from his occasional visitors—the Silken Folk, that his mother had often seemed unable to see—and he knew his reputation for wickedness and cruelty. He remembered very little of what had happened the day they met. He had been angry and upset, grieving for his mother. All he remembered was how they had flown together, over the village. How the villagers had screamed. And to know now that this was his *father*—

And so the Prince stayed in hiding, deep in the heart of the forest. He fed on wild honey, berries, and nuts, and sheltered in the hollow trunk of an ancient oak-tree. And it was here that the Spider Queen discovered him, asleep in the tree, and summoned her servants to bring him to the gates of her forest lair.

Over twenty years had passed since the Lacewing King had robbed the Queen of her coronet of eyes, and since then she had remained in her lair, surrounded by the high stone wall and the monstrous garden. But though she was unable to *see* beyond the walls of her domain, her web extended much further. Her long and sensitive fingers had grown so attuned to the movements of the world beyond, that, she could sense the presence of an ant on a wall a mile away; or feel the hairs on a moth's wing against a window-shutter at night. And though she had withdrawn from the world, into the safety of her lair, she had not forgotten her vow to take revenge on the Lacewing King, and break his cold and arrogant heart.

Over the years she had observed him through the silken skeins of her web. Though she could not see his face, she knew his every movement. She knew the tone of his voice; where he went; the nights he slept like a child and the nights he paced the floor of his chamber. She knew when he was bored, and when he visited his concubines. She knew the names of his horses; his favourite dishes; his favourite books. And little by little, she had come to know things about her enemy that even the Glow-Worm Chancellor—even the Honey-comb Queen—did not. But as for breaking his heart, the Queen was no closer to finding a way than she had been two decades ago. As far as anybody knew, the Lacewing King was heartless.

But now, at last, she began to believe she might have found his weakness. She had followed his quest for an heir and knew how badly he had wanted a son. And now, the Wasp Prince was in her grasp, and she would have her vengeance.

First, she had her servants escort him to her forest lair in a carriage drawn by emperor moths and upholstered in dragonfly leather. She came to greet him in person as he arrived at the rust-red gate; but not in the Aspect she had assumed when she had first met his father. Gone was the queenly apparel; the crown; the train of ten thousand dewdrops. Instead the Spider Queen came to the boy as a woman of the Folk—a woman not unlike his mother—dressed in a simple homespun gown, with an apron knotted about her waist. So like his mother was she, in fact, that the boy was not in the least bit suspicious, but went with her willingly into her lair, which she had cleverly camouflaged to look like a little cottage, humble but inviting, in the heart of the overgrown garden.

"Forgive a poor widow, my Prince," she said. "But I saw you sleeping out in the woods, and though my home is humbler than your father's underground citadel, I would be glad to offer you whatever poor hospitality I can provide."

And she offered the young Prince homely meats of the kind his mother used to cook; dishes of fried potatoes; river-fish cooked in jackets of leaves; mutton stew with dumplings and wine. The Prince, who was hungry, ate his fill, while the Spider Queen stood by and smiled. And then the Wasp Prince turned to her, and thanked her for her kindness, and asked her exactly what she knew of the Lacewing King, his father.

The Spider Queen told her tale; of how the King had stolen her crown through treachery and falsehood (although she omitted to tell of her plans to devour the young King on their wedding night). She told him of her poverty; of her withdrawal from the world; and then of her desire for a son to comfort her in her old age.

The boy listened to her tale in growing indignation. The Spider Queen's story confirmed everything he'd heard about the Lacewing King. His cruelty; his deception; his guile.

"And to think that you are his son," said the Queen, clicking her mandibles beneath the human Aspect she had assumed. "His only son, my Prince; his heir. To think that, one day, *you* will wear his crown—"

The Prince shook his head. "I don't want it."

"Why not?"

The young Prince explained how he and the King had taken revenge on the villagers, and how much horror he still felt at the memory of that day. The Spider Queen listened attentively. Until that moment, she had planned to simply devour the troubled young man. But now she had a better idea.

She poured the Wasp Prince a cup of wine. "It still disturbs you, doesn't it? How easily your rage took flight? How crisp and keen the air felt? The joy that filled you, the joy of revenge?"

The boy looked up with tears in his eyes. "Am I a monster?"

"My Golden One. There is no shame in enjoying revenge. I've enjoyed those pleasures myself." And the Queen took the boy in her many arms and rocked him gently, and sang to him in the voice of his mother:

"Long ago, and far away,
Far away and long ago.
The world's our honeycomb, you know;
The world's our honeycomb."

And at this the boy wept and rested his head in the lap of the Spider Queen, and said, "Oh, Mother. I miss her so much."

The Spider Queen smiled and poured the boy another cup of wine, and said, "I can be your mother, my Prince. I can keep you safe from the King. I will teach you all I know; and when you are fully-grown and strong, I will help you claim your crown. All I ask in return, my Prince, is what your father stole from me. My coronet of a thousand eyes that he plundered in my sleep. Promise me this, my Golden One, and I shall be your mother."

The boy looked at the Spider Queen, who looked so like his mother. She even used the childhood name his mother had used when she was alive.

He nodded, eyes still wet with tears. And the Spider Queen smiled and said, "Good boy."

21

THE CLOCKWORK PRINCESS

Once, there was a Clockwork Princess who lived in a land of forgotten things. The King of this land had long since been forgotten, as had the circumstances of the Princess's creation, though some told tales of a craftsman, a genius with ceramics and machinery who, half a century ago, had built a girl so perfect, so lifelike in every way, that the King, childless and a widower, had ordered the craftsman to give her up, meaning to adopt her as his own daughter.

Reluctantly, the craftsman had done as he was ordered. But he had hidden the silver key that wound up the clockwork girl's mechanism, so that within a few days she became increasingly listless. Too late, the King had tried to find the mysterious craftsman. However, the man had already fled, taking the silver key with him; and so the clockwork girl remained, silent, sad, and motionless.

Time passed. The old King died, leaving no heir but the clockwork girl. For a time, the Clockwork Princess reigned over the people. The actual business of ruling was all done by the King's old Regent; a kindly old man who understood the Princess's role as a figurehead. But soon her ailing mechanism ran down completely, and the Clockwork Princess went to sleep and would not re-awaken. And yet, for a time, there was no change, and things went on as normal.

But a kingdom needs a ruler. A sleeping Princess is no substitute for a King. For a time, the old Regent ruled in her place, trying to fight off foreign kings and warlords trying to take control. Meanwhile, the Clockwork Princess lay in state, right at the top of the castle tower, looking so like a real girl that over the years, people forgot that she was only clockwork.

But economic collapse, disease, and finally, the passing of time did its work. The kindly old Regent died, and soon the kingdom fell into lawlessness. The castle was looted; the servants fled; and finally, the grounds fell into such decay that all the paths were overgrown; the gate was rusted closed; the trees grew to monstrous proportions, each trying to steal the others' light, and in the end, the place was first shunned, and then almost forgotten, except by a few old wives, who told the tale of a sleeping girl under a curse, doomed to sleep for a hundred years until her prince awakened her.

Meanwhile, the Clockwork Princess still slept in the ruined tower. She might almost have been alive, except for the dust that filtered through the broken roof onto her porcelain skin, and the fact that she was not breathing. Meanwhile, outside, the legends grew, embellished by the telling. People spoke of trying to find their way into the castle grounds; but it had become so overgrown that many folk were afraid to approach, fearing wolves and witches and worse. Most who ventured in turned back long before they reached the tower; a few went inside but were daunted by the broken stairs and the gaping roof. One young man, alone, found his way through the garden and up the stairs, but when he saw the girl, asleep, under an inch-thick shroud of dust, he lost his mind on the instant, and never spoke a word again.

And so, in time, the Clockwork Princess was well and truly forgotten. Until one day, a watchmaker's boy came wandering through the forest. A hundred years or more had passed since the death of the old King, and even the walls of the castle grounds were broken-down and covered in moss. The boy, who was a stranger both to the place and to the tales that haunted it, had taken the short-cut through the woods to deliver a watch to a customer—a wealthy merchant who lived nearby.

The watch was as large as a turnip, and the key required to wind it was as thick as the boy's thumb, but the merchant felt that the size of his watch added to his consequence, and so was most

impatient to have it returned to him as soon as possible. The watch-maker, a stern employer, had sent the boy with instructions not to waste time, but the boy craved adventure, and when he saw the ruined tower in the woods, his curiosity overcame him and he went in for a closer look.

The stairs were rotten; the balustrade, once-gilded and carved with roses, was all that kept him from falling as he climbed up the tower. The stained-glass windows were all gone, shot through with sprays of briar. But the boy was light-footed and nimble and reached the top without difficulty, finally opening the door that led to the Princess's bedchamber.

The Princess had lain there a hundred years, under rain and sun and snow. Moss had grown on her porcelain face, and a colony of spiders nested in one sunken eye-socket. Her hair had mostly fallen out, and a piece of falling masonry had knocked off her right arm to the elbow, exposing the intricate system of cogs and wheels that it contained.

The watchmaker's boy came closer. He had understood at once that this was no ordinary girl, but a wonderful machine of sub-lime and intricate craftsmanship. Water had rusted the mechanism, but, on closer inspection, the boy believed that maybe she could be mended.

He tried to move her. No result. The Clockwork Princess was rusted fast. But, with the aid of his bottle of oil, his toolkit, and the big key from the merchant's turnip-watch, the watchmaker's boy finally managed to loosen, then to wind up the ancient, long-dead mechanism.

There came a terrible squealing of gears and rusty cogs in motion. Then the Clockwork Princess sat up. In spite of the ravages of time and the damage done by the elements, a part of her beauty still remained, as she fixed her remaining eye upon the watchmak-er's boy.

"Father?" she said in her rusty voice. "Father? Father? *Father?*"

It was the first word she had ever learnt from the craftsman who made her. It was the only word the old King had ever heard the Princess speak. It was the first word she'd spoken for well over a hundred years, and it sounded strange and sad.

The boy said, "No, I'm not your father."

The Clockwork Princess got to her feet. "No," she said. "No. No."

Her voice was quite expressionless, and yet it seemed to the boy that there was a world of sadness in the single syllable. A tear of rust came from her sunken, dead eye and trickled down her porcelain face.

The boy took a rag from his pocket and wiped away the rust and moss. Then he picked up her broken arm. "I'm pretty sure I could fix you," he said. "Will you come back home with me?"

The Clockwork Princess tilted her head. "Home."

"That's right," said the watchmaker's boy, and told her about the workshop; the watches waiting for repair; the cuckoo clocks; the grandfather clocks; the endless, quiet ticking. The watchmaker was not a kind man, but he was a very skilled craftsman. He would be able to mend the Princess—but what would become of her afterwards? The boy suspected she would be sold; maybe to a travelling show, or to a museum of curiosities, or even to a merchant, who would use her to enhance his prestige among the other merchants.

"Home," repeated the Clockwork Princess, and the boy thought there was doubt in her voice. "No. Home. No. Father."

The boy looked at the broken arm with its ruined, rusty clockwork. He knew that at the workshop, there would be plenty of spare parts. Then he looked at the turnip-watch he'd been paid to deliver, the key of which he had already used to wind up the Princess's mechanism. Slowly he became aware that she, too, was looking at the watch, a gleam of hope in her one blue eye—

He opened the watch and took out the works and used them to mend the Princess's arm. She waited in patient near-silence, occasionally whirring rustily. When the arm was re-attached, she flexed it experimentally. Although the porcelain shell was damaged beyond the boy's skill to repair, the arm itself still worked;

and when the Princess pulled the sleeve of her dress down over the exposed joint, the illusion was complete.

The boy looked at the ruined watch. "Well, that's done it. I can't go home now. That watch was worth a fortune."

"Fortune," said the Clockwork Princess, and the boy thought she sounded wistful.

He looked at her. "What's that you say?"

"*Fortune,*" repeated the Clockwork Princess, and lifted her delicate porcelain hand to point at the distant horizon.

The watchmaker's boy had always dreamed of travelling and adventures. "You think I should go *seek* my fortune?" he said.

"Fortune," said the Clockwork Princess in her sweet and toneless voice, and the gears and cogs in her abdomen moved a little faster, almost as if she had a heart under the silk and porcelain.

"But what about you? Would you stay with me?"

"Stay. With. Me," said the Clockwork Princess.

"All right," said the boy. "I will."

And so the two of them climbed down the stairs and into the ravaged garden, where the watchmaker's boy and the Clockwork Princess went off into the wilderness, she whirring occasionally to herself, he whistling a cheery song.

The watchmaker hired another boy, one who was nervous of the woods and not remotely curious. As for the merchant, he never got his watch back. Instead he bought a stovepipe hat and an amber-clouded cane, and set such a trend among his peers that watches went quite out of fashion.

22

THE WATCHER AND THE GLASS

There once was a woman who liked to watch. Her life was small, and she lived alone, but she liked to watch through her windows. Through glass, the world seemed smaller, somehow; safer and less threatening. And so, every day, the woman watched the world outside through her window.

She watched the people in the street. She watched the lives of others. She watched the cats and dogs go by. She watched the passing tradesmen. But most of all, she watched herself every day in the mirror, and wondered at the way in which she seemed to grow smaller every day.

One day, a journeyman came to the door. She watched but did not open it. The journeyman was old, and tired. His pack looked very heavy. He knocked once more at the door, but when the woman still did not open, he sighed and went on his way again, leaving behind him an object wrapped in cloth, on the doorstep.

The woman made sure that he had gone before retrieving the object. It was a viewing-box, made of wood, cunningly inlaid with silver. It looked valuable, and the woman wondered why the journeyman had left it there, and why he had been carrying it at all. Perhaps it was stolen, she told herself, and she took the viewing-box away into the backroom of her house and looked through the tiny glass window at the world around her.

Through the glass, the world looked so small and perfect that she almost wept. She went to the bedroom window and watched the passers-by through her viewing-box. Everything looked to her neater that way; clean-edged, bright and gleaming. Anything she preferred not to see was hidden by the wooden frame; everything she viewed became new and fresh and interesting. The woman spent the rest of the day watching the world through her viewing-box; and at the end of the day she looked at herself through the little glass window, and saw every detail, crisp and sharp, and marvelled at her reflection.

After that, the woman only watched the world through the viewing-box. Through the tiny window, even household duties became a source of daily pleasure; food became more enticing; visitors more amusing. There was no scent in the viewing-box; no tastes and no sensations. But through the box, the sun always shone; the world was always entrancing. Through the box, the world was safe; and the woman used it day and night. It was the first thing she reached for as she opened her eyes in the morning; the last thing she put aside before closing her eyes at night.

Time passed. Through the viewing-box, the woman watched as her friends moved away; got married; had children; lived their lives. The woman continued to watch them as they grew smaller and smaller. She fell in love through the viewing-box; watched as at last, her man went away. And time passed, until the day the woman lay on her deathbed, watching the world through her viewing-box and wondering at how small it all was; how delicate and perfectly formed.

Then there came a knock at the door. The priest, who was waiting by her bedside to perform the Last Rites, went to open it. The visitor was an old man; an old man the woman recognized. It was the journeyman who had left the viewing-box on her doorstep so many years before. He went to the woman's bedside and sat beside her on the bed. The woman looked at him through the tiny lens of the viewing-box, marvelling at how small he looked; how ancient, yet how oddly untouched by Time.

"You have something of mine," he said gently to the woman.

The dying woman shook her head. She was very weak, and yet her hands were still clutched tightly around the viewing-box.

"I left you this box on loan," said the man. "Now it's time to give it back." And he reached out and took it from the dying woman's hands.

Suddenly, for the first time in years, the woman could see the world as it was, without the glass or the wooden frame. Everything looked so huge to her now; huge and dark and frightening. Suddenly, she realized that she was actually going to die; and Death was like an enormous cloud, yawning, bleak and shapeless.

"Please, give me the box," she begged.

But the journeyman simply shook his head. "You have chosen to watch your life go by unlived," he told her. "Everything you might have been; everything you might have achieved; everything you might have seen, you hid inside this little box. And now I have collected your life, as I have collected so many lives from people who were afraid to live."

The woman looked at the journeyman, and now she saw him clearly, she saw that under his rags he was one of the many servants of Death; stern and dark and implacable. And she realized, too late, that she had given up the whole world for the sake of a little security. And then she died; and the journeyman collected the woman's dying breath, and sealed it inside the viewing-box, and put it gently into his pack, and went on with his journey.

No one ever saw him again in that part of the Middle Worlds— except maybe for the honeybees, from whom I heard the story.

23

THE COURTSHIP OF
THE LACEWING KING

In his court deep under the ground, the Lacewing King was lonely. A long, long time had passed since the disappearance of the Wasp Prince; still longer since he had last sought a bride. Even someone as wicked as he undoubtedly was sometimes feels in need of love, and after ruling alone for years, he began once more to look for a Queen.

It wasn't as easy as you might think. The King's requirements were many; and none of the ladies of his court seemed entirely to his taste. But somehow, word soon got around that the Lacewing King was contemplating matrimony; and foreign queens came from far and wide to present themselves and to solicit his favour.

The Cockroach Queen, all in black leather, with her retinue of armoured guards. The Mantis Queen, in eight-inch heels and a dress the colour of poisoned absinthe. The Scarab Queen, wearing the white crown of Isis (and absolutely *nothing else*).

But the King, in his coat of a thousand eyes, just watched them from his throne and yawned. The truth was, he was already in love. Madly, desperately in love. In love, or in lust, he barely knew—but whichever it was, it had consumed him utterly.

He knew her by reputation alone—they had never formally met. He knew that she was whimsical, volatile, and hard to please.

But with his coat of a thousand eyes, he had admired her from afar as she flitted across the countryside in her tumbleweed chariot, drawn by its team of Monarch butterflies, and gradually, he had come to believe that only she could satisfy him. She was the Butterfly Princess; as bright as the Lacewing King was dark; as kind as he was cruel. She lived in her treetop castle in the heart of the forest, and cared nothing for wisdom, or power, or wealth. *Love* was what she wanted.

But she wanted to be loved for herself. Not for her beautiful butterfly wings, or the narrowness of her waist, or the size of her brilliant eyes, or the thickness of her hair. She wanted something that would last beyond the attractions of physical beauty. And so, when the Lacewing King's envoys came to woo her on his behalf, she sent them back without even a word of encouragement. She knew of the King's reputation just as he knew of hers; she knew of his cruelty and his pride, his arrogance and his vanity. So she sent back his gifts unopened; the rolls of silk spun from the wings of dragonflies; the carpets woven from grasshopper silk, the candied wasps, the honeycomb, the mantles made from bumblebees. The Butterfly Princess refused them all, saying:

"Love is humble. Love is plain. If the King will come alone, without his crown or retinue, empty-handed and on foot, I *may* accept to hear him."

And so, for the first time in many years, the Lacewing King dismissed his court, dressed in his plainest, simplest clothes, and travelled on foot through the countryside to the court of the Butterfly Princess.

She watched him in secret, from afar. He was much more handsome than she had thought, and touchingly pale and lovelorn. She decided to put his love to the test. And so, on arriving, the Lacewing King found himself face-to-face, not with the Butterfly Princess herself, but with her mother.

This was the Caterpillar Queen, as pale and lumpen and loathsome as the Princess was lovely and delicate; sitting on her green velvet throne and watching him through tiny dark eyes. She herself was mute, but a servant (a golden dragonfly) translated her message to the King.

She said, "I will live in your court for a year, and if I am wholly satisfied, then my daughter will be yours."

Reluctantly, the Lacewing King agreed to the proposal. A year was not so long, he thought, and then the Princess would be his.

But he found that even the journey home was fraught with unexpected difficulty. The Caterpillar Queen was too heavy to walk. The Lacewing King had to carry her all the way back on his shoulders. She was a prodigious burden, and before the King had even left the forest, he was already sore and aching. She was also very demanding, making all her comments via the dragonfly servant.

"My lady asks why we are stopping again," it whirred, as the King collapsed to the ground. He was unused to heavy lifting, and the task of carrying the monstrous Queen had quickly brought him to his knees.

"My lady craves sweetness," said the dragonfly servant. "She asks that you fetch her some honeycomb."

And so the King had to walk for miles to raid the nearest bee's nest, by which time the Queen was asleep again, and could not be awoken.

"My lady is fatigued," said the dragonfly servant. "She wonders that the journey home is taking such a long time."

It says much for the King's self-control (and for the power of his desire) that he did not simply throw the Queen off his back and leave her to crawl back home on her own. But worse was to come. On arrival, he realized that his problems were only just beginning. The Queen was perpetually ravenous; devouring ten thousand honey-fried ants in a single meal, with three jars of mealworm marshmallow, and hundreds of candied cockroaches. She never said a word to the King, except through her intermediary, but ate so much that the royal chefs were obliged to work all day and night to sustain her enormous appetite, after which she was thirsty, and drank all the King's reserves of wine. She also smelt disgusting, and left a trail of pale slime on everything she touched.

Within six weeks the Lacewing King was in despair, and his court was close to mutiny. Within six months, his chef had resigned, most of his other servants had left, and he was forced to wait upon her alone. Soon, the Queen's demands began to take their toll upon the King. He became careless and neglectful. He would go out for days at a time, forgetting to see to her dietary needs. Once he left for a whole week, roaming the woods, going hunting, swimming in the cool green streams and trying to get the stink of her out of his clothes and from his hair.

But when at last he returned to his court, he found the Glow-Worm Chancellor in a state of extreme anxiety. His Majesty's guest had been unwell for some days, and that morning, the Chancellor had found her lifeless in her bed. Her dragonfly servant could not explain exactly what had happened, but clearly blamed the Lacewing King for his neglect of the royal visitor.

The Lacewing King was surprised and ashamed—but also secretly relieved. He immediately sent word to the Butterfly Princess, explaining that her mother had died unexpectedly in her sleep and expressing his humble condolences. Then, as he awaited the arrival of the Princess, he worked to make his underground court as magnificent as it could be.

He had the walls hung with black crepe, and veiled every mirror in spider's web. He placed a thousand black candles in every crystal chandelier. He ordered a lavish funeral, with mourners and weeping and incense, and a carriage topped with fine black silk and drawn by an army of carrion beetles.

Then, assuming an air of grief, he went to keep watch by the bedside of the Caterpillar Queen. He sat by her body for three days, awaiting the Princess's arrival, during which time he amused himself by telling the dead Queen exactly what he thought of her.

He told her how much he had always loathed her miserable appearance; her lack of conversation, her greed, her rudeness, and her laziness. He told her how she disgusted him, with her stink of rotten fish. He told her that the only reason he had tolerated her for so long was that he was in love with her daughter.

By then, the Caterpillar Queen's body had turned hard and brown, and still the Princess had not arrived. And then, on the fourth day of his watch, the Lacewing King was horrified to see the hard brown shell split open with a sudden crack, revealing a silken envelope that opened in its turn to reveal the elegant form of the Butterfly Princess; as beautiful as ever; veiled in nothing but her wings.

For a moment, she stood, blinking in the torchlight. Then she stretched her golden limbs and turned her luminous eyes to the King.

"I would have been yours," she told him. "But you broke our agreement."

Then she spread her butterfly wings and flew away into World Above. The Lacewing King ran after her, pleading for a chance to explain, but the Princess had already gone back to her court in the treetops.

He never did marry, in the end. Perhaps he always secretly feared having to care for a mother-in-law. As for the Butterfly Princess, he never mentioned her again, although some said they had seen him, in summertime, at the edge of the woods, watching the butterflies at play. And from that day forth, his head chef's signature dish of honeyed, roasted caterpillars—once a favourite in his court—was no longer served there.

24

THE BULL AND THE SNAIL

Once there was a farmer who kept a wild, ferocious bull. The bull was so savage that he had to be kept locked up in the barn, but even so, the other farm animals were terribly afraid of him. The hens and geese trembled in fear every time they crossed the barnyard, and the sheep and ducks and donkeys lived in terror of his horns.

"What can we do?" said the animals. "That bull could get free any time."

They became increasingly nervous. Just thinking about that bull and his horns made life in the farmyard unbearable. Hens and ducks stopped laying eggs. Horses threw their riders. Sheep became tangled in hedges. Pigs and rabbits ate their young. Soon, the very mention of horns, or even the sight of a cow in a field, was enough to provoke a near-stampede as the climate of panic grew.

The animals all agreed that this was a sorry state of affairs, and that something drastic would have to be done. Finally, they came up with an idea. They appointed a pack of dogs to protect them. The dogs patrolled the farmyard, identifying potential threats. Horned creatures—goats and cows—were cautioned to make sure they didn't intimidate the other animals.

One rainy day, a Snail appeared on the farmyard gate. As a flock of geese went by, it put out its horns and waved at them. None of the geese seemed to mind very much, but the dogs gave the Snail a caution.

"Put those horns away," they said. "That's threatening behaviour, that is."

The Snail ignored them and wiggled its horns again.

The dogs went to the farmer and complained about the aggressive snail. They presented such a convincing case that the farmer agreed to investigate. He spent the rest of the week killing snails in and around the farmyard. By the end of that time there wasn't a snail to be seen within miles, and the animals all agreed that the threat had been well and truly addressed.

Meanwhile, the bull broke out of the barn and ran amok, trampling and goring everything in his path. A flock of sheep was scattered, and some ducks were badly frightened. The dogs (and indeed, the farmer) saw this as further proof that you can never be too vigilant, and extended their war on invertebrates to include slugs and caterpillars, as well.

25

THE CAT WHO WAS KING

There once was a cat who longed to be King. He lived near the palace kitchens, and he had often seen the King, regal in his tall white hat, distributing food to the populace. (In fact, that stately personage was only a third apprentice pot-boy, but the cat had no idea of this, and longed to be just like him.)

And so he went to the Council of Cats and declared, "O Cats, behold your King!" But the other cats just laughed at him.

Then he went into the stables, where the King's horses were kept, and where an army of stable-boys worked to keep them ready and fed.

"Behold your King!" he mewed at them. But the stables were far too noisy for anyone to hear him.

And so the cat who longed to be King went out into the forest alone, searching for his subjects. And in due course, he came across a flock of chattering green parakeets.

"Behold, your King!" exclaimed the cat.

And the parakeets echoed; *King! King!*

The cat was delighted. "At last!" he said. "At last, a people who will appreciate my magnificence!" And he made himself a royal crown of grass-green parakeet feathers and sat upon a grass-green throne to listen to his subjects. And all through the day, the parakeets circled him, squawking; *"King, King!"*

The cat was overjoyed, and swore to himself that he would be a good ruler and only eat his subjects very occasionally, to keep discipline and to vary his diet of capons and cream.

But when night fell, the cat grew hungry. And so he addressed his new subjects, saying; "I hunger. Bring me meat."

The parakeets flew round him, *crawk*-ing and squabbling.

Meat! I hunger! Meat! Meat! squawked the flock of parakeets, and all the predators in the woods heard their call and came prowling. Wolves; foxes; weasels; owls; all followed the cries of the parakeets, and came to where the King sat, crowned; reclining on his grass-green throne. And all the parakeets flew away.

"Don't go!" cried the King.

"*Go! Go!*" called the parakeets as they vanished into the tree-tops. But still the wolves and foxes came, eyeing the cat with hungry eyes.

Seeing that his subjects had flown, the cat made a rapid decision. "I don't think I want to be King after all," he said, and jumped off his regal throne and ran away as fast as he could. He ran away through the forest, leaving a trail of grass-green feathers as he went, back to the palace kitchens, where the king of the kitchens, in his tall hat, was fast asleep by the dwindling fire, and dreaming of becoming a pastry chef, or even, one day, a sauce-boy.

26

THE RETURN OF THE WASP PRINCE

During this time, the Wasp Prince had grown into young manhood. Under the care of the Spider Queen, he had grown strong and fearless; skilled in combat; silver-tongued; and brought up in the certainty that vengeance was sweeter than honeycomb.

The young Prince had his father's powers; the ability to take any form, or to walk among the Sightless Folk in the shape of a handsome young man. He could sleep, cocooned in silk, in the top of the highest trees. The Sightless Folk feared him—he was cruel— just as they feared his father, whom they blamed for the son's cruelty. And as time passed, the Wasp Prince learnt to enjoy his power in the world, and, with the Queen's encouragement, to revel in causing fear and death. Throughout the summer and autumn he would gorge himself on honey and fruit; and in winter, he would sleep beneath silken sheets and thistledown in the heart of the Spider Queen's lair. No one dared approach him. No one dared stand up to him.

His cruelty took many forms. Sometimes, he would take the shape of a swarm of wasps and attack at random, and without warning; here an old man on the market road; there a group of children playing around a mulberry-tree. But this was the least of his malice. In his guise as a young man, he would seduce a girl of the Folk—or sometimes, a boy—make them love him; then, when they were naked and in the throes of passion, the Prince would revert to his swarm Aspect, blanketing his victim in fire; stinging and remorseless.

Some died in his embrace; some, too, were left insane. The wasps—his special envoys—became the scourge of the Silken Folk; doing whatever they wanted; taking whatever they wanted; terrorizing humankind and living only to serve the Prince who had given them power and life.

From afar, the Lacewing King heard of the Wasp Prince's exploits. Through his coat of a thousand eyes, he watched his son's activities with growing curiosity. The Spider Queen had secret ways of shielding herself from prying eyes; and so the King was unaware of her influence in the young Prince's life. Besides—as he told the Glow-Worm Chancellor, when that gentleman cautiously inquired as to whether His Majesty proposed to curb his son's erratic behaviour—it was not the place of a King to meddle in the affairs of Princes. And as long as the Prince did not threaten him, he was content to leave him alone. Perhaps he was even flattered by the way his son had turned out—the Wasp Prince had already proved himself as ruthless and strong as he was himself.

Finally, the Honeycomb Queen came to hear of the newcomer, and traced his arrival back to her son. The Honeycomb Queen was the only one who had ever dared speak up to the King, and it was to her that desperate folk came to beg to intervene. She had a court of her own, deep in the heart of the woodland; a court that some called Tír na n'Óg, and others called Fiddler's Green. There, she cared for her daughters, the bees, and watched over her son from a distance. But as the Wasp Prince and his folk grew stronger and more dangerous, she could no longer stay silent. Robed in bees, golden from head to foot, she came in state to the court of the King and found him in his throne room.

It had been a long, long time since the Queen had seen her son. It may be that he feared her a little—she was, after all, his mother. It may be that he felt guilty at not having visited her more often. Or it may be that he was simply bored: with the King, it was hard to tell. In any case, he greeted her politely enough: the bees on his coat of a thousand eyes winked and hummed and shimmered.

Bowing low, the Queen explained the reason for her visit. "Your rebel son, the Wasp Prince, has become too great a threat to ignore. You must exercise some control over him, or he will one day defy you."

The Lacewing King laughed at that. "That little boy? Defy me?" he said.

The Queen pointed out how many years it had been since the Prince was a little boy. Then she recounted some of the tales that her bees had told her.

The King looked thoughtful. In fact, until then it had suited him to ignore the boy he had brought into the world, whose vengeance against the Sightless Folk he himself had abetted. Had it really come to this? He himself could be cruel, but the tales that the Queen now told him were beyond anything he had ever dreamed. And this boy—this *man*—was his son.

He felt a pang of something that might almost have been remorse. "Send for the Prince," he told the Queen. "Have him come to my court. It's time."

Time passed, and the Lacewing King waited impatiently for his son. But the Wasp Prince showed no sign of obeying the summons. Instead came word that the young Prince was gathering his resources and building an army of warriors to terrorize the neighbouring kingdoms. Complaints came in from every side, from the Cockroach Queen to the Butterfly Princess, and the Lacewing King became angry. How dare the Wasp Prince disobey? How dare he defy his father?

Of course, the King had no idea of the Spider Queen's role in all of this. He still believed the Wasp Prince would come to him eventually. And so he ignored the growing complaints and hoped for a resolution. But still the Wasp Prince gave no sign of obeying his orders.

Once more, only the Honeycomb Queen dared say what everyone was thinking. "You made him what he is," she said. "He's your responsibility. Either you curb his excesses now or risk an open rebellion."

The King knew that the Queen was right, and with a heavy heart, he prepared for a confrontation. He gathered together a hundred of his most ferocious warriors. Leaving the Glow-Worm

Chancellor to care for things in his absence, he put on his cock-roach armour and rode off in search of the Wasp Prince.

Through the web of the Spider Queen, the Wasp Prince sensed his father's approach. "What shall I do?" he asked the Queen.

The Spider Queen looked at him tenderly. Over the years, she had come to be very proud of her Golden One. Handsome, ruthless and clever, he had exceeded all her expectations, and now she was looking forward to seeing him face the Lacewing King in battle.

"Make him angry," she replied. "The Lacewing King is arrogant. Send out an envoy to greet him, then provoke him to combat. With my help, you will surely win; and then I shall finally have my revenge."

The Wasp Envoy was massive; fanged and clawed in his yellow-and-black. Marching to the enemy camp, he levelled his giant, fac-etted eyes on the Lacewing King and said:

"What business do you have with my lord the Wasp Prince?"

The Lacewing King was unused to dealing with envoys. He was equally unused to dealing with the young Prince's kind of arro-gance. He had come out expecting deference, welcome, maybe even repentance. Instead he was faced with veiled contempt. It made him angry. The Lacewing King was not at his best when angry.

He said, "My business is with my son."

The envoy sneered. "My lord the Wasp Prince is occupied. Send me your proof of fealty and I will convey your words to my lord."

At this insult, the King's entourage gave a collective hiss of rage.

"My proof of fealty?" he said.

The envoy looked down at the Lacewing King from eyes that reflected him a hundred—no, a thousand times. "Your time is over," the envoy said. "Too long have you ruled the Silken Folk. You are old. The Wasp Prince is young. His message to you is this: swear fealty, or prepare for war."

In all his life, the Lacewing King had never yielded to anyone. The thought that he might do so now was utterly unthinkable. And yet the Honeycomb Queen was right. The Wasp Prince was his—and *only* his—responsibility.

"Tell my son to meet me at dusk by the edge of the forest," he said. "There, I will meet him face-to-face, and we shall resolve this once and for all."

The envoy agreed, and later, at dusk, the Wasp Prince and the Lacewing King met, their armies at their backs, to determine which one of them would rule. Both were in human Aspect: the King in his cockroach armour; the Prince resplendent in yellow-and-black. The King was wearing his coat of eyes; the Prince, a mantle of living wasps. Both were tall and golden-eyed; except for the difference in age, they might as well have been brothers.

"Come with me," said the Lacewing King. "I will teach you all I know. I will make you heir to my throne and instruct you in the ways of our people."

The Wasp Prince laughed. "But you have *already* taught me," he said. "You've taught me how to fend for myself. How to be fearsome and ruthless and strong. Why would I want any help from you now? All I want is your kingdom, and the crown that belongs to me by right."

The Lacewing King tried again. "There's more to being King than power," he said. "There's patience—loyalty—and love—"

"So it's true," said the Wasp Prince, and laughed. "They told me you were going soft. The King *I* remember was proud and strong. He would never have humbled himself for a woman."

The Lacewing King remembered the Butterfly Princess and winced. Once more, he tried to be reasonable. "When I brought you into the world," he said, "I was young and thoughtless. I had nothing to teach you then but cruelty and vengeance. But I've changed. And you can, too. You can be a better King than I was. All it takes is patience, and time."

The Wasp Prince laughed again at that. "Time?" he said. "I don't think so. I'll take my inheritance now, *Father*, with or without your blessing." And at that, he drew his silver blade and cast his cloak of wasps at the King, who took a step back just in time and drew his sword to parry the blow.

And so they fought in earnest, Wasp Prince and Lacewing King. Both were fast and skilled and strong; but the King had greater experience. Sometimes the Wasp Prince became a furious swarm of yellow wasps, forcing the King to change Aspect, but the King responded by taking the form of a cloud of tiny pale-green gnats that drifted through the swarm like smoke.

The battle went on, and the Wasp Prince changed his tactic, becoming a phalanx of dragonflies with giant, vicious mandibles. The King returned to his human form just in time, but the Prince changed back into a giant hornet, and stung the King so hard on the hand that he could barely hold his sword.

The Wasp Prince laughed. "Yield to me now, and save yourself further embarrassment. Who knows, I may even let you live, if you promise to serve me."

Grimly, the Lacewing King shook his head and moved his sword to his left hand. He was the better swordsman by far, but the Prince was aiming to kill, whereas the King was simply trying to disarm his opponent.

"Don't be a fool," he told the Prince. "Can't you see I don't want to kill you?"

But the Wasp Prince only laughed, and fought back more fiercely than ever.

Deep in her lair, the Spider Queen followed the battle through the skeins of her web. She could sense every movement, every step the combatants made. She knew when one of them faltered, or when the other landed a blow. And with every blow that was struck, her joy increased, until it was almost unbearable.

The fact was, she had never meant the Wasp Prince to defeat the King. The Prince was an able fighter, trained and taught by the Queen herself, but she had no intention of letting him steal her vengeance. Her vow had been to break the King's heart, and from the way he was fighting, she knew that whenever he struck a blow, he felt the pain of it himself. And so she watched from the heart of her web, teasing the strands with her fingers; and with every moment that passed, with every blow, her pleasure increased.

The battle went on. The stars came out. Both combatants were wounded and stung, but still they went on fighting. The Wasp Prince fought with all his might, but the Lacewing King was holding back, hoping the Prince might see reason. But the Prince was unstoppable, leaping from Aspect to Aspect, passing from a swarm of wasps and back to his human form again, his sword flashing through the shadows, his voice ringing out in defiance.

Finally, the Lacewing King, feinting and dodging among the swarm, landed a final, fatal blow. They fell together on the battlefield, the Wasp Prince pierced through the heart; the King on his knees beside him.

"Why did you defy me?" he said. "I would have given you everything."

The Wasp Prince shook his head and laughed through the blood that welled from his mouth. "Not everything," he whispered. Then, knowing his time had come, he sent one last command to his troops.

"Vengeance," he whispered.

The Spider Queen, at the heart of her web, felt a banner of wasps unfurl across the battlefield on which the Lacewing King knelt by his son. The wounded Prince lay dying; his blood soaked into the trampled ground to mingle with that of his father. He looked into his father's eyes and saw them filled with sorrow.

"You see," he said. "You *are* going soft." And then he died, and a curtain of death descended onto the Lacewing King—

But just as the avenging swarm was about to reach the enemy, a swarm of bees flew to meet them, sent out by the Honeycomb Queen to protect her son from danger. They were only honeybees, but their loyalty was to the death, and they covered him over, head to foot, so that no harm could come to him. One by one, the honeybees died in defence of their master. But as they fell, more took their place, so that finally, leaderless, drained of their venom, the angry wasps were forced to retreat, and the King was left alone.

The Spider Queen watched him through her web, and though she had won a victory, she knew that the war was not over. Her enemy had suffered a blow, but his heart was not broken. In fact, he returned to his underground court just as if nothing had happened; his evil reputation intact; his royal crown unchallenged. And the Honeycomb Queen went back to her hive, satisfied that her son was safe. But though he showed no sign of it, she knew that *something* had changed in him; and she continued to watch over him from afar, in the hope that one day he would learn to love someone as deeply as she loved him.

27

THE OLD WOMAN
AND THE ROCKING-HORSE

Once there was a little girl, who very much wanted a rocking-horse. But only boys could play with such things, and so she would sit and play with her dolls and dream of wooden horses.

Her brother had a hobby-horse and a wooden lance to go with it, and sometimes she would stroke its mane, but she never rode it. Instead, she would watch her brother play, and when he left his toys outside, she would bring them in out of the rain and tidy them away for him. She always left the horse till last, lingering over its horsehair mane and running her hands down its wooden flanks. But she never dared ride it.

Time passed. The girl grew up. She married a man who kept horses. But she was always so busy looking after the children that she never learnt to ride. Instead, she would look out of the window at the horses in the fields and wonder what it would feel like to simply ride away.

Her husband died. Her children grew up. The woman was left alone. Her children sold the horses and gave her the money for her old age.

"It's time to think of yourself," they said.

But then they asked her to babysit for all her little grandchildren, so that she had no more time than she'd had before. But in her dreams, the old woman rode horses of every colour; with flowing manes and gleaming eyes and nostrils flaring in the wind.

Time passed. Her grandchildren grew up. She grew too frail to be useful.

People started to whisper that the old woman's wits were wandering; that she had entered a second childhood. Her children and grandchildren moved away; lived their lives; hoped for their inheritance.

But the old woman had a secret. Every morning, she would walk up the hill to the wood-carver's house and talk to him for an hour or more. Sometimes she gave him money.

She did this every day for so long that finally all her children and grandchildren and great-grandchildren became suspicious. What was the wood-carver making for her? Why was she paying him so much of her life's savings?

So they followed her to the wood-carver's house, and found out the old woman's secret. She had ordered the craftsman to make a magnificent rocking-horse. It was the king of rocking-horses: carved from a massive piece of oak; with eyes that flashed green fire and a mane like sea-foam. But neither they nor the wood-carver knew the person for whom she intended it.

Every child and grandchild and great-grandchild assumed that the horse was a gift for them. Every child believed himself to be the old woman's favourite. Family members who had not paid her a visit in years now became regular callers. Children who had once complained about coming to see the old woman now came with gifts of flowers. They listened to her anecdotes. They sat on her knee and smiled at her. They brought her cakes and honey and bottles of elderflower wine, and wondered when she would tell them about the marvellous wooden horse.

The old woman received them all with a twinkle in her eye, but she never mentioned the rocking-horse.

Christmas approached. The old woman's family eagerly awaited news of the gift. Surely now the old woman would reveal her long-kept secret?

Meanwhile, the wood-carver worked to complete his work in time for the celebrations. And at last, on Christmas Eve, it was done. The old woman went out in the snow to the wood-carver's house, to make the final payment. She looked at the horse. It was perfect.

She stroked its mane with a trembling hand.

"To whom shall I deliver it?" asked the wood-carver at last.

"No one," said the old woman, and smiled. "This rocking-horse belongs to *me*."

And at that, she climbed up onto the horse's back, held the reins in both hands, and began to ride. She rode so hard and so high that she rode right out of the wood-carver's house and out into the snowy night, with the wind in her hair and the stars in her eyes.

Some people say they've seen her, galloping across the sky.

28

THE POOR KING

The king of a certain country dwelt in a palace of marble and gold. He had servants to deal with his every need; master chefs to prepare his food; musicians to play and sing him to sleep. He had pages to entertain him; courtiers to keep him company; and dancing girls and French masseurs, along with an army of gardeners, all trained to cater to his tastes and to grow all his favourite flowers.

But the people of his country lived in the worst kind of misery: working for barely enough to feed themselves and their children. The people who were not able to work were even more wretched; forced to beg along the streets and under the bridges of the city. And when the King walked in his garden, he would hear the cries and complaints from outside, distracting him from his meditations.

And so the King sent his servants to clear the road outside the palace gardens; and for a while, he was at peace. But the beggars kept on coming back; poor people; orphan children; crippled folk and blind. They clung to the palace railings and stared in from between the bars. It made the servants uncomfortable, and neglectful of their duties. The head Chef, who was temperamental, was so upset by this that on one occasion, he actually wept, ruining a lemon soufflé and a delicate Hollandaise sauce.

This could not go on. The King ordered for a higher wall to be built around his palace, with more guards to remove the loiterers. But the cries of the people could still be heard; and the shadow of despair could still be seen in the faces of his servants.

The King did his best not to notice. He had the gardener plant even more flowers in his garden. He had his chefs prepare him ever more succulent dishes. He had his musicians play day and night, to drown out the pleas of the people: the old; the orphaned; the crippled; the blind. And yet he still heard them in his dreams, and was filled with misery.

"Was ever a man so tormented?" he cried, locking himself in his chamber. "Was ever a man made to suffer so, in all the history of suffering?"

The King grew pale, and refused to eat; exhausted, but unable to sleep. And still the despair of the people continued to torment him. Finally, he went to seek help from the Silken Folk, who lived in the wild woods outside his realm. Under the ground, in the darkness, he came face-to-face with the Lacewing King.

"How can I combat this tyranny?" he begged. "How can I escape these visions that so disturb my quietude?"

The Lacewing King, in his mantle of bees, and wearing his crown of centipedes, smiled at the unhappy King. Then he leant forward and whispered a few words into the man's ear. The King's expression changed. First he looked puzzled, and then his face broke into a radiant smile.

"Of course!" he cried. "Of course! Now why didn't I think of that before?"

The next day, when the King did not return to his palace of marble and gold, his servants went to look for him. They sought him, but did not find him; called him, but he did not reply. Only his Chancellor thought he saw a beggar by the side of the road who slightly resembled the missing King. But, the Chancellor knew it could not be so; for this man was mad, and had blinded himself with a sharpened reed, and had cut off his ears so as not to hear, and so the Chancellor was sure that he could not be the missing King.

And so he and the rest of the servants went back to the palace of marble and gold, and flung open the gates to the folk outside. While, far behind them, on the road, the madman cried in a broken voice:

"Pity the blind! Pity the blind!"

29

THE BLUE SASH

During the reign of the Clockwork Princess, there was a young Commander who was as handsome as he was vain and mean-spirited. All the men admired him; all the women dreamed that one day, he would choose them to be his bride. But the Commander despised the company of women, preferring his entourage of men; eager and adoring.

"Love me," he would say to them. "Worship me, and we shall be kings!"

And his followers—peasants, and merchants, and men who had been disappointed in love, and men who felt that their destiny was to be something greater—all bowed to the handsome Commander and tried to be just like him.

The Princess never spoke a word, but watched the Commander in silence. With his blue sash of office and his golden hair, he looked as regal as a prince—and in fact, he secretly believed that he would become king someday. To his followers, who had no idea that the Princess was only clockwork, he hinted that he was her son, and that it was just a matter of time before she would acknowledge him. To the Princess, he was all flattery, although she seemed as unmoved by his sycophancy as by his ambition. She simply listened in silence from her carved and cushioned throne, until the Commander reminded himself that she was only clockwork, and probably couldn't understand him anyway.

The thought made him bold. To his followers, he grew even more boastful, bragging of his influence, his power and his wealth. To women, he was arrogant, expecting them to serve him and cater to his every need. Some of the women accepted this, perhaps still hoping he would notice them. Others spoke against him, saying:

"What right do you have to speak to us thus? Who gave you this authority?"

To which the Commander always replied, "The Princess gives me authority. See how alike we are, she and I. We have the same regal deportment. The same flawless complexion. The same golden hair and elegant demeanour. And see here, my blue Commander's sash, given to me by the Princess herself. Who could doubt my superiority over you other poor mortals? One day, I shall rule you all, and all my followers will be kings."

The men of his retinue applauded this with great enthusiasm. They began to ape his mannerisms; his speech; even his golden hair. Like him, they looked down on the womenfolk and the ladies of the court, criticising their clothes, their speech, scorning and ridiculing them as he did. They laughed at the fat palace housekeeper; they took liberties with the housemaids. Some even grew bold enough to throw stones at the Princess's ladies-in-waiting as they passed, and although the Commander pretended to deplore this kind of action, he was well-pleased with his success.

"Everyone wants to be me," he said. "What a fellow I am, to be sure!"

Finally, the ladies-in-waiting came to complain to Her Majesty. They found the Princess in her chamber, her mechanism almost at rest. But she listened to the ladies' complaint, and when they had finished telling their woes, she very slowly lifted her hand and beckoned to them to come closer.

It had been months since the Clockwork Princess had done anything so strenuous. The ladies-in-waiting moved closer, and the Clockwork Princess whispered her orders in her rusty, dying voice.

"*Take. His. Sash. Away,*" she said. "*Take. His. Blue. Commander's. Sash.*"

And at that she closed her blown-glass eyes and fell into a deep, deep sleep, from which not even her favourite musicians were able to rouse her. But the ladies-in-waiting had understood the final message of the Princess. As the Commander slept, they took his blue Commander's sash from its place by his bedside and burnt it in the kitchen fire.

When the Commander awoke the next day and found his sash missing, he was enraged. "Where is my blue sash?" he demanded of the maid, who had come in to clean the room.

But the maid simply shrugged. "I don't know. Perhaps the housekeeper can help."

"Return my blue sash immediately!" said the Commander to the housekeeper.

But the housekeeper simply shook her head and said, "Maybe the ladies-in-waiting . . . ?"

In growing fury, the young man sought out the Princess's ladies-in-waiting. "I *know* you've taken my blue sash. Return it at once!" He stamped his foot.

The ladies looked at him and smiled. "Our orders come from the Princess," they told him. "Why don't you ask her for your sash?"

And so the Commander went to the Princess, who was asleep in her chamber. Not a sound came from her mechanism; not a flicker from her eyes. For almost an hour he pleaded, he raged, he questioned, and he shouted. He demanded the return of his sash; spoke of persecution; and finally, in a fit of pique, vowed to overthrow the Princess and seize the kingdom for himself.

But none of this moved the Clockwork Princess. Her mechanism finally at rest, she slept a dreamless, peaceful sleep. The Commander, understanding at last that he would receive no answer, went out into the city streets to rally his loyal supporters: young men with golden hair just like his; with voices that were just like his; with arrogant hearts that were just like his.

"Listen to me, men!" he cried. "It is I, your Commander! Now is our time to take the throne! I can be king! *We* can be kings!"

But without his blue sash, the Commander looked just like every other angry young man trying to make his voice heard. No one listened: no one cared. Everyone was calling out:

"*I* can be king! We can be kings!"

"You idiots!" cried the Commander. "*I* am your King. Can't you see that?"

But even he was uncertain now: without his blue sash, there was nothing to make him special. Still protesting, he found himself swept away from the palace gates and into the heart of the city. Soon, he was lost in the winding streets; trampled underfoot by the crowd; laughed at by women; taunted by men; forgotten, in the gutter. And there he remained, so the bees always said.

No one even missed him.

30

THE HONEYCOMB CHILD

Since the death of the Wasp Prince, the Lacewing King had become fatigued. Nothing pleased him anymore. Not one of his twenty thousand books could sustain his interest, with their pages made of moths' wings, bound in dragonfly leather and cunningly illuminated in butterfly colours and rosewater ink. Neither did his gallery, lined with his ancestors' faces, where the kings and queens of the Silken Folk looked down at him from their gilded frames.

Neither did his army of chefs, all specially trained to bring him every subtle dish and exquisite wine that might tempt his jaded palate; from the rose-gold wines of Faërie, aged for a thousand years in cedarwood casks, to his favourite dish of damselflies' tongues, slow-cooked in honey and saffron, and served under silkworm pastry. His entertainers gave him no pleasure, nor did his many courtesans. Neither his centipede contortionists, nor his dung-beetle jesters, nor his butterfly dancers managed to keep his attention, and as for his circus of performing fleas, all they did was make him itch.

And so he sat on his termite throne, encrusted with beetles'-wing casings, and brooded silently to himself, occasionally leaving his reverie to heave a deep sigh, or to toy with the sapphire that hung round his neck, casting a ladder of wintry light onto the marble pavement.

"The King is lonely," murmured his folk as they tiptoed around him in fear and concern.

Certainly, ever since his disastrous attempt to woo the Butterfly Princess, the King had been silent and withdrawn. Was it love? Probably not. The Lacewing King was too selfish to give his heart to another soul. Or so they whispered among themselves (keeping well out of earshot) as they crept around the silk-lined halls and the labyrinthine corridors of his underground palace, lit by glowworms and fireflies.

"This place needs a child," said the King. "Someone to run down these passageways. Someone to tumble across these floors and startle the cockroach soldiers. Someone to entertain me with questions and laughter and stories and games. Someone to—"

Someone to love, perhaps? Who knows? He never said it aloud. And yet, his longing for a child had grown into an obsession. Since the death of the Wasp Prince's mother, he no longer trusted the Sightless Folk. No more would he dare to place one of his children into their care. And after two unsuccessful attempts to seek a Queen, his pride was hurt, and his faith in women was shaken. There was only one woman in whom the King still had the utmost confidence. And so that night he went to the court of the Honeycomb Queen in the greenwood and told her that he wanted a child.

"I want a son," said the Lacewing King. "A son who will wear my crown one day. A son to keep me company and to—well. You know what I mean."

The Queen looked at him for a long time. "You don't know what you're asking," she said. "A child is not a plaything. Have you learnt nothing from the death of your son, the Wasp Prince? A child needs parents—affection, *love*—"

"I can do that," said the King. "I'll reward you for your trouble."

The Queen gave him a sad smile. "You don't know what you're talking about," she said. "You've never brought up a child before.

How can you know what you're going to feel? More to the point, how do I know that the child will be raised as it should?"

The Lacewing King looked dangerous. "Just give me the child," he told her. "Too long have I given my favour to the little builders of honeycomb. It's time you gave something in return. A son, in my image, that's what I want. And if you defy me, you'll suffer."

The Queen gave a sigh. "All right," she said. "But you have a lot to learn about love. Love can't be bought with wealth and rewards. Love can't be earned by anger or threats. Love is like a honeybee— one-half sweetness, one-half sting. We get the half that we deserve. Remember that, Your Majesty."

The King shrugged. "I'll do as I please," he said. "Now when do I get the baby?"

"Give me nine days," said the Queen. "Then you may come and collect it. But remember—this baby needs patience and love. It isn't one of your courtiers. If you treat it badly, it will not simply bow and retreat. You asked for son in your image, and that is what I shall give you. Let's hope you don't live to regret it."

The King waved his hand impatiently. "It's just a baby," he told her. "You make it sound like a monster."

"If it grows into a monster," she said, "then you will be the one to blame." And she went back into her hive to prepare for the baby's arrival.

Of course, the Honeycomb Queen had no intention of giving up any of her precious children to the Lacewing King. Her little queens-in-waiting were all tucked away in their beeswax cradles, sucking on honey, surrounded by love. Besides, she did not respond well to threats, and she meant to punish the Lacewing King a little for his arrogance.

And so she created a manikin that would look just like a baby; grow just like a baby—and maybe show the Lacewing King a thing or two about fatherhood. She made a skin from spun silk and wax, dark honey and golden pollen. She made it plump and soft and sweet, with big brown eyes and honeyfuzz hair; and then she filled the skin with bees, so that every part was warm and alive, down to the tiny fingers. And then, nine days later, she handed it, wrapped in a shawl, to the Lacewing King.

The King looked at the Honeycomb Child and saw nothing amiss. Of course, it was the closest he'd ever been to a baby, and he had no idea that the manikin was just a silken cocoon filled with bees. He looked into its big brown eyes and heard the small contented sounds it made as it sucked its fat little thumb, and a strange kind of feeling came over him; a feeling of pride, and of wanting to protect the little creature in his arms from anything that might harm it.

And so he took the baby home to his underground palace of caverns and roots. He fed it on honey-sweetened milk and placed its crib by the side of his bed, so that if it should awake during the night, he would be there to attend to it. He gave it toys to play with: dragonfly mobiles and rattles made from beetles'-wing casings, and dolls made out of earwig husks with wigs made from real caterpillar-hair. Sometimes he even sang to it the ancient lullaby of the bees.

The baby was good; it never cried, though sometimes it made a buzzing sound that the Lacewing King took for contentment. Fed on milk and honey, it grew; learnt to sit up and walk within weeks; within a month it was talking.

The King was very proud of his new son, and dressed him in silk and butterfly wings and tiny suits of armour with stag-beetle helmets and bumblebee boots. He taught it how to say: *Fetch me my rattle immediately, or I shall have you eviscerated*, and, *Take back this milk, it is tepid*, and, *Amuse me, servants, I am fatigued.*

The Honeycomb Child grew much faster than any ordinary boy, although the Lacewing King saw no problem with this, having always assumed that his son would be different to other children. By the time the child was nine months old, he was the size of a six-year-old. He could read and ride a pony. He could fight with a tiny sword. He had a natural air of command, and no fear of upsetting the servants. In fact, he was the image of the Lacewing King in miniature, and the King was immensely pleased with himself. If, at certain times, the child seemed fractious or defiant, he simply took it as a sign that his son was a natural leader, born to command, unwilling to be ordered about, and his pride in the boy continued to grow, along with a kind of tenderness that he could not express, not even to himself.

The Honeycomb Child had no name, being simply addressed by servants as "His Young Majesty" and by the Lacewing King as "Son." He had no friends; no access to boys and girls his own age. He had no idea of how others lived, no contact with the world outside. It was a sad life, had he but known it; but the young prince did *not* know, any more than did the King. He spent his days in the underground court, playing with his many toys. He rode his pony through the silk-lined tunnels that ran for miles through World Below. He sat in the library and read from the Lacewing King's collection of books. He fed on honey-roasted grubs and mantis tongues and caterpillar marshmallow. He grew strong and handsome—handsome enough to break hearts, if he had cared to—but the boy cared for no one but himself. How could he? No one had ever taught him otherwise.

Within a year, the Honeycomb Child had grown to the size of a twelve-year-old. He was tall and athletic, skilled in all kinds of games and sports. He rarely smiled and never laughed, but in this he was just like his father, who found himself doting on the boy more and more as time went on.

Was it love? Perhaps it was. But love cannot be bought with toys, or gifts, or ponies. The more the Lacewing King rejoiced in the boy's presence, the less the boy seemed to want to be with him. He became sullen and withdrawn, shouting at his servants and refusing to leave his chambers. He flew into terrible rages over the chef's inability to find wild strawberries out of season; smashed the antique mirror that hung over his bed because he disliked his new haircut; threw tantrums because his food was too hot; his wine too cold; his spider-silk shirt the wrong shade of grey.

The Lacewing King saw nothing unreasonable in this. He himself was particular about what he ate, and drank, and wore. He himself had a temper. But he *did* regret the fact that his son did not seem to care for his company. He went out of his way to try and find games that they might play together; hired troops of entertainers; searched out books from his library that might appeal to a young boy. But the more the King tried to engage him, the less the boy seemed to like him. In fact, he seemed to take pleasure in rejecting the King's advances.

The Lacewing King, who was not used to rejection, tried his best to be patient. But patience was not in his nature, and soon he became angry instead. There followed a quarrel, after which he ordered the boy to stay in his rooms until such time as his manners improved. Secretly, he hoped that the boy would miss him, feel sorry and ask to be forgiven. The Lacewing King had even prepared a little acceptance speech, to be used when the time arrived. But days passed, and then a week, and still the boy had made no move. He simply remained in his chambers, reading, or playing solitaire, seemingly indifferent to his incarceration.

Time passed, and the Lacewing King began to regret his anger. The more he considered his actions, the more he realized he'd been at fault. The boy needed guidance, he told himself; kindness and understanding. How could he learn how to behave properly if his father failed to give him the right example? He remembered the words of the Honeycomb Queen; that if his son grew into a monster, he would only have himself to blame.

And so he resolved to seek out the boy, and mend the rift between them, even if it meant losing face, or having to apologize. This was a new experience for the Lacewing King, who in all his life, had never apologized to anyone, or ever acknowledged that he had been wrong. But over that week he had suffered more than he ever had before. He had discovered loneliness, regret, self-doubt, and jealousy. It was unendurable.

And so on the eve of the ninth day, he went to his son's quarters, bringing with him a silver box of the boy's favourite sweetmeats—violet-sugared scorpion tails—firmly resolved to end the feud. But when he unlocked the door and went in, he found that the boy had disappeared.

The King was puzzled and anxious. How could the young prince have left his rooms? Two cockroach guards had been watching the door, which had been locked with a double bolt. He looked around for a possible route, and found, behind the chimney, a vent, just large enough for a boy to escape.

The King's anxiety redoubled. The boy was still too young, too inexperienced, to be allowed to roam in World Above without any supervision. Anything might happen to him; he might be attacked by brigands; he might be lost in the wild woods or drowned in the fast-flowing river. He might be abducted; held for ransom; murdered; torn to pieces by wolves. The King was so anxious and afraid that, when he finally picked up the trail a mere hundred yards from his underground realm, his first reaction was relief, rather than his customary rage.

He followed the trail and found the boy less than half-an-hour later. The Honeycomb Child was sitting on a fallen tree by the riverbank, his travelling-bundle by his side, his hat on the ground beside him. His face, sweetly pensive a moment before, hardened as he saw the King.

He turned his back. "Go away," he said.

The King was puzzled and hurt. He said, "Aren't you happy? What do you want? Whatever it is, I can give it to you."

The boy only shrugged and would not reply.

"Why did you run away?" said the King. "Why did you want to leave me?"

Once again, the boy only shrugged.

"What about me?" said the King. "Didn't it occur to you that I might worry? Didn't you care?"

"No, not really," said the boy.

"I *command* you to care," said the Lacewing King, finally losing his temper. He grabbed the boy by the shoulders and pulled him roughly to his feet. "I *command* you to return. I order you to *love* me—"

The young prince struggled to escape, but the King was too strong, too angry. He picked up the boy like a sack of flour and slung him over his shoulder, meaning to take him back by force—

But the silken skin that the Queen had spun to clothe her manikin of bees was as fragile as it was deceptive. At the King's rough handling, it split, releasing the trapped bees. For a moment, they kept the shape of the prince; and then they spilled out of the silken skin and into the air, their golden wings blurring into movement, the prince's voice becoming the drone of a hundred thousand bees.

The Lacewing King soon realized that something was amiss. He felt the weight on his shoulder lift; heard the humming of the bees. He dropped the silken envelope—now nothing but an empty cocoon—and turned to face the swarm of bees, still forming the ghostly shape of a boy in the honeyed forest air.

For a moment the King's surprise was enough to make him weak. And then, as he realized how he'd been tricked, his rage was uncontrollable.

"*No!*" he cried, and took a step towards the cloud of honeybees, trying to take the ephemeral shape of the Honeycomb Child back into his arms. "No! Please! Please come back!"

But the bees only stung him, making him howl, stinging him through his clothes and hair, stinging his face and his bare hands until he was burning all over; until at last he retreated, maddened, in pain, stumbling blindly back through the woods to the safety of his citadel.

There, he locked himself in his rooms and would not speak to anyone. He took to his bed with a fever, and for three days he shivered and burned and whimpered with the pain of it. But it was not simply the bees' venom that troubled him. As the fever abated, he began to feel a deeper hurt, a hurt that seemed to penetrate all the way into his heart, as if the stinging of those bees had delivered some lingering poison that wounded him to the very soul. Never had he suffered so much, or been made to feel so wretched, and the fact that it was all his fault made it all the more frightening.

It was many days before he was seen by his folk again, looking a little paler, perhaps, smiling even less often. And when one of the cockroach soldiers was fool enough to ask after the Honeycomb Child, the King's explosion of rage was enough to ensure that no one else ever dared ask the question again, or even referred to the fact that, once, their King had had a son.

Only the Honeycomb Queen knew the truth. But she never told anyone. She had only intended to punish the King, not to ridicule him. But that was the end of the Lacewing King's desire for a son in his image. For, as the Honeycomb Queen had said, love is often half-sweetness, half-sting, and he had been stung once too often. And yet, sometimes, it seemed to the Queen that something about him was different. She hoped so. In spite of all his many faults, she *was* his mother, after all.

In any case, the Lacewing King never did take revenge on the honeybees. In fact, in his way, he always seemed closer to them than to any of the Silken Folk. Nor did he threaten the Queen again, or ever try to coerce her. But he never spoke of his son again, or gave any further sign of wanting someone with whom to share his life. Hopeful queens and princesses began to look elsewhere for a husband. His selfishness they could live with, they said, as well as his temper and cruelty. But for all his wealth and power and looks, he just wasn't made for fatherhood.

31

PENANCE OF THE LACEWING KING

Soon after that, for the first time since the restless days of his boyhood, the Lacewing King decided to leave his underground court and travel the roads of World Above. No one could guess his reasons for abandoning his kingdom, his comforts, and his servants—except perhaps for the Honeycomb Queen, who may have had her own ideas, and who knew him better than anyone.

In any case, once he had made up his mind, no one could force him to change it. He left his Glow-Worm Chancellor and his Cockroach Commander in charge of the court, and, stopping only to pack a few necessaries—his sword, two shirts of spider-silk and a pound of earwig cracknel—set off into the forest towards the mysterious world of the Sightless Folk—in other words, the world of *Men*.

The Sightless Folk had always held a peculiar fascination for the King. Perhaps because he had been delivered by a human midwife; perhaps because he felt the need to atone for some of his cruelties. Or maybe it was just because they seemed to lead such frantic lives, fraught with hope and hate and love, while his was uneventful, and had been so for a hundred years. And so he set off alone, at first light, leaving his people wondering.

"I'll give him a week, maybe two," said the Glow-Worm Chancellor.

But the Honeycomb Queen was not so sure. Since the loss of the Honeycomb Child, the Lacewing King had been different. She had seen him angry; impatient; bored; but never so sad—at least, not until now.

So, he has a heart, after all, she thought. And she sent her bees to follow him, to report to her where he went, and to give him any help they could.

It was autumn. The nights were cold. For the first time in his life, the King slept on the hard, cold ground, and not in a bed hung with gnats'-wing drapes, under a caterpillar quilt. But while he was sleeping, the bees came down from out of the forest canopy and covered him from head to foot in a warm, thick blanket. The King never noticed them, of course; but was surprised at how well he slept, and from afar, the Honeycomb Queen was reassured that her son was safe.

Day by day, the Lacewing King continued through the forest. The leaves were mostly fallen now, and the air was white with mist. He soon finished all the provisions he'd brought, and looked around him for berries and fruit; but the season was past, and pickings were few, and so the King went hungry. Though he was used to eating such things as cockroaches and woodlice, these were always served to him deliciously prepared, by chefs who had been trained for years to braise a roach to perfection, or to make a tart from dragonfly tongues that melted as it touched the lips.

But the King had no idea how to do those things for himself. And so he fed on rose-hips, and drank the rain that dripped from the trees, until once more the Queen sent her drones to show him where the wild bees slept, and to feed him straight from the honeycomb.

By now it was very clear to the Queen that this quest was no whim of her son. Seven days had already passed, and the Lacewing King was undaunted. What was he looking for? She did not know.

Perhaps he did not know himself. But until he found it, the Queen understood that he would not return to her. She wanted to protect him, but knew that he must find his own way, and so she simply watched from afar and hoped that he could take care of himself.

On the eighth day of his quest, the King came to a village. It was years since he'd cared to venture so far from his underground court, and yet he seemed to remember it. Hidden from sight by the trees, he watched as the villagers came and went; the washer-women by the stream; the blacksmith with his horses. As night began to fall, he watched as the children came out of school and the smoke from the evening's cooking-fires came curling out of the chimneys. It was all quite unremarkable, and yet for some reason it drew him.

Night came. The Lacewing King continued to watch, as fires burned, and windows lit up all around the village. But as he watched from the shadows, he suddenly sensed that he was not alone. He turned and saw a little girl, no more than nine or ten years old. She was barefoot; her dress was too short; her eyes were bright and curious. And around her neck, on a piece of thread, was a string of blue beads and feathers.

Above them in the canopy, the honeybees were restless, rising and falling among the leaves and humming a little song:

"The heart is like a honeycomb,
A honeycomb, a honeycomb.
The heart is like a honeycomb,
And love will make you blind."

But the Lacewing King was not listening. "You can see me?" he said to the girl. Of course, he was used to going unseen—except when he chose otherwise.

"Of course I can," said the little girl. "My grandmother told me to keep watch."

"Your grandmother?" said the Lacewing King.

"Yes. She needs me to help. She's blind."

The Lacewing King looked at the child, feeling vaguely uneasy. There was something strange about her, something he almost recognized. Was it her eyes, that seemed hardly to blink as they watched him so directly? Was it her curiosity, the fearless way she spoke to him? The Lacewing King was used to being feared and hated by the Sightless Folk. Why was this girl different? And why was she so familiar?

Above him, in the tree canopy, the hum of the bees grew louder.

But the King had no time for them. Suddenly, he had realized that he *knew* the village. He had been there, long ago—almost long enough ago to forget a girl who had loved him. Surely, she must be dead by now. The lives of the Folk were so brittle, so brief. But had it really been so long?

"Take me to see her," said the King, and followed the girl through the forest to a tiny cottage hidden away under a mountain of bracken. Inside, in a rocking-chair, he saw a woman, old and grey. There was no lamp in the cottage, but by the light of the moon, the King saw that she had no eyelids; only a scribble of scar tissue over her dead and sightless eyes.

"Who's there with you, child?" she said.

"A traveller," said the Lacewing King.

"Come in," said the blind woman. "Though we don't have much to offer you."

Outside the cottage, the honeybees sang:

"The heart is like a honeycomb,
A honeycomb, a honeycomb.
The heart is like a honeycomb,
And love will make you blind."

But once again, the Lacewing King ignored them, and went inside. The door of the cottage closed behind him, cutting off the sound of the swarm. The child lit a single candle. The King found

himself in a tiny room with only one window, a table, a stool, and the old woman's rocking-chair by the hearth.

"Sit down," said the crone. "It's been a while."

"Do you know me?" said the King.

The old woman said, "How could I forget? I hear you every night, in dreams. I see your face in memory. I even cut off my eyelids for you, hoping I could see you again."

The Lacewing King sighed. "So it *is* you," he said. "I had no idea it had been so long."

"A lifetime," said the woman. "At least, a lifetime for such as I. For you, no more than a season's growth, a single ring in the trunk of a tree destined to stand for a thousand years."

"And the child?" said the Lacewing King.

The old woman rocked to and fro in her chair. "My daughter died too young," she said. "The girl you see is your grandchild, cursed with your blood and your powers. All these years I waited, hoping you would come for me. But now all I want is to die in peace, and never hear your voice again."

According to legend, the Lacewing King never feels remorse or regret. His cruelty is the one thing upon which all the storytellers agree. But this time, something was different. He felt a terrible pain in his heart. The bees had tried to warn him—and now, he had fallen into a trap as cruel as any he had devised.

For a moment, the Lacewing King found himself unable to speak. In all his time, he had never felt pain as visceral as this. He had no idea what it was; all he knew was that it was unbearable. And as he realized that the child for whom he had longed so badly had been within reach all the time; and that, through his wickedness and neglect, she had died in misery, he was overwhelmed with shame, and fell to his knees on the ground, and wept.

The old woman did nothing to stop him. She simply rocked herself in her chair, her dead eyes like those of a painted doll. "Don't think tears will redeem you," she said. "Forgiveness comes at a higher cost."

The Lacewing King looked up. "How much?"

She shook her head. "I don't want your gold."

"Then what do you want?" said the Lacewing King.

The old woman held out a hand as papery as a wasp's nest. "I want you to take the child," she said.

"You want me to—what?" said the Lacewing King.

"I love her dearly," said the crone. "But she is a child of your people, your blood. I want you to take her to where she belongs. I want you to be a father to her. I want you to love her, care for her, as you never loved your daughter."

The King looked at the little girl. She was no beauty, certainly. And yet, there was something that set her apart from the children of the Folk. Maybe her unblinking eyes; or her hair, the shade of a moth's wing. In any case, there was no doubt in his mind that the old woman was telling the truth. The girl was his grandchild; the daughter of a daughter he had never seen; whose eyes had never been treated with the nectar of the flower of dreams—

"Is this what you want?" he said at last.

The old woman nodded. "Take her," she said. "Take her to your citadel. Show her the Silken People. Love her if you can, and perhaps you will find forgiveness."

The Lacewing King gave a sigh of relief. If he was forgiven, he thought, the pain in his heart would surely fade. But instead, the pain grew even worse, as if a colony of fire-ants had moved into his rib cage.

"What have you done to me?" he said.

The old woman shook her head. "Forgiveness from others comes easily," she said. "But, my love, to forgive *yourself* may be the work of a lifetime." And then, having spoken, the old woman died, right there in her rocking-chair, her sightless eyes still open wide, a tiny smile on her ruined face.

The little girl wept. The Lacewing King put a hand on her shoulder. "Dream is a river," he told the child. "Dream is a river than runs through Nine Worlds, and Death is only one of them. *Look—*"

And he touched the dead woman's face, and spoke a word in a secret language. And as the child watched in wonder, her grandmother began to dissolve, softly and sweetly, into the air; becoming transparent, becoming diffuse; so that, minutes later, she was nothing but a cloud of tiny, golden bees that clustered in the candlelight.

The Lacewing King turned to the child. "Don't be afraid," he told her. "Now she has ten thousand eyes to see you and watch over you. Now she'll always be one of us, and never be old, or hungry, or sad, but live forever in my court among the Silken People."

The little girl looked at the Lacewing King. "Is that where we're going?" she said.

For a moment the King did not reply. He did not know if it was because of what the child had said to him, or because of the trusting look in her eyes, but the pain in his heart intensified.

"I'll be coming later," he said. "But first, there are things I have to do."

He took off his coat of a thousand eyes and draped it over her shoulders. "Here. Wear this. It will keep you warm. And that way, I shall always be with you."

Then he opened the cottage door and addressed the swarm of bees. "Look after this child, and protect her," he said. "Take her to the Honeycomb Queen. Tell her to care for her while I am gone, and to give her everything she wants, for she will be the heir to my throne."

And then he sent the bees with the child and went on through the forest alone.

32

THE BAREFOOT PRINCESS

After that, the Lacewing King disappeared for a long time. No one saw him—not even the bees; no one knew where he had gone.

Stories sprang up about him, of course, and were carried all over the Middle Worlds; but no one could confirm them, or even prove that he was alive. Some said he was in exile; some said he had met his end. The rumours flew wildly around the court, where the Barefoot Princess, as the Silken Folk now called her, was under the care of the Honeycomb Queen. And as those rumours grew and grew, voices all over the kingdom began to speak of a coronation.

The Barefoot Princess, however, would not hear of taking the throne. The King would come home in his own time, she told the Glow-Worm Chancellor. During that time, she would wait for him, however long he took to return. Alone of all the Silken Folk, she had nothing but love for the man who had rescued her from misery, and the only time she ever lost her sunny disposition was if anyone spoke ill of the King, or tried to change her opinion of him.

The Honeycomb Queen said nothing, but watched her with approval. The child the King had rescued was growing into young womanhood—not with the beauty of the Silken Folk, but she was

good and kind and honest. No longer barefoot, she was clad in the finest of court finery; dresses of caterpillar silk, boots of scorpion leather—and of course, the Lacewing King's magical coat of a thousand eyes. Her hair, which was now always neatly brushed, was plaited through with silver thread, and she wore a crown of fireflies that flashed and twinkled as she moved. She had everything a girl might want; beautiful clothes and jewelry; entertainers; musicians; a dappled-pink pony, which she rode in the woods, or along the tunnels of World Below; an easel and a writing-desk equipped with silken paper, dragonfly quills, caterpillar-hair paintbrushes, and three hundred different colours of ink.

But her favourite place was the library, where the Lacewing King kept thousands of books, bound in the finest materials, hand-inked in the tiniest of script. And her favourite stories were about the land of World Beyond, where buildings sometimes scrape the sky, and everyone is a Queen or a King, and most folk are blind, not because they *can't* see, but mostly because they don't want to.

In these books, most of the tales were about a young man or woman who discovered a way into Faërie and had a lot of adventures there; but the Barefoot Princess was much more interested in the World those people had left, and she dreamed of finding a doorway (perhaps through a wardrobe, whatever *that* was) that would lead her into World Beyond and to the land of the Sightless Folk.

She never told anyone else about this. The Silken Folk had been so kind, and the Honeycomb Queen so good to her that she felt ungrateful, dreaming of other Worlds. Besides, she felt that she owed it to the Lacewing King to await his return. And so she waited patiently, and read her books, and lost herself in dreams of science, and skyscrapers, and supermarkets, and plastic, and trains.

33

THE SAND RIDER WHO DREAMED OF THE OCEAN

In a desert as vast as the ocean, there lived a boy who dreamed of the sea. His tribe were the Sand Riders, herders of camels and dwellers in tents, who moved from one watering-place to the next, faces veiled against the perpetual lash of the sand. The boy's family was wealthy, with more than a hundred camels to their name, and he was the favoured eldest son; born to inherit his father's herd and to move on with the Sand Riders.

But the boy dreamed only of the sea beyond the desert; a place where the blue salt water rose and fell in waves as high as the tallest dune; where the wind blew spray instead of sand; where fish leaped and mermaids swam.

His father, who had never seen the sea, was first scornful, then impatient. "There are no mermaids," he would say. "These things have only ever existed in the heads of foolish old women."

But the boy's old grandmother said, "Don't listen to him. All this desert was ocean, once, a thousand thousand years ago."

And she showed him, under the crest of a dune, where the rocks still bore the traces of the bones of sea-creatures long dead; starfish, and shells, and fronds of weed, frozen in time beneath the sand; etched in salt against the stone.

And so the boy continued to dream; and everywhere the Sand Riders rode, he searched for the people of the sea. He searched around the water-holes; he looked for them in the waves of sand. And in his dreams he saw them; their long hair gleaming with ocean salt; their tails sending up great rockets of spray. When he rode his camel across the endless waves of the desert, he always imagined the waves of the sea rising and falling around him.

Then, one scorching midday, he saw a blue shimmer on the horizon.

"It's a mirage," his father said. "There's no water here for a thousand miles."

But the boy did not believe him. Eyes narrowed against the burning sands, he thought he could see the ocean. And when night fell and they pitched their tents, he set off in secret to find it.

He walked all night under the stars, and although he could not see the sea, he thought he could hear the sound of the waves, so like the pounding of his blood as he drew closer to his dream.

Morning came; and the desert grew rose-gold, then red, then bone-white. The blue at the horizon had gone. And yet the boy kept walking, alone, watching his shadow rise and fall against the frozen waves of sand.

Behind him, only his footprints: the Sand Riders had already moved on.

On the second day, his water ran out; but the blue shimmer was back in the sky, and he could hear the cries of gulls above the pounding of the waves.

On the third day, his legs gave way, and he was forced to crawl towards the shimmer of blue on the skyline. But now he could see the waves on the shore, and the jumping fish, and the mermaids, and his heart swelled with inexpressible happiness.

But although he could see it, and hear it, and smell it, the ocean never came nearer.

On the fourth day, the boy stopped. Even crawling had become impossible. "Perhaps it *was* a mirage," he thought, as he dragged himself to the crest of a dune and waited for the sun to set. "Perhaps my father was right," he thought, "and there never were any mermaids." And he laid his head against the sand that had been there for a thousand years and prepared himself for the inevitable.

And then, just then, he noticed a piece of rock pushing out of the sand. It was a flat and silvery rock, etched with writing a thousand years old. And the boy, in wonder, realized that it was a map of the ocean, embellished with pictures of mermaids and flying fish and sea monsters and ships. He smoothed away the sand from around the crest of the dune, and as he did, he realized that this was what his grandmother had described: the fossilized remains of the People of the Sea, their scales gleaming silver against the stone; their fine, sharp bones standing out like tiny shards of mica.

The boy, exhausted, closed his eyes and slept, the silvery stone against his cheek. And in the morning, he was gone—swallowed, perhaps, by the tides of sand.

Or maybe he'd found his way home at last—for Dream is a river that runs through Nine Worlds, and Death is only one of them.

34

THE PERSUASIVE PARROT

In a certain farmyard, the animals were choosing a king. The Dogs said, "We are the cleverest. The king should naturally be one of us."

The Sheep said, "We have the majority. We should choose the new king."

The Cart-horse said, "I'm the strongest. Obviously, I should rule."

The Chickens said, "We are the most productive. The king should naturally be one of us."

The animals, unable to agree, decided to put it to the vote. "Every animal has a voice," said the leader of the Dogs. "I suggest that every group of animals here elects a representative. Then, we lay out our agenda. After that, every animal will speak out in favour of his choice. The winner will be king for a year. Agreed?"

All the animals agreed. The Dog was *very* convincing.

And so the barnyard election began. Every species had a champion; from the rabbits in the hutch to the ducks on the duck-pond. And every species had its agenda; better swill for the pigs in their sty; superior pecking rights for the hens. But it soon became very clear that some voices were louder than others.

"Why vote for a chicken?" said the Dog. "Chickens are not natural leaders. If chickens vote for a dog to be king, then we promise never to chase you again."

And so the chickens gave up their voice and voted for the Dog to be king.

"Why vote for a Dog?" said the Cart-horse, addressing the smaller animals. "Dogs kill chickens, and rabbits, and ducks. Vote for a Horse as your king, and I promise to protect you."

After that a number of chickens, hens, ducks, and pullets all voted for the Cart-horse.

"Why vote for a Horse?" said the Sheep. "Sheep are clearly the future. Sheep stand for greener meadows; peace; good feed; plenty of space for everyone." This sounded quite attractive—especially if you were a sheep—so some of the braver chickens and ducks—and all of the sheep, of course—voted for a Sheep to be king.

Sheep were in the majority, which means that they might have won the vote, had the Dogs not managed to convince so many of the other animals to vote for a Dog. As it was, the vote led to a draw between a Dog and a Sheep.

"Hooray for democracy!" said the Dog. "I suggest we share the crown."

The Sheep, who was afraid of dogs, agreed. And for the next twelve months, the Dog and the Sheep shared both the crown and the farmyard. The Dog generously gave the Sheep control over the grass in the south pasture, while he and his friends ate as many chickens, rabbits, and ducks as their appetite demanded.

Occasionally, the chickens, ducks, and rabbits complained at this treatment. It generally fell to the Sheep to try and address their grievances. And when the year was over, the Sheep had become so unpopular that none of the other animals (not even the other sheep) would even consider voting for him.

And now the elections began again. But the animals were discouraged. None of the chickens, rabbits, and ducks wanted a Dog to be king again. But they had no confidence in the Sheep, and the Cart-horse had lost faith in the system.

"Why bother voting at all?" said the red-and-green Parrot who lived in a cage in the farmhouse, and therefore technically had no vote. "What voice has a duck, or a hen, or a pullet, against the voice of a Dog?"

Gently, the Cart-horse pointed out that *every* animal had a voice, but the Parrot squawked so loudly at this that hardly anyone heard him.

"The only way you can protest," he squawked, "is to say *nothing at all*! That will teach those Dogs and that Sheep to take advantage of their position." He was a very persuasive Parrot.

And so the day of the vote arrived. The dogs all voted for a Dog as king. But the Sheep, discouraged by their leader's lack of leadership, followed the persuasive Parrot's advice. The smaller animals, too, who felt that the Parrot was the only one speaking any sense, decided to stay silent when it came to choosing the king. And so, when the votes were counted, the Dog was re-elected by an overwhelming majority.

"Hooray for democracy!" cheered the Dogs, tucking into a shepherd's pie with a side-dish of fried chicken.

As for the Parrot, safe in his cage, he pecked at a piece of cuttle-fish bone and went back to sleep, head under his wing, thinking that he had never seen a more entertaining election.

35

FIVE PRINCES IN SEARCH
OF THEIR HEART'S DESIRE

In a far-off land lived five princes, who went off one day in search of their heart's desire. One prince went in search of love. The second, in search of riches. The third craved knowledge; the fourth fame. Only the fifth and youngest prince had no particular goal in mind; he simply wanted to see the world, and to enjoy what it had to offer.

The others mocked him, saying that he had never been serious; that he had no ambition and therefore, that nothing he did would amount to much. Then they set off in different directions, the four eldest princes on horseback, the youngest idling on foot, stopping every now and again to investigate a flower, a stone, or to follow the tracks of a spider ant on the dusty highway.

Meanwhile, the four elder brothers rode as fast as they could through the countryside, heading for the gleaming spires of cities, with their promise of wealth, love, knowledge, and fame.

The eldest prince soon found himself in a city of women of all kinds, many of them hungry for love. But he was proud and impatient, and Love remained elusive.

The second prince rode into a town where the streets were paved in brass, the air was spiced, and even the beggars wore velvet.

But for all the town's beauty, there was no gold to be found in the place, and so he was disappointed.

The third young man arrived in a city known for its magical storytellers. But there were no libraries in the town, or schools, or places of learning, and so the prince rode off again.

The fourth prince, after many days, came to a city of theatres. Actors, singers, and dancers thronged the busy marketplace, each vying for the attention of the audiences that came and went. One look at the competition, though, and the fourth prince was discouraged, and he set off home without delay, or attending a single audition.

And so the four young men went home, opened a keg of wine, and recounted their adventures. As each of the princes told his tale, describing the landmarks and buildings and gardens of the cities they had seen, the brothers came to realize that the city of women, the city of beauty, the city of stories, and the city of theatres were all one and the same city, which they had approached from different gates, each prince thinking he was alone.

"What bad luck," they said, "to find the one city in the whole world with no one to love, no wealth, no books, and no chance of finding artistic success." And they drank, and nodded sagely, and agreed that their luck had been terrible.

And then they looked around and saw that their youngest brother had still not returned. They opened another keg of wine and waited. Surely the youngest Prince would not be long.

Time passed: weeks, then months, then years. Still the young prince did not return. His four brothers stayed in the palace (which by then was in some disrepair), drinking wine and discussing their dreams and disappointments.

Occasionally, travellers who came by the palace spoke of a young man—a prince, they said—who had come to a city nearby. The boy had started out penniless, telling tales in the marketplace of his travels and of the many things he had learnt as he roamed the countryside. One day the queen of the city—a woman famed for her beauty—had heard of the marvellous stories told by the young traveller. She had come to hear him speak, and they had fallen deeply in love. Their wedding had been the richest that the country had ever seen, and their love the most passionate and lasting. And now, years later, the young man was famed throughout the land for his wisdom, his wealth, his talent, and his knowledge.

The four elder princes at last understood that this young man was their brother.

They opened another keg of wine (their cellars were greatly depleted by then) and said: "Well, he was lucky. He must have accidentally found his way to another city; one in which Love and Fame and Wealth and Learning were present in abundance."

They never left their palace again, not even to see their brother. Instead, they emptied the wine cellars, one by one—until the wine had all been drunk. Meanwhile, reports of their brother's fame grew, but by then they had all stopped listening.

36

TRAVELS OF THE LACEWING KING

Meanwhile, and for many years, the Lacewing King had been travelling. Far from his kingdom, he wandered alone, learnt to fend for himself, and had many strange adventures.

For a time, he travelled the roads, living rough from day to day. For a time, he worked on a farm, where he learnt to plough the soil. For a time, he sailed the sea in a ship from the Outlands, and saw the sun set in a green flash over the islands of the West. He walked across deserts of blood-red sand and mountains crowned with ice and snow. He entered one city as a king and left another as a condemned man. He slept by the roadside and under the turf; learnt how to find food and water. He clothed himself with glamours so that he could walk among the Sightless Folk, appearing to them as a tall man with hair the shade of a moth's wing. Sometimes he stole supplies as he went—his spun-silk shirts and dragonfly boots having long since been reduced to rags—and travelled now in the battered boots and leathers of a journeyman, hiding his face with a broad-brimmed hat and carrying a satchel.

He seldom spoke, and seldom smiled, and no one—not even the bees—could say what he was seeking so far from home, or whether even he would know when he eventually found it.

One day, the King was passing through a city like many others. A grey and cheerless city on the banks of a river that smelt of mud and dead fish. On the far bank of the river, he came across a floating market of barges, rafts, and river-boats. Here was trade of all kinds: fruit; flowers; spices; wine; fried Fat Boys; bacon; bread; chickens; carpets; magic charms. Here, too, were entertainers; rope-dancers; drummers; tellers of tales; prophets in rags and scarlet paint; talking parrots; dancing bears; jugglers and acrobats. And here too, of course, were the Silken Folk; cockroaches and woodlice; gnats and water-boatmen and wasps, brought there by the promise of food and the scent of warm-blooded creatures.

For a time, the Lacewing King wandered idly from barge to barge. Then he noticed a couple who were standing by the quayside: a young man and a woman of strange, inhuman beauty, whose head was wrapped in a ragged scarf and who carried her broken arm in a sling.

No one approached the couple. They stood apart, the young man cautious, the woman serene. For a moment, the King observed them. His eyes saw things that the Sightless Folk could not, and he understood that the woman, for all her beauty, had no soul. This did not trouble him. Neither did he. But he sensed the fear in the hearts of the Folk when they ventured close to the strange pair, and he knew that trouble was not far away.

Finally, a Lawman came to investigate. He demanded the young man's papers, and seeing that he had none, ordered him and his woman to leave.

"We're doing no harm," said the young man. "All I want is a few supplies. I have money. I can pay."

The Lawman shook his head. "Be off. No one wants your money here."

And so the strange couple turned away and seemed about to leave. But the exchange had attracted the attention of a crowd of market-goers, who now clustered around the pair, taking courage from the Lawman's presence.

The Lacewing King was curious. He had no reason to interfere, and yet he felt sympathy for the outsiders. He came a little closer, using the crowd for cover. He saw that the young man was *very* young, but that the beautiful woman was old. A hundred years old, or older, he thought, and with a silent, inhuman grace. The crowd grew bold, and pushed closer, plucking at the ragged clothes of the young man and the woman. One woman in the crowd took hold of the woman's scarf and pulled, revealing the hidden part of her face, a crazed and sunken eye-socket and a broken arm, inside which secret machineries worked and gleamed—

"It's a demon!" the woman cried. "A soulless, mechanical demon!"

The crowd took up the woman's cry. Rough hands took hold of the young man and the clockwork woman. The Lacewing King watched from afar, feeling increasingly curious. He had encountered many unusual things, but never a clockwork woman before, and besides, he sensed that things were about to go very badly for the strange pair.

Sure enough, as the King watched, the young man and his clockwork companion were seized and carried to the water's edge. The young man cried:

"Please! Don't! She can't swim!" But the mob was howling for blood, and no one paid attention.

The Lacewing King now remembered a tale that the bees used to tell, of a Clockwork Princess asleep in a tower, and of the watchmaker's boy who had saved her. He realized that this unlikely pair must be the couple of whom he had heard. But the prejudice of the Sightless Folk was too much for such a strange love as theirs, and their pleas were in vain as the mob took ropes and tied them back-to-back. Then they pushed the Clockwork Princess and the watchmaker's boy over the edge of the quayside and into the water, where they sank.

The Lacewing King, who had watched all this, now considered the tools at his disposal. Water favours the Silken Folk, and though he was far from his kingdom, his word still carried authority.

He uttered a secret cantrip, and deep in the river, the Silken Folk, the water-boatmen and river-beetles and dragonfly larvae began to gather, blowing and gathering air into a giant silver bubble, that surrounded the drowning boy and his lady. Then, with their sharp little mandibles, they cut the ropes that bound the pair, so that the boy was able to swim back towards the surface and downstream. But the Clockwork Princess was too heavy to float, and simply lay on the riverbed, her undamaged eye staring up at the light, tiny bubbles rising all around her.

The Lacewing King had seen her plight. He spoke another cantrip, and the creatures that lived on the riverbed crawled into the eye of the Clockwork Princess, and into the gash in her damaged arm. They rebuilt her damaged interior, nibbling away at the rust inside. They mended her skin with mother-of-pearl, replaced her hair with gossamer silk, and set back her eye in its socket. Then, with a million blown bubbles, they floated her back to the surface, downstream to where the young man was grieving for the loss of his love.

Behind them, hidden in the trees, the Lacewing King was watching. He watched the happy reunion and listened to the couple talk. He had no idea of why he had intervened on their behalf, or why he should care if they lived or died. But maybe his travels had changed him. Or maybe it was something else that had begun to work in him, a secret transformation like that of larva to chrysalis. In any case, it was done, and he prepared to go on his way again.

But the Clockwork Princess, whose mechanical eye was unaffected by glamours, saw him, and recognized him at once. And in so doing, she understood who had saved her and her friend. She stood up, shaking her wet hair, meaning to thank him for what he had done—

But by the time she reached the edge of the woods, the Lacewing King had already gone. And so she spoke to the forest instead; to the bees in the woodland canopy; to the earwigs in the ground; to the ants and the beetles and the wasps and dragonflies. And she said:

"If ever one day he needs help—whatever the reason, wherever he is—I want you to tell me. I owe him a debt. *Will* you tell me?"

In the leaf canopy, from the ground, came a murmur of acquiescence.

The Lacewing King did not hear it, of course. And even if he had, perhaps he would not have believed in the loyalty of a creature without a soul—after all, the Clockwork Princess was only a thing of gears and levers and porcelain, now held together with spider's web and river-bottom mother-of-pearl. How could such a creature feel gratitude, let alone love?

But Love is a strange emotion; infinitely adaptable. And those who at first seem least deserving of it are sometimes those who need it most. The Lacewing King went on his way without even a second thought for the two strangers he had saved, but the Clockwork Princess did not forget. One day, she told herself, she would repay her debt to him.

She went back to where the watchmaker's boy was drying his clothes on the riverbank. She had lived a hundred years. She could wait a little longer.

37

THE SILENT SONGBIRD

To a kingdom far away, there came a man, selling singing birds. The Queen of that country, a proud and tyrannical ruler, heard of the stranger and his birds, and came to see them for herself.

The man was nothing special, but pale, like the men of the distant northlands. His clothes were worn and colourless, his hair the shade of a moth's wing. His birds flew freely around him, as he fed them with handfuls of dried insects, and their song was bright and powerful, wild as the wind and sweet as the sky.

The Queen was enchanted. She paid the man in gold and took one of the beautiful singing birds back to her palace among the sands. She placed it in a golden cage, sat on a chair beside it and waited eagerly for it to sing. But the bird remained silent.

The Queen summoned her Master of Birds and ordered him to make the bird sing. But for all his skill, the Master of Birds, who knew only hunting hawks and peregrines, was unable to do so.

The Queen then summoned her Master of the Kitchens to bring dates, pistachios, and honey pastries to tempt the bird into song. But no amount of fruit, or nuts, or sesame biscuits, or camel's-milk sweets would tempt the bird to sing a note.

The Queen grew very angry. She summoned her Captain of the Guard and ordered him to find the man who had sold her the singing bird. The Captain brought her the man in chains: she demanded that he make the bird sing for her.

But the seller of birds just looked at her. "Lady," he said. "I sold you the bird. The song was not mine to offer."

The Queen was angry. She had the man flung into her deepest dungeon. But the man just shrugged and said to her:

"Lady, I have seen dungeons before. Rarely does anyone sing there."

The Queen's rage grew. She tore her hair. But no amount of pleading, or threats, would force the man to make the bird sing.

Months passed. Winter came. The prisoner grew even paler. His hair grew matted, and his clothes more ragged and filthy than ever. According to the Master of the Dungeons, he never spoke, never slept, and ate nothing but the cockroaches that ran up and down the dungeon walls. But still, the man gave no sign of defeat, and still the songbird did not sing.

Finally, the Queen gave up. The passing months had changed her, too: had made her less certain of herself. Alone in her tower of gleaming brass with its mosaics and its silken draperies, she seemed to hear the sound of the wind and the distant roar of the ocean; and the silent songbird in its cage seemed almost to taunt her.

And so she released the seller of birds and prepared to let him go. She dressed him in silks, fed him on dates, and scented his hair with sandalwood. Then she sent him on his way, the caged bird as silent as ever. But as the man vanished over the crest of a distant sand-dune, the Queen heard him singing to himself, a song she almost recognized:

"Long ago, and far away,
Far away and long ago.
The Worlds are honeycomb, we know;
The Worlds are—"

And hearing the song, in its gilded cage, the silent songbird started to sing. It sang a song of such sweetness that the Queen was moved to tears. It was a song of the wild wind; of the skies above the dunes; of rising moons and setting suns; of distant oceans that she had never seen. And so she opened the door of the cage and let the singing bird fly free. Its song unfurled into the air like a volley of rainbows.

It still sings in the Queen's gardens, and when it does, she listens. But cages are no longer allowed in that land; and as for the seller of singing birds, he was never seen again.

38

THE SINGING FROG

In a certain forest, near a farmyard we know well, the animals were very excited. The song of a new, unidentified creature had been heard in the treetops. It was a song of surpassing beauty; infinite sadness; unspoken joys. It rang over the treetops at dusk, putting the nightingales to shame. The animals of forest and farm were filled with curiosity.

"What is this creature?" they asked themselves. "A song thrush? A skylark? A warbler?"

The thrushes, skylarks, and warblers assured them that it was not.

"Could it be some foreign bird, from distant lands over the Sea?"

But search as they might, the animals could not discover the source of the beautiful song that had moved them all so deeply.

"This creature must be very shy," said the Squirrel, who was not, and who liked to know everyone's business.

"Perhaps we should leave it alone, then," suggested the Dormouse, who suffered from social anxiety.

"Ridiculous!" said the Owl, who was generally thought to be clever (mostly because he said so, very loudly and often). "We owe it to the community to reveal this creature's identity," said the Owl.

Meanwhile, the unnamed creature sang a song of such piercing clarity that the Rats (who were sentimental) wept, and even the Hens in the barnyard said that they had never been so moved. Such was the excitement surrounding the strange and lovely song that all the animals set themselves the task of finding the singer.

The songbirds searched the treetops; the beetles searched the forest floor. The pullets searched the henhouse (even though it was very unlikely that such a song could ever come from the throat of a pullet). The song was elusive; coming from all directions at once, it seemed, and at any time of day.

But the animals refused to give up the search, until finally the Squirrel tracked the song to a hollow tree by the pond. The tree was home to a small green frog, which had a remarkable vocal range. And after the rain, it would sing to itself, amplified by the hollow tree.

The animals were outraged.

"Frogs can't sing!" said the Nightingale.

"Frogs are drab and ungainly!" protested the Skylark.

The Rat, who had been moved to tears by the song of the little Frog, said, "Frogs are the antithesis of the Sublime."

In fact, all the animals agreed that a Frog, however talented, was a ridiculous person, and that its song was really quite dull. They quickly turned their attention to a talented Turkey who seemed to show some promise, and left the Frog to its hollow tree.

The Frog was secretly quite relieved, never having sought their attention in the first place. But the Dormouse took to sitting on the bank by the hollow tree, listening to the beautiful song. The other animals sneered at the Dormouse for its plebeian tastes, but the Dormouse—being a Dormouse—paid them no attention.

39

THE GARDENER

On the edge of a ruined city, in a disused, overgrown lot, a man decided to build a garden. For years he worked; finding the earth under the broken concrete; digging it; sifting it; building the paths and borders. For years he cared for his garden, until at last it was ready; a perfect acre of summertime in the blasted landscape.

There were flowers of all kinds: hollyhocks and wallflowers; roses and lavender and peonies. There was rosemary and bay; pear trees, scarlet poppies; golden honeysuckle; daisies; bitter rue; shaggy bronze chrysanthemums and purple morning glories. And the gardener tended them all year round and was proud of his handiwork. Little by little, people from the city began to notice the garden, and visit. They did so carefully at first, and always thanked the gardener. It soon became a fashionable place to come on Sunday afternoons; for elegant ladies to meet their friends; for children to play on the soft green lawns. Soon, it was busy every day, and the gardener was proud.

But as time passed, people forgot who had built the garden. Ladies in their summer frocks, carrying silken parasols, would look at the old man working there with haughty disapproval.

"Who is that old man?" they would whisper behind their embroidered fans.

"I suppose he is just the gardener," their companions would reply.

Sometimes the old man heard their words, and he realized that the people believed that he and his work were theirs to command. It did not stop him working. The old man lived for his garden. But some of his pleasure had gone from the task, and this filled him with sorrow.

As time passed, the visitors grew more and more outspoken. "These rose bushes are in the wrong place," said one elegant lady.

Another said, "And why is there not an arbour, that I may sit and rest, or an herb garden for my kitchen?"

"See to it, fellow," they told the old man as he leaned on his spade one fine day, enjoying the morning sunlight. "And hurry! I'm sure your masters are not paying you to waste time."

The old man realized that they thought he was a public employee, and he began to get angry.

"This is my garden!" he shouted. "You are all here because of me!" And the spoiled and elegant ladies shrank, and ran back to their husbands, telling them how the old man had frightened them.

The next day, the gardener was faced with a crowd of angry people, protesting against his behaviour.

"How dare you alarm these good people," said the Mayor of the town. "You should be grateful for all this attention. What would you do if people stopped coming to walk in your garden?"

"I don't know," said the old man. "Let's find out, shall we?"

And he built a high wall around the place; so high that no one could climb it, or look into the garden. And inside, there were hollyhocks; and peonies; and roses; and all the birds came there to sing—for walls meant nothing to them. And in summer, the garden was alive with honeybees and butterflies.

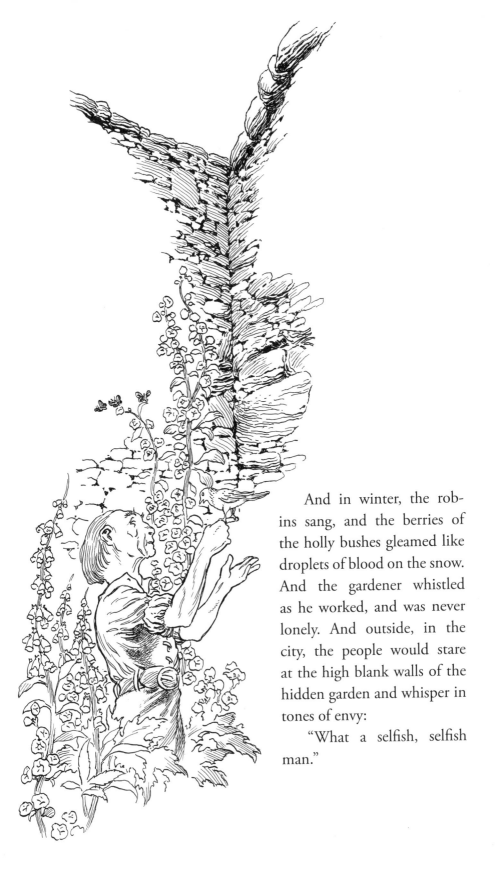

And in winter, the robins sang, and the berries of the holly bushes gleamed like droplets of blood on the snow. And the gardener whistled as he worked, and was never lonely. And outside, in the city, the people would stare at the high blank walls of the hidden garden and whisper in tones of envy:

"What a selfish, selfish man."

40

THE ARROGANT BAKER

In a city of many people there lived a baker, whose bread and cakes were the finest in the land. Folk came from all quarters to buy, and the baker grew first proud, then conceited. While his underlings worked in the kitchens, he would stand behind the shiny front counter, watching the queues of people arrive, and his sense of self-importance grew and grew and grew.

One day he noticed a stranger standing under his awning. The man was dressed like a beggar, though the baker never saw him beg. He did not come into the shop, but stood under the awning instead, to smell the scent of baking that came from the open door. This angered the baker, who had always done what he could to discourage beggars and loiterers. There were spikes on the pavement to discourage the homeless from sleeping there. There were placards on the door warning beggars to stay away. But the stranger seemed not to notice these, and the baker grew increasingly annoyed.

Every day, the man would come to stand outside the baker's shop, enjoying the delicious scents of baking bread and cakes and pies that drifted out into the street.

Finally, one foggy day, the baker came out to confront the stranger. "If you're going to stand here, enjoying the scent of my baking," he said, "then you'll have to pay me."

"You'd make a man pay for the scent of your bread?" said the man to the baker.

The baker replied, "Of course I would. My bread is the best in the city. Why would I allow beggars and thieves to benefit from my hard work? Now pay me my money, or begone."

The stranger gave a little smile. His eyes were dark as comb honey, and his look was not that of a beggar. It made the arrogant baker feel a little uncomfortable, and he raised his voice a little and said:

"I told you, pay me or be off. Otherwise, I'll call the police!"

For a moment the stranger did not move. Then he reached into his pocket and brought out a coin in the palm of his hand. The baker did not recognize the currency, but he knew the gleam of gold well enough, and he understood that the stranger was not as poor as he appeared, and might even be someone of consequence. He saw his customers staring, and he began to stammer and fawn, but it was already too late. The man bent down and rang the coin lightly against the cobblestones.

"I might have made you rich," he said. "But I see that you are a heartless man. Henceforth, everything you bake will taste of ash, go stale, be burnt, or be infested with weevils. But, I'll pay you for the scent of your bread—with the sound of my money."

And at that, the stranger picked up his coin and walked away into the fog, leaving the baker open-mouthed.

And all the customers followed him.

41

THE MOON QUEEN OF
THE UNDERSEA AND
THE MOON KING OF THE SKY

Once, in the depths of the Undersea, there reigned a strong and beautiful Queen. She was wise and powerful and luminous as starlight, but she had never been in love.

She was not without suitors, however. Many came to beg for her hand. The Rainbow Prince of the Angel Fish, in his cloak of many colours. The proud Prince of the Warrior Sharks, in his steel-blue armour. The noble Prince of the Sea Urchins, in his waist-coat of rose-pink spines. But the Moon Queen would have none of them. Her folk were the Moon Jellyfish, and like them, she was a dreamer. And at night, when the business of ruling was done, she would leave her coral throne and put aside her starfish crown and her gown of gilded sea-foam, and rise to the ocean surface, naked but for her long train of tiny silver bubbles. There, the Moon Queen would drift and dance in a midnight darkness shot like phosphorescent silk, and she would watch the starry skies and dream of World Above.

Night after night, she would gaze at the stars, which looked to her like silver fish in a midnight-blue ocean. She would gaze at the purple clouds, which looked to her like forests of weed cloaking the shoals of sky-fish. But most of all, she looked at the Moon; the Moon King of the Sky-Sea, and saw him cross the sky every night, and watched his pearly movements across that mysterious ocean.

But the Queen did not see a lifeless rock circling from a great height: she saw a Moon Jellyfish; a powerful ruler like herself; the Moon King of the Sky-Sea; proud and alone and beautiful, in command of an ocean kingdom filled with adoring subjects; and finally, the Moon Queen felt the joyful turbulence of love.

* * *

The more she considered it, the more obvious it seemed to her that only the Moon King of the Sky would make a suitable consort. They could merge their territories, make of the Worlds one vast ocean that would stretch all the way into Dream. They would ride across the sky in a starlight chariot drawn by a thousand sea horses. And their marriage bed would be a ship with sails of phosphorescent silk that would drift between the Worlds on a sea of Northlights.

The Moon Queen of the Undersea whispered all these things to the King when she rose to the surface to watch him. She spoke of her regard; her love; her vision of the future. But the Moon King never heard, and went his way, oblivious.

The Queen began to spend more and more time on the ocean surface. She grew impatient with her throne, impatient with her subjects.

"What do those things matter?" she said. "When I am Queen of the Sky-Sea, I shall rule over everything. My joy and that of my consort will fill the whole of the Nine Worlds."

Time passed. Years waxed and waned. The Queen spent less and less time in her own realm, and more and more gazing at the sky, looking for the Moon King. She tried to attract his attention by singing her most beautiful songs; tried to bewitch him from afar with her most seductive dances.

But the Moon King of the Sky-Sea never seemed to notice her, but kept to his allotted course, dispassionate; indifferent; drifting calmly through the clouds in a trail of star-bubbles.

One night, there was a lunar eclipse. The Queen had never seen one before. She watched as first, the Moon turned red, then began to disappear. She watched in horror. Could it be that some predator—a shark, a whale, a Kraken—was devouring him, that her beloved Moon King was bleeding to death before her eyes?

Desperately the Moon Queen tried to warn him from below. But even then, the Moon King did not respond to her urgent calls, until finally, even his shadow had vanished from the night sky.

The Moon Queen was filled with grief and despair. She fled back to the Undersea, vowing never to visit the surface again. She handed over her coral throne and her starfish crown to another Queen, and warned her never to go up Above, for that world was filled with sorrow. And there she remains, to this day, in the deepest ocean—for jellyfish are immortal, unless devoured by predators—rising; falling; luminous; languid in the inky depths; still searching for something that never was; still grieving for her lost love.

And that is why moon jellyfish never go to the surface—except perhaps to die of grief at the sight of that ocean they will never know.

42

THE BAREFOOT PRINCESS
AND THE SPIDER QUEEN

Meanwhile, in the court of the Lacewing King, the Barefoot Princess was fully-grown. She had grown to be clever, and wise, compassionate, and extremely well-read, but in spite of these advantages, she still refused to take the throne, or consider the likelihood that the Lacewing King would never return.

The Glow-Worm Chancellor had ruled the kingdom for over a decade. A loyal servant, both of the King and of his father before him, he loved his master, in spite of his faults, and still hoped for his return. But his love for the Barefoot Princess was nothing short of adoration. He pleaded with her to take the throne, to relieve him of his burden. But still the Barefoot Princess refused to believe that her protector was gone for good.

"There must be a way of finding him," she said to the Glow-Worm Chancellor.

The Glow-Worm Chancellor pointed out that in ten years, there had been no trace of the King, except in stories told by the bees. No one could find him, the Chancellor said, except maybe for the Spider Queen—

The Princess's eyes lit up at once. "The Spider Queen?" she repeated.

The Chancellor shook his glowing head. "I should not have spoken, Your Majesty. The Spider Queen is a recluse. She does not stir from her silken couch, or concern herself with our affairs."

The Barefoot Princess shrugged and pretended to show no further interest. But the following day, at dawn, she saddled her pink pony and pulled on her coat of a thousand eyes, and rode in search of the Spider Queen, to ask for her help in finding the King.

The Barefoot Princess knew the Queen only by reputation. She knew that the Queen's network of spies saw everything Above and Below, and that her web, which was so intricate that even she did not know all its complexities, had strands in all of the Nine Worlds. What the Princess did not know was how much the Spider Queen hated the King; how he had stolen her coronet, and how the Queen had brought about the death of his son, the Wasp Prince. All she knew was that the Queen was old, and wise, and mysterious, and that if anyone could find news of the King, she would surely be the one.

Of course, the Princess never thought to use her coat of a thousand eyes. The King had never told her its use, and the bees in its lining simply had orders to watch over her. And so she rode to the Spider Queen's lair, and stood in front of the rust-red gate, and called to her:

"Your Majesty! I come to seek your gracious help in a matter of great importance!"

The Spider Queen watched her approach from her web. Time had not dulled her hatred. From afar, she had watched the Princess, and she knew how much the King cared for her. And so she welcomed the Barefoot Princess into her hall of spider-silk, and, through her veil of cobwebs, she listened in silence to her tale.

"So, you're his adopted daughter?" she said. "I wouldn't have thought it of him." (In fact, she knew perfectly well the identity of her unexpected guest, having watched her from afar from the moment she arrived.)

Earnestly, the Princess explained that the Lacewing King was misunderstood. "So many people hate him," she said. "And yet, he has been so kind to me."

In her silkiest voice, the Spider Queen agreed that people were very cruel and unfair. "Never mind them, child," she said. "I'll help you—for a favour."

The Barefoot Princess opened her eyes very wide. "What favour?" she asked.

The Spider Queen looked down at the coat of a thousand eyes. "That coat. Where did you get it?" she said.

"It was a present from the King."

"Give it to me, and I'll find him for you. You have my oath and my promise."

The Barefoot Princess was reluctant to give up the King's first gift to her. But although she loved the coat, she had no idea of its value. And so she took it off and gave it to the Spider Queen (the bees in the lining scolded and buzzed), and the Queen gave a slow and poisonous smile. She had no use for the bees, of course. But the eyes that the King had stolen from her were stitched into the fabric like gems.

She passed a white hand over the coat, releasing the bees with a word of command. The thousand eyes of her coronet fell into her silken lap.

Then she led the Barefoot Princess to a bed all draped in white silk, surrounded by gossamer curtains and covered with a thistle-down quilt.

"Why don't you stay the night?" she said. "I'll comb my web for news of the King, and in the morning we'll find him."

And so the Barefoot Princess slept, while the Spider Queen thought hard. She had been very tempted at first simply to devour the Princess. But now she understood that the King actually *cared* for this human child, and her wicked old heart rejoiced at the thought that through her, she might have her vengeance at last.

And so she combed her web of dreams for news of her old enemy, and, through her coronet of eyes, she finally discovered him, sailing to a distant land. The Glow-Worm Chancellor's dream had been at least partly accurate. The Lacewing King *was* in danger. And if the Queen was to have her triumph, she would need to find him before the fate that threatened him robbed her of her vengeance.

Meanwhile, the bees from the Lacewing King's coat continued to guard the Barefoot Princess. Although they had lost the thousand eyes, they still had their orders. And when, in the morning, the Barefoot Princess awoke from a sweet and dreamless sleep, to find her new friend the Spider Queen ready to go on a journey, they followed the royal party as it set off in search of the Lacewing King; the Princess on her pink pony; the Queen in her funnel-web chariot drawn by a dozen red spiders; and the swarm of honeybees following behind them, towards the place where the Lacewing King would face his most perilous trial. . . .

43

THE RETURN OF THE KING

On an island, Worlds away, there was a tribe of people who lived under the shadow of a great black rock. Only one person lived in the light: he was the High Priest of the tribe, and he lived at the summit of the rock, crossing the line between light and shade by means of an intricate trellis of vines. The villagers lived in darkness and fear: food was never plentiful. But the High Priest lived well, enjoying the fruits that grew at his feet in the canopy of the trees, and sleeping all day on the sun-warmed stone.

And yet, his people were grateful to the High Priest for his work. This consisted of watching the sky and checking the sea for omens. No one else dared leave the rock, or had for generations. It seemed that once, many years ago, a King had discovered the island. The terrible King and his army, they said, had laid waste to everything, slaughtering the inhabitants and sending the few survivors into hiding under the rock. A hundred years later, the tribe was still there, and though there was no one left alive who remembered the terrible King, the villagers still feared his return.

"When the King returns," they said, "the trees will fall beneath his tread. The earth will tremble, and the island sink into a lake of boiling fire."

"When the King returns," they said, "the sky will crack open, and even the stars will fall from the sky like fruit from the tree."

"When the King returns," they said, "he will devour every one of us."

The High Priest listened in silence, smiling from his place on the rock. He had no fear of the absent King. In fact, he had long ago decided that the King would never return; and yet, he enjoyed his status. He knew that, if the villagers ceased to fear the terrible King, he would lose his position of privilege. This is why, every day, he would climb down to the foot of the rock, and address the villagers solemnly:

"The omens are bad," he would tell them. "The ocean was red this morning. The crows were flying above the sea, and the sky was black as murder."

Given that none of the villagers had ever seen the ocean, or even dared to look at the sky, this sounded all the more ominous.

"Is there sign of the King?" they would say.

At this, the High Priest always shook his head. "Not yet," he would say. And then he would return to his vantage point on the rock, to enjoy the rewards of his labours. These rewards took many forms. The villagers, in their gratitude, gave him the best of everything. They gave him the best of their food and wine; even, sometimes, their daughters. In these cases, the girl was always drugged and blindfolded before the High Priest took her up to his rock. This added to the priest's mystique, and heightened his sense of power.

"What a man am I!" he would say. "What a King among men am I!"

One day, a girl more spirited than most caught the eye of the High Priest. But when he asked for her to be sent up to him, the girl refused, saying:

"Why should I sacrifice myself for the sake of an absent King?"

This only inflamed the High Priest's desire. And so, the next day, when he came to report to the tribe, he assumed an air of even greater solemnity than usual, announcing:

"I have terrible news. The King has finally returned."

The folk of his tribe were stricken with fear. "What must we do?"

The High Priest shrugged. "Word of your defiance has already reached His Majesty. Much as I hope to placate him, I fear that it may be too late."

The terrified people pleaded with him to intercede on their behalf, seizing the girl who had rejected him and saying, "Not our defiance, but hers. Take her, give her to the King!"

The High Priest pretended to hesitate. But inside he was smiling. Finally, he accepted the girl, drugged and blindfold, as was the custom, and had her lifted to the top of the rock. But the girl, who was as cunning as she was spirited, only pretended to swallow the drug, so that as soon as she reached the top, she pulled off the blindfold and looked around.

The High Priest was relieving himself over the side of the big rock. There, in the sunlight, he looked much smaller to the girl, who had only ever seen him in the semi-shadows.

"Where is the King?" she said at once. "Where are the terrible omens?"

The High Priest turned. He was furious. "Why have you defied me *again*?" he said in his most impressive voice. But the girl was not impressed. She looked at the sky, and the clouds, and the sea, and the green canopy of the forest below the rock on which she was standing. And she understood that the terrible King—if he had existed at all—was now nothing more than a story to frighten the weak and gullible.

The High Priest saw her expression and understood that he had lost. If he had been braver or stronger, he might have tried to push the girl off the rock to her death. But his power was all in illusion, and now the illusion was broken. Besides, there was a look in the girl's eye that suggested she would just as happily fling *him* off the rock instead—and so he ran away to the shore of the Sea, where he lived out the rest of his life as a recluse, eating nothing but shellfish, and occasionally weeping at the ingratitude of his people.

As for the girl, she went back to her tribe and told them everything she had seen. Most of them did not believe her, and stayed there in the darkness, afraid of what they might find outside. But some of the brighter, more spirited girls followed her into the sunlight, where they live happily to this day, filling the clear and salty air with the sound of their laughter.

44

THE PEACOCK

The animals of a certain farm were under a dreadful pall of fear. It seemed that an elderly Hen had once encountered a Peacock, which had startled her considerably. Since then, tales of this Peacock had grown, spreading all around the farm.

"'Twas a terrifying sight," said the Hen to her comrades. "Blazing eyes, a thunderous voice, and a tail like a wheel of fire."

The other hens listened in silent awe, and were duly terrified. The Hen, who was rather enjoying the attention, widened her audience to include the Ducks, the Geese, and even the Sheep, and soon, every group of animals, from the cows in the field to the guinea pig in its cage, knew about the Peacock.

"This Peacock will devour us all!" squealed the suckling pigs in their sty.

"The Peacock will burn down the farm with its eyes!" said the Horse, who was fond of drama.

"The Peacock will take us to Heaven in the wheel of its glorious tail!" said the Cows, who were inclined towards religion.

Before long, the Hen who had actually *seen* the Peacock had quite forgotten what it had really been like, and the rumours spread further and further still, becoming increasingly menacing. Every day, more facts emerged about the mythical Peacock.

"The Peacock can change its appearance," said the Donkey with authority, "taking on the aspect of all manner of baneful creatures, including foxes, rats, and even wolves."

"Wolves!" echoed the Sheep in terror.

The Donkey looked mysterious. "Who knows whether, even now, the Peacock is among us?"

This caused the Sheep to bleat very piteously. After that, whenever a Sheep seemed to behave unusually, or show any kind of initiative, the others would whisper and say to themselves, "Maybe it's the Peacock, spying on us in secret!" This led to a great deal of unrest in the Sheep community.

Then, one day, a Gosling heard the Farmer talking to his wife through the bathroom window. "There's a leak in the cistern," he said. "We'll have to fit a stop-cock."

The Gosling, who was very young, misheard, and assumed that the Farmer was bringing *a Peacock* into the farm. He told the other Geese, who told the Hens, the Ducks, the Pigs, and the Rooster.

Immediate pandemonium ensued. The Hens drew up a petition, demanding that the Peacock not be allowed to stay. The Rooster, rather grandly, announced that he would never mate with a Peacock, however hard it begged him. And the Geese began a protest chant, calling:

"What do we want? Peacocks *out!* When do we want it? *Now!*"

The following day, the Plumber arrived to deal with the leaky cistern. The Plumber's car was rather grand, with big, bright headlights and an engine that roared.

"*It's the Peacock!*" squawked the hens, running madly round the yard.

The rest of the animals followed suit. Cows stampeded; dogs barked; even the old Horse in the barn kicked over his bucket and feeding trough.

"I wonder what's got into the animals today?" said the plumber, fixing the stop-cock above the leaky cistern. Then he drove away in his car, as the animals howled in triumph at having sent off the Peacock.

Some time after the fuss had died down, a fine Peacock arrived at the farm. He was a plump and handsome bird, and the animals looked at him curiously. "What kind of bird are you?" they said.

Now the Peacock had heard from a passing Vole about the recent events at the farm. He pecked at some corn and thought to himself. Then he spread his beautiful tail.

"Just call me Dave," he told them.

45

THE GIRL WHO NEVER SMILED

There once was a girl who was beautiful from the very day she was born. She was a very beautiful child; but by the time she reached young womanhood, she was turning heads everywhere she went. Her skin was cream and honey; her hair was gold and fallow silk; and she walked with the grace of a shadow. And yet, she never smiled. Not once; nor ever laughed at anything.

Her sister, who was plain, once asked, "Why do you never smile?"

The beautiful sister looked at her with pity and disdain, saying, "I decided long ago to never compromise my beauty. Smiling causes wrinkles and lines. By never smiling or laughing as you do, I shall always be flawless."

And she was right; as they both grew older, the plain sister, who was merry and smiled often, grew to look older than her age. The beautiful sister, however, did not; and people marvelled at the fact that they were even related. As middle age approached, the plain sister grew dumpy from a lifetime of enjoying biscuits and cakes, and from the children she had brought into the world, who made her smile and laugh all the more.

The beautiful sister, however, had wisely restricted her diet to green leaves and yoghurt, and still had the figure of a girl. Of course, she had never had a child, and therefore had avoided stretch marks and laughter lines and all the signs of ageing that were now so apparent in her poor sister.

The pair grew old—well, the plain sister did. At seventy, she had become a winter apple, all wrinkled and brown, while her beautiful sister looked forty still; with never a line on her flawless face. And still the plain sister refused to see how old and ugly she had become, and went on laughing and eating cakes, heedless of the consequences.

The beautiful sister felt quite revolted by this, and by her sister's family and friends, who seemed not to be repelled at all. In fact, the plain sister (who had now become positively ugly), seemed only to be loved by all, and spent her days in laughter.

In time, both sisters died. The plain sister was put in the ground in a closed coffin, and everyone grieved. The beautiful sister, who, in old age still made a handsome corpse, had ordered a glass-fronted coffin. The whole of the village came to her house to pay their last respects. One by one, they looked through the glass, marvelling at the flawless skin that had never known a smile; whispering at the slender bones that had never once succumbed to any kind of pleasure, and wondering at the terrible sight of a face and a body that had never once been loved or used, and never would be.

Then they went home, and hugged their children, and laughed, and smiled, and drank wine, and ate cake, and promised themselves to take what they had, and to treasure it for as long as they could; for Life is short, and Death is long, and Love lasts longer than Beauty.

46

THE COCKROACH QUEEN

Meanwhile, far away, the Lacewing King had joined the crew of a sailing-ship, heading West, bound for the islands of spices and silk. In disguise, he worked below decks among the beetles and cockroaches. In the heavy darkness it was like being home again, and for the first time in many months, he was almost happy.

Down in the bilges, during the night, the cockroaches sang as the ship rocked, and the King rocked with them as he slept in his silken hammock. Sometimes he came out onto the deck and looked up at the alien stars, and dreamed of places still to be seen, of adventures still to be had.

One day, when they had been at sea for weeks without a glimpse of land, the travellers came across an island, ruled by a fearsome Cockroach Queen. Her people were the Cockroach clan, a fiercely warlike, tribal race, who feared strangers above all else. If a stranger came ashore, or even approached the island, the Queen would send her warriors to throw them back into the sea. And when a ship came into view, the Cockroaches would line the shore, claws raised, shields up and ready to attack.

Now the Lacewing King and his companions had been at sea for a long time. Their supplies had run low. They needed food and fresh water. The island of the Cockroach Queen was green and rich and beautiful, and so they steered their ship towards the near shore of the island and prepared to risk its inhabitants.

The Cockroach Queen, on her high throne, sensed the approach of strangers. She stood well over thirty feet high; resplendent in her black armour; agleam from every link and plate of her intricate carapace. No man had ever seen her face under her shining helmet. Her fists were like granite; her tread was like doom; her eyes were like ice under the jet-black visor.

But it was her voice that struck the most fear into all her people. It was a voice like thunder; like steel; like a volcano erupting. Her people had learnt to obey that voice, and to do their Queen's bidding immediately. It had been years since she left her seat overlooking the ocean; now all she had to do was raise her voice, and her people would obey.

Now, from her seat on the mountain, the Cockroach Queen saw the ship approaching her island and gave a great cry of anger. "Intruders!" she cried in her thunderous voice. "Find them at once and bring them to Me!"

Her people, always on the alert to obey their Queen's commands, clustered round. They were small but hardy folk; resilient and hardworking. They had to be; the appetite of the Cockroach Queen was boundless. She ate over forty meals a day; meals of nectar, fruit, and flesh. When supplies on the island ran low, she fed on her own people, who lined up in their thousands for the privilege of serving their Queen. Now, in reply to her summons, they swarmed towards the shoreline, where the Lacewing King and his companions were collecting fresh supplies; fruit and grains and honeycomb; and water from the many springs that were on the island.

The travellers were quickly surrounded by a swarm of the Cockroach clan; armoured; fearful; hungry. And yet the creatures knew the King, even without his coat of bees and his crown of living centipedes, and dared not tear him to pieces.

Instead, they warned him: "Leave this place, before our Queen comes here for herself. For our Queen is as terrible as her hunger is insatiable."

The Lacewing King considered this. Many, many years ago, he had known a Cockroach Queen. She had been a warrior then, but never a ruthless tyrant. What could have happened, he asked himself, to make her into this monster? How could she feed on her people, and slaughter the strangers and travellers who came to her for shelter?

And so he decided to find out. While his companions hunted for food, he sat on the sand and waited for the Cockroach Queen to come to him. But the Cockroach Queen did not move. Instead, she called from her high seat in a voice like doom and thunder:

"Who dares invade My sacred shore? Who dares eat of My sacred fruit, and drink from My sacred fountains? Bring Me the strangers, my people; or feel the terrible weight of My wrath!"

The Cockroaches trembled and cowered low, but dared not lay hands on the Lacewing King.

Still the Cockroach Queen did not move. "How dare you keep Me waiting!" she cried in a voice like boulders rolling down a mountainside.

The Cockroaches wept and writhed in fear, and yet they still could not obey.

Once more, the Cockroach Queen did not move. "This is My final command!" she called in a voice like the howl of the wind through a thousand tunnels of stone. "Bring Me the strangers immediately, or I shall show no mercy!"

The Cockroaches wailed and gnashed their teeth, and yet could not harm the Lacewing King.

And so the Queen left her high seat and came to the shore of the island. She moved very slowly; trees fell in her wake; her giant tread shook the mountainside. At last, she came to the beach, where the King was sitting in the shade, and stood above him, terrible; thirty feet tall and in armour.

The Lacewing King stood up and said, "Your Majesty, I am honoured."

The Cockroach Queen looked down at him. "Who are you, you insect, to dare address Me as an equal?"

He smiled. "Do you not know me? I am the Lacewing King," he said, "and I do not address you as an equal, but as your lord and ruler of all the tribes of the Silken Folk."

The Cockroach Queen said in a voice like stone, "The Lacewing King is dead and gone. You are an impostor."

The Lacewing King shook his head. "A King is not his crown," he said. "Or a Queen her armour." And picking up a handful of sand from the beach, he blew it into the face of the Queen.

The Queen drew a single sharp breath, and sneezed.

It was a colossal sneeze. It rolled across the island like thunder. It rolled across the sea, where it dispersed into several tropical storms. It caused a tidal wave to submerge several neighbouring islands. Such was the force of the mighty sneeze that it blew off the Cockroach Queen's helmet. The helmet flew through the air, bounced and went crashing through the undergrowth.

The Cockroach clan averted their eyes at the blasphemy, expecting terrible vengeance to descend upon the culprit. But the Lacewing King just smiled, and when no retribution came, the Cockroach clan dared, one by one, to look up at the face of their Queen. But where the face of the Queen should have been, there was nothing but a space.

The Cockroaches grew bolder; first moving towards the foot of the Queen, then swarming up her burnished sides to peer into her armour. The armour was empty. Inside the gleaming carapace, there was nothing but darkness and dust and a fleeting scent of decay. The Cockroach Queen had been dead for years, leaving her armour for some other being to inhabit in secret; the space inside the helmet serving as an echo chamber for some other creature to take her place, and to issue its commands to them; commands to feed it; to worship it; to sacrifice their children.

The Cockroaches were first puzzled, then stunned, and then, fiercely, desperately angry. "We have been duped!" they exclaimed. "Let us find this parasite and make it pay for what it has done!"

They combed the island. They scoured the shore. They searched and searched for the creature, but in vain. Meanwhile, the Lacewing King and his companions went back to their ship with their supplies and sailed off into the twilight.

Some time later, the ship's cook discovered, in the bilges, a single fat white cockroach, hidden away in a barrel of beef. He pulled out the helpless, bloated thing, wondering how it had got there. But there was no room on the ship for a parasite, and so he flung the stowaway out to sea, where, lacking the means to swim, it sank.

The Cockroach clan elected a King, who ruled the island wisely, and well; and made sure to give hospitality to any travellers landing there.

And the Lacewing King and his crew sailed on, through the blue archipelago towards the unknown horizon.

47

THE SPIDER QUEEN SAILS WEST

Meanwhile, half a world away, the Spider Queen and the Barefoot Princess looked up at the same sky, and each in her way remembered the King and wondered how to reach him.

Every night, the Barefoot Princess would close her eyes and see his face; his hair the shade of a moth's wing; his golden, melancholy eyes. And every night, the Spider Queen would spin the skeins of her web of dreams and finger the strands of gossamer. Every night, she would put on her crown and watch the sleeping King from afar. And every night she would tell the Princess that they were getting closer.

At last, one night, they reached the sea. A vastness of ocean so dark and huge that the Barefoot Princess was moved to tears.

"How will we ever find him now?" she said, as she clung to the skirts of the Spider Queen, so like those of the waves on the beach that whispered so relentlessly. The Spider Queen watched her in silence, her coronet of a thousand eyes shining in the moonlight. Then she spoke a silent command and set to work spinning another web. She spun it from starlight and coral dust, and from the sound of the ocean. And she summoned her spider servants to join her in the great work, to build a ship that would take them as far as the islands of spices and silk, where the Lacewing King had just arrived, weighing anchor in a cove at the foot of a giant cliff.

For three days and three nights, the Spider Queen spun her web of dreams, a web more complex and beautiful than any made, before or since. And on the third day, the Barefoot Princess saw that the Queen had made a ship as light and strong as spider-silk and as flexible as steel. The crew were spiders of every kind; clinging to the gossamer sails; watching from the crow's nests; scuttling up and down the rigging. The hull was as light as a silken cocoon; but strong enough to withstand even the most relentless of storms. Inside, there was a state cabin, draped in the finest gauze, in which the Spider Queen and the Barefoot Princess would rest during the voyage.

And so they set sail on a moonlit tide, using the stars to pull them along. And as they sailed, the spider crew sang a little lullaby as they ran up and down the masts, adjusting the sails to suit the wind. And the Princess slept. But the Spider Queen stayed out upon the twilit deck, her coronet of a thousand eyes watching the horizon, and she dreamed of the day when she would have her final revenge on the Lacewing King.

For thirty nights, the Queen sailed west in her ship of silk and starlight. Meanwhile, halfway across the world, her enemy the Lacewing King was standing in the shadow of the tallest cliffs he had ever seen. These cliffs were so tall that their summit was wreathed in clouds; and their heels dug deep into the sea, a mile beneath the surface.

The Captain of the vessel had heard that there was rare profit to be had in the islands of silk and spices, which was why they had come this far, right to the edge of the Middle Worlds, where Pandaemonium meets the Sea. Here it was said that Dream went untamed; gold dust lined the seashore and men lived like wild animals. It was also the territory of two opposing, warlike tribes; one that lived at the top of the cliffs, another that lived below the sea, inside a labyrinth of caves.

The Captain took a dozen men and started to climb the tall cliff, using the purple vines that grew all the way down the rock-face. His First Mate stayed to explore the caves, taking a dozen men with him. And the Lacewing King sat on the beach and watched a cloud of dragonflies circle around the moored ship, and knew that this was not a good sign.

For the dragonflies were the warriors of the Dragonfly Queen, an ancient and pitiless ruler. The King had encountered her before—but with his royal entourage, and never alone or unguarded. He knew her to be bloodthirsty, cruel, and vindictive—and deeply suspicious of anyone who dared to enter her domain.

Soon enough, the dragonflies saw that the King was watching them. Even without his coat of bees and his centipede crown, they knew him. They descended upon him, a thousand strong, and lifted him into the air, and flew with him to the top of the cliffs, where the Dragonfly Queen and her folk had ruled, unchallenged, for centuries.

The Dragonfly Queen was a warrior, savage from the tip of her dragon-glass sword to her silvery, razor-edged wings. Aware of the

King's reputation, she assumed that he must be allied with her mortal enemy, the Queen Below the Water, whose realm in the shadow of the cliff was the mirror of her own. In fact, the only reason she had not ordered her people to kill him on sight was her own curiosity. The Queen Below the Water was as much of a mystery to her as she herself was to the Queen Below—neither could enter the other's realm, and both were equally hostile. If the Queen Below had sent the Lacewing King as one of her spies, then maybe this could be her chance to find out more about the enemy.

But she also knew that the Lacewing King was far too clever to come alone, unarmed, into her island realm. If he was a spy, then he must have some kind of protection. And so she welcomed him into her court, hoping to discover his plans. She greeted him politely, brought him wine and honeycomb, and led him to a flower throne decked with cushions of silk-moth damask. For a pleasant time, they talked; but whenever the conversation turned to matters of war or strategy, the Lacewing King always managed to somehow change the subject.

Meanwhile, the Captain and his men had run into the Queen's guard, a squadron of wingless warriors with no eyes and massive jaws. The guards were always hungry; and their favourite food was still-moving flesh. While the Lacewing King fed on honeycomb, the guards made short work of the sailors. And then the Dragonfly Queen brought out a flagon of her favourite wine and suggested a drinking game.

"Truth or dare?" she asked the King. "Winner eats the loser."

The King, who knew what was happening, knew that if he refused the game, the Dragonfly Queen would kill him. If he won, however, the Queen's code of honour forbade her to go back on a promise. And so he nodded politely and gave her his most insectivorous smile. "Why not?" he said. "Let the game begin."

And, pouring himself another cup of flame-green grasshopper nectar, he settled down to play for his life—which currently, was all he had.

48

TRUTH OR DARE?

While the Lacewing King and the Dragonfly Queen were playing Truth or Dare, the ship of silk and starlight was reaching the shores of the island. Its crew of tiny spiders began to gather in the sails, and the Barefoot Princess, almost speechless with excitement, climbed up to the crow's nest to watch the shore through her spy-glass.

"Do you really think he's here?" she said again to the Spider Queen.

The Spider Queen gave a narrow smile. The thousand eyes in her coronet blinked and glittered balefully.

"Oh, yes. He's here," she said. "I can already see him."

But there was a trace of doubt in her voice. Yes, she could see the Lacewing King through her coronet of eyes, but he was in danger. Weaponless, surrounded by Dragonfly Guards, without even his coat of bees, he was at the mercy of his hostess. The Dragonfly Queen's reputation was known everywhere in the Nine Worlds. She was cruel; she was clever; she liked to play games with her prey, and she was always hungry. Not that the Spider Queen didn't welcome the prospect of seeing her enemy eaten alive—but she meant to do it herself, and not before taking her revenge.

She stood high up in the bows of the ship and ordered her spiders to unfurl the sails. Sailing in at maximum speed, it would still take them hours to reach the shore. Surely, by that time, she told herself, her enemy might already be dead. Anxiously, she resumed her watch from the bows of the spider ship, while the Barefoot Princess watched from above, eagerly and with fast-beating heart, for the first sight of her protector.

Meanwhile, at the top of the cliffs, the Lacewing King and his hostess were engaged in a dangerous game, for which the stakes were higher than the Lacewing King could afford.

"Truth or dare?" said the Dragonfly Queen. "My turn to start." And she poured herself a goblet of the flame-green grasshopper nectar and smiled.

"First question: Who sent you here, and why?"

It was not an idle question. The grasshopper nectar was spiked with a drug, a very potent truth serum. If, as the Queen suspected, the Lacewing King was working for her enemies, then he would have to admit his guilt, or run the risk of a forfeit that would almost certainly claim his life.

He looked into her eyes and took another draught of the flame-green wine. "No one sent me here," he said. "I came here on a passing whim, unarmed and unprotected."

The Dragonfly Queen's eyes opened wide under her warrior's helmet. Her truth drug was infallible; and yet she could not believe that the King could have done such a reckless thing. Certainly, he was unarmed: she could see for herself that he carried no sword and wore no crown. Even his coat of a thousand eyes, stolen from the Spider Queen, was gone, which meant that, if his story was true, he was virtually helpless. But still, the Queen did not believe that he was unprotected. She knew his reputation, and she was sure he had a plan.

"Very well. Your question," she said, and swallowed a mouthful of the wine.

The Lacewing King smiled at her. "What's your name?"

Now, that may seem a harmless question. But names are things of tremendous power, not to be given lightly. *A named thing is a tamed thing*, or so the old saying goes, and the Queen was not about to give hers away so easily to the enemy. So she gnashed her razor teeth and said:

"I'll take the forfeit."

The King shrugged. "As you wish," he said. "Then, your forfeit is—a dance."

"A *dance*?" repeated the Dragonfly Queen.

"Why, yes, if it pleases my Lady," he said. "I've heard of your grace and elegance."

This was flattery, of course. The Dragonfly Queen was a warrior; fierce and merciless in combat, but neither graceful nor elegant. But she had no choice, and so she prepared, most reluctantly, to dance. But she could not dance in full battle-gear. So she took off her belt and her dragon-glass sword, and her armour (which was flexible as spider-silk, but as hard as Damascus steel), leaving only her helmet over her veil of dragonfly lace. Then she ordered her cricket quartet to play a rasping melody.

The King was an excellent dancer, taught as a child by a water-skater of tremendous skill and renown, and he led the Queen into the dance, holding her gently by the waist. The Dragonfly Queen, disoriented, and feeling her rage and hunger increase, vowed that her next question would put the King at her mercy.

At last, she pulled away and said, "Second question. Whom do you fear?"

It was a dangerous question. To know a man's deepest fear is to wield a weapon of terrible potency. The Lacewing King thought for a moment, taking more of the spiked wine.

"Whom do I fear? My mother, of course. My turn again."

The Dragonfly Queen hid her displeasure. There was no doubt he was telling the truth. What man does not secretly fear his mother's disapproval?

"I came here with a ship and its crew. Where are they now?" asked the Lacewing King.

Once more, the Dragonfly Queen gnashed her teeth. Her warriors had devoured the crew the moment she had captured the King. To warn him would be madness—she needed him to finish the game.

"I'll take the forfeit," she said at last, promising herself to use a particularly small, blunt knife when she cut him into pieces.

"Very well, I want a kiss," said the Lacewing King, and smiled.

The Dragonfly Queen became ashen with rage. She slashed at the air with her razor claws. But she could not abandon the game. And so she took off her helmet and kissed the Lacewing King on the mouth. She made sure it hurt, too; like kissing a mouthful of razor-blades.

But the Lacewing King made no comment. He simply dabbed the blood from his mouth and said, "Your turn, my Lady."

Now the Queen thought very hard. By this time, she was certain that the King was in league with the enemy, and she needed a question that would tax him to the utmost. She knew that the best way to destroy a man is to find his heart—and the Lacewing King had a special knack for making folk want to destroy him. And so she poured the last of the wine and asked him:

"Whom do you love most?"

Until then, the Lacewing King had seemed to have the upper hand. But the Queen's third question troubled him. To answer it was out of the question. He had no intention of telling her that the one he loved most was a human child—the Barefoot Princess, whom he believed to be safe and sound in the care of the Glow-Worm Chancellor. However, he knew that his forfeit would be designed to kill him—and probably in the slowest and most painful way imaginable. And yet, he simply smiled again, and said:

"I'll take the forfeit."

"Very well," said the Dragonfly Queen. "You know the rules of the game. If you fail—"

"I won't fail," said the Lacewing King.

The Dragonfly Queen gave her venomous smile. "Very well, my Lord," she said. "Then bring me the head of my enemy, the Queen Below the Water."

49

THE QUEEN BELOW THE WATER

Now the Dragonfly Queen and her rival, the Queen Below the Water, had been enemies since before the days of the Moon Queen of the Undersea. In fact, they had been enemies since anyone could remember, although the cause of their enmity had long since been forgotten.

The Dragonfly Queen lived on top of a cliff, with her army of cannibal warriors. The Queen Below the Water lived in her pale-green palace under the shadow of the cliff. And each of the two Queens was convinced that the other meant to destroy her. There was some truth in this; the Queen Below the Water regularly lost her folk if they approached the surface, and as for the Dragonfly Queen, she found that her eggs and larvae disappeared whenever she left them unsupervised. But, in spite of incursions from both sides, neither side was strong enough to win the war outright, and so they had remained at a standstill for years, neither of them bold enough to launch a direct attack on the enemy.

But now, at last, the Dragonfly Queen saw a way to strike back at her rival. She believed that the Lacewing King was spying for the Queen Below the Water—but either way, the rules of their game meant that he must take her life, or forfeit his own in consequence.

As for the King, he was well aware of the danger in which he now found himself. But, as always, he had a plan, and he was not quite unprepared. He left his seat on the flower throne and looked down from the edge of the cliff. Far below, he could see the realm of the Queen Below the Water. He knew she was as ruthless as the Dragonfly Queen herself; an ancient, cunning ruler, with as little tolerance of spies as her cliff-top counterpart. Her undersea guards were armoured things with massive, crushing teeth and jaws, armed with brutal whips that were made of hundreds of drifting tentacles. Their jaws were twice the size of their heads, and they were always hungry. They could smell an intruder a mile away, under or over water, and they were sworn to protect their Queen from her foes in World Above.

But the Lacewing King had arrived at the court of the Dragonfly Queen alone and unarmed; and during the course of their drinking game, he had already managed to make her discard her weapons and her armour. Now he quickly slipped them on: the feather-light armour; the helmet. Then, before the Queen could protest, the Lacewing King took a deep breath, and dived from the top of the cliff into the ocean far below.

The armour fitted him perfectly. The helmet, light as a soap-bubble, but strong as a piece of tempered steel, contained enough air for a minute or two. This was all he needed; and, making for the forest of weed that surrounded the pale-green palace, he set about making things ready for the second stage of his plan.

First, he took off his armour and hid it in the forest of weeds. Then he added the war helmet on top of the suit of armour, and with his last, precious breath, he swam for the pale-green palace.

As he had expected, the Undersea Guards were quick to sense an intruder. They came after him almost immediately, with tentacle whips and weighted nets. The Lacewing King did not resist, but allowed himself to be taken. His air was almost gone by then, but from the cliff-top he had seen that the undersea palace was built upon a number of hollow chambers, like a honeycomb in shape,

many containing pockets of air. It was into one of these chambers, larger than the rest, that the Undersea Guards dragged the Lacewing King, and threw him, gasping, before the throne of the Queen Below the Water.

For a moment the Queen looked down at him from her throne of coral and pearl. Her lidless eyes shone like opals; her hair was silver as the sands. Even without his crown and retinue, she recognized the King at once, and, like her counterpart, was convinced that he was a spy for the enemy.

"Do you know what I do with spies?" she said in her silky, watery voice.

The Lacewing King stood up and bowed graciously to the Queen Below. He knew his position was dangerous, and that his reputation was no better in the Undersea than it was elsewhere. Over the course of his long reign he had made a great number of enemies; and he guessed that the Queen knew half-a-dozen rulers, at least, who would have paid any amount of gold to get their hands on her prisoner.

But he had been hatching a plan ever since the Dragonfly Queen had suggested her game of Truth or Dare; and now, it was time for the next stage.

"My Lady, I am no spy," he said. "The Dragonfly Queen took me prisoner. I managed to escape with my life, but my ship and my crew are lost. And yet, I have information that can help you defeat the Queen for good; information that—for a price—I would be willing to share with you."

The Queen Below the Water looked sceptical. "What price?"

The King replied, "A ship of my own, and safe passage out of these waters."

The Queen Below considered this. But she did not trust the Lacewing King. "I think this is a trick," she said. "Look me in the eyes and swear that you were not sent here to take my life."

The Lacewing King felt a tremor of fear, knowing that he was still under the influence of the Dragonfly Queen's truth serum. But if he refused to speak, he knew the Queen would kill him. And so he looked into her eyes, and said:

"My Lady, you are right. I *was* sent here to kill you. But also believe me when I say that I can end this war of yours, alone and without bloodshed."

The Queen Below the Water looked into the eyes of the Lacewing King. She was suspicious, and yet she could see that the King was telling the truth. How could *both* his stories be true? How could he not be lying?

"End it how?" she said at last.

"You must meet the Queen face-to-face, unarmed and unaccompanied. I have already persuaded her to give up her helmet and armour."

The Queen Below the Water laughed. "Do you expect me to believe that?"

"I hid them in the weeds," said the King, "not far from your palace. Have your guards search, and they will find them."

The Queen Below was troubled. His story was incredible. And yet, her people had suffered so long that she would have done almost anything to put an end to the Dragonfly War.

"This is some kind of a trick," she said.

"Yes," agreed the Lacewing King, still under the spell of the truth serum.

"Explain," said the Queen.

The King shook his head. "If I told you, it wouldn't work."

The Queen Below grew angry. She turned to her thick-jawed, tentacled guards, standing by the entrance to the royal chamber. "Take him to the dungeons," she said. "Leave him in a coral cell. Then go and search for the armour he claims he hid away in the weeds. Let's hope—for his sake—you find it."

And so the guards took the Lacewing King to the honeycomb of cells that formed the base of the Queen's undersea fortress. These were made of coral, not wax, but the resemblance was striking. From below, the whole fortress looked like part of a giant hive, moored in place by ropes of weed, suspended in the water.

Some of these cells were flooded; some held pockets of trapped air. And it was into one of these half-flooded cells that the Undersea Guards flung the Lacewing King and lowered the trapdoor into place, leaving him standing waist-deep in the icy water. The floor of the cell was covered with tiny, sharp little coral spikes that cut into his bare feet, and the air was stale and brackish. The King guessed that he might have an hour or so of breathable air before he started to suffocate.

But this was not his greatest concern. His greatest concern was the creatures he now glimpsed through the holes in the floor. Drawn by the scent of blood, they came scuttling up from the indigo depths; their claws biting into the coral and their eyes swivelling madly atop their armoured bodies. *Spiders.* Spiders of the sea; some spiky-bodied; some smooth-clawed; some tiny and nacreous, no larger than a fingernail, others as long as nightmare, trailing their legs in the darkness.

From his cell, the Lacewing King listened to the creatures below. He could hear the sound of their claws against the brittle coral. He wondered whether the air would run out before the creatures reached him, or whether he would be eaten alive. Most of all, he wondered whether he could persuade the Queen Below the Water to meet her rival face-to-face and discharge his obligation. Because the Lacewing King had a plan; a plan that hinged on a lucky guess; which, if it were revealed to be true, might solve all his problems.

He thought of the face of the Dragonfly Queen under her warrior's helmet. Then he thought of the Queen Below, pale and stern and beautiful. He remembered how each of the warrior Queens claimed that the other had started the war, although no one really remembered the cause of their age-old rivalry. But the Lacewing King had suspected the truth from the moment he had first seen the realm of the Queen Below the Water, mirrored in the shadow of the cliff-top realm of the Dragonfly Queen. And when he had seen the face of the Queen Below the Water, so like the face of the Dragonfly Queen underneath her helmet, he had known that he was right. The Queen Below the Water was the image of the Dragonfly Queen—softer; paler, younger, perhaps, but unmistakably her child.

Of course, the Lacewing King was aware that dragonflies are born underwater, living for a time as nymphs, to emerge as warriors and queens. But the two opposing Queens had no idea of this at all. They had been at war for years, unaware that their differences were just a question of maturity. The Lacewing King knew that, given time, the Queen Below the Water would grow hard, shiny armour and beautiful wings, just like her mother before her. Whether he could explain all this to an angry, juvenile Queen was quite a different matter. But now, with the spiders of the sea making their way through the walls of his cell, his time was quickly running out.

He tried calling out to the Undersea Guards. But the cell was half-flooded, and the sound was swallowed up by the walls. Below his feet, the scrabbling of the spider crabs grew louder. The floor of the cell was almost breached. For the first time in his long, strange existence, the Lacewing King was truly afraid.

Then there came a terrible crunching sound as the floor collapsed beneath him. The Lacewing King fell through the hole in a shower of coral pieces. He fought in vain to escape, but the sea-spiders were on him now, dragging him down to the sea floor. He lay there helpless, his air almost gone, with thousands—*millions*—of the creatures swarming all over his body. He closed his eyes, and his final thought was of the Barefoot Princess, and how he would never see her again. Perhaps that was a good thing, he thought. He would not have wanted her to see him die in this horrible way, stripped to the bone and screaming blood into the turquoise ocean.

But when he opened his eyes again, he found himself breathing and unhurt. And now he began to understand that, far from eating him alive, the undersea creatures had saved his life. Each of the spiders was carrying a bubble of air from the surface—some as small as a pinhead, others as large as a pumpkin—to make a kind of chamber, in which the Lacewing King could survive. And slowly and laboriously, the creatures were *rolling* the bubble of air across the sand of the sea-bed, towards the wedge of shadow that marked the ship of silk and starlight, in which the Spider Queen awaited delivery of her victim.

50

TRIAL OF THE LACEWING KING

As the Lacewing King made his escape across the floor of the ocean, he wondered who could have rescued him. He knew of only one person who commanded the spiders of the sea. But the Spider Queen was his enemy. Why would she want to save his life?

There was, of course, only one answer to this. *Because she wanted to take it herself.* And as the spiders carried him steadily towards the ship, the King began to understand that, far from being safe, he had simply exchanged one peril for another. But he showed no sign of fear. He was, after all, the Lacewing King.

Finally, the bubble of air reached the surface of the waves. The Lacewing King looked up and saw the ship of silk and starlight, with the Spider Queen looking down at him, and said:

"What a charming welcome."

The Spider Queen's thin lips twitched in satisfaction. She had made a special attempt to look as captivating as possible; her dress was of moths'-wing velvet, stitched all over with tiny pearls, and she was wearing a silken veil over her coronet of eyes.

"I'm so glad you think so," she said. "In fact, I've brought some- one to see you." And with that, she indicated something that hung from the top of the crow's nest. It was the Barefoot Princess, tightly bound in spider-silk, with only her face, feet, and hands showing from beneath the cocoon. Around her, the swarm of honeybees that had once adorned the King's coat buzzed and scolded helplessly.

The Spider Queen saw her enemy flinch, and felt an exquisite pleasure.

"Your ward was so eager to find you," she said. "Your ward—or is she something else? Your daughter? Maybe your granddaughter?"

The Lacewing King just looked at her with eyes as cold as starlight. And yet, he knew that the Spider Queen had finally found the way to his heart.

"I brought her here to find you," said the Queen in her silky voice. "And of course, for you to watch as I feed on her delicious young flesh." Shifting to her spider Aspect, mandibles clicking hungrily, she started towards the crow's nest, moving deftly along the ropes, singing a little song under her breath.

"Long ago, and far away,
Far away and long ago—"

In his bubble, the Lacewing King fought and struggled to escape.

"Don't waste your time," said the Spider Queen. "That bubble is made from sea-spider silk. It's as flexible as steel and virtually unbreakable. It's certainly strong enough to contain any Aspect you choose to take—a swarm of bees, for instance."

"Please. Can we talk?" said the Lacewing King.

The Spider Queen's smile broadened. She perched herself on the yardarm, swinging her legs beneath her skirts, looking down at her prisoner.

"Of course we can," she said warmly. "In fact, I was rather hoping we would. Maybe you'd like to start with a threat. Then, we'll move on to the pleading."

"The girl is innocent," said the King. "Let her go, and then we can talk."

"An *innocent?*" said the Spider Queen. "I can smell your blood in her. Your lying, thieving, treacherous blood. Your warm, *delicious* blood—"

"Please," he said. "Just let her go."

The Queen pulled a face. "Call that pleading?" She moved a little closer to the Barefoot Princess's cocoon. Inside, the Princess struggled, but she could not free herself. "You owe me more than that, my Lord. You lied to me, deceived me, stole from me, humiliated me. *Blood* is what you owe me."

"Then take it," said the Lacewing King. "Take my life, but spare the girl."

The Spider Queen laughed. "But I don't want your life. I want you to be sorry."

"I *am* sorry," said the King. "What else do you want from me? Do you want my kingdom, my crown? Take them. Only let her go."

"Do you mean it?" said the Queen.

"More than anything," he said.

The Spider Queen gave a long, sweet sigh. "That's all I needed to hear," she said. "Honesty from you, at last." And, reverting to Spider Aspect again, she opened her massive jaws and prepared to bite off the Barefoot Princess's head.

But just as the Spider Queen picked up her prey, there came a cry from the spider-ship's bows. Turning, the King saw the Dragonfly Queen, in her armoured chariot, drawn by twelve of her Dragonfly Guards. Her silk-and-titanium bow was drawn, the dart pointing straight at the Spider Queen.

"Unhand your prisoner," she said.

The Spider Queen put down her prey. "This is none of your business," she said. "I have no quarrel with you."

But before the Dragonfly Queen could reply, the sea began to boil at her feet, and something began to emerge from the waves. It was the conch-shell chariot of the Queen Below the Water. Beside her lay the armour and helmet of the Dragonfly Queen, and her escort was twelve of her Undersea Guards, their tentacles raised in a strong-arm salute.

The opal eyes of the Queen Below came to rest on the Lace-wing King. "Return my prisoner at once," she said, addressing the Spider Queen.

The Dragonfly Queen looked scornful. "Your prisoner, or your spy?" she said. "Lady, this man is *my* prisoner. I demand you return him to *me*."

The Spider Queen gave a dry hiss. "My claim is older than yours," she said. "His blood is mine, and mine alone."

And so they argued, the three of them: the Spider Queen and the Dragonfly Queen and the Queen Below the Water. All three felt they had a claim on the life of the Lacewing King: one for spying, one for theft, and one for failing a forfeit in a game of Truth or Dare.

The Lacewing King let them argue awhile. Then he said, "If I might speak?"

The three Queens turned to stare at him.

"Much as I hate to contradict three such noble ladies," he said, "I feel I ought at least to respond. My Lady the Dragonfly Queen," he went on, "ordered me to bring her the head of the Queen Below the Water. Well, here it is, as I promised her—although I have chosen to leave it attached to the body of the Queen. That completes my forfeit. As for you, my Lady," he went on to the Queen Below, "I promised you I would end the war if you met the Dragonfly Queen face-to-face."

"End the war?" said the Dragonfly Queen, staring at the Queen Below.

"Face-to-face?" said the Queen Below, staring at the Dragonfly Queen.

The Lacewing King nodded. "Whatever your feud, it is fear, and not hate, that has kept you apart for so long. But with mother and daughter together again, how can the war continue?"

And as they faced each other at last, the two Queens finally understood the truth behind their rivalry. Two profiles; one young, one hardened with time; two pairs of opal eyes, each with an identical line of doubt between the arched and delicate brows—

"*Daughter?*" said the Dragonfly Queen.

"*Mother?*" said the Queen Below.

"This is all very touching," said the Spider Queen from the high ropes. "But when you've both finished catching up, I have an execution to carry out."

"Execution, or murder?" said the Lacewing King from his bubble. "Execute me, if you must, but leave the Princess out of this." He indicated the spider-cocoon hanging from the crow's nest, the anguished face of the Barefoot Princess just visible beneath the silk.

The Dragonfly Queen and the Queen Below agreed that this was reasonable. In spite of the Spider Queen's protests, the Dragonfly Guards cut down the cocoon, and soon the Barefoot Princess was free. The cloud of bees surrounded her, buzzing and swarming fretfully. At a sign from the Lacewing King, they settled onto her shoulders.

"Very well," said the Spider Queen. "But I have the right to justice."

The two other Queens exchanged glances.

"Justice," said the Dragonfly Queen, "would suggest a trial."

The Spider Queen managed to hide her anger. "And who would preside?" she said at last.

"We would," replied the two Queens. "Let us hear the charges."

For a moment, the Spider Queen hesitated. Then, she shrugged. "So be it," she said. And turning to the two Queens, she began to enumerate the crimes committed by the Lacewing King; which were many, including; trespass, theft, perjury, and making a false promise of marriage, with all the subsequent pain and expense that this had entailed the would-be bride.

Inside his bubble, the Lacewing King acknowledged that the Queen had a point, but wondered if the return of her crown, plus a heartfelt apology, and maybe a share in his personal fortune (which was large) might perhaps help take the sting from an insult given over a century ago.

"I don't think so," said the Queen. "The Worlds will be better without you." And, shifting back into her primary Aspect, she started to move towards her prey.

But the Barefoot Princess appealed to the court, saying, "If this is a trial, then where is the counsel for the defence? If my guardian has done wrong, then let the wrong be righted. But I refuse to believe that the wrongs he has done outweigh the good."

The Spider Queen looked sceptical. "Your *guardian*, as you call him," she said, "has never done anything in his life but lie, and steal, and cause misery. Is there anyone here who can speak for him?"

"I can," said the Barefoot Princess. "He was good and kind to me."

"Out of *guilt*," sneered the Spider Queen. "You think I don't know how he rescued you? How he seduced your grandmother and let her die, blind and helpless? Even without my thousand eyes, my web still brings me all the news, and if your King has ever had a single moment of altruism, if he has ever selflessly brought happiness to *anyone*, then I swear I will give up my revenge and go back immediately to my lair."

For a moment, the Barefoot Princess considered the words of the Spider Queen.

"Do you mean it?" she said at last.

The Spider Queen flexed her jaws. "I swear it on the Old Ones."

"Very well," said the Barefoot Princess. "Give me three days to prove you wrong. If I can find what I'm looking for, then you must give up your revenge. If not, then take my life. I owe it to him, anyway."

The Spider Queen agreed to the plan, although the Lacewing King did not. Trapped inside his bubble, he gave full vent to his protest. But the Barefoot Princess was his granddaughter in stubbornness as well as in blood, and she refused to listen. Instead she had him lowered back safely into the depths of the Sea. The Dragonfly Queen and her daughter remained to supervise the proceedings, and the Princess then sent out the swarm of bees that had been her constant companions, telling them to search the Worlds for someone who would speak for the King.

Meanwhile, the Spider Queen found a place high in the rigging of the ship, and began to spin a funnel web so lovely and so intricate, stitched throughout with symbols and runes, that even her spider crew could not see where in the Worlds the funnel led. No one asked why she was doing this. No one suspected foul play. She was a spider, after all; and spiders weave—it's their nature.

The first day passed. The Lacewing King begged for release, offering his own life in return for that of the Princess. But the Spider Queen simply smiled and said, "A promise is a promise," and flexed her giant mandibles, and spun her web, and watched for the bees. But at the end of the first day, none of the bees had found what they sought. There were many stories of the Lacewing King's cruelty, stories of his restlessness, many tales of his lies and deceit, but nothing wholly selfless.

The second day passed. The Lacewing King pleaded once more with the Spider Queen. But the Spider Queen ignored him, her ghastly smile growing broader. By that evening, when the sun had vanished beyond the distant horizon, try as they might, none of the bees had found as much as a rumour of a selfless deed, or an act of honest love carried out by the Lacewing King.

The third day dawned. By now the bees, short of nectar, were beginning to fail. The Barefoot Princess sent them off from the crow's nest of the ship, while the Spider Queen spun her web and smiled, and the Lacewing King stood silent and pale inside his bubble of sea-spider silk and waited for the inevitable.

The evening of the third day came. None of the bees had yet returned. The Barefoot Princess, in her crow's nest, had started to doubt they ever would. The sky grew red; the sun sank low. Only a sliver of brightness now showed on the purple horizon. The Spider Queen smiled at the other two Queens, awaiting the outcome of the game. But even they had given up hope of seeing the Princess evade her fate.

But then, just as the sun began its final journey, there came a flash of something green upon the far horizon. And in its glow, the

Princess saw a cloud of bees, and a tiny boat, in which two figures were standing. The bees were all but exhausted, but they managed to guide the tiny boat to the ship of the Spider Queen just as the green flash of sunset dispersed, sending its shadows into the sky. And from the boat came a young man and a beautiful woman, whose face was half-obscured by her hair of spiderweb gauze, and from whose nacreous china skin came the sounds of clockwork.

"We will speak for the Lacewing King," said the erstwhile watchmaker's boy. "We have searched the whole Nine Worlds for a chance to repay him."

And now the boy told his tale to the court, while the Clockwork Princess stood beside him, looking down at the Lacewing King imprisoned in his bubble.

"It seems the Lacewing King has found someone to speak in his defence," said the Barefoot Princess to the Spider Queen (who was no longer smiling). "By the terms of our agreement, you must now give up your case and return to your own domain."

The Spider Queen said nothing, but her eyes gleamed with anger. She looked down at the Dragonfly Queen and the Queen Below the Water. Both of them nodded agreement.

"Release the King," said the Dragonfly Queen. "This court has made its decision."

With a gesture to her servants, the scuttling spiders of the sea, the Spider Queen had the Lacewing King released from his bubble of sea-spider silk.

For a moment, she watched as the King celebrated his victory. The Barefoot Princess flung her arms around him. The Clockwork Princess and the watchmaker's boy held hands, smiling shyly. The Dragonfly Queen and her daughter, who had reason to thank the Lacewing King for bringing them together (even though his actions had been far from selfless), added their voices to the chorus of applause and merriment.

And in that moment, the Spider Queen reached for the strands of the web that she had built high in the rigging of the ship. "Congratulations," she said to the King. "You have evaded my justice once more."

And, with these words, she pulled at the web, releasing the intricacies of its design like a bouquet of flowers. For a moment the funnel gaped like the throat of a spider lily, and at its heart was darkness and a silence sure as Death.

And then she smiled and said to the King, "But at least I can make sure that I never see your face again."

And at that, she cast her web at him, and the darkness swallowed him whole.

"Bring him back!" cried the Barefoot Princess, but the Spider Queen simply smiled and spun the silken thread tighter and tighter, closing the throat of the lily.

And so the Barefoot Princess did the only thing that she could think of to do. She ran headlong at the Spider Queen and tore the silken thread from her hands. For a moment it twisted in her grasp like a living creature. And then she jumped from the bows of the ship into the funnel of darkness, which snaked and collapsed into itself, then winked out of existence.

The Spider Queen blinked her thousand eyes. "Well, that's the last we'll see of *them*," she said at last to the two other Queens.

And so—at least in *that* world—it was.

Book Two
Far Away

My mother used to say to me: There are no such things as fairies. Ignorant people saw butterflies and imagined they were fairies. But my old grandmother said: That's not true. People saw the fairies, all right, but just believed they were butterflies.

TABLE OF CONTENTS: BOOK TWO

51 Moonlight 227

52 The Builder of Boats 231

53 Rescue of the Lacewing King 236

54 The Engine Driver
Who Left the Tracks 240

55 The Scarlet Slippers 245

56 The Mermaids 249

57 Return of the Harlequin 254

58 The Clockwork Tiger 260

59 The Night Train 266

60 Dreams of the Barefoot Princess 268

61 The Harlequin's Kiss 270

62 The Barefoot Princess
on the Night Train 274

63 The Barefoot Princess in Hel 279

64 The Sparrow 282

65 The Prince 284

66 The Dancing-Shoes 287

67 The Lion Who Had No Roar 291

68 The Lacewing King
Between the Worlds 294

69 The Hallowe'en King 297

70 The Girl in the Candy-Pink Castle 303

71 The Very Popular Piglet 306

72 The King's Canary 308

73 The Lacewing King in Exile 311

74 The Spider King 316

75	The Moth Wars	321
76	The Lacewing King and the Spider Moth	325
77	Blinding of the Lacewing King	327
78	The Mermaids and the Mirror	330
79	The Petulant Pullet	335
80	Dead Man's Poker	339
81	The Lacewing King in Darkness	345
82	The Insects' Alliance	347
83	Three Buckets	350
84	The Labyrinth of Forgotten Things	354
85	The Story of the Hallowe'en King	359
86	The Watchman	366
87	The Empress's New Dress	370
88	The Master Chef	372
89	Flight of the Barefoot Princess	376
90	The Man Who Had Everything but Time	379
91	Apples	383
92	The Editor	386
93	Dishes	389
94	The Lacewing King in the Labyrinth	392
95	Descent of the Night Train	395
96	The Reaper of Clouds and the Spinner of Stars	398
97	The Cat Who Looked Out to Sea	402
98	Dead Man Walking	404
99	Dead Men's Shoes	408
100	Honeycomb	414

51

MOONLIGHT

There are many doors between the worlds of the Faërie and the Folk. Some look like doors; or windows; or books. Some are in Dream; others, in Death. And some simply wait for one person—the *right* person—to find them and to pass through.

So it was with the Lacewing King. Banished by the Spider Queen, he was dragged through the space between the Worlds into a different place and time; into a different ocean. He found himself drifting there, alone; under strange stars, with no land in sight; and no sign of his ship, his crew, the Spider Queen, or the Barefoot Princess. Exhausted from his long ordeal, lost and at the mercy of the waves, he drifted in the darkness, watching the river of stars above and the glimmer of phosphorescence below, thinking about the Barefoot Princess, and what might have befallen her.

Beneath him, shoals of angel fish swam through arches of coral. Great whales passed like shadows; Moon Jellyfish rose and fell in the depths. For a moment the Moon Queen herself glanced up from her midnight cradle, and saw the man floating far above her. Her tentacles had grown so long that they almost reached the surface, drifting like a bridal veil, and for a second they brushed the soles of the feet of the Lacewing King, and he looked down and saw her.

It had been five hundred years since the Moon Queen had last come to the surface. In that time she had grown so large that she rivalled even the Moon himself, glowing pale and perfectly round on the floor of the ocean. Against that ghostly circle of light, the King looked small and helpless. But although he would have made easy prey, the Moon Queen did him no harm. Instead, for the first time in centuries, she found herself growing curious. How had he come to be there? What was his story? What was his name? Why was his skin so pale; his hair so silvery in the starlight? Where were his people, and why was he floating above her so calmly?

None of her people could tell her these things, or even guess at the answers. And so at last she broke the rule of five hundred years of solitude, and, slowly, rose to the surface to see what the tides had brought her.

By this time, the Lacewing King had been in the water for hours. He had shed his clothes in an effort to stay afloat; and, drifting naked in the dark, now waited for Death to claim him. But the Moon Queen came instead, in her gown of a thousand frills, and in the glow of her tentacles, she saw that he was handsome.

And now a thought occurred to her. She looked into the clear night sky. There was no moon. She quivered with hope. Could this be her lost Moon King? Could he have survived somehow, and come to her to declare his love?

The Lacewing King was too weak to reply to her eager questions. Barely alive, and delirious, he drifted in and out of consciousness. And so she took him in her arms, and combed the wet hair from his face, and kept his mouth above water (for she knew that her King was a creature of air), and fed him on morsels of urchin and scraps of tender seaweed.

"My King is tired," she declared to the watchers of the deep. "Dolphins, sweeten his slumbers."

And so, in her arms, the Lacewing King slept; and the Queen held him close as dolphins sang their lullabies, and the Moon Jelly-fish circled around like a chain of floating lanterns. All through the night, the Moon Queen cradled him in her white arms; kissed him with her soft mouth; investigated his body with a thousand loving tentacles. And throughout her embrace, the Lacewing King slept, until finally he awoke, refreshed, just as the first soft light of dawn coloured the far horizon.

Finding himself in the arms of the Queen, he soon understood what had happened. He knew the story of how she had fallen in love with the Moon King, and he knew that his life was in danger. The moment the Queen realized her mistake, her vengeance would be terrible. The sun was already rising; and with it, the threat of discovery. He had to act quickly to save his life, and so he turned to the Moon Queen and gave her his most winning smile.

"My love," he said. "Here comes the dawn, and with it, my kinsman, the Sun. Soon you must return to the Deeps, and I must attend to my kingdom. But I will meet you here again, tonight, as soon as the sun has set."

It was a cruel lie, of course, and a tremendous risk to take. But the Lacewing King had no choice. The following night would bring the New Moon, and the Queen would know his deception. And so he smiled and kissed her mouth, and swore he would meet her at sunset.

Then, as soon as the Queen had withdrawn back into the dark-est Deeps, the Lacewing King began to swim as fast as he could towards the West. He was an excellent swimmer, trained in the underground lakes and ice-cold rivers of World Below, and he had regained his strength, thanks to the Queen's attentions. But there was no land in sight, and he knew that if he failed to reach safety before the New Moon rose in the sky, then the Queen would dis-cover his ruse, and she would tear him apart.

The Lacewing King swam for hours that day. The hot sun burned his shoulders. He grew thirsty; his head hurt; his limbs ached and were heavy. And still there was no sign of land in that rolling ocean. Even the nearest islands were a thousand miles away, and there was nothing to cling to; not even a piece of driftwood.

Finally, the sun set and darkness crept across the sky, and the King knew that the Moon Queen would be waiting at their meeting-place. It was hopeless. The miles he had swum were nothing compared to the speed at which the Queen and her servants could travel. Already, the sea around him was filled with leaping dolphins, messengers sent by the Moon Queen to locate her absent lover. And in an hour or less, he knew, the New Moon would rise, and he would be lost.

The King trod water and looked around. Still, there was no land in sight. He could think of no plan to save himself. He was parched, exhausted and sore, and this time, he knew there could be no reprieve. And so once more he waited for Death, while around him the endless ocean glowed with the pale light of Moon Jellyfish as they rose from the distant Deeps to greet the coming of their Queen.

52

THE BUILDER OF BOATS

On an island in a far ocean, there lived a humble builder of boats. She was happy in her work, which consisted of building little craft of coconut bark and banana leaves, which sliced through the water like darkened knives, leaving barely a shimmer of wake. She had everything she wanted: food; the ocean; the forest. But in the evenings she would sit and watch the sun go down in flames, and look for the fabled green flash that followed the moment of vanishing, and dream of other places, other worlds to experience.

And so one day she began to build a boat that would take her far away. Not a fishing-boat, this time, but an elegant craft thirty feet long, with a hull of intricate pieces, all interleaved and sealed with wax, and a sail of scarlet silk that stood out bold against the sky. It took the builder of boats six months to make the craft seaworthy, to stock it with food and water and to launch it from the beach. Her friends and family mocked her work, and the elders of her village frowned in disapproval. But finally, the builder set sail, and left her island far behind, travelling to the Edge of the Worlds in her red-sailed barque of dreams.

Now, on another island nearby, there lived a King, who saw the red-sailed boat skimming past, and understood its mission.

"But what a very *small* boat it is," he said. "I could build a bigger one."

And so he summoned his master boat-builders, and commanded them to build him a ship larger than any ever yet seen. And so they did; with purple sails and a mast that was topped with a golden crown. And with much pomp and excitement, the ship was launched, with the King aboard, and set sail for the Edge of the Worlds.

Now the King of the neighbouring island heard of the first King's plans, he knew that he, too, had to build a boat. And so he commanded his builders to make him a mighty longship, with

space for a hundred oarsmen and a saffron-coloured sail. And when it was ready, he too set off in search of other places.

But the King of the archipelago saw the longship sailing past, and he too was envious. And so he had his craftsmen build him a schooner with a hundred sails, and he set off for the Edge of the Worlds, leaving the other two ships in his wake, and the red-sailed barque of dreams far behind.

But the builder of boats did not give up. She sailed on towards the Edge of the Worlds. Her boat was slow in comparison with the three great ships built by the Kings, but she was not discouraged. Instead, she watched them from afar, trying to avoid their wake, which disturbed the sea and attracted sharks and Kraken and sirens, and other kinds of predators.

But as they passed through the archipelago and into the Ninth Ocean of the Worlds, the Kings of the Outer Islands saw the three great ships approach, and set to building their own to compete. And so, as time passed, it became a fleet of schooners and long-ships and catamarans, and heavy-bellied galleons, and great canoes and coracles, and ships with masts that scraped the sky. All sailing towards the Edge of the Worlds, while far behind, and losing hope of ever overtaking them, the builder of boats in her red-sailed ship (now bleached to rosy-pink by the sea) urged her small craft dog-gedly towards the pale horizon.

By now, the fleet had grown in size and fame, and every-one cheered as it passed. But no one cheered for the builder of boats. No one flung ribbons and sweets, or blew kisses or waved flags as she passed. Instead, the islanders laughed at her and said:

"Look at that tiny boat, trying to copy the big ships!"

The builder of boats tried to explain that she had been the first to launch, but the crowds only laughed at her all the more. And still she was not discouraged but sailed on, ever more painfully, towards the Edge of the Worlds.

Time passed. Storms blew. The fleet of tall ships weathered them. But the tiny red-sailed boat (its sail now worn thin as a dragonfly's wing) was tossed and smashed and broken. Even so, the builder of boats carried on, making repairs as she sailed to the Edge of the Worlds, braving the ridicule of the Folk who saw her pass, and urged her to give up on her dream.

By now, the main fleet was far ahead, and the builder of boats was obliged to endure the stench of the refuse they flung in their wake, and repeated attacks from devil-fish. But still she did not turn back from her goal. The sunset was filled with the masts of the fleet, and the green flash obscured by their turbulence, but still she sailed on, wretched, half-blind, towards her destination.

The fleet was thirty miles ahead, racing towards the horizon. The schooner of a hundred sails was still in the lead, with the longship close behind, and the rest of the fleet—the galleons, tall ships, catamarans—racing behind on the light wind. Of course, the little red-sailed boat could never dream of catching up. Which is why her captain could only watch as the great fleet sailed off the Edge of the Worlds and down into the bottomless gulf of the stars, and was lost forever.

The builder of boats sailed up close to the Edge of the Worlds and looked down into the darkness. There was no sign of the great fleet, not even a piece of wreckage. Then she hoisted her sail again and travelled back from the gulf of stars and had many more adventures.

There are a hundred stories about what happened to that fleet; of how they battled the Kraken; braved the song of the Sirens; then sailed off the Edge of the Worlds and were lost forever. But few (except, perhaps, for the bees) know what became of the red-sailed boat—bleached to nothing by the salt; dry as driftwood under the stars—or to its single occupant. Because, where dreams are concerned, it is not the size of the vessel that counts, but the power of the dream, and hers were inexhaustible.

And yet, just one of her stories survives, amongst the legends of the Folk. Because, when hope had failed him, and with Death only moments away, she alone was the reason that the Lacewing King was rescued.

53

RESCUE OF THE LACEWING KING

The builder of boats had steered her craft halfway across the Ninth Ocean. It was the widest of oceans; clear and filled with teeming life; and, knowing the ways of oceans, in spite of its vastness, the builder of boats had managed to keep herself alive, thanks to the bounty of the sea as well as her own ingenuity.

Thus, she had food in the form of fresh fish; water, collected from rain-barrels; shelter, made from the branches of green sea-palms and coconut trees, and even company, in the form of gulls, sea-turtles, and dolphins. She had seen storms and shark attacks and great continents of drowning weed. In fact, she thought she knew everything the sea could possibly throw at her. Which is why, on the evening of Midsummer's New Moon, she was astonished to discover a man in the sea; naked; a thousand miles from land.

It was the Lacewing King, of course. Hearing the sound of sails as the boat moved across the water, he had summoned the last of his strength to swim towards the little craft. All he could hope for now was that its single occupant would have mercy on his plight and agree to take him on board.

The builder of boats was wary at first. The Sea Folk could be treacherous, and it was not beyond them to lure unwary travellers

to their deaths with tales of misadventure. Besides, the man in the
sea looked very different to the people she knew: to begin with,
his skin was white, not brown, and his hair, which was long and
straight, was the shade of a moth's wing in the starlight. A string of
Moon Jellyfish circled him; his skin shone in their pearly glow. And
beneath him, moving up from the Deeps, was a shape like that of
the full Moon, dressed in a gown of a thousand frills.

"Help me," said the Lacewing King.

"Who are you?" said the builder of boats. "And what are you
doing so far from land?"

The King looked down at the glowing shape that was racing up
to meet him. "Please," he said. "Just take me on board. I swear on
my name I'll repay you."

"Your *true* name?" said the builder of boats, who knew the
value of such an oath.

The Lacewing King had no choice but to swear, and to give the
boat-builder his true name.

"*A named thing is a tamed thing*," said the builder of boats with
a smile. "Henceforth, you will serve me, until your debt to me is
discharged."

Once more, the King had to agree. It was that or be torn apart
by the Moon Queen in her rage and grief. So the builder of boats
hauled him aboard; and there she gave him food and drink, and
clothes like those of the islanders; a sleeveless tunic, tied at the waist,
and a woven blanket wrap in the bright colours of the islands.

Meanwhile, the Moon Queen had risen to the surface but
could not see the Lacewing King, hiding in the red-sailed boat. In
her gown of a thousand frills, she searched the waves; she searched
the skies; she called him, but he did not reply. At first, she was only
anxious. Could her King have suffered some kind of misadventure?
Could he have missed the rendez-vous, and be waiting for her elsewhere?

Finally, the New Moon rose. The Queen saw it riding pale in
the sky and knew that her King had failed her. And in her grief

and sorrow and rage, she raised the creatures of the Deeps; the sea-serpents, the Kraken; and they thrashed the sea with their tentacles until it was red with sand and blood.

The little red-sailed barque of dreams was tossed and tumbled on the surface. But the builder of boats had built it well. Boat and passengers survived. And by the time the Moon had set, and dawn was on the horizon, the red-sailed boat had almost reached the Outer Archipelago, in which ten thousand undiscovered reefs and islands awaited them, and where a thousand thousand tales were carried on the wind by the bees.

54

THE ENGINE DRIVER
WHO LEFT THE TRACKS

In a land of metal things, and plastic, and concrete, and sooty buildings and speeding trains, there lived a little girl who dreamed. On sunny days, she liked to sit by the railway line. On rainy days she would watch from inside, tracing the tracks of the raindrops as they trickled down the window and listening for the sound of the trains like music in the distance.

The little girl knew where the railway led. It was a steel road connecting two cities, equally grey, with equally sooty buildings. But secretly the girl believed in special trains along the line, leading to secret stations. She often dreamed that if she believed, then one of these trains would stop for her and take her to a world in which magic was as everyday as science was in her own world, where animals spoke; where Kings and Queens rubbed shoulders with monsters, and witches, and fairies, and where Love was an adventure, not an ending to a story. Sometimes, on rainy days, she felt almost close enough to touch those secret walls between the Worlds, and to hear the sound of a passing train slowing to allow her on board. But they never did, of course, and in time she came to believe that they were only stories.

Time passed. The girl grew up to become an Engine Driver. She drove a train between cities, but every stop she made was the same.

The cities were grey and sooty and dull; the stations were busy with people going from one place to another. But the Driver still sometimes dreamed of those secret stations, and listened for the passing trains in the spaces between the Worlds, and wished that she could drive them instead, and travel with them between the stars. But she never told anyone, and instead, continued to drive her train from one dull place to another, but never going anywhere.

One day, when it was raining, the train she was driving broke down between stations. The passengers were all transferred, but the Engine Driver stayed with the train to wait for the repair crew. She sat in her cab and watched as the rain trickled down the window, and looked around her at the place in which the train had been stranded.

The train had stopped in a siding, deserted and overgrown. Willow-herb grew on the bank, and nettles in the ditches. Beyond were fields and hedges and woods, all summer-green and drenched with rain. The Engine Driver thought it was the most magical place she had ever seen. The trees were wild with blossom; the birds sang with unusual grace; and all around her, the air was alive with golden swarms of tiny bees.

Then she noticed a lake by the side of the tracks; a lake that, in years of driving that route, she had never seen before. The woman got down from her driver's cab and walked over to the lake. It was small and perfectly round, and looked very dark and mysterious. And from the depths, the woman thought she could hear the sound of the ocean.

Heedless of the rain now, the Engine Driver knelt by the lake. Now she could *smell* the ocean, too, and hear the cries of seagulls. And in the water, she could see the reflection of a ship; a great, three-masted ship with sails of spider-silk and starlight. And behind the dream-ship shone a blue and cloudless summer sky.

The Engine Driver sensed that something magical was within her grasp. Without thinking of the risk, she plunged her hand into the water. Ripples moved across the lake, obscuring the ship and

the summer sky. For a moment she saw her hand in the darkness of the lake. Then another hand grabbed it.

The Engine Driver was amazed. She held on as tightly as she could to the hand in the water. She felt the weight of a living being struggling to the surface. And finally there emerged from the depths a young woman with weeds in her hair, and covered from head to foot with bees. It was the Barefoot Princess, of course, flung through the window between the Worlds by the power of the Spider Queen.

The girl and the Engine Driver stared, both astonished by what they saw. Then the girl saw the broken-down train and her face lit up in astonished delight.

"What kind of vessel is that?" she said.

"A railway train," said the Driver.

"A *train*?" said the Princess joyfully. She ran to the train and put out her hand to touch its metal hide. For a moment her joy was so great that it overwhelmed everything else. Then she turned to the Driver and said:

"But why am I here? And where is the King?"

The Engine Driver shook her head. "Which King? Why would he be here?"

The Barefoot Princess told the tale of how she had followed the Lacewing King all the way to World's End, only to lose him once again, just when she thought she had found him at last. She told the tale of the Spider Queen, and the coat of a thousand eyes. She told the tale of the Dragonfly Queen and the Queen Below the Water. She told the tale of the Clockwork Princess and how she and her young man had saved the Lacewing King from a sentence of death. And then she wept, because she was lost and alone in a foreign land, and because in all her dreams of travel and adventure, she had imagined the Lacewing King by her side, and now he was lost to her again—this time, maybe, forever.

The Driver listened in silence to the tale of the Barefoot Princess. Not since her childhood had she heard stories anything like these. Never had she known a world in which such things were possible. And never had she encountered anyone like the Barefoot Princess; so vivid, brave, and yet so sweet—and, in the eyes of the Driver, at least—so very beautiful.

"I'll help you," she said. "Wherever he is, I'll help you find the Lacewing King."

"Why would you help me?" said the Princess.

"Because," said the Driver, "I too was lost. But you have made me believe again."

The rain had stopped. The Princess's bees dried their wings in the sun and took nectar from the flowers that grew along the side of the railway-tracks. Then they settled around the Princess; on her shoulders and in her hair, for bees are the most loyal of all the Silken Folk, and they were bound to serve her.

"Couldn't your train help us find the King?" After years of reading about them in books, the Barefoot Princess staunchly believed in the magical power of trains, though her faith had been somewhat shaken by the fact that this one had broken down.

"That's not quite how trains work, I'm afraid," said the Driver. And she explained about railway lines, and timetables, and advance fares, and first class, and economy class, and minding the gap at stations. The Barefoot Princess was entranced, and it took the Engine Driver some time to convince her that the train could not be commandeered to leave the tracks and to go in search of the Lacewing King.

"But there are other trains than this," said the Engine Driver. "Trains that can take you to other worlds; stations lost between the stars. The Lacewing King, wherever he is, may be at one of these stations."

"So how do we find him?" said the Princess.

"The way you found *me*," said the Driver.

By the time the engineering crew came to make their repairs, there was no one aboard the train. Nor was there any sign of a lake by the side of the railway tracks. Of course, they had never heard of the Barefoot Princess, and so could not notice her absence; but the Engine Driver had disappeared, leaving no sign of where she had gone except for her engine-driver's cap, covered in seaweed, on the rails, and a distant murmur of bees.

55

THE SCARLET SLIPPERS

In the land of the Sand Riders, where women go veiled from top to toe, there lived a young man who dreamed of love. But he was too young to think of marriage, and according to the customs of his land, he was forbidden even to speak to any of the unmarried women he saw. Instead, he would picture their faces; try to overhear their words as they spoke to each other in their lowered voices. And he dreamed of one day having a woman of his own to love; to cook for him and sing to him; a woman whose face would be veiled to the world; and that only he would ever know.

And then one day, in a strange town, in a crowded marketplace, the young man finally fell in love. She was veiled, like all the rest, and yet she seemed very different to him. Slender as a reed beneath her robes, she held her head high; and on her feet she wore slippers of scarlet silk. It was those slippers that moved him. And the slippers were how he followed her through the market-day crowds until he came to her neat little house, set in a tiny walled garden of mango trees and jasmine.

In the land of the Sand Riders, women do not live alone. The woman in the scarlet shoes lived with her mother and father. She cooked for them and cleaned for them, and ran their errands and washed their clothes, and the only moments she had to herself were in that tiny garden, with its sleepy jasmine scent, and the fountain that sang a three-note song that echoed the song of the nightingale. And yet she too had dreams. But they were never dreams of love. Instead the woman longed to see beyond her father's walls; to ride a camel through the desert and to hear the sound of the ocean waves. In her dreams, she sometimes walked barefoot on the sandy shore, or swam naked in the water, far away from the gaze of men. But these things were forbidden; and so, the woman never spoke of them.

That night, the young man waited for his love to come into the garden. And through the iron bars of the gate, he told her of his great love. She listened in modest silence, as the young man spoke of his plans for them; of her life with the Sand Riders; of their future children; of the care he would take to shield her from the eyes of other men.

"Come with me," he told her. "Be mine, and I will protect you. I will love you and cherish you. No man or woman will trouble you or speak to you with disrespect. You will live at the heart of my tribe, surrounded by camels and warriors. Your body will be mine alone; no other man will see your face. You will drink only the finest wines, and taste the most delicate spices. You will be my Queen; my all; the mother of my children, if only you will come with me today, and be mine forever."

Finally, the woman spoke. "I will come with you," she said, "but only on one condition. I have never seen the Sea, or walked on a beach, or heard the waves. Take me to the Sea," she said, "and I will be yours forever."

And so the young man opened the gate and led the girl to the place where his people had their camp. He stole a pair of camels, and by the time their absence was known, he and his love were far away, riding hard towards the coast. They rode for three nights, resting by day, and every day the young man asked his lady-love to show him her face.

But she always said: "Not yet, my love. Only when we are married may you see what no man has ever seen." And so the young man waited, congratulating himself on having chosen such a virtuous bride.

Finally, they arrived at the Sea; a wild and lonely stretch of coast where only the sound of the waves could be heard. No one lived here; but there were stories of mermaids that lived in the sea; luring unwary men to their deaths; proud, and beautiful, and free.

The woman in the red slippers stood for a long time by the shore, looking out to sea. The wind tugged at her robes and veil, showing the young man the gentle curves of her body. Finally, she said, "This is the place," indicating a tiny beach at the base of the rocky cliff. "This is where I shall take off my veil, stand barefoot on the sand, and be yours. But you must be patient and wait for me."

The young man waited on the cliff as the girl climbed down to the beach. "Are you ready yet?" he called. But there was no answer.

He waited for a long time, and then, when his love still did not call him, he too climbed down to the little beach. But his lady was not there. Instead, all he found was her slippers, laid neatly on the seashore, the last in a long line of women's shoes that stretched right across the little beach and disappeared around the base of the cliffs.

And opposite the line of shoes was a line of bare footprints— dozens, maybe *hundreds* of them, leading to the water's edge—but none of the footprints ever led back. Because, of course, mermaids have no need of embroidered slippers—or of silken veils, or even men. Mermaids recognize their own—even when they are in disguise.

The young man sat by the water's edge and wondered what he might have done wrong. "I would have kept you safe," he wept. "I would have watched over you day and night. I would have made sure no other man ever came anywhere near you."

But there came no answer from the Sea, except, maybe, far in the distance, the sound of the mermaids laughing.

56

THE MERMAIDS

Meanwhile, the red-sailed barque of dreams had reached the archipelago. Ten thousand islands lay before it. To the West lay the End of the Worlds. To the East, an ocean that no man had crossed. But the builder of boats had no wish to go back to her home in the islands. She wanted to know what lay beyond that undiscovered ocean. And the Lacewing King was bound to her until he had repaid his debt, which meant that he, too, must journey on. But this did not trouble him. However luxurious his exile might have been in the islands of the archipelago, the King had only one wish, which was to find the Barefoot Princess again, and to return to his people.

At every island at which they had stopped to seek fresh water and pick up supplies, the Lacewing King had asked the bees to give him news of his grandchild. But the bees of the archipelago knew only the islands. They had never crossed the Sea or seen that other world from which the Spider Queen had banished him. And yet, the island bees understood that he was their King in exile, and swarmed about him wherever he went, and told him all the stories they knew. But none of them were stories of the Barefoot Princess, or the Spider Queen, or the clockwork woman and her young man; and the Lacewing King had begun to believe that they were lost forever.

And so he and the builder of boats set off across the uncharted sea. The red-sailed boat had weathered storms; braved the Edge of the Worlds; and faced the terrible wrath of the Moon Queen. Now, laden with supplies, it sailed into the gold of the morning sun. Bleached and dried by the salt and the sky, the boat was almost as light as air, skating over the water like a crane fly on a gilded lake, and the builder of boats sang a happy song as she steered it into the sunrise:

"Up above and down below,
Down below and up above,
The world's a honeycomb, my love,
The world's a honeycomb."

It was not quite the same song the bees used to sing in the world of the Lacewing King; and yet it was not quite different. It made him homesick, but it was also strangely comforting, as if the space between the Worlds were nothing more than the breadth of a dream away. And so he sailed, while the island bees followed in the wake of the boat, and the woman who had rescued him sang as they left the islands behind.

Days passed; then weeks. The Lacewing King's pale, northern skin veered from moon-white to honey-brown. The builder of boats sometimes caught fish, but even so, as the weeks went by, their food and water supplies grew low. They endured both storms and weather so calm that the red-sailed boat, feather-light as it was, could barely be seen to be moving. They saw great whales, and giant sea-turtles, and heard the songs of dolphins. They watched the moon change from a shred of rind to a perfect silver apple. And still, there was no sign of land as they sailed into the sunrise.

One day, the travellers came across a great flock of birds, circling low over the sea. Approaching, they saw, from the bow of the ship, what looked at first to be dolphins. But as they came closer, the builder of boats stood up and gave a joyful cry.

"Not dolphins," she said. "*Mermaids*. Legend says they were women once, who fled to escape the tyranny of men."

The Lacewing King looked into the sea; and sure enough, here were the mermaids, swimming alongside the ship; sometimes diving beneath the hull or leaping ahead in the sunlight. Unlike the mermaids of his own world, which had been pale and silvery, these were brown-skinned, like the islanders, with long black hair and powerful tails of every colour: yellow, red, or striped with black like angel fish; or dappled brown like manta rays, or iridescent butterfly-blue. Sometimes they surfaced, calling out to the travellers:

"*Come play with us, come play,*" they sang.
"*Come play with us under the Sea.*"

The Lacewing King knew that mermaids were seldom to be trusted. Their games were not the games of the Folk, and they were often treacherous. And yet, there was such joy in them; such fierce beauty in their eyes and in their rainbow colours, that many men had succumbed to their call, and leapt in pursuit of them to their deaths. But he knew that while they despised men, they often took in women and girls. Could they have seen the Barefoot Princess? Could they even have helped her?

But when he asked them if they'd seen a girl with hair and skin like his own, travelling with a swarm of bees, they only laughed and sang at him:

"*Buzz, buzz, little bee, in your nest of honeycomb.*
Buzz, buzz, little bee; on the sea, and far from home."

The Lacewing King was curious. Their song suggested they had heard of him; knew him, perhaps from stories. But cajole and plead as he might, they would not give him any news of the Barefoot Princess.

"*Buzz, buzz, little bee,*" they sang from under the water.

"Buzz buzz, little bee, fleeing from the Spider.
Spider's web has many strands in my lady's garden,
But for those who love the land, there will be no pardon."

Meanwhile, the builder of boats was scanning the horizon. Mermaids seldom inhabit the Deeps, preferring the reefs and coral caves, and she hoped at least for an island nearby, where she and her companion could find fresh food and water.

"Is there land nearby?" she said.

"*Ocean,*" sang the mermaids. "*Ocean without ending.*"

But the builder of boats looked up at the flock of seagulls circling over her head and knew that the mermaids were lying. There must be land somewhere nearby; something large enough to sustain a colony of sea-birds. That meant food and water, too; maybe even people.

"*This way, this way, this way,*" sang the mermaids, holding out their strong brown arms and pointing to the western sky. Once more, the builder of boats looked up, then set sail towards the East, the Lacewing King sitting in the bows, a mantle of bees on his shoulders. The mermaids followed till nightfall, following in the wake of the ship; sometimes leaping across the bows; sending out great plumes of phosphorescence in their wake. Sometimes they called out and sang:

"Buzz, buzz, little bee, far from home and sailing.
Buzz, buzz, little bee, sailing on the endless Sea."

But the sailors ignored them, and finally, during the night, the mermaid shoal moved on at last and left them to their journey, the King more melancholy than ever, the builder of boats filled with new hope. And, in spite of their taunting, the mermaids must have brought them luck, because, the next morning, for the first time in months, the builder of boats sighted land.

57

RETURN OF THE HARLEQUIN

The Lacewing King and the builder of boats had reached land in the evening. It was a rocky, featureless coast, lined by a narrow stretch of beach. The builder of boats moored her craft in a sheltered inlet, and together, she and the Lacewing King set off to explore the land.

There was little to explore. Beyond the tiny strip of beach were cliffs of rust-red sandstone. After that, the desert; a desert that seemed to reach as far as the ocean from which they had come. There were no trees, no bushes; only a sprawl of blue thistles at the top of the sandstone cliffs, and the occasional small shrub, leaves burnt grey by the hot sun; roots sunk deep into the sand.

There were shellfish on the rocks. The hungry travellers ate their fill. But with so few supplies left aboard the red-sailed boat, they needed to find water, or die. The Lacewing King went one way down the seemingly endless strip of beach; the builder of boats took the other path. The bees, which had followed the Lacewing King all the way from the islands, now flew inland into the dunes, to see how far the desert lay. All three parties agreed that they would meet again in the morning.

The Lacewing King walked down the beach. The night was cool, the stars were bright, and it was the first time in months that he had been completely alone. It was pleasant, and for a time, he considered keeping on walking, leaving the builder of boats to face whatever awaited her. But he still owed her a debt, sworn on his true name to repay, and so, when the night began to turn, he set off back the way he had come, and was back at the boat by sunrise.

But although the bees had already returned, bearing news of a city some three days' march into the sands, there was no sign of the builder of boats. The sun rose, and then grew hot; but still there was no sign of her, and the Lacewing King began to believe that something had befallen her. And so, with the swarm of bees following him along the beach, he followed her footsteps in the sand. He took what was left of their water; he fed on urchins by the shore. When the sun grew unbearable, the island bees flew over his head in a cloud that sheltered him from the glare. Once or twice he thought he saw mermaids in the distance, and heard their distant, mocking song; but there was no sign of the builder of boats.

Instead, he came across pair after pair of abandoned shoes on the shoreline; some already bleached white by the sun; some richly jewelled; some plain. All left in a neat row, side-by-side at the top of the beach; a row that went on for miles and miles. And as he walked, the Lacewing King once more heard the distant sound of song and laughter from the sea, and began to understand what this was; a place where women came to cast off their unhappy lives on land, to be reborn into the sea, to follow the call of the mermaids.

The King began to wonder if the builder of boats had followed it too. But her footprints on the sand told a different story. Finally, as the sun began to set on the beach behind him, he saw a figure by the shore. It was the builder of boats at last, sitting immobile on the beach; wide, unblinking eyes now fixed upon the fiery sunset. Around her, fashioned from the sand, was a garden of dusky roses; blooming petal and flower and bud; coils of briar and sharp thorns and drifts of shining, lion-toothed leaves, all of them spun entirely from sand and gleaming in the rosy light.

The Lacewing King understood at once that there were powerful glamours here. His instincts told him to flee the place, but the builder of boats would not move from her spot or answer him when he spoke to her. Looking into her sun-filled eyes, he realized that she had lost her mind—and then he heard a voice at his back that he recognized only too well.

"Welcome to my garden," said the voice of the Harlequin.

The King turned slowly to face his foe. It had changed Aspect since their last meeting, and stood before him as one of the Folk; naked but for its long hair, its warning colours of red and black painted onto its body. Its skin was brown, like that of the islanders, and its savage claws were unsheathed; but its eyes were still those of the Harlequin, dark and ancient and filled with hate.

"I knew we'd meet again someday," said the Harlequin, smiling. "I knew you'd cross my path again if I waited long enough. And here you are, my enemy, the son of the man who cheated me of my kingdom and my crown; who sent me into this desert world; now alone and helpless."

"Not so helpless," said the King, and took the form of a cloud of bees, which swarmed among the island bees that still hung in the air like smoke. The Harlequin hissed with rage but was unable to focus its gaze, trying in vain to isolate the parts of her enemy's Aspect.

But although this was his chance to flee, the Lacewing King knew he had to remain. He still owed the builder of boats a debt, and could not leave without paying it. He guessed that she had fallen victim to the gaze of the Harlequin, her soul now lost between the Worlds, and severed from her physical form. The Harlequin could release her—but could he persuade it to do so?

He resumed his human Aspect, standing at a safe distance from the Harlequin's razor claws. The Harlequin watched him avidly, its eyes filled with troubling lights.

"Release my friend," said the Lacewing King, taking care to avoid the creature's eyes. "And then perhaps we can discuss terms."

The Harlequin bared its teeth, exposing its fearsome mandibles. "Terms?"

"You must have a price," said the Lacewing King.

The Harlequin began to laugh. "My price?" it said. "My price is a kiss. The chance to hold you in my arms and look into your eyes again."

The Lacewing King sighed. "Really?" he said. "You wouldn't accept an apology, or the promise of a favour, or untold wealth, or fame, or something like that?"

The Harlequin said nothing, but its mandibles worked furiously.

"I didn't think so," said the King. "Very well. I'll grant your wish."

The Harlequin gave a rusty laugh. "Another of your tricks!" it said.

The King shook his head. "No tricks," he said. "An oath, sworn on my true name."

The Harlequin's eyes were hungry. "Explain."

The King explained to his enemy the debt he owed to the builder of boats; how she had saved his life, and how he was bound to repay her. The Harlequin, who understood the binding power of such an oath, listened to his story. It knew that, though he was devious, in this case, he was telling the truth; and it smiled to itself as it realized that the King was in its power.

"Very well," it said at last. "But now your life belongs to *me*."

And it knelt down beside the builder of boats and touched her face with the tip of a claw. Then it looked into her eyes, whispering in an ancient tongue that not even the King could understand.

The builder of boats began to stir. Her dark eyes came into focus. They widened in fear at the Harlequin's touch—and then she saw the Lacewing King, watching the last of the sunset, the island bees draped around him like the most regal of mantles.

In that moment, she understood how he had redeemed her, and leapt to her feet with a cry of alarm as the Harlequin turned on its enemy. The razor claws hissed through the air, but the King made no move to evade them.

Instead he looked back at the builder of boats. "Consider my debt repaid," he said.

And then he took a step forward and looked into the eyes of the Harlequin.

58

The Clockwork Tiger

A toymaker had two daughters. One was good and beautiful, the other, wayward and brilliant. Their father was old and losing his sight; their mother had been dead for years. The two girls lived by a forest but were forbidden to walk there; for the woods were dangerous, a home to packs of savage wolves.

The good and beautiful daughter was obedient and stayed at home. But the brilliant, wayward daughter longed to hunt and explore the wild woods. But she had no weapons, no hounds, or anything to keep her safe. And so she stole into her father's workshop one night and started to build a guardian, a fearsome mechanical guardian, to protect her from the wolves.

For twelve nights she worked in secret, by the light of a single lamp. She used her father's work tools; his watchmaker's kit and his soldering irons and the many cast-off mechanical parts from the toys he had discarded. Night by night her creation grew, until on the twelfth night it was complete; a magnificent clockwork tiger, with eyes of luminous amber glass, a shaggy, magnificent growling head and stealthy, terrible, silent paws that would strike in defence of its mistress.

But, awakening that night, the good and beautiful daughter sat up to find her sister gone from her bed. She called her father immediately, and together they found the sister in her father's workshop, putting the finishing touches to the marvellous clockwork tiger.

The father was very angry that his daughter had entered his workshop. "How many times have I told you," he said, "that good girls do not work with tools, or build tigers from clockwork!"

The wayward daughter tried to explain; but he was too angry to listen. He fastened a padlock on the door and kept the key around his neck so that his daughter could never again enter without his permission. But he himself had grown too old to use the tools in his workshop, and so for many years afterwards, the place remained abandoned, and the clockwork tiger was left in the dark, growling softly to itself.

Time passed. The sisters grew up. The good and beautiful daughter married a man from the village and had two good and beautiful daughters of her own. But the brilliant, wayward daughter preferred, against all her father's warnings and threats, to go hunting in the forest. She would have liked to ride a horse, and maybe carry a crossbow, too—but her father always refused.

"How many times have I told you," he said, "that good girls do not ride, or hunt, or handle dangerous weapons!"

But the wayward, brilliant daughter never listened to his words. Instead she built ingenious traps, until one day she fell foul of the largest and most savage wolf in all of the forest, and, having no horse or crossbow, was killed.

The good and beautiful daughter grieved for her brilliant sister. And the father, relenting (too late), now opened his old workshop with the key that he kept around his neck, and found the clockwork tiger there, still growling softly to itself. For a long time, he inspected the work of his brilliant, wayward daughter, marvelling over her craftsmanship. Then he fastened a heavy chain around the clockwork tiger's neck and gave it to his daughter.

"Soon I shall be gone," he said. "This tiger will be your guardian. Keep it close as you walk near the woods, and you will be spared your sister's fate."

The good and beautiful daughter did just as her father commanded. Until the day she died (giving birth to her third and youngest daughter), she was never without the clockwork tiger by her side, and neither wolf nor wild boar ever ventured anywhere near. And as she lay on her deathbed, she called her daughters to her side, and gave them the clockwork tiger, telling them never to go into the woods without it.

The good and beautiful daughters duly obeyed their mother. But it was their sister, who had entered the world just as their mother had left it, who was most fond of the tiger. She grew up as wayward and brilliant as the girl who had built it, and she would often roam in the woods, with the tiger at her side, while her good and beautiful sisters stayed at home with their needlework, or eyed the young men on the way home from church, or looked after their father.

"Let her have the beast," they said. "What do we need with a clockwork tiger?"

Time passed. The father died. The wayward, brilliant sister had already grown into young womanhood. The good and beautiful sisters had moved away into homes of their own. But the younger

sister did not move away, but chose to remain in her grandfather's house, and opened up his workshop, and marvelled at the many things he had made in the days of his youth. But there was nothing as marvellous there as the clockwork tiger, even though it was old now, and its amber eyes were milky with age, and there was a tremor in its paws on some cold and wintry days. But the brilliant sister was sure that she could help revive the beast, and she spent many months in the workshop, discovering her grandfather's tools, and slowly but certainly learning his trade.

The older sisters laughed at her. "How ridiculous," they said. "How will she ever find a man? Fancy spending all your time in a dusty old workshop, getting oil under your nails, and all for a stupid old tiger that doesn't even work anymore."

But the brilliant, wayward sister paid no attention to them. Instead, she made a new pair of eyes for the clockwork tiger, and oiled its secret machineries, and took the rust from its ancient claws, and made it purr like a kitten, and run as smoothly as a pocket-watch.

The good and beautiful sisters began to laugh more openly. "What a silly girl she is," they said to their husbands and friends from church. "Why does she need that old thing anyway? There haven't been any wolves or bears near the village for years and years." (Of course, the reason there were no wolves or bears was precisely *because* of the wayward sister and her clockwork tiger.)

But the young girl paid no heed. In her grandfather's workshop, she made herself a fine mechanical crossbow, which she would take into the woods, with her tiger by her side. And there she would hunt the wild wolves, driving them further and further away, making the forest safe again for everybody to enjoy.

As the months and years passed, her good and beautiful sisters became more and more contemptuous, both of their sister's obsession, and of the dangers of the forest.

"All the wolves have been hunted to death," they said to their friends. "If anything, we should be protecting these animals, not encouraging their destruction."

The ladies in the village agreed. To be fair, it had been such a long time since wolves had presented any danger at all that many had never seen one. Led by the two sisters, they went to the toy-maker's workshop, bearing placards and chanting, "Save the wolves! Tigers, *out!* Save the wolves! Tigers *out!*"

The brilliant, wayward sister heard their protest and went outside. "Don't you understand?" she said. "The role of the clockwork tiger was to *protect* you all from the wolves. It is the reason you are all still safe."

"Safe?" repeated the ladies. "*You* are the threat to our safety. You spend all your time in this workshop, doing things no lady would do. *You* have disgraced our family, made us into a laughing-stock."

"That isn't true," said the brilliant, wayward sister. "In my grandfather's workshop, I have discovered many things. Things that will change our lives for good. I have made a mechanical horse that will never need to rest. I have made crossbows for all of you; weapons for your protection. Come inside, let me show you."

But the brilliant sister was all dusty from the workshop. Her hair was unkempt; her dress was torn; her nails were broken and grimy with oil, and the ladies would not listen to her. Instead they took their placards into the heart of the forest, where the wild wolves still roamed free.

"Tigers out! Save the wolves!" chanted the ladies, dancing and waving their placards.

The wolves, attracted by the noise, came slinking out of the undergrowth. Several of the poor ladies, hampered by their long skirts, were immediately savaged to death. Others ran and were lost in the heart of the forest. And the good and beautiful sisters returned in tears to the village to find that the wayward sister had taken her clockwork tiger and her crossbow and ridden off on her mechanical horse to new and exciting adventures.

The good and beautiful sisters never mentioned her again. They both married well, to handsome men who promised to look after them, and had good and beautiful children. The wolves moved back into the outskirts of the village, but since no one dared enter the woods anymore, none but the most reckless (or drunk) ever came to any harm.

As for the wayward, brilliant sister, the villagers never saw her again. But there are many stories of her, and of her clockwork tiger, and of the many things she did, and of the many places she saw. And as far as anybody knows, she never ceased to be wayward and brilliant, but travelled the world with her tiger, scandalizing right-thinking folk and beautiful ladies everywhere.

59

THE NIGHT TRAIN

There is a story the bees used to tell, about a train that passes through every station between Hel and Pandaemonium, without ever stopping. The stations are places from legend, and run from the topmost branches of the World Tree to the cliffs of Damnation; to the Northlands, always in darkness; to the Southlands, always in flame, and thence to the shore of the River, where the bees first discovered the nectar of dreams and took it back to their Queen as she lay in her fortress of velvet and honeycomb.

The train is built from the bones of the dead; bound together with runes and sheathed in a casing of polished black steel. The engine runs on the dying words of men who have ended their lives in regret; compressed into shining coals, that, when burnt, release their cries and complaints to the wind, so that the train can always be heard, although its wheels are silent, rushing through the night to the sound of distant, relentless sobbing.

They say that no one alive has ever seen the Driver of the Night Train. His cab is hidden behind a door, sealed with lead and inscribed with runes. No sound ever comes from behind it. And all the passengers are dead, staring out at the scenery; lost souls too fearful to enter the Kingdom of Death; now doomed to ride the train forever on its journey through the Worlds.

All but one: a boy of the Folk, who boarded the train from the islands of Dream, and now, unable to leave, remains, watching the signals, ever alert for a red light in the darkness. For the red light would mean a stopping-place—maybe a chance for him to escape. But in all the years of his service, the boy has never known the Night Train to stop, or to take on a living passenger.

On the night of each New Moon, the snack trolley trundles down the train. The boy feeds on ancient sweetmeats; cakes long past their sell-by dates; wrapped in plastic; crystallised; slices of eternity. Sometimes he writes little stories, just to pass the endless time. He writes them on scraps of paper and throws them out of the window. The scraps of paper sometimes catch in the bushes along the track. He hopes that someday, someone might read one, and come aboard. Until then, he rides the train; doomed to watch the Worlds pass by; moving ever closer to whatever awaits at the end of the line.

All this is true—or at least, it *was*. Trapped in his nightmare, the boy from the train had no idea that change was afoot. But in another world, events were aligning, like two distant stars coming into conjunction.

60

DREAMS OF THE BAREFOOT PRINCESS

There are many different ways to reach the River Dream. One is Sleep; but certain dreams thrive best in the waking world, and these are among the most powerful. The Driver and the Barefoot Princess were both in pursuit of one of these dreams; and here, at the junction between two Worlds, it seemed to the Engine Driver that Dream must only be a whisper away.

"That's how you found me," she told the Princess. "And that's how we'll find the Lacewing King."

The Princess looked uncertain. "How?"

"When I was young," said the Driver, "I used to believe in stories. Now you have made me believe again that stories are real, and dreams can come true."

And then she kissed the Barefoot Princess by the side of the broken-down train, with the bees humming all around them:

"Up above and down below,
Down below and up above,
The Worlds are honeycomb, my love
The Worlds are honeycomb."

The Barefoot Princess had read about Love. But in the Lace-wing King's library, Love had seemed very far away. Now it felt close, as close as Dream, and sweet; as sweet as honeycomb.

She looked at the Engine Driver. "Will you follow me?" she said.

"Anywhere," said the Driver at once.

"I haven't even told you where," said the Princess with a smile.

The Engine Driver shrugged and said, "I've worked this line for twenty years. I know exactly where it leads. And I've always known there were other worlds, other stations along the line. And then *you* came from another world, and I knew that together we could go anywhere, even to the end of the tracks."

The Princess smiled. "All right," she said. "I'm going to tell you a story."

"A story?" repeated the Driver.

"*That's* how we find our way into Dream. That's how the bees have *always* found their way. Because, what else is a story but a dream that has been shared with the world?"

And as the Barefoot Princess spoke, the cloud of bees began to dance. It was the ancient dance of the honeybee, leading its folk to the nectar. It was a complicated dance, and the Princess watched in awe as they twisted and turned in the rapturous air, making a kind of spiral.

"A honeycomb has many cells," said the Barefoot Princess. "They look like separate chambers, but really, they're just part of the whole, linked by a narrow wall of wax. All we need to pass through the wall is to listen to the bees."

And then, the Barefoot Princess began, in the words of all the best stories: "*There is a story the bees used to tell, which makes it hard to disbelieve. . . .*"

61

THE HARLEQUIN'S KISS

Meanwhile, in another World, the Lacewing King and the Harlequin were locked in a close and cruel embrace. She who had once been the Hallowe'en Queen might have lost her kingdom, but the Harlequin's gaze still had the power to open the gateways to the Worlds. And now, as she clasped her enemy tightly in her razor claws, she flexed her giant mandibles and prepared, with relish, to tear him apart.

The King looked into the Harlequin's eyes. For a moment, he saw a maelstrom of stars, and realized in wonder that each was a World—thousands, maybe *millions* of worlds—an ocean of possibilities. And even as the Harlequin's claws sank into his back and shoulders, he thought he heard a humming sound, as if something were approaching.

For a moment the Harlequin's attention was diverted. Its gaze lost focus. Its claws relaxed—though not quite enough. But the builder of boats, recovering, had seen her chance to intervene. She had only the faintest memory of what the Harlequin had done to her, but she knew that the Lacewing King had saved her from a dreadful fate, condemning himself in the process. Of course, he owed her a life's debt—but she had never imagined that he would forfeit his own for hers. And so, seeing her chance, as the Harlequin seemed distracted from its prey, summoning all her courage and strength, she flung herself at the monster.

By now the mysterious humming sound had grown. It was nearly inaudible, and yet they all felt it distressing the air; shaking the trees; shifting the ground; tumbling birds from out of the sky. The island bees could sense it too. Something was coming, not of this World. Something made from the sound of a million untold stories; something that burned with the energies of a million million lives—

The builder of boats struck at the Harlequin just as it tightened its hold once more. The Lacewing King was caught in its grasp; pinned in the glare of the creature's eyes. The blow was not a powerful one; but it took the Harlequin by surprise, and, dropping its prey, it turned again, as just at that moment something emerged from out of the space between the Worlds; something like a very bright light, with a sound like approaching thunder.

For a moment, the Lacewing King was aware of two realities. On one side, there was the World he knew; the sea; the beach; the Harlequin; the anxious face of the builder of boats, her mouth forming words he could not hear. One the other, he seemed to see a shining beast of polished steel rushing towards him from out of the dark. His head was filled with black smoke; his arms and back were bleeding. And then something knocked him off-balance; he fell, and suddenly he was tumbling through the space between the Worlds. The Harlequin went after him, its powerful jaws working furiously. But he was already out of reach, and soon both he and the Harlequin were lost in a cauldron of darkness.

The builder of boats could only watch as the Lacewing King and the Harlequin plunged together into the void. There was no way of knowing if either of them had survived, or if the shape that she had glimpsed—a dragon, an unknown leviathan—had already devoured them. She sat down on the sand and wept for the loss of her mysterious friend, who during all of their travels, had never

told her his story, or even the reason for his exile. And then she looked for the bees that had been the King's constant companions, and saw that they too had vanished in the wake of their master.

This cheered her a little. Perhaps the bees would bring him some comfort, wherever he was. And then she stood and looked out to sea, and thought of her own predicament: lost, without food or water, between an endless desert and an equally endless ocean.

Far away, the builder of boats could hear the mermaids singing:

"Leave your shoes upon the shore,
Castaway, castaway.
Leave your shoes upon the shore
And listen to the ocean's roar
And leave the land for evermore
My little castaway."

For a moment, the builder of boats wanted nothing more than to join the mermaids; to swim away and to forget everything. But sometimes, an adventurer has to follow the path ahead, regardless of the danger, or of what she may find there. And so she walked back along the beach to her little red-sailed boat, and set sail once more for the open sea, where, in the face of all odds, she survived, living on fish and rainwater, and had many more adventures.

But, in all her travels, she never saw the Lacewing King again.

62

THE BAREFOOT PRINCESS
ON THE NIGHT TRAIN

There are many different ways to reach the River Dream. One is Sleep, one is Desire; but the greatest of all is Story: brought from out of the Land of the Dead by the bees in search of nectar. And as the Barefoot Princess told her tale, the humming of the swarm increased, and the spiral dance of the bees blossomed in the gilded air. And now she could hear a different sound approaching along the railway tracks. A sound, or a vibration, growing progressively stronger. No trains were scheduled to come that way—or so the Engine Driver had said. Nevertheless, she almost believed that that she could hear the hum of a train—

Some dreams are islands out of Time. Some dreams are doors into the past. And some are trains, approaching like Death; relentless and unstoppable. There came a silent thunderclap. The Princess's hand tightened on that of the Engine Driver. And then, in a soundless blaze of light, the approaching train was upon them.

For a moment, frozen in time, the Barefoot Princess and the Engine Driver seemed to be at a junction, with many different railway tracks, like lightning-trails across the sky. Stations flashed by that were glimpses from other Worlds, other stories. An island in an endless sea; a desert as broad as the ocean; an underground citadel lined with books; a silent vortex, with, at its heart, a spinning mael-strom of stars. In that instant, *all* Worlds were linked, like the cells of an intricate honeycomb, making a pattern that stretched beyond even Death; even Dream. And then, for a moment, the Barefoot Princess thought she saw the Lacewing King, falling—silently call-ing her name—away from her into the darkness.

The Barefoot Princess watched him fall. He looked very small, very far away, just-glimpsed, already out of reach. And the fact that she had come so close only served to increase her distress.

"We almost had him! He was there. Did you see him? He was *there*—" Then, addressing the bees, she cried, "Take me to him! Take me back! Take me back to where he is!"

But the bees had ceased their dance. The air was still, almost stagnant. Looking around, the Barefoot Princess saw, with some surprise, that she was in a railway carriage. The carriage windows were milky with age; the seats bled colourless; the scent a com-pound of dust and bone and dreams forgotten and gone to waste. The Engine Driver was at her side, looking dazed and shaken.

"Where exactly are we?" she said.

Then the two became aware of a presence beside them. They turned and saw a ragged boy, wearing a cap much too large for him, and watching them with frightened eyes.

"Excuse me—are you *alive*?" he said.

The Barefoot Princess and the Engine Driver looked at one other. Both of them were wondering what kind of a train they had boarded. Around them, in the shadows, sat the other passengers: all of them still and grey-faced and sad, looking blindly through the glass at the Worlds that passed outside. And then, at last, they understood. This was the train that runs through all Worlds, from Hel to Pandaemonium, consuming the hopes and dreams of the Folk in its bottomless furnace.

For a moment, the Barefoot Princess was afraid that perhaps both she and her new friend had died, back there on the railway track, and that this was their final journey. But the Driver's hand in hers was warm, and her heart was beating fast. Both of them were still alive; and they were on the Night Train.

"How can this be?" said the Barefoot Princess.

The boy shook his head. "I don't know. The Night Train only serves the dead. The living have no place here."

"But *you're* alive," said the Barefoot Princess.

"If you can call it life," said the boy. Brightening a little, he said, "Shall I bring you the snack trolley? I always feel better after a snack. Then I'll tell you everything."

And so the travellers ate and drank—sweets and cakes and chocolate bars that were powdery with age; brightly coloured fizzy drinks with names like *Buzz* and *Elektro-Lyte*. The Barefoot Princess, at the window, ate a packet of stale nuts and watched the stations flashing by. Surely, she thought, this marvellous train could take her to the Lacewing King.

But when she asked the boy when the train was next due to stop, he looked at her in puzzlement and said, "But I thought you understood. This is the Night Train. It never stops."

"Then how do we leave?"

"No one can leave. All you can do is ride the train, until the End of All Things."

The Barefoot Princess was filled with alarm. Had she, in pursuit of her dream, doomed herself and her new friend, either to death, or to the eternal life of a passenger on the Night Train? But she did not lose heart. She had not crossed between the Worlds, braved the wrath of the ocean, or escaped the clutches of the Spider Queen only to give up hope at the very moment at which the Lacewing King seemed to be within reach again.

"I want to speak to the Driver," she said.

The boy opened his eyes wide. "No one does that," he said. "Not even I have seen him. His cabin is sealed with runes and lead. Even his door gives me nightmares."

But the Barefoot Princess was undeterred. She marched along the Night Train, passing from carriage to carriage. She passed through a hundred carriages before reaching the locomotive. She stopped by the door to the driver's cab and looked at the runes upon it. Then she reached out her hand and touched the dismal surface of the door; a door that was made of human bones and sealed with giant knuckles of lead.

Then, she knocked.

Nothing happened.

The Barefoot Princess knocked again. "Open this door!" she demanded. (In spite of her sweetness of character, she must have inherited *something* of the Lacewing King's imperious manner.) "Open this door, in the name of the Silken Folk, guardians of the honeycomb, who were the first to bring the nectar of Dream into the Worlds!"

Behind the door, there came a sound; a soft and somehow loathsome sound, like something large and soft and slow moving over paper.

The Barefoot Princess knocked again. "Open this door!" she repeated. "In the name of the Lacewing King and the Honeycomb Queen, I command you!"

The sound came again. Then, silence. Then, at last, there came the sound of many bolts slowly being drawn. On the near side of the door, the Barefoot Princess watched as the chain of runes that bound the door began to unravel slowly. They made an unpleasant clicking sound, like the claws of some giant crustacean. Then the door began to move, until it was standing slightly ajar, and finally, the travellers saw the Driver of the Night Train.

He might have been a man once; many, many years ago. But time had long since taken that, and now he was a withered thing, all sinew and parchment, bound together by wire and will, his hands on the wheel worn down to the bone. Only his eyes were alive; but as she looked closer, the Barefoot Princess saw that this was because the sockets were crawling with insects: woodlice; termites; death-watch beetles. But they *saw* her, nevertheless, which was somehow worse than if he had been wholly dead.

The eyes moved up and down her. A sound came from the lipless mouth. A voice, which was neither human nor sane, said, "What do you want?"

The Barefoot Princess stood her ground, even though she wanted nothing more than to run. "I need to find the Lacewing King," she said. "Can you take me to him?"

For a long time, the eyes remained fixed on her. Then, the rasping voice replied, "The Night Train only serves the dead."

"Then take me to the Land of the Dead," said the Princess. "Take me to Hel."

63

THE BAREFOOT PRINCESS IN HEL

There is only one infallible way to reach the kingdom of Death. But to reach it as a living soul demands a great deal of courage. The Barefoot Princess had that, as well as determination and zeal. The Driver of the Night Train had never had a passenger who *wanted* to be taken to Hel, and the dim intelligence that lurked behind its dead eyes puzzled and sought for an answer to this strange conundrum.

Finally, the dry lips moved. "I will take you there," it said. "Whether or not you remain there is your own responsibility."

Thus began the journey of the Barefoot Princess and her friends into the territory of Death. Death has no boundaries; no geography. Death is at the same time everywhere and nowhere. It can be found in a second; or vainly sought across continents. The journey can take many years, or can be over in a single lightning-strike. And the Kingdom of Death is endless; a vast expanse of featureless dust, bleaker than any desert. The Night Train tore through the darkness, Worlds flashing by in an instant, and its passage was like the sobbing of a thousand voices in the night. The Barefoot Princess and the Engine Driver watched through the windows in silence, until at last the engine slowed, and they saw a red light in the distance.

"This is where the line ends," said the Driver of the Night Train.

The Princess looked out of the window. Outside, nothing but darkness, except for the glow of that distant red light. "Where do we go from here?" she said.

The Driver of the Night Train shrugged. From his desiccated throat came the sound of laughter. "This is Hel," he said. "No one here *goes* anywhere."

The train stopped at last. The Barefoot Princess and her friends prepared to get out onto the platform. But as the boy stepped out onto the boards, there came a low, moaning sound, like that of wind through a tunnel, and in the light of the carriage, they saw the boy disappear in a cloud of dust, that vanished into the ceaseless wind that blew from the dismal plains of Hel.

"What happened?" said the Barefoot Princess, dismayed at the loss of her new friend.

The Driver of the Night Train gave a rasp of laughter. "That boy had been with me a hundred years," he said. "His time, like mine, was long past. Now he sleeps in the Kingdom of Death. If only we could do the same."

The Barefoot Princess looked around at the passengers of the Night Train. Grey-faced and silent, they looked back; the hopeless faces of the damned.

"Then why don't you leave?" she asked him.

The Driver of the Night Train gave a dreadful, crustacean sigh. Behind its dead eyes, insects moved. "I and all my passengers," he said in his dry and creaking voice, "are here until the End of Days. We all feared Death too much to accept to enter the realm of the Hallowe'en Queen. And so she cursed us to this half-life; to travel the Worlds, without respite; without finding peace; forever."

The Barefoot Princess thought for a moment. "If I can persuade the Ruler of Hel to lift the curse, then will you help me—one last time?"

The Driver nodded. "I can try. But I cannot delay the train longer than an hour."

"Very well," said the Barefoot Princess. "Wait for me here on the platform. If I am not back in an hour, then you'll know I have failed in my task. But if I return with good news, then you must find the Lacewing King, and take me to wherever he is."

Slowly, the Driver nodded. "An hour it is. But no longer," he said. "After that, the Night Train leaves." And he brought out a great dark hour-glass and set it down on the platform. "The sand in this glass was taken from the furthest plains of Hel," he said. "When the last grain of sand has run through the glass, I will know that you have failed."

"I won't fail," said the Barefoot Princess.

The Driver of the Night Train shrugged. "Everyone fails," he told them in his dry and dusty voice. "But if you can help me find peace, I will give you what you ask."

And so the Barefoot Princess and the Engine Driver stepped out into the dust of Hel and started the strange and weary walk towards the hall of its ruler.

64

THE SPARROW

In a distant land there lived a King, who kept a bird in a golden cage. It was a small, brown, humble bird, with bright dark eyes, and a cheery song. It was in fact a sparrow; but the King and his courtiers did not know this. The court was filled with exotic birds. There were parakeets from the islands, and macaws from beyond the Ninth Sea. Peacocks roamed the gardens, their tails spread proudly behind them, and there were dovecots and hunting hawks—but there was only one sparrow.

The King was very proud of this rarest of specimens. And the sparrow seemed to sense his joy. All day long, it would chirp and sing; and the King and his courtiers would listen and dream of freedom and faraway places; of distant mountains; forests; fields; the cloudlands; and the open sky. These were things the folk of the court could only know from stories; and yet they never tired of dreaming and hearing about them.

"Behold, my singing bird," said the King. "Have you ever heard such a marvellous song? Have you ever seen such plumage, or felt such passion in music?"

And the courtiers would nod their powdered wigs, click their gilded nails and smile—oh, just a little, to avoid cracking their makeup.

Every visitor to the court was shown the marvellous singing bird. Emperors; kings and pontiffs came to hear its song of freedom. They all agreed that the King's lovely bird was the most wonderful and unique creature they had ever seen or heard.

As for the sparrow, it sat and watched the royal court through the golden bars. It watched the fawning courtiers in their silken coats and high heels, bowing so low as the King approached that their wigs almost brushed the parquet floor. It watched the servants in their grand liveries, and the musicians in the gallery. It watched the battery of chefs that brought the King his meals every day, and the Royal Taster, who tried every dish. It saw the royal children in their whaleboned corsets and taffeta skirts, pale from lack of sunlight and melancholy from lack of play. It saw the dancers and courtesans, the eunuchs and the pages; and sang its song of freedom as they listened in envy and wonder.

But by night, when the courtiers were asleep, the other sparrows would fly in through the open window, and there they would perch on the furniture and on the silken draperies, and talk to their friend in her golden cage, and try to persuade her to leave with them.

"Why do you stay here?" they asked. "The bars are surely wide enough for you to squeeze between them and escape. Why do you not fly from your cage and join your people in the sky?"

But the sparrow always replied, "I could never do such a thing to my King and his people. You see, these folk are all prisoners here. And if I fled, they would never hear the song of another sparrow."

65

THE PRINCE

In a neighbouring land there lived a prince who longed to be King in his father's place. But the King was reluctant to give up his crown; besides which, his only son was arrogant, and stubborn, and rude, and the King feared for his kingdom. The people, however, favoured the Prince, not because he was good or kind, but because he was quite the opposite.

"A Prince should not be ordinary," said the Prince to his servants. "He should be noble, contemptuous, and proud. Common politeness and courtesy are for the common people. I am a King, not a commoner."

The servants nodded politely, as their Prince expected. No one even dared point out that he was not yet King. Besides, they thought, the old King would die, and then the Prince would claim the throne. And those who had earned his favour would be rewarded for their loyalty.

And so the Prince continued to grow in arrogance and cruelty. He poured contempt on everyone: women; foreigners; the old. He flew into violent rages if he did not have his way. And when the King, his father, criticized his behaviour, he screamed such insults at the old man that the King was close to disowning him.

But the Chancellor said, "Your Majesty, beware of acting hastily. The common people admire your son, and if you were to take action, then there might be serious consequences."

And so the King forgave the Prince, hoping for better next time.

But the Prince soon got used to his father's tolerance. He spoke out ever more loudly against anyone who offended him. Servants who failed to cater immediately to his whims, day or night. Courtiers who did not laugh at his jokes. Ordinary people, just for being too ordinary to understand his regal commands. Most of all, he spoke out against the reigning monarch, his father.

"When will the old fool abdicate?" he said. "Better still, when will he die?"

The King overheard these comments and was angered and hurt by them. Once more, he came very close to banishing the Prince from his court. But his advisors, who feared the Prince and wanted to earn his favour, said, "Patience, Your Majesty. He will learn. Surely, your wise example will calm his youthful high spirits."

And so, once more, the King allowed his son to insult him, hoping that his own dignity would eventually mellow the young man's pride.

Years passed. Nothing changed. The Prince grew increasingly arrogant. The old King, though now very frail, seemed no closer to passing on the throne. But the Prince's behaviour, if anything, grew more unreasonable than ever. Even for his most fervent admirers, it was no longer possible to blame his behaviour on youthful high spirits. He insulted everyone he met. He seemed to respect only wealth, and those who were as offensive as he was himself. He poured contempt on the ordinary folk, and if anyone spoke against him, would fly into a rage, saying:

"I am a Royal Person! Your common rules do not apply to me! How *dare* you expect me to conform to the manners of the populace?"

Finally, after one such fracas, the old King lost his temper. "You have learnt nothing," he told his son. "Henceforth, I disown you as my heir, and shall pass on the throne to my brother's kin."

At first the arrogant Prince was stunned. Then he, too, lost his temper. He said to the old King, "You sad old man. You have no power. The people will never stand for this."

And he was right. The people, having been told for so many years that kings should be above the rules of ordinary folk, rebelled and came out in protest against the old King's decision. They mobbed the palace; attacked the guards; threw stones at the old King's carriage. In fear for the kingdom, the old King finally gave up his crown, and his son became king in his place.

But the new King was not happy. He found that Kings had duties to perform, and that many of them were burdensome. He found that he had no more time for pleasure and carousing. Most of all, he found that his people were difficult and rebellious, violent, angry and uncouth. Keeping order took up all his time, and the King found it very wearisome.

"What is the world coming to?" he said one evening as he sat on his throne, drinking a small cup of cocoa and nursing a nagging headache. "Why aren't people considerate and kind, the way they were when my father was King?"

No one answered. But that was all right, because no one was listening.

66

THE DANCING-SHOES

In a city of towers and spires, there lived a girl who loved to dance. During the day, she dressed modestly; eyes lowered, head veiled. But alone in her bedroom at night, she would put on her satin slippers and dance in secret on the polished floor, to the sounds of passing trains and the heartbeat of the city.

But the girl came from a family that disapproved of dancing. And at night, the parents heard the sound of their daughter's shoes on the parquet floor and knew that something was afoot.

"A virtuous woman does not dance," her mother told her sternly. And her father, who meant for his daughter to make a splendid marriage one day, said, "If I hear of you dancing again, there will be serious consequences."

But the girl did not listen. Dancing was in her heart and her blood. And besides, if no one *saw* her dance, she thought, what harm could it do?

And so she bought herself a rug on which to dance unheard. And every night, when she was alone, she would unbind her long black hair, slip on her satin shoes, and dance away to the city lights below her bedroom window.

But the girl's family had a neighbour whose daughters were ugly, and whose son was cruel and mean-spirited. This woman was jealous of the girl; her beauty and her sweetness. And so she ordered her son to keep watch at the girl's window every night. And when he saw the girl dancing, his mother quickly spread the word that the girl was flaunting her body to men, to the disgrace of her family.

The girl's family soon heard the rumours. The splendid marriage the father had planned succumbed to the growing scandal. Women smiled behind their veils when the dancing girl went by; men made suggestive comments. Angry, the father gave orders to his wife to fetch their daughter. And when she had brought her to him, he took his largest chopping-knife, and cut off one of his daughter's feet, so that she would never disgrace him again.

Time passed. But although the girl never danced again, the splendid marriage never came. Instead, her parents married her to the neighbour's son, who gracefully accepted to take a crippled bride for the sake of her dowry. And she went to live with her mother-in-law, who treated her like a servant. Her dancing-shoes were left behind, under the bed in her parents' house, so that even the small comfort of holding them in her hands was denied her. But when she was alone at night, she still sat by the window, and dreamed, and remembered when she was a dancer.

One night, at supper, a beautiful moth flew into the house. It danced at the window, trapped by the glass, its wings as pale as moonlight. The mother-in-law would have killed it, but the girl quickly opened the window.

"Dancers should be free," she whispered to the moth, as she let it fly.

The girl did not know it, but the moth was the servant of the Moth Queen, who lived beneath the city. Flying back to her domain, she told the Queen her story. The Queen listened with interest; and then she summoned her people. They flew to the house of the girl who had danced. They crept in through the windows. They crept down the chimneys, and under the doors, and into the room where

the girl was asleep, secretly dreaming of dancing. And when the girl opened her eyes, she saw the Moth Queen standing there, regal in her ermine robes, her long black hair unbound and decked with many shining jewels.

"Dancers should be free," she said, and touched the girl's face with her fingertips. And at her touch, the girl became a moth, all silk and velvet. Through the open window, she flew, into the heart of the city, towards the towers and the spires, and the moonlight on the water. Her family never saw her again.

But under the bed, her satin shoes, filled with moths, shifted and stirred. And sometimes, at night, as they lay in bed, the girl's parents would sometimes hear the sound of their daughter's slippers dancing on the polished parquet floor above them.

67

THE LION WHO HAD NO ROAR

There once was a lion who had no roar. He stood on a massive plinth of stone in the centre of a park, overlooking the lawns and beds in stern and hollow silence. He looked imposing, but the birds had long since discovered that he was powerless. He could not flick his tail at them when they perched on his hindquarters. He could not blink when they sat on his nose, or even growl when they called him names in their twittering voices.

Knowing this, the birds grew increasingly bold. They hated cats, and this King of Cats was theirs to torment, and could not fight back. The Lion hated the birds, of course, and he was very unhappy. The birds gave him no peace, day or night; they even roosted on his back and left their droppings like pale scars across the smoky bronze of his flank.

One day at the end of summer, the Lion noticed a man in the park. The man was not a beggar, though he moved as if his body hurt, and his clothes—strangely colourful among the city's palette of greys—were ragged and torn. And there was something about him—perhaps a madness in the eyes—that spoke of other places; lost worlds; strange things glimpsed by moonlight. Strangest of all, the madman travelled with a swarm of golden bees, which clung to him like a mantle.

The nights were drawing in by then, and the ragged stranger was cold. The space between the Lion's feet looked safe and inviting. And so the stranger and his bees curled up in the space underneath the bronze lion, and prepared to go to sleep.

At first, the Lion was displeased. But there must have been some power in the mysterious stranger, because the birds dared not approach him, not even as he was sleeping. And so, for the first time in many years, the Lion, too, slept in peace, with the man between his great bronze paws.

In the morning, the stranger made as if to move on. He picked up his blanket and bedroll and prepared to go on his way. But there was a restlessness in the bronze lion, as if he were struggling to speak.

The stranger looked up at the Lion. The Lion tried once more to speak. But only the tiniest sound emerged from between its open jaws.

The stranger reached up and put his hand gently on the Lion's flank. His eyes met those of the Lion. And in his eyes the Lion saw both madness and understanding.

The Lion, with a tremendous effort, managed to summon a pitiful squeak, no louder than a bat's cry. But the stranger had heard him. Slowly, he took off his mantle of bees and whispered a word in a foreign tongue. At once, the bees took flight and began to swarm around the Lion's head. Softly, they settled onto him; covering his head and ears with a mane of gold and black. And then, one by one, they entered his mouth, and crawled into the tiny space at the back of the Lion's throat, and from there, into his belly.

It was warm inside the Lion, and the bees buzzed happily. The stranger, who, for all his faults, never left a debt unpaid, listened, nodded, and then moved on. The Lion never saw him again. But when the birds returned to perch on the head of the Lion, and to mock him for having no voice, the Lion gave a low *growl*—

And from that day forth, the Lion was never tormented by birds again, as the bees in his belly swarmed and buzzed, and sometimes gave voice to the dull golden roar of approaching autumn.

68

THE LACEWING KING
BETWEEN THE WORLDS

That was the first of many tales of the Lacewing King in World Beyond, carried by the island bees that had followed him into the honeycomb. What happened to the Harlequin was a tale they did not tell, but, released from his enemy's grasp by the courage of the builder of boats and the unexpected arrival of the Night Train, the Lacewing King had evaded Death, and had slipped between the Worlds to find himself in another place.

This was a world of concrete, and trains, and cities of many people. It was a world in which magic had died and long since been forgotten; where bees were only insects, and where folk were blind to most things—at least, things of any importance.

Bloody from the Harlequin's claws, the Lacewing King was thrown into this world; alone, but for the island bees; robbed of his mind and his memory. He had no knowledge of who he was, or how he had come to be there; except for a few dreamlike fragments, which gave him little comfort. Everything he cared for was lost; his world; his people; his sanity. He could not even remember his name—the true name that held the secret of his power and his identity. The wounds on his body healed quickly, but in spite of the scars on his back and arms, he forgot how he had been wounded.

Instinct alone drove him now: and instinct it was that took him at last into a city of the Folk; a city of towers and sewers and spires, and beggars, and bishops, and bandits, and kings.

In this city, the Lacewing King seemed almost invisible. It was a skill that had served him before; now he rediscovered it. And thus he was content to be, living his life from day to day; eating what he could find among the leavings of the Folk; sleeping in alleys, on rooftops, in tunnels and under bridges. Sometimes the police moved him on. Sometimes he was beaten. Sometimes there were kind folk who gave him food and clothing. But he never spoke a word, or ever cried out, not even in dreams. He was among the Sightless Folk; and in silence, he endured.

One day, he saw a young girl passing the mouth of the alley-way in which he had spent the night. She was carrying a basket, and something about her suddenly reminded him of the Barefoot Princess—whose name he had forgotten, but whose face still some-times appeared in dreams. There was something about this memory that filled his heart with sorrow, but try as he might, the Lacewing King could not remember what it was.

The girl looked into the alleyway, and as the King looked back out at her, he met her gaze for a moment, and knew that she had seen him. This was very unusual. Most of the Sightless Folk were as blind to the poor and the homeless as they were to the rare and magical. And yet this girl did not look away, but stepped into the alley instead, and looked closely at the Lacewing King.

"Don't I know you from somewhere?" she said.

The Lacewing King said nothing. His golden eyes shone in the darkness. His skin was powder-pale once more, and his hair was matted and long, but still, there was something in his face that spoke of distant places. Under the rags of the blanket wrap given to him by the builder of boats, he was thin, and shivered with cold.

The girl reached into her basket and took out a piece of flat-bread. "Are you hungry?" she asked him.

The Lacewing King said nothing.

The girl put the bread into his hand, and the King, who had not eaten for days, tore at it with his sharp teeth. He had no memory of a time when he had *not* been hungry; and yet, through the mist of his suffering, the young girl's kindness had moved him. The look in her eyes had moved him, too; and the fact that she could see him. He seemed to remember a time—a place—where someone else had looked at him thus, and he felt a sudden certainty that *something* was about to change.

He finished the bread, and in silence, held out his closed hand to the girl. Then, he opened his hand to reveal a beautiful moth resting in his palm. The Lacewing King, in his exile, was unaware of his powers, and yet the Silken Folk in that place—the moths, and bees and cockroaches—knew him and served him in silence, knowing him to be their King.

For a moment the moth remained in the palm of the Lacewing King's hand, then it took wing and flew upwards, out of the alley towards the light. The girl understood that this must be the stranger's way of thanking her. And in her bed that night, she dreamed of a golden citadel lined with silk, deep underground, and awoke with the taste of salt on her lips and a fleeting scent of honeycomb.

69

THE HALLOWE'EN KING

Meanwhile, the Barefoot Princess and the Engine Driver were crossing the barren plain of Hel. Death's kingdom has no boundaries; no geography; no rules. A person can walk there forever without ever meeting another soul—although the dead are everywhere, their dust distressing the stagnant air. Nothing ever happens in Hel without the consent of its ruler; and he was a stern individual, whom some folk called the Hallowe'en King; some Alberon; some Hades.

From his citadel of bone, the Hallowe'en King watched the travellers. His hair, the shade of a moth's wing, was held in place by a circlet of gold. One side of his face was a fleshless skull; the other, that of a handsome young man. Such is the traditional Aspect of the Kings and Queens of Hel, whose eyes see both into the world of Dream and into the world of the living.

It had been many, many years since he had tricked the Hallowe'en Queen into surrendering her crown. Since then, he had lived alone, surrounded only by the dead, watching the world that he had lost from his blue and living eye. His son, whom he had last seen when the boy was an infant, had grown to be very like him, but this had given him no joy. The Ruler of Hel has duties that cannot be evaded; and, from the day he accepted them, all he could do was watch from afar, as the boy grew ever more selfish, arrogant and cruel, until finally, he had turned his eyes away from his son forever.

Thus, the Hallowe'en King had not seen the Lacewing King's change of heart. He had not watched as his wayward son had sowed the seeds of his exile and been banished into the world of the Folk with no memory of who he was. And now, as he surveyed his realm (for the ruler of Hel sees into all Worlds), he did not recognize the girl who now approached from across the plain, or know her as his blood kin.

The King was not used to visitors. Since his arrival, years ago, no one alive had dared to come within sight of his borders. His blue eye saw the living Worlds; his golden eye saw the World of the Dead. He levelled it now at the Barefoot Princess and on her companion. He was suspicious—he himself had taken the throne through trickery, much as his son had stolen the crown of a thousand eyes from the Spider Queen. Could this girl be a spy, perhaps some envoy of the Harlequin? Could she be here to take back his crown and make him pay for his treachery?

And yet the King was curious. Power was all that remained to him, and though sometimes he hated it, he feared that others might steal it away. Besides, it had been so very long since he had spoken with a living soul. His life as Ruler of Hel was bleak, and he longed for diversion. This girl, whose footsteps in the sand left a shimmer behind her, was no ordinary child: and her friend, a woman of the Folk, seemed unusually alert to the secret pathways of Dream.

Who were they? What did they want? And what was the swarm of golden bees that followed them between the Worlds? It was too much for the Hallowe'en King. He had to know the answers. And so he opened the bone-white gates of his floating citadel and allowed the travellers inside.

The Barefoot Princess and the Engine Driver looked around in amazement. There was hall after hall of marble and bone; corridors of dancing dust. There were mosaics of human teeth and passage-

ways of polished skulls. And at the centre, the Hallowe'en King, regal on a throne that was made from a mountain of dead man's ivory. The Barefoot Princess looked up at his face. One side was a death-mask. The other was that of a living man, who looked so like the Lacewing King that her heart almost broke with joy.

But the Barefoot Princess had listened well to the tales told by the bees. She knew that, whatever his kinship to her, the Ruler of Hel was by his nature, treacherous. She whispered to the Engine Driver:

"If he offers you food or drink, refuse. And take care to touch only his living hand."

The Hallowe'en King looked down and smiled. "To what do I owe this pleasure?" he said.

The Princess told her story. She explained how the Lacewing King had been flung out of his World by the Spider Queen, and how she and her companion had vowed to find him and to bring him home. She told him how she had seen the King, bloody from the Harlequin's kiss, lost and falling between the Worlds. She told him about the Night Train, the curse upon its passengers, and her promise to its driver. She told him how she had promised to return to him in an hour. Then she knelt in front of the throne and said:

"Will you lift the curse, my Lord? Will you help me find your son?"

For a long time, the King did not reply. He was thinking deeply. For the first time in a hundred years, he found himself taken by surprise. He had a great-great grandchild, he understood: and this child had promised to save his son. But was his son worth saving? He had ruined the Kingdom; deserted his throne; wasted his time among the Folk; murdered his own son, the Wasp Prince; left his bastard daughter to die; stolen, lied, and cheated his way across Nine Worlds with impunity. Most of all, he had grieved his mother, the Honeycomb Queen. Perhaps he deserved to be punished. And the Hallowe'en King was lonely. This child, he thought—the child of his blood—could be his companion in Hel. Her youth, her vigour, her laughter, would banish the shadows from his heart. If only he could persuade her to stay—

He showed her his living profile. He looked so like his son it hurt. "There's no hurry, is there?" he said. "An hour in Hel is longer than a whole day in the waking Worlds. First, let me offer you refreshment after your long, weary journey."

And with a gesture, he summoned a table laden with food and drink of all kinds; sugar plums and new-baked bread and honeyed, roasted caterpillars; and wines from every one of Nine Worlds, from the golden wines of the islands to the green wines of the frozen North; and fruit of every imaginable kind; pineapples and strawberries and grapes with a bloom like a butterfly's wing—

But the Barefoot Princess simply shook her head and said, "Thank you, my Lord. But your favour is all the refreshment I need."

The Hallowe'en King clenched his fists and smiled. "But where are my manners?" he told them. "You haven't introduced your friend. Come here, both of you; kiss my hand." And he beckoned with his skeletal hand for the pair to step forward.

The Princess smiled. "Your Majesty, I am not worthy to kiss your hand. Let me kiss the hem of your robe." And, kneeling, she kissed the hem of his robe, which was stitched all over with finger-bones and embroidered with runes of binding.

The Hallowe'en King clenched his fists so hard that blood dripped from his living hand. But still, his smile did not falter as he looked down at the travellers.

"Very well. I will grant your wish. But stay with me for a little while. Play a game of cards with me. I've been alone here for so long, with none but the dead for company."

The kind-hearted Princess heard his plea and was filled with pity for the King. "I will play a game," she said. "But in an hour, the Night Train will leave, and my friend and I must be on board."

The King's living profile remained serene. But beneath the mask, he grinned like a corpse. Time works differently in Hel, and he knew that if he could trick the Princess into either neglecting the time, or eating his enchanted food, or simply touching his skeletal hand, then she would be forced to stay by his side forever.

He gestured with his skeletal hand and summoned an inlaid card-table. Around it were three velvet chairs, upon which the players sat, facing one another. Then, from the pocket of his robe, the King brought out a deck of playing-cards and began to shuffle them. The cards were made of ivory, cunningly polished and painted. Every King and Queen was black; every card a spade, a skull, a gravestone, or a blackheart. The Hallowe'en King dealt the cards, moving so fast that the Barefoot Princess hardly saw the movement of his skeletal fingers. Quickly, she pulled her own hand away, and felt the terrible closeness of Death, and knew that she must be on her guard.

"What are we playing?" she asked the King, smiling in spite of her narrow escape.

"The only game I know," he said. "I call it Dead Man's Poker."

70

THE GIRL IN THE CANDY-PINK CASTLE

On one of the furthest skerries of Dream, there lived a girl who refused to die. She lived on the edge of the Kingdom of Death, so close that she could sometimes see the haze that rose above its wastes, and hear the howling of the wind over the steel-grey desert. She often heard the Night Train as it passed her island, heading for the heart of Death with its cargo of passengers, and she promised herself she would never set foot, either on that dreadful train, or on the shores of the Kingdom of Death that lay across the water.

And so, on her island, she built a wall to keep out the sight and stench of Death. She made it from dreams and picture-books; from coloured candies and teddy bears; from birthday candles and parasols; from ribbons and rainbows and ponies and dolls. She built it very high, so that even the sky she shared with Death was obscured in a haze of ice-cream clouds. And then she built within the walls a candy-pink castle of marshmallow fluff, with turrets made of raspberry glass, and pavements made from honeycomb.

There were parlours filled with cushions and cakes, and treasure-chests filled with candies. There was a park with a rosewater lake, and alleys of sherbet fountains. There were orchards of blossom, and lollipop trees, and herds of pastel-pink ponies. And there were many, many toys: for Death is a cold and lonely place, and the girl was afraid of being alone.

There were dollies, and pandas, and rabbits, and cats; and soldiers with tiny pink rifles that fired flower petals and stars. There were princesses in flouncy skirts, and teddy bears, and happy clowns. There were china dolls with cupcakes for heads, and talking pandas with lollipop paws, and dragons that breathed candyfloss clouds, and cats that grinned like monkeys.

And the girl, who was the Queen of them all, looked at what she had built, and smiled, and knew that she had conquered Death. The sun always shone on her kingdom, although sometimes there were clouds that rained showers of petal-pink popcorn. Nothing ever died there, because nothing had ever quite been alive; and the cold sound of the wind outside was drowned in laughter and music.

Every day was a birthday, filled with cakes and candles. Every day was a holiday. A hundred thousand days went by; and yet the girl did not grow old, or sick, or sad, or lonely. Every day, she would choose a new dress from one of her many changing-rooms, and dance and sing to adoring crowds of children, toys, and animals. She would sing songs about candies and kites, marshmallows, cupcakes, and rainbows. Sometimes she would accompany herself on one of her ice-cream coloured guitars. And every day, surveying her realm, the girl in the candy-pink castle would congratulate herself on having conquered Death.

And then, one day, there arrived in her castle a little girl just like herself. She was almost as pretty, and very nearly as beautifully dressed, and her hair was the palest pistachio-green, held back with a pair of plastic barrettes shaped like tiny coffins. Her gloves and matching platform shoes were painted with little black roses, and she carried a silken parasol, printed with pastel candy skulls.

The girl in the candy-pink castle came to greet the dainty newcomer. "Who are you? Where did you come from?" she said.

"You've made quite an impression," said the newcomer to the girl. "My own little Kingdom almost pales in comparison with yours."

The girl in the candy-pink castle frowned for the first time in many years. For the first time in years, she seemed to feel a mysterious chill, as if a cold wind had somehow found its way through the rosy, raspberry walls. And there was a sound, too; a sound like that of an oncoming train, approaching through the gardens of lollipop-trees and candy-canes.

She looked again at the newcomer. "Who are you?" she repeated.

The newcomer took off one of her gloves. Beneath it, her hand was skeletal.

"I'm just a little girl, like you. Like you, I have many outfits. Like you, I love to play little games. Like you, I enjoy being surrounded by toys, and pets, and playmates."

The girl in the candy-pink castle paled. "How did you get in here?" she said.

The little girl, who was Death, gave a smile. "You silly," she said, and took her hand. "I've been in here all the time."

71

THE VERY POPULAR PIGLET

In a farmyard we know well, a certain Piglet had achieved an astonishing popularity. Part of this was to do with the Piglet's charming manner; its winsome little face; its sleek silvery side-whiskers; its wealth of knowledge on all aspects of piglet diet and grooming. The other piglets adored it; but geese and hens and pullets and ducks also found it inexplicably fascinating. As far as they were concerned, the popular piglet could do no wrong, and they admired it even to the extent of grooming their feathers and polishing their beaks and claws in the styles that the piglet had made fashionable.

One day, the popular Piglet announced to the farmyard that it had laid an egg. "I've always wanted to lay one," it said, beaming at the animals. "And now, my lifelong dream has come true!"

The other piglets were filled with ecstatic admiration. The Piglet's popularity grew to a hitherto unprecedented level. Even the sheep and the cattle, who until then had had little to do with the Piglet, were filled with condescension.

"What a marvellous achievement," they said, sagely chewing the cud. "Especially for a piglet, who, let's face it, does not represent a group primarily known for laying eggs."

But in the henhouse, the subject was hotly debated. Some of the younger pullets really believed that the popular Piglet had laid an egg. But the older, wiser hens maintained that the egg must have been laid by someone else, and delivered to the Piglet under a veil of secrecy.

Finally, the oldest hen asked the question directly: "Did you really lay that egg?" she said to the popular Piglet.

The Piglet looked furtive for a time, and then admitted that, although the laying of the egg *had* been mostly its own idea, it *had* had a certain amount of help from a speckled Hen, who had done the actual laying.

The other piglets were outraged. "We have been grossly deceived!" they exclaimed.

The speckled Hen was quite surprised. "But—didn't anyone wonder," she said, "how a piglet could lay an egg?"

But the piglets were too indignant to listen. "We have lost all confidence," they said. "Henceforth, how can we ever be sure where *any* of our eggs are coming from?"

The elderly Hen tried to explain that most eggs came from a bird of some species or another. But the piglets refused to listen. The popular Piglet retired to a private stall of its own, where its remaining admirers continued to visit, and it continued to dispense its peculiar kind of wisdom. The egg hatched, and the resulting chick, assuming from the moment of hatching that the Piglet was its mother, grew up in blissful ignorance of the fact that it was actually a chicken—at least until the day on which the farmer's wife roasted them both for Sunday lunch, the farmer declaring afterwards that he had never had a chicken so plump, or a piglet so tasty.

72

THE KING'S CANARY

In a city of World Beyond, there lived a woman who loved to sing. She was poor; her life was hard, her voice was nothing special, perhaps, but singing was her comfort and joy.

On Sundays she would stand in the square barefoot and sing for pennies. But secretly, she was singing for love. Every week she would come and sing, and every week the little crowd that gathered there grew larger. These people were mostly children, but their parents liked her too, and the woman who loved to sing saw the crowds grow and was happy.

One day the King himself heard her sing, and he was so impressed that he asked her to sing at his palace to entertain the royal children. The royal children loved her too, and the King, seeing her shabby clothes and the poverty of her home, offered her a place to live in the grounds of his palace, where his children could enjoy her songs anytime they wanted.

The woman could not believe her luck. Overnight, her life had been transformed. She had fine clothes; a carriage; a horse; a beautiful house on the palace grounds. And those who came to hear her sing now came in their hundreds, then in their thousands; more than enough to fill the town square ten or twenty times over. And so the King suggested that instead of singing in front of the church, she sang from the palace battlements, where everyone could see her. And so she did—she had no choice—and still the people kept coming.

But, much as they still loved her songs, the woman felt that something had changed in the people who came to watch. There were fewer children now, and more adults with envious eyes. People started to laugh at her and call her the King's Canary. Even the King felt uncomfortable, and had a protective cage built around her to make sure no one threw stones at her. And every week, the woman sang to the crowds from her gilded cage. But she was no longer happy.

From the battlements she could hear every word that was spoken below. "Her voice is nothing special," she heard. "Who on earth does she think she is?"

She heard when other singers came to discuss her intonation. "There are far better singers out there," they said. "Why did the King even choose her?"

She heard when children cried because she wouldn't come down to talk to them. "Why won't she talk to us anymore?" they said to their parents.

And she heard when the parents said, "She's far too grand for the likes of us."

Some people had started throwing stones at the bars of the golden cage. The stones never hit the woman inside, but of course, she heard them, too, and she grew still more unhappy. But still, the crowds kept coming. And still the woman sang and sang, and looked for the love in their faces.

One day the woman lost her voice. She went out onto the battlements, sat inside her gilded cage, opened her mouth—and nothing. The crowds went mad with frustration. They shouted; they screamed; they begged; they threw stones. And the woman watching in silence from her cage understood that this *wasn't* love; it was a kind of madness.

And so she went back to her fine house in the palace grounds. She took off her fine clothes and her shoes. From the bottom of an old chest, she found the ragged dress she'd worn when she was still singing for pennies. She wrapped an old shawl round her head to hide the face that too many knew. Then she went back to the marketplace, barefoot and in rags, and started to sing.

It was a busy market-day. Hardly anyone noticed her. The face that too many people knew was hidden underneath the scarf, and her voice was just an ordinary voice, pleasant, but nothing special. Hardly anyone listened to her. But for the first time in a long time, the woman was truly happy.

Every day after that she came to the marketplace and sang for pennies—but mostly for love. The people who stopped to listen to her singing were few, but every one of them loved her. And then, one day, a man passed by who recognized the woman's face.

"It's *her!*" he cried in excitement. "It's the King's Canary! Or should I say *the King's Cuckoo?*"

More of the onlookers crowded round. The cry went up, half-joy, half-rage. Some of the folk were angry that they had been duped by the woman's disguise; some were simply overjoyed that their idol was there among them. A fight broke out at the back of the group. Someone threw a stone. Someone pulled at the woman's scarf to show the face that everyone knew.

"How dare you pretend to be poor?" they cried. "How dare you pretend to be ordinary!"

"Please!" cried the woman above the noise. "All I want to do is sing!"

But singing was out of the question. The noise of the people was far too loud. And finally, the woman left the square and went back to her gilded cage, and put on her shoes and her fine new clothes.

But she never sang again.

73

THE LACEWING KING IN EXILE

Meanwhile, in a city of concrete and spires, the Lacewing King lived in exile. Hunting by night, sleeping by day, and living on what he could scavenge or steal, he survived alone and unseen by the Folk, who mostly went about their lives without suspecting he was there.

However, unbeknown to the King, he was not quite unobserved. Beneath the city, and during the night, the Moth Queen, mistress of deception, ruled the city unchallenged. Her spies were on every rooftop; in every wardrobe; on every street. Her people were hidden in plain sight, their wings camouflaged against the stone, and they moved freely among the homeless, the exiled, and the destitute.

Thus it was that the Moth Queen's spies first encountered the Lacewing King. To the Sightless Folk he was almost invisible, but to the Moths he stood out like a beacon in the darkness. Insects swarmed to be near him: moths and hoverflies and bees. Beetles in their thousands guarded his sleep in the alleyway. Wasps never stung him, even when he disturbed their nests on the rooftops. And although the stranger never spoke, the Moths knew he could see them.

The Moth Queen had watched him from underground throughout the long, cold winter. She found him both troubling and incomprehensible. He looked like a beggar, but she could sense a power in him. He looked like one of the Folk, but was not. He lived like one of her tribe, but was not. He made her uncomfortable, and from her royal chamber, she watched, and wondered how to deal with him.

The Moths of that world were very like the Silken Folk of the World he had left. They had their own rulers, their own wars, their own peculiar history. Once again, the Lacewing King was caught between two rival factions: the Moths and the Butterflies. The Butterflies were flamboyant; moving by day and preying mostly on the Sightless Folk. The Moths moved by night, and worked in stealth, and preyed mostly on the Butterflies. Both sides hated each other, and both sides were deeply suspicious of each other and of strangers.

Thus it was that these warring tribes never spoke with the honeybees, the messengers to the Silken Folk who link the Worlds through stories. The Moth Folk and the Butterflies both had stories of their own, passed down through generations, but over the years, these tales had become tangled and twisted beyond repair, so that the truth had been long lost, although both sides believed themselves to be the only ones in possession of it. And now that the Moth Queen was certain that the Lacewing King was no Butterfly, she wondered how she could use him in her war against the enemy.

And so, one night, she summoned her guards and had the stranger brought to her. The guards were ready to bring him with force, but the King came quietly. He barely glanced at the Moth Guards in their sumptuous livery, or at the Queen on her sable throne. He had looked into the eyes of the Harlequin, and all places looked the same to him. Faërie and Folk existed for him in a kind of dreamlike haze; the people that came and went around him seemed no more than shadows.

The Moth Queen addressed him from her throne. "Who are you?" she said. "What brought you here? What do you know of the Butterflies?"

The Lacewing King said nothing. His face was hidden in the shadows.

"Speak," said the Queen, "and I will be kind. Be stubborn, and you will suffer."

Still the King said nothing. From behind his matted hair, his strange eyes looked through the Queen as if she were a column of glass.

"Where are you from? Who are your kin? What do you know of the Moth Folk?"

Once more, the Lacewing King was silent. With one finger, he traced a spiral in the dust at the foot of the throne. A colony of ants began to march from the heart of the spiral. The Barefoot Princess would have understood that this was his way of answering her. But the Moth Queen did not understand, and she soon grew angry.

She summoned the Moon Moth, her Chancellor, and the Death's-Head Hawk Moth, her Chief of Police, and ordered them to question her guest. But neither the Chancellor's subtle cajolery, nor the Chief of Police's more vigorous style of interrogation, provided any answers. The Lacewing King had forgotten more than the Moths had ever seen; and he answered their questions with a sullen, contemptuous silence.

At last, the Queen summoned her shaman, the subtle, shadowy Spider Moth, whose eyes were said to look beyond the boundaries of their World, even to the shores of Death and into the waters of Dream.

"Find out who he is," she said. "There is something about him that troubles me."

The shaman clasped her pale hands under her robe of velvet. "Do you think he's a spy?" she said.

"Perhaps," replied the Moth Queen. "Whoever he is, I need to know."

The Queen had ordered the King to be locked in a cell below her court. He had still not spoken a word to her, or to her interrogators. Now he slept, and the Spider Moth made her way into his cell and sat cross-legged beside him, silently, to watch his dreams.

This was the shaman's speciality. She lived her life between the Worlds, watching for spaces and entry-points. The Moths had been exiled from their home many, many years ago, but their Queen had never ceased to hope that, in time, they might one day return. And so the shaman watched the King, and followed him into Dream as he slept, and when she had gathered what information she needed, she quietly returned to the Queen and told her what she had observed.

"Your Majesty, as you suspected," she said, "your guest is from another World. His mind is damaged, but his dreams reveal knowledge of the Silken Folk. He has committed many crimes, and, in different circumstances, might have been dangerous. But now he is a nameless thing, divorced from his World and his memory. I doubt he presents any threat to us."

"But who is he? Did you find out?"

The shaman shrugged. "Not with any certainty. But, from the fragments of memory I was able to gather from him—memories of the Spider Queen, the Silken Folk, even the Harlequin—I believe I can hazard a guess."

The Queen leaned forward. "Tell me."

"I may be wrong," said the Spider Moth. "But all the omens point to it. I think your prisoner may be the lost groom of the Spider Queen, whose gaze is keen, whose reach is long, and whose web reaches into all Worlds but one."

The Moth Queen took a sharp breath. "You really think it could be him?"

The shaman nodded. "My Lady," she said, "I believe we have found the Spider King."

74

THE SPIDER KING

There is a tale, of how, long ago, the Spider Queen fell in love. In those days, her kingdom was not as vast as it was to become, and her web reached only to its borders, instead of far beyond the Worlds. In those days she was very young, and beautiful, and wilful, and spoilt, and more than a little naïve. And the object of her affection was a visiting Prince from the distant North; older and more experienced, and therefore irresistible.

The courtship was brief, and one-sided. The Spider Queen was besotted. Neither the advice of her Chancellor, who cautioned her against making too hasty a choice, nor the words of her Chief of Police, whose earnest enquiries had failed to reveal the lineage of the newcomer, caused the Queen a moment's pause. Even the fact that the Prince's face was always concealed behind a jewelled helm—a marvellous helm of a thousand eyes, that gleamed with secret intelligence—did nothing to dissuade her. The Prince was all the more alluring for his air of mystery.

After less than a week, the Queen announced her betrothal to the Prince, as well as her decision to make him King, with powers equal to her own, and not, as custom dictated, Prince Consort.

"My love and I shall be equals," she said. "We shall share the Spider Crown and make all decisions together."

Once more, the Spider Chancellor tried to warn his mistress. But the Queen was determined. The royal couple were wed in nine days; she resplendent in her train of silver-spangled spider-silk, he handsome in his armour of hand-stitched dragonfly leather. But the bridegroom's face remained hidden, as it had been throughout all their courtship, beneath his helm of a thousand eyes.

It was partly this mysterious aspect of her new consort that had first attracted the Queen, and now she imagined their wedding night with a girlish eagerness.

I will take off my wedding gown, she thought, *and there, in the moonlight, piece by piece, I will remove his armour and his helm of a thousand eyes, and look into his face, and at last, I shall see my beloved.*

But when the time came, the bridegroom said, "Have patience, my love. My helm of a thousand eyes sees beyond our kingdom. Let me wear it a few days longer, and I will ensure that no danger will come to threaten our future happiness."

The Spider Queen was touched at her new husband's concern for her safety. She was a strong and independent Queen, and the novelty of seeing herself perceived as a fragile, vulnerable creature was strangely intoxicating. And so she continued to tolerate her husband's helm of a thousand eyes, until, after twelve whole days and nights—blissful in all ways but one—she finally grew impatient.

Surely, one glimpse of my beloved will not endanger the kingdom, she thought. And that night, she crept to the bed of her bridegroom while he was sleeping.

The Spider King was lying in his four-poster bed of gossamer silk, hung with curtains of the finest gauze. Through the curtains, the Queen could hear the sound of his breathing, soft as thistledown. One hand lay on the bedspread. One dappled shoulder, too, lay bare, and the helm of a thousand eyes glittered in the moonlight. The Spider Queen put out her hand—and just at that moment, her husband turned, murmuring softly in his sleep, and she saw against his skin the red-and-black marks of the Harlequin—

For a moment, the Queen stood frozen with dread. Young as she was, she already knew the Harlequin's reputation. Devious, treacherous, hungry for power, its kind were masters of disguise, travellers through Worlds and Time, and charm was their greatest weapon. Now she could see clearly how, in the guise of the mysterious Prince, the creature had managed to insinuate itself, first into her own heart, and then onto the throne of her kingdom. And then she realized—too late—that thanks to her pride and stubbornness, if she were to meet with her death, the Harlequin and its descendants would rule forever in her place.

Now the young Queen understood how she had been deceived from the start. She saw how the Harlequin had assumed the pleasant disguise of a stranger, hiding its markings beneath its clothes; its eyes beneath the jewelled helm. She understood that she would be in danger if the Harlequin awoke and saw she had discovered its ruse. And so she crept back to her chamber, and spent the rest of the night awake, wondering what she was to do.

She could not bear to call her guards. They might keep her safe from the Harlequin, but if she revealed the treachery, then everyone would know how their Queen had been deceived, and that would be unbearable. On the other hand, she could not tolerate the thought of the interloper by her side for a moment longer. The thought of it there, on the Spider Throne, clothed in the flesh of one of her kind, feeding on her people by stealth, filled the Queen with horror.

And so as soon as dawn broke, she called her Court Physician, complaining of a sickness. The Physician, seeing her pale and wan, agreed that she was gravely ill, and she kept to her bedchamber all day, curtains drawn, cocooned in a shroud of spider-silk.

Her new bridegroom expressed concern and came at once to her bedside. "What ails you, my darling?" he said.

From her cocoon, the Spider Queen watched him; eyes narrowed in silent rage. Beneath the silken coverlet, she began to spin a thread, lighter than thistledown, stronger than steel. Quickly and nimbly she spun the thread, her fingers working furiously. But her voice was soft as she said, "My love, my dreams have been terrible. My head aches, I cannot sleep, my body is racked with tremors."

The Spider King's voice was soft and concerned. Beneath the helm of a thousand eyes, his face was, as always, in shadow. But now, the Spider Queen could hear the rasping voice of the Harlequin, and hear the sound of its razor claws beneath its silken tunic.

She turned away, feigning sickness, and whispered in a feeble voice, "Oh, my love, come closer. Hold me in your arms, I beg."

The Spider King came closer and put his arms around the ailing Queen.

"Rock me," she said. "My head aches so."

And so the Spider King rocked her, and, as he did, the Spider Queen half-closed her eyes and pretended to sleep, all the while spinning her thread and watching the interloper from beneath her lowered lashes.

When the work was finished, and the King thought she was asleep, the Spider Queen then reached up behind the marvellous helm of a thousand eyes. With delicate fingers, she started to unbuckle the many fastenings. Slowly and cautiously, she worked, taking care not to alert her consort. Then, when the helm was finally free, she wrenched it from the Spider King, and, leaping from her sick-bed, her thread of spider-silk in her hand, she looped the skin of spider-silk twice around the Spider King and, lifting the helm of a thousand eyes, placed it onto her own head.

For a moment, the Harlequin was unveiled, its eyes widening in anger as it understood the treachery. Its eyes met those of the Spider Queen—but instead of a single pair of eyes, the thousand eyes of the helmet reflected its rage and astonishment. Then, as the Spider Queen pulled at her thread, she opened the doorway through the Worlds and spun the Harlequin like a top, projecting it into the darkness.

The Queen's guards, hearing the sound of a disturbance in the royal chamber, came running to find nothing left of the King but the helm of a thousand eyes, now lying by the bedside, and the Queen, distraught, in her nightdress. Unwilling to confess to her guards how she had been deceived, she spun them a tale of how the Harlequin had planned to attack her in her sleep, and how her new consort had saved her, and had been lost between the Worlds. Then she wept—for she was young, and this was her first affair of the heart—and swore that she would never again give her love to anyone.

It was a vow she was to keep. Although the Spider Queen married again—many times—her consorts never lived beyond a single night of passion. She consumed them, every one, at the height of her pleasure, and theirs, and used their vigour to strengthen her own, their blood to enhance her power. As for the helmet of eyes, it became part of the crown of the Spider Queen, enabling her to look far beyond the borders of her kingdom. With it, she now reigned supreme—until at last the Lacewing King had robbed her of her supremacy.

But she never told anyone the truth about the Spider King; and although the stories of his fate were carried far across the Nine Worlds, only the honeybees knew the tale, and whispered it to the passing winds.

75

THE MOTH WARS

It was through one of these many stories—not quite lies, but distortions—that the Moth Queen, Worlds away, had discovered the Lacewing King. Through the shaman's power, she had looked into his dreams. And now a dream of her own began to take shape once more in her mind: a dream of returning home again, in triumph, with her people.

There is a story of how, long ago, Moths and Butterflies were part of the same great family. Both were brightly coloured; both were active night and day. Their King and Queen ruled together, though their natures were very different. The Moth King was sullen and taciturn; the Butterfly Queen was frivolous. Both led separate lives; he studying in his library, she making merry with her courtiers. But in spite of their differences, they stayed together for the sake of their son, the Clearwing Prince, who was loved by the whole court for his gaiety and sweetness.

One day, the young Prince disappeared. Suspicion fell on the Spider Moth—a powerful shaman, like all his kind—who was tutor to the Prince and a close friend of the Queen. It was known that the Spider Moth had long dreamed of reconciling the pair, and, on his loom of silk and stars, had spun threads into many Worlds in the hope of finding an answer. As it happened, on the day of the young Prince's disappearance, the Spider Moth had been working on a web of particular complexity; a web that led into a World so different and new in every way that the Clearwing Prince, craving adventure (and against his tutor's instructions), had followed it into that alien World, unable to find a way to return.

Too late, the Spider Moth had discovered his charge's escapade. Following the silken thread that linked the Worlds together, he had gone to bring back the Prince. He might even have managed it, but for the anger of the King, who, on hearing of the disappearance of both his son and the shaman, was seized with a violent, terrible rage.

He marched to the shaman's studio, to find the Queen already there, staring with dismay at the loom upon which the shaman had spun his thread. From the loom, a thousand skeins of finely spun moth spider-silk floated in the dusty air, each one leading to a World. For a moment the Moth King stared at the loom, then angrily addressed the Queen.

"This is your fault!" he told her. "If you had taken care of the boy instead of spending all your days in dancing and frivolity—"

The Queen was angry. "How dare you!" she said. "If only you had paid more attention to him, instead of to your dusty old books—"

"The Spider Moth was your creature!" said the Moth King. "Perhaps you and he concocted this plan to steal my son away from me!"

At this unfair accusation, the Butterfly Queen's anger grew. "How dare you accuse me?" she said. "That child—our son—is the only good thing that you and I have ever achieved together. The shaman is like a father to him—more of a father than *you* ever were—"

At these words, the Moth King was seized with a terrible jealousy. The Spider Moth's studio was filled with rare and precious artefacts. Blindly, in his rage, he lashed out: tumbled furniture;

hurled ancient grimoires to the floor; smashed vials of precious spices; scattered papers to the winds. Then, finally, disastrously, he pushed over the loom of silk and stars upon which the shaman had spun his web, so that the skeins that linked the Worlds were broken and lost forever.

Seeing this, the Butterfly Queen gave a cry of grief and despair. The Moth King was instantly sorry for his moment of madness. But, without the Spider Moth, there was no way of mending the loom, or of repairing the broken threads. And so the King and Queen parted ways, bitterly, and forever. Their courtiers were divided: some went with the Moth King; some with the Butterfly Queen. And from that day forth, they never met again, except as enemies. The Butterflies kept to the daytime, and the Moths to the darkness, although they were always drawn to the light, reminding them of what they had lost. And wherever they went, throughout the Worlds, the two tribes sought the vanished Prince, not knowing whether he had grown up to be a Butterfly or a Moth—or indeed, if he had grown up at all.

And until they find him, the story says, Butterflies and Moths will always be enemies, each keeping to their half of the day, forever alone and incomplete.

76

THE LACEWING KING
AND THE SPIDER MOTH

The Moth Queen was a descendant of these rival factions. For many years she had ruled underground, fighting her rivals, the Butterflies, and their leader, the Butterfly King. For many years, the two factions had kept to their own territories, the Butterflies ruling the day, the Moths coming into their own at night. Both factions hated each other with a terrible bitterness. Both blamed the loss of the Clearwing Prince on the other faction; both firmly believed the lost Prince to be one of their own.

But now, with the arrival of the Lacewing King, the Moth Queen thought that maybe she could see a way to end the war. Not that she wanted peace; no. Her hatred of the Butterfly King had consumed her too much for that. What she wanted—with all her heart—was to find the long-lost Prince, and with his help, and under his flag, to bring about the extermination of the Butterflies.

The Lacewing King, she told herself, with his eyes that had looked into those of the Harlequin, must surely know where to find the Prince. And with the Prince to lead them, the Moths would then possess the means to eradicate their rivals for good. Of course, she said none of this to the King. Instead, she summoned her shaman again, the shadowy, treacherous Spider Moth.

"The eyes of the Spider King have seen into all the Worlds," she said. "Somewhere in his mind, there lies the secret to our lost Prince."

"His mind is in pieces," the shaman said. "Only the Harlequin itself can restore his sanity."

The Moth Queen drew her feathery cloak around her slender shoulders. "But we don't *need* his sanity," she said to the Spider Moth. "All we really need, after all, is to see what the Spider King has seen; to go where the Spider King has been, into the spaces between the Worlds."

The shaman frowned. Her dark eyes shone. Her face was awash with shadows.

"Majesty," she said at last. "Dreams are unreliable. Like pieces of light from a crystal, they flit from one thought to another, never settling for long; never focusing long enough to make a connection with this world. But—" Now the shaman frowned again, her gaze moving to that of the Queen. "Perhaps we do not need his dreams. All we need, after all, is to see what the Spider King has *seen*. And for that, all we really need from him is—"

"What?" said the Moth Queen.

"My Lady. An eye."

The Moth Queen stood very still. "An eye?"

"The eye remembers," the shaman said, "more than memory ever could. Every image, every face, is held within its orbit. Give me the eye of the Spider King, and let me build a web of dreams with which to catch his memories."

Once more, the Moth Queen was silent. She hated the thought of what she must do, and yet, a Queen must sometimes make the cruellest of choices. Who was this man to her, after all, compared with the good of her people? And what use was an eye to a man with no understanding of what he saw?

"Your Majesty," said the shaman. "We must."

The Moth Queen sighed and turned to her guards, who were awaiting her command. "Very well," she said at last. "Bring me the eye of the Spider King."

77

BLINDING OF
THE LACEWING KING

And so they seized the Lacewing King, and held him while they cut out his eye. He did not give it up easily, but fought them like the madman that he was, cursing them in a language that he had long forgotten he knew. But the Moth guards were innumerable, and the King was only one man, and finally they took his left eye, and brought it to the shaman.

Meanwhile, on her loom of stars, the Spider Moth began to spin. She spun a marvellous, intricate web of magical and exquisite design. It was made from nine panels of silk, one for each of the Nine Worlds, and embroidered in runes with the secret names of the Silken People. And at the centre, like a gem, she placed the eye of the Lacewing King, which shone like a piece of amber. Then she began to turn the web, like a shadow-lantern, about the eye of the Lacewing King. Round and round went the amber eye, projecting the things the King had seen and the Worlds through which he had passed, onto the woven panels of silk.

Here was the court of the Moon Queen, with its floating lanterns. Here was the court of the Dragonfly Queen, its cliffs all draped with scarlet vines. Here was the court of the Honeycomb Queen, all decked with velvet and gold brocade. And this was the realm of the Harlequin; the rose garden; the mermaids. But as yet, there was no sign of the Clearwing Prince of the Moth Folk.

The shaman became impatient. The Queen was awaiting her findings. The Harlequin's gaze reflects *all* Worlds—so surely the eye of the Lacewing King must have seen the Clearwing Prince? Over and over she turned her web, spinning it restlessly this way and that. Still the web did not reveal any sign of the lost Prince. With delicate fingers, she pulled at the threads to re-position the eye in the web. Dark as honeycomb it gleamed, but did not deliver the information she sought.

Of course, the Spider Moth did not know how the King had lost his mind. She did not know of the Harlequin's kiss, or the builder of boats' intervention. She did not know that, at the very moment at which the Harlequin had prepared to gaze into the eyes of the King, the Night Train had burst unexpectedly through the space between the Worlds, breaking the link between them and projecting them into darkness. In other words, she did not know that the Harlequin had failed to consume the mind of its victim entirely, but had merely stolen his memory and his awareness of who he was.

The Lacewing King, however, was unable to tell the shaman this, and the shaman was too preoccupied to read the signs he had given her. Obsessed by the thought of finding the Prince, and convinced that her theory was right, she continued to search the intricate web, her frustration growing with every hour.

Finally, the Spider Moth came to a galling conclusion. The left eye of the Lacewing King had *never* seen the Clearwing Prince. Perhaps, in the split-second horror of the Harlequin's embrace, his field of vision had been obscured, and only the *other* eye had seen the immensity of the Worlds.

Her hands froze on the silken web. For a moment, she hesitated. But there was too much at stake to hesitate for very long. The Moth Queen was getting impatient. And after all, the prisoner was not one of *their* people. And so the shaman summoned the guards, and told them to bring her his *other* eye; and when she had it, she set it in place at the heart of her loom of stars, and looked through its amber-coloured lens into a world of honeycomb.

Meanwhile, the guards, on her orders, carried the Lacewing King from his cell. A blood-spattered bandage covered his face; his body was limp and lifeless. Death would have been a mercy then— and yet, the guards were gentle. They carried him to a secret door, down many flights of narrow stairs. They covered him with a sable cloak and pressed a flask into his hand. For a moment, they lifted their torches, revealing a hall of immeasurable size. And then, they left him lying there, and closed the secret door again, and climbed the stairs as fast as they could, and left him to whatever dreams might come to him in the darkness.

78

THE MERMAIDS AND THE MIRROR

In a great city under the Sea, there lived a kingdom of mermaids. They lived in a labyrinth of caves, where curtains of phosphorescence lit corridors of crystal. Flickering fish swam in and around; Moon jellyfish floated like lanterns. The mermaids dwelt in this silvery space, singing; surrounded by bubbles; combing out their long pale hair with combs of gilded fishbone.

The mermaids were all very beautiful, with skin like palest mother-of-pearl, and hair of milled gold and spun silver; and tails that shone like the moon and the stars—not that they had ever *seen* the stars, for they never came to the surface, but stayed in the safety of their caverns, dancing and singing and playing games.

Except for one lonely mermaid, who was different to the rest. No one knew how that could be; but her skin was as brown as buttonweed, and her hair was black as a tiger shark's eye; and her tail was striped like an angelfish in markings of yellow, orange, and blue.

The other mermaids had no idea how she had come among them. Perhaps she had been left behind by some passing shoal from the islands. Or maybe she was simply a freak—the lonely mermaid did not know. But she did not belong with the others, and yet she had no other place to go: the kingdom of caves was all she knew, and all that she had ever known.

And the other mermaids were not unkind. They tried to include her as much as they could. But everything they did for her served only to highlight how different she was. The jade and silver bangles they liked to wear on their long pale arms only emphasized how brown she was. And the combs they slid through their silken hair only caught in her thick black curls, or broke when

she tried to use them. When she swam with the shoal, she felt garish and unnatural, and the colours of her angelfish tail looked strange and dangerous to them. And so the mermaid was lonely, and longed for just one friend like herself, with whom she could share her secrets.

Now, in that labyrinth of caves there was a crystal chamber. It was round, with a hole in the roof; and in this mirror, the mermaids could see their reflections in the water. All the mermaids loved this room, and spent many hours there, admiring themselves in the mirror. But the lonely mermaid avoided the room whenever the other mermaids were there. She did not like to see her reflection next to theirs in the mirror. She did not like the way her colours in her tail shone out; or like to see her sunny skin in the shoal of silver shadows.

And yet, the mirror drew her. At night, she would sometimes go there alone and look at her reflection. On these occasions, she would talk to the mermaid in the mirror. She told her all her secret thoughts; her sorrows and her loneliness. She would tell her all the things she dared not admit to the others. And all alone, in the crystal cave, the lonely mermaid did not feel quite so sad, or so different. Instead, she would look at her angelfish tail, and her golden eyes, and her close black hair, all filled with a mist of bubbles, and think:

Why, I'm just as beautiful as all the others, in my way.

But she dared not say so to the rest of the mermaid community. She knew they would laugh at her if she did. The other mermaids sometimes liked to tease and spy on her; and the lonely mermaid felt that she would die if they ever found out her secret.

And so she continued to hide away, and to creep to the mirror-cave at night. But one night, the other mermaids followed her in secret. They had noticed her habit of slipping away, and were curious to know what she did. In the silvery darkness, the others went almost unnoticed, pale against the nacreous walls; veiled in phosphorescence. Silently, they followed the lonely mermaid to the mirror-cave, and watched her approach her reflection, and speak to it in the shadows.

That day, the lonely mermaid was feeling especially sad. As always, she told her reflection; and then, as she combed her curly hair, she sang to it in a low, sweet voice—not the songs of the chilly North, but the merry, warm songs of the islands, where the mermaids in their vivid shoals would swim and sing with the dolphins, their tails flying colours of yellow and black, and brilliant orange, and butterfly-blue. She sang:

"Leave your shoes upon the shore,
Castaway, castaway.
Leave your shoes upon the shore
And listen to the ocean's roar
And leave the land for evermore
My little castaway."

And as she sang, the other mermaids started to laugh from the shadows. Not because they were wicked, but simply because they were foolish, and she had surprised them. None of them had ever seen the land or heard the waves on the shore. None of them had ever sung the songs of the southern islands. And the thought that the lonely mermaid might be homesick for a place that she had never even seen seemed to them so strange and absurd that they could not hold back their laughter.

The lonely mermaid heard them. Wildly, she turned, and saw them behind her, in the chamber. There was nowhere for her to hide; and yet, in her discomfiture, all she could think of was escape. And so, with a flick of her angelfish tail, she leapt right through the mirror and found herself, not in the Deeps, but on the surface of the Sea.

For a moment, the mermaid stared at the sky and the sunlight. It was all so different to the life that she had known. The sea was sparkling and blue; the sky was warm and cloudless. And all around her, on the rocks, were the *other* mermaids. Not the silvery shoals of the North, but the merry brown girls of the islands. And all of them were just like her: with vivid tails of orange and black and yellow and electric-blue, gleaming in the sunlight.

They smiled at the lonely mermaid, and stretched out their arms to her, and said, "We've been watching you for so long. We heard you singing every night. Why did you stay down under the Sea when you could have been here, with us?"

And the lonely mermaid (who knew right then that she would never be lonely again) replied:

"All this time, in my loneliness, I thought I was looking at myself. Now I understand that my mirror was really a window." And off she swam, with her new shoal of friends, to warmer, happier places, and was never seen again down in that crystal kingdom.

79

THE PETULANT PULLET

In a certain farmyard, there lived a petulant pullet. She was not high in the pecking order, but she did so *much* pecking that over time she had earned herself quite a reputation. She pecked the other pullets. She pecked the hens and the bantams. She even pecked the old Rooster who liked to perch on the chopping-block, and because she was such a young pullet, highly-strung and temperamental, the others seldom pecked her back, believing that she might someday outgrow her petulance.

As a result of this, the petulant Pullet grew in confidence. She acquired a number of followers among the other pullets. Some of these joined her entourage simply in order to avoid being pecked. Others enjoyed being in a gang and felt there was safety in numbers. They began to go around the farmyard in a tight little feathery group, discussing the other birds in the yard (most often in unflattering terms).

"Oh, look at that old Houdan hen over there," said the petulant Pullet one day. "She thinks she's so much better than us. She thinks she's terribly grand, you know."

At this, the Houdan, who thought no such thing, felt impelled to protest. But the petulant Pullet set up a screech, calling her friends to surround her.

"That hen was going to *peck* me!" she said, fluffing her red feathers. "I could see it in her eyes!"

An elderly Minorca hen, who had witnessed the whole thing, said, "Really, I don't think so. But perhaps you shouldn't have said what you did."

The petulant Pullet screeched again. "That Minorca threatened me! The Houdan sent her after us! Did you hear how she tried to silence me?"

A Norfolk Grey pullet, known for her excitable temperament, distinctly recalled having once heard the Minorca say something very nasty indeed, though she could not recall the details. Another pullet, a Scots Dumpie, remembered that a friend of hers had once been attacked by a Minorca hen and viciously pecked in the eye. A third pullet remembered seeing two hens—who looked suspiciously like the Houdan and the Minorca—talking to a visiting fox.

The petulant Pullet's screeching grew increasingly pitiful. "I thought she was going to kill me!" she cried. "Or send her friend the fox after me! I've never been so afraid in my *life!*"

The other pullets clustered round, protesting their loyalty and love. The petulant Pullet, still shaken, bravely squared up to the Houdan hen, squawking, from behind a line of angry, protective pullets:

"You don't frighten me, Houdan hen! You can't stop my voice from being heard!"

The Houdan hen, who had a kind heart and who didn't want to frighten anyone, took herself to the far side of the yard. The pullets cheered and cackled.

"That's right!" said the petulant Pullet. "We'll teach those uppity hens that this farmyard belongs to *us!* Let them stay on *their* side of the yard. *This* space is *pullet space!*"

After that, the pullets set up a squawk every time any other bird tried to come into "pullet space." When the hens and roosters protested that the farmyard belonged to everyone; or that "pullet space" was the sunniest spot and the closest to the grain-bins, the pullets screeched and protested. And so, for the sake of a quiet barnyard, the hens and bantams kept away from the place where the petulant Pullet held court.

But this made the petulant Pullet worse. Emboldened by her success, she began to discuss all the other birds with her friends, very loudly, and in the most unflattering terms. Predictably, the Houdan and the Minorca hen were often the butt of their comments.

"Look at that Minorca," would say the petulant Pullet in a voice that was clearly audible right across the fields to the piggeries. "I hear she's been at her tricks again, frightening innocent pullets and threatening them with the fox."

"I heard she sometimes wears a fox *skin*," said the Norfolk Grey.

"Well *I* heard from a pullet who actually witnessed it," said the Scots Dumpie, not to be outdone, "that she and the Houdan hen are both *really* foxes, dressed in feathers, only *pretending* to be hens."

"That's ridiculous, and you know it," said the Minorca, pecking the ground.

The petulant Pullet flapped her wings. "I can't believe she's still doing it *now*. Attacking us in our space. Why doesn't she stay in her own space? This space is for pullets only!"

"Hens *out*! Pullets *in*! Hens *out*! Pullets *in*!" chorused the other pullets.

The Minorca hen tried to protest but could not be heard because of the noise.

And so, once more, the other hens tried to keep clear of pullet space. Time passed; soon the henhouse also had a "pullet zone," in which the petulant Pullet and her ever-increasing group held forth in comfort, showering vitriol and abuse on any bird that questioned them, and pecking at those who came too close.

Finally, the other hens simply went to roost elsewhere, leaving the henhouse empty—except for the petulant Pullet, of course, and her gang of hangers-on.

Then one night, an old fox got into the henhouse. He squeezed in through a crack in the door, moving as softly as oiled smoke. He moved along the rows of sleeping pullets and ran his long tongue over his teeth.

The petulant Pullet awoke and found herself gazing into a pair of green eyes.

She started to screech, "*Pullet spa—*"

And then the fox bit off her head.

As it vanished down his throat, the petulant Pullet's erstwhile friends exchanged nervous glances. "Er . . . welcome to pullet space, Mr. Fox," quavered the Scots Dumpie. "We're *tremendous* fans of yours—"

The fox grinned redly and opened his jaws. "Likewise, dear lady, I'm sure," he said.

80

DEAD MAN'S POKER

The Hallowe'en King's favourite game was played with a pack of fifty-two cards. These were like everyday playing-cards, except that every card was black. Every Jack and King and Queen; every heart; every diamond was as black as the Ace of Spades. The suits—all four of which were black—were spades, skulls, grave-stones, and blackhearts. But the rules were simple enough, and the Barefoot Princess and the Engine Driver were very soon ready to start the game.

"But what are the stakes?" said the Princess. "I don't have any money."

The Hallowe'en King turned his living profile toward her and smiled. "Why would you need money here? I'll wager ten years of your life against whatever you choose to ask of me."

The Barefoot Princess and the Engine Driver looked at one another. "All I want is the Lacewing King," she said. "What else would I ask for?"

The Hallowe'en King shrugged. "My dear, it isn't my place to suggest. But if I were you, I would make it worthwhile."

The Princess thought for a moment. This was a test, of course; and she knew that if she failed it, she was lost. But what did the Lord of Death possess, that might be worth ten years of her life? Wealth? Power? Knowledge?

Around her, the honeybees started to hum, urgently and persistently. The Princess waved them away. "Not now. I'm trying to think."

But the bees only buzzed more persistently, and finally, she realized that they were singing their old, old song:

"Long ago, and far away,
Far away and long ago—"

The Barefoot Princess was perplexed. "What are you trying to tell me?" she said. "What must I ask of the Hallowe'en King?"

But the bees would only answer in song, repeating the words she already knew:

"Long ago, and far away,
Far away and long ago.
The Worlds were honeycomb, we know;
The Worlds were honeycomb."

It sounded like a story. But what could stories teach her, here, in the citadel of Death? And then, it struck her. After all, stories were what had brought her here. Stories had nourished her childhood. Stories were how the Lacewing King had tricked the crown from the Spider Queen; a story was how the Hallowe'en King had made himself the Ruler of Death. Perhaps the bees were right, she thought. Perhaps what she needed most was a story—and if so, the Princess knew *exactly* which story she needed. She looked at the Hallowe'en King and smiled straight into his living eye.

"How can I know you're not cheating?" she said.

The Hallowe'en King turned his skeletal face towards her, and said, "Cheating?"

"Well, be fair," said the Barefoot Princess. "Your eyes can see into all the Worlds, and into the hearts and minds of the Folk. How do I know you won't use your powers to see the cards I'm holding?"

The Hallowe'en King gave a low growl. "Is my word not good enough?"

The Barefoot Princess laughed. "Perhaps. But I've heard deviousness runs in the family."

The Hallowe'en King was not displeased. The child was as witty as she was astute. "Very well," he told the Princess. "Be assured, I will play fair." And he took out his dead, all-seeing eye from out of its socket of bone and laid it on the table, where it shone like a piece of amber.

"But what shall be my stake?" he said. "Wealth? The knowledge of ancients? The dying whisper of a man who learnt the secrets of the stars, but never lived to tell them?"

"A story," said the Barefoot Princess. "*Your* story. That is all I ask."

The Hallowe'en King gave a frown. "What kind of a stake is that?" he said.

But the Princess just smiled and dealt the cards. "Shall we play, Your Majesty? Remember, my time is running out. The Night Train must not leave without me."

"Very well," said the Hallowe'en King. "Let us play, then. And don't be afraid. Time works differently in Hel. Your train is far from ready to leave."

And so the three began to play a hand of Dead Man's Poker. The Engine Driver was the first to deal. Then the three players looked down at their cards.

"Well? Will you wager?" said the King. "Ten years of your life for a tale?"

The Barefoot Princess smiled. "I will."

"Then I will, too," said the Driver.

The Hallowe'en King shrugged. "As you wish. Now let me see your cards," he said.

The Barefoot Princess had three blackhearts. The Engine Driver had a pair of Queens. But the Hallowe'en King had a full dark house, and so he claimed the victory. With a wave of his skeletal hand, he prepared to collect his prize.

"Your Majesty, wait," said the Barefoot Princess. "Surely, ten years is not enough."

The Hallowe'en King raised an eyebrow.

"Double or quits," said the Barefoot Princess. "I'll wager twenty years of my life, Your Majesty, for your story."

The Engine Driver was looking at her—of course, *her* life was also at stake—but she trusted the Barefoot Princess, and would have followed her anywhere.

"Very well," said the Hallowe'en King, and dealt the cards—the Barefoot Princess and the Engine Driver taking care to avoid his skeletal hand.

They looked at the cards. The Engine Driver had a pair of spades and a pair of blackhearts. The Barefoot Princess had a rising flush. But the Hallowe'en King had a Graveyard Flush; five rising cards of the same suit, which made him, once more, the winner.

Once more, he turned to the Barefoot Princess. "You owe me twenty years," he said. "Don't be alarmed; twenty years at my side may not be the nightmare you think it is. I can be kind, when I choose to be. I can even be generous."

The Barefoot Princess looked him in the eye. "One more game," she said evenly. "I'll wager my life—the rest of my life—just to hear your story."

The Hallowe'en King turned away. The living side of his face was smiling.

"Very well," he said. "One more game. If you win, I'll tell you my tale and send you off on the Night Train. But if you lose, you and your friend will stay with me forever."

The Princess dealt. The cards were like ice, but her hands did not tremble. And this time, as she dealt, she glanced—just glanced—into the eye of the Hallowe'en King, which was lying on the table. Not to see his cards, no—that would indeed have been cheating—but to see if she could catch a glimpse of the Driver of the Night Train and know how much time had already elapsed.

And there he was, holding his hour-glass, looking out into the darkness. The sand in the glass was fine as soot and slightly phosphorescent, and the Barefoot Princess could see that almost half of it was already gone. For a moment, she almost allowed her self-control to slip. But she knew that if she did, her advantage would be lost. Instead, she looked down at the cards in her hand and allowed herself a little smile.

"Well?" said the Hallowe'en King. "Will you wager your life on the cards?"

The Engine Driver put down five spades. The Hallowe'en King had a Charnel House—three Kings, and two matching skulls. But the Barefoot Princess had all four aces, and the King of Skulls, which made her the winner.

For a moment the Hallowe'en King stared at the cards as if he couldn't believe he had lost. But then he looked up, and he levelled his most charming smile at the Barefoot Princess.

"Well played, my child," he said. "You win."

In actual fact, he was not displeased. The child was capable, he thought, and would be excellent company. He was far from having given up hope of claiming her—in fact, the card game had only been the first of several schemes whereby he hoped to delay her. If she missed the Night Train, he knew, she would be stranded in Hel for good, and a hundred swarms of bees would not be able to save her. And so he smiled and said to her:

"And now for the story I promised you."

The Barefoot Princess allowed herself a tiny moment of victory. Time was short—even in Hel—and the Driver of the Night Train would not delay forever. But stories take their own time, even the ones that most need to be told, and the Barefoot Princess had a plan.

The Hallowe'en King, however, was in no great hurry to begin. "Will you take a glass of wine to celebrate your victory?" With his living hand, he poured a goblet of wine for the Barefoot Princess, and handed it to her, still smiling. She knew that the touch of his skeletal hand would bind her eternally to his command, and that even a taste of the wine would make her his slave forever.

And so she shook her head and said, "Your Majesty, wine would cloud my thoughts. I want to give all my attention to the story."

The Hallowe'en King said, "I expect nothing more. But will you not take refreshment? Here are the finest fruits in Hel. Pomegranates; sugared grapes; purple figs and pineapples: or if your taste runs to sweeter things, there are candied locusts, honeycomb, ants in ginger syrup—"

"Thank you, no," said the Barefoot Princess. "Your Majesty's words are sweet enough."

The Hallowe'en King raised his goblet to her. "Then I shall tell you my story," he said, and started his tale in the usual way.

"There is a story the bees used to tell . . ."

81

THE LACEWING KING IN DARKNESS

Meanwhile, in darkness, the Lacewing King slept uneasily and dreamed. In this World, his dreams were often the only thing that made sense to him. Now, he dreamed of the Barefoot Princess, playing cards at a table, opposite a one-eyed man with hair the shade of a moth's wing—

Waking, in pain, he seemed on the verge of remembering something. He *knew* that man; he *knew* that girl—and the sudden pain in his heart was infinitely more than that of his blinding. The memory of another place seemed to drift through his consciousness—another place, long ago, far away, where a girl had cut off her own eyelids.

What was her name? He did not know. Perhaps, he thought, he had never known. And yet, he sensed that the story was part of why all this was happening. Passing once more into Dream, he heard a low and somehow familiar song:

"Long ago, and far away,
Far away and long ago—"

Was it a dream? He put out a hand and touched the cloak around him. It was thick and warm, and yet he knew it did not belong to him. And with that, came the memory of another cloak, both soft and warm, that lay across his shoulders and hummed with its own secret melody.

The King sat up. The darkness was dense and full as a beehive with movement. Tiny rustlings from below; sinister creaking from above; the sound of water from far away, and all around, an echo, as of some vast and cavernous space that seemed to go on forever. The bees were in his head, too, buzzing—or were they *stinging*?

He put out a hand and touched the flask the Moth Queen's guards had left him. Because he was thirsty, he opened it and tried a mouthful of what was inside. It was a kind of spirit; sweet and flavoured with green ginger. That, too, evoked a memory; of dragonfly candies, ant cracknel, and pastries filled with wild strawberries and caterpillar marshmallow. And then came more of those memories: a golden chamber of velvet and silk; the scent and feel of ancient books; torchlight shadows in a darkness that was murmurous with bees.

The sweetened spirit stung his mouth, but he felt a little better.

"Where am I?" he said. "*Who* am I?" and, for the first time since the Harlequin's kiss, the words he spoke made sense to him. He raised his fingers to his eyes, and felt the memory of their loss, and his anger and pain were tempered by a sudden sense of wonderment.

Something new was happening—something both dreadful and marvellous. Whether it came from the spirit, the dream, or the distress of what had occurred, the Lacewing King was unable to tell; but somehow, in the darkness, his memory was returning.

82

THE INSECTS' ALLIANCE

In a forest, Worlds away, there was discord among the Silken Folk. Woodlice and termites, cockroaches and ants, battled with the bumblebees, the solitary bees, the moths and mayflies and honeybees, who were themselves at war with the spiders, the earwigs and crane flies and bluebottles, so that the woods were a hive of unrest, where no insect or spider felt safe.

One day, badgers moved into the woods. They were fierce and warlike, and they were always hungry. They ate the eggs of songbirds; they raided the nests of termites and wasps; they even broke into beehives to steal the precious honeycomb. The bees knew they must act quickly. And so they convened a meeting of all the insects—centipedes and cockroaches, shield bugs, greenfly, lacewings, even down to the ladybirds—to discuss the new arrivals.

It was a long and earnest debate. Many of the forest creatures had been enemies in the past. And yet, they were united in their fear of the badgers.

"Together, we have a chance," said the bees. "Let us put aside our differences and form an Insects' Alliance."

And so the Insects' Alliance was formed, and the honeybees led the rest in a plan to drive the enemy from their door. The badgers lived in a sett in the woods. Their young were left there alone, except for one old, half-blind badger who was left there to guard them. An army of insects could surely find a means of luring out the old badger, then attacking the young ones. And if their young were under threat, the adults would surely then leave the woods and move to somewhere safer.

This at least was the theory. The Insects' Alliance set to work.

First, a delegation of bees was to tempt the old badger away from the sett, using the promise of honeycomb. While he was away, a team of Devil's Coach-Horse Beetles would burrow into the sett itself. A specially chosen squadron of Moths would hover over the attack site, ready to give the signal. The newly exposed burrow would be guarded by a team made up of Cockroaches, Wasps, and Hornets. A cricket with an exceptional voice was chosen to deliver the warning: "GO AWAY, OR WE WILL STRIKE!"

It was a very intricate plan. The Honeycomb Queen would have been proud. But the Honeycomb Queen was far away, and the Barefoot Princess was combing the Worlds for a sign of the Lacewing King, and the Glow-Worm Chancellor was old, and cautious in matters of discipline, and over time, the bees had become quarrelsome and disorganized.

The drones complained that the honeycomb they planned to use to lure the badger represented months of hard work. "Why don't you use royal jelly, instead?" they said to the queenlets. "Queenlets never appreciate everything we do for the hive."

The queenlets responded by saying that drones were *supposed* to do the work. "That's the way it has always been," they said.

"So drones don't matter?" said the drones, and in a fit of pique, refused to go ahead with the plan. The queenlets went to the wasps instead, and explained that a complication had arisen.

But the Wasps, too, were experiencing difficulties. Hornets had recently broken into one of their hibernating nests and eaten many wasp larvae. "We refuse an alliance with the hornets," said the Wasp Queen to the honeybees.

Meanwhile, the Cricket had refused to co-operate with the Centipedes—as a gesture of solidarity with the Water-skaters, whose larvae they ate. And the Moths, being creatures of the night, had a historic problem with daytime creatures, like wasps and bees.

The argument between them all became increasingly passionate. So passionate, in fact, that the leader of the badgers heard the commotion and came shambling along to find out what the problem was. The leader of the badgers sat down and listened to the debate for a while.

And then, because he was hungry, he helped himself to some of the delicacies the Alliance had so thoughtfully provided for him.

Between alternate mouthfuls of bee, moth, and wasp, he listened with growing interest to the tale they had to tell—a tale of conflicting values, racial and historic feuds, philosophical differences and elevated principles.

"Funny, that," said the badger, as at last he finished his meal. "They all taste just like insects to me."

83

THREE BUCKETS

A village was ruled by three elders. All three were heads of their family. All three were respected and venerable. All three had their own customs and ways, all three had their own followers. Each felt himself to be the *real* leader, and the other two, subordinate. And yet the three elders lived in peace, in the same little village.

Now in the village, there was a well, which served all three of the families. The water from the well was clear and sweet and was drawn every day from a plain wooden bucket. One day, the first elder was waiting to drink, when he saw the second elder there, drinking from the bucket.

"Why should I wait in line?" he said. "In future, I shall have my own bucket. It shall be made of silver, as befits my superior rank, and only my people will use it."

And so the first elder had a magnificent silver bucket made, and whenever he needed water, would send one of his people to draw from the well in the silver bucket. "How sweet and clear this water tastes," announced the second elder, "now that I am rid of the inferior wooden vessel."

The third elder, hearing of this, decided that he, too, would have a bucket of his own. "But mine will be made of gold," he announced. "As befits my seniority."

And so the third elder commissioned a magnificent golden vessel, to be used only by his people. It was very splendid indeed, and the other two elders watched him with barely concealed envy.

"In this golden vessel of mine, water tastes like sparkling champagne," said the third elder. "How anyone could bear to use anything less, I do not know."

For some time, the elders went on, watching each other with varying degrees of envy, complacency, and contempt. The elder still using the original bucket remained steadfast, saying:

"I keep to the old traditions. That makes me the superior man."

The elder with the silver bucket replied by saying, "I have refined the well water. In my superior vessel, it tastes infinitely purer."

The elder with the golden bucket smiled and said, "But nothing beats the purity of water drawn from a golden cup."

Time passed. Resentment grew between the three elders and their families. They moved to the furthest corners of the village and took every precaution never to meet. But their servants still met by the well, as they came every morning to fetch the water, and their hostility increased.

Time passed. Such a long time, in fact, that the elders barely remembered why they felt such resentment against each other. The families lived far apart and told dreadful stories about each other: how the people of the wooden bucket lived like pigs in squalor and filth; how those of the golden bucket lived in decadence and debauchery. In fact, they lived very similar lives, in very similar houses, and all of them drank the same water from the same well in the village.

Then, one summer, the well began to show signs of running dry. The water was no longer clear; it tasted foul and brackish.

The people of the golden bucket blamed those of the silver bucket. "What have you done to the water?" they cried.

The people of the silver bucket indignantly denied this. "Obviously, the people of the wooden bucket have maliciously tainted the water," they said.

The folk of the wooden bucket were angry at these accusations. "We were the first at the well," they said. "What right have these others to accuse us?"

Tensions rose. The three families became more hostile than ever. The folk of the golden bucket said, "Why do we tolerate these people, living so close to our boundaries? Why do we share our precious well with those who taint our water?"

The summer grew hot. The water ran dry. Only mud was left in the well, and the families had to send people out to the river for water. The river was far beyond the borders of the village, through a forest of bandits and wild wolves and bears. There were several casualties. The three rival factions at once assumed that one of the others had murdered their folk, and the tensions between them mounted still more. Between the drought, the bandits, the wolves, and the tensions within the village, they found it increasingly hard to survive.

Then a stranger came to the village, from a long, long way away. A warrior, on a mechanical horse, and carrying a crossbow. A clockwork tiger followed her, watching them from golden eyes.

The elders of the village explained their predicament to her. Each one, of course, blamed the others for the state of the well, and explained about the three buckets. Each one begged the stranger to help, and to rid them of their enemies.

"*We* were the first. You should support *us*," said the one with the wooden bucket.

"But we are clearly superior," said the one with the silver bucket.

"Silver is nothing, compared with gold," said the one with the golden bucket.

The woman, who had travelled far, and had seen many strange things, was puzzled. "You've been enemies all this time for the sake of three *buckets*?" she said.

The elders nodded.

The stranger laughed. "I can help you," she said. "Give me the buckets of silver and gold, and I will give you my expertise."

The elders looked in wonder at the stranger's marvellous mechanical horse, her crossbow and her tiger. Surely, with her help, each one thought, they could be free of their enemies. And so the warring elders gave up their gold and silver vessels, and the stranger put them into her pack, which was already stuffed with treasure. Then, from out of her pack, she brought out three large and irregular parcels.

Handing one each to the elders, she said, "Open these when I am gone. Take care to use them as befits your status."

The elders did as she had commanded. Each one was sure that his gift would be something that would reflect his superiority over the rest. But on opening the packages, all three elders found themselves holding a simple wooden spade.

The third package came with a note inside. The elders crowded to read it.

"But what does it mean?" they said. "Is it in code? Surely, this arcane motto must contain some secret wisdom?"

For hours, they pondered the message. It was only nine words long. They looked at each other wordlessly. Then, they looked back at the wooden spades in their old and wizened hands. Then, they read the message again. Nine words, and yet it seemed to them to contain all the secrets of the Worlds. Then they looked back at each other, as slowly, they started to understand. The message said:

DIG A NEW WELL.
YOU CAN KEEP THE BUCKET.

84

THE LABYRINTH
OF FORGOTTEN THINGS

Memory, or so say the bees, is one of the tributaries of Dream. Its waters are almost as magical—as magical, and as dangerous. In Memory, Death has no foothold; and even Dream is a distant haze, like smoke upon the water. The Lacewing King had lived between the Worlds of Dream and Insanity ever since the Harlequin had looked into his eyes; but now, blind, his memory returned, and with it, his sense of purpose.

There is a story among the Folk about a labyrinth of lost things. Far under the ground it lay, buried beneath the many layers of an ancient city. Many centuries had passed since that city's founding. Many times had it been rebuilt, and as many times, lain in ruins. Now, as the city soared above, all glass and stone and concrete, the city *beneath* stretched in darkness, ten times vaster and more powerful than any city of the Folk or stronghold in the Nine Worlds.

Here it was that the lost things, the forgotten things, the broken things, all found their way to where they belonged. Toys that children had put aside; love letters from folk long dead; unfinished novels; unwanted pets; wedding bouquets under glass; old sepia photographs; pieces of bad taxidermy; terrible family recipes. Then there were the people: soldiers from forgotten wars; sellers

of dubious magic; purveyors of antiquated cures; priests of long-dead religions. Here were submerged cathedrals, and fallen stars, and vanquished kings, and all the lost and forgotten things that can lead a man to Damnation.

Here, too, were the passions of childhood; the rocket-shaped beds and the wooden swords, and the jewel-cases filled with glass, in which tiny plastic ballerinas danced to a tinkling melody. Here were presents still in their packaging, and streets of houses lost in fog, and bright ideas that never bore fruit, and promises made to be broken. All hidden away in this cavernous space, lit by stray phosphorescence, with the ghosts of long-ago campfires illuminating the towering walls, and the discarded folk around them, warming their hands, and drinking beer, and searching through the Forgotten things, and playing Dead Man's Poker.

But The Labyrinth of Forgotten Things was not a place of sadness. For some, it was the only place where they could find acceptance. Down among the forgotten things, no one was ever unwanted; no one ever was turned away. Outcasts found their way down here to a different kind of life; the broken came to be mended; the unloved, to search for love. And many of them found it—for here, nothing was impossible. One man's trash can sometimes be another person's heart's desire. And so the folk of the city below lived more happily than most of the Folk who dwelt on the surface.

It was here that the Lacewing King, blind and abandoned by everyone, rediscovered his memory, broken piece by broken piece—although what good was memory, when all that remained to him was regret? And yet, he was himself again, after a long estrangement, and it felt good to know who he was, and to feel his strength returning.

He drank a little more of the sweetened spirit in the flask. Then he sat up and carefully began to explore his surroundings. He found that he was in a kind of narrow corridor, the walls of which were made of all kinds of disparate objects, all stacked on top of each other. With his fingers, he could feel the spines of books; the edges of cardboard boxes. He felt his way along to the end of the narrow passage, which then opened up into a broader space, too large for him to touch the walls.

For a moment he stood uncertainly, hands outstretched in front of him. Then, in the darkness, he heard a voice; harsh, and somehow familiar.

"Your Majesty, welcome," said the voice.

"Who are you?" said the Lacewing King. "How is it that you know me, when I barely know myself?"

There came a croak of laughter. "I've followed you across the Worlds. Others may have forgotten you, but even here, I remember."

"Who are you?" said the Lacewing King.

"A friend," replied the voice, and the King heard the sound of beating wings, and felt something land on his shoulder. Sharp claws dug into his flesh: soft feathers brushed his face. "I am the one who remembers. I am the only one you can trust. All the others are dead: your friends; your courtiers, and your family. Only I remain, as I was right at the beginning." And now the creature started to sing the ancient song of the honeybees, and the Lacewing King would have wept, if he could, at the familiar melody. Instead, he simply sighed and said:

"My mother?"

"Dead," said the harsh-voiced bird.

"My people?"

"Also dead," said the bird.

"And the Barefoot Princess?"

"Dead; wandering the plains of Hel. All of them dead; their names unknown, forgotten, except in stories. And when you join them—which will be soon—even those stories will be gone, washed away, like footprints on the seashore."

The Lacewing King gave another sigh and sat down on the dusty floor. The joy of regaining his memory had given way once more to despair. Why had he survived so long? What use was his life to him now, if everyone he cared for was gone? A dry sob racked his body; he raised his voice in an anguished cry, and his heart—the cold and cruel heart that had survived intact for so long—was finally, fatally broken. He sank to his knees on the ground and wept, and genuinely wished for Death. And at that moment, his Aspect shattered into a million pieces. A million stuttering fireflies scattered like fireworks into the air; scrawling his grief in letters of fire across the Labyrinth of Forgotten Things.

From the heart of the Labyrinth, people saw the fireflies, rising like stars into the sky. Mostly, they ignored them. The people of the Labyrinth were used to unusual happenings. But one man saw the trail of stars and felt his heart quicken abruptly. He turned to the woman at his side—a woman of marvellous beauty, with a face unlined by Time, although she was many centuries old—and said:

"At last. We've found him."

85

THE STORY OF
THE HALLOWE'EN KING

There is a story the bees used to tell," said the Hallowe'en King to the Barefoot Princess. "But mine is *not* that story. This is a story not even the bees have ever had the chance to tell, and that is because I have never told anyone—not my wife, nor my infant son—the tale that you are about to hear."

The Barefoot Princess smiled and tried not to let her anxiety show. Time works strangely in Hel, and although she knew that the hour had not yet passed, she also sensed that the Hallowe'en King was trying to trick her into missing the Train. But there is a power in stories. Power to cross into other Worlds; power to live alternate lives; power even to raise the dead. And so she listened to the tale, as, far across the plains of Hel, the Driver of the Night Train checked the sand in his hour-glass and looked out into the darkness.

"Far away, among the Folk, there lived a boy unlike the rest. A foundling, brought up by the Folk, and yet not of their people. Handsome, with hair like a moth's wing, the boy was ambitious from the start, and though his parents were humble folk, he knew that he was born to be King. His mother indulged these fantasies, but they annoyed his father, an honest, dull, hard-working man, who did not believe in Destiny.

" 'The boy needs to learn a trade,' he said. 'What use is he otherwise?'

"But the mother, who doted on the boy, said, 'He was always different. Why should my boy soil his hands with work when he was born for greatness?'

"The father sighed and shook his head. 'That boy was born for nothing good,' he warned. 'He'll come to a bad end, mark my words.'

"The boy grew into a handsome young man, but he was never popular. Folk found him proud and arrogant, and women mocked his ambitions. But the man who would be King was unmoved by their ridicule. He knew he was different from the rest: he knew he had a destiny. And so, one day, he decided to leave his home and set off for great adventures.

"His father was happy to see him go; but his mother wept bitterly.

" 'Before you leave,' she told him, 'there is something I must tell you. It is the story of how we came to adopt you.' "

At this point, the Barefoot Princess glanced into the eye of the Hallowe'en King, still lying on the table. Through the gleaming lens, she saw the Driver of the Night Train looking into his hourglass. The phosphorescent sand was now more than three-quarters gone.

"May I remind His Majesty," she said to the Hallowe'en King, "that he promised to return me to the Night Train within the hour?"

Thoughtfully, the Hallowe'en King poured wine into his goblet. "A story takes its time," he said. "But I will keep my promise." He took a mouthful of the wine, smiled, and went on with his tale.

" 'It was a cold, midwinter's night,' said the mother, remembering. 'Your father and I were by the fire, when there came a knock at the door. Opening the door, I saw a child—a boy, no more than three years old—standing outside in the snow. That boy was you,' he told her son, 'and I loved you straightaway.'

"Continuing her tale, she described the boy she had brought in from the snow. He was beautiful, she said; dressed in rich, unfamiliar clothes. One of his eyes was butterfly-blue; the other as dark as honeycomb. And around his neck, on a golden chain, there was a golden pendant, on which there was an inscription so small that even if she had known how to read, she could not have fathomed it. But the strangest thing about him was that there was not a single footprint in the snow behind him, or any sign to indicate how he had come to be at her door.

"She wrapped the boy in a sheepskin cloak and gave him tea from a china cup. He smiled at her, but when she asked him where he had come from, and who he was, all he would do was sing this song:

"*'Long ago, and far away,*
Long ago and far away.
The world was honeycomb, they say;
The world was honeycomb.'

"And for a long, long time, those words were all the boy seemed able to say. But as the weeks and months went by, he began to talk at last, although he never explained how he had come to be where he was. Nor did he seem to remember anything about his previous life, except that little fragment of rhyme, and the knowledge that he was born to be King.

"Now the mother reached into her pocket and brought out a golden pendant, inscribed in tiny, delicate script. 'Your father sold the chain,' she said. 'But I kept the pendant. It's yours.'

"The son, who had listened with interest to his mother's story, took the pendant and, narrowing his eyes, read the words. He had no idea of what it was, or memory or who he had been, but he must have known, even then, that it held the key to his memories. The inscription read:

"*Dream is a river that runs through Nine Worlds, and Death is only one of them.*

"The young man pondered the words for a while, but they brought back no memories. Nevertheless, he kept the pendant and wore it around his neck, hoping that one day, he would meet someone who could explain the inscription to him.

"For three years the young man travelled the Worlds. He made his fortune playing cards, and lost it again at chequers. He crossed over nine oceans. But though he saw many marvellous things, he was still unsatisfied. He knew that he was born to be King, and until his ambition had been achieved, his quest could never be at an end.

"One day, the young man found himself at the edge of a forest. It was a green and magical place, and the young man was drawn to its beauty. He followed a path into the woods until he came to a clearing. There, he sat with his back to a tree, and went to sleep in the sunshine. When we awoke, he found himself looking up at a woman of marvellous beauty. It was the Honeycomb Queen, of course: and the forest was her domain. The young man was astonished. He felt as if he had been blind all his life, and that she had restored his sight.

"And with his sight, came a memory of a time when he had lived somewhere else, in a place not unlike this one. He remembered a forest of silver trees, with a canopy of rich green leaves. And in the canopy, butterflies; and under the canopy, moths of all kinds, brushing the air with their feathery wings.

"The Honeycomb Queen looked down at him. She had been watching him for some time. Even without the pendant that was hanging around his neck, she knew him for one of the Silken Folk, and longed to know more about him.

"'Who are you?' she said. 'Where are you from?'

"But the young man could only tell her the story his mother had told him; of how she had found him in the snow, and of his continuing certainty that he was destined to be King."

At this point, the Barefoot Princess, still listening attentively, stole another glance into the all-seeing eye of the Hallowe'en King.

Through it, she saw the Driver of the Night Train with his hour-glass. Only a trickle of sand remained, shining pale in the darkness.

"Your Majesty, the Night Train," she said.

The Hallowe'en King looked at her keenly from his living eye. "My story is not yet finished," he said. "And as you know, these things take time."

By now, the Princess was beginning to think that the story would *never* be finished. Like the World Serpent, tail in its mouth, the Hallowe'en King's story would grow to fill the Nine Worlds, and still it would never quite come to an end. But around her, the bees continued their song, urging her to listen.

"I'm sorry, Your Majesty," she said. "I know you would not break your word. Please, tell me the rest of the story. Did the young man marry the Queen? Did he ever get to be King?"

The Hallowe'en King smiled. "Oh, yes. He did. The Honey-comb Queen fell in love with him, and gave him, as her token, a tiny crystal vial containing the last of the nectar of dreams, brought by the bees from the shore of Dream; precious beyond understanding. And he gave her his heart, his soul, for Love is also a river that runs through Nine Worlds of enchantment."

The King paused for a moment. To the Barefoot Princess, it almost seemed as if a tear gleamed in his living eye.

"And yes, he did become King," he went on. "But he became King of the Land of Death; ruling alone, and in bitterness. And the son in whom he had placed his hope grew up to be just like him—cold, treacherous, and arrogant. And he never saw his Queen again, except as the stars look down at the earth; from a great height, and with frozen hearts."

"Oh," said the Barefoot Princess. "Is that the end of the story?"

The Hallowe'en King smiled. "Not quite," he said. "There was a girl, a lovely girl, like summertime and honeycomb. She was the last of the Silken Folk, although her eyes had never known the nectar of the flower of dreams. But she had dreams enough of her own, and courage enough to fill Nine Worlds."

And at these words, the Hallowe'en King reached inside his silken shirt and brought out a crystal vial.

"This should have gone to my son," he said, handing it to the Barefoot Princess. "Now I want you to have it instead. A drop in the eyes will show you the Nine Worlds as they really are. A single droplet on the tongue, and you will know what the honeybees know; the darkest mysteries of Dream. Take it, drink, and know what I know—"

And at those words, the Hallowe'en King offered the nectar to the Princess, who opened her mouth to receive it, forgetting, in her eagerness, the rule of never eating or drinking in Hel—

The Engine Driver saw the danger in time. She reached out her hand to take the vial before the Barefoot Princess could drink. But as she did, her fingers touched the skeletal hand of the Hallowe'en King—

The Barefoot Princess gave a cry of dismay. But it was too late—the damage was done. Death's touch is irreversible. The Engine Driver was bound to stay forever in the Kingdom of Hel—unless she could somehow outrun Death and catch a seat on the Night Train.

For a moment, the Barefoot Princess was frozen with uncertainty. And then, almost without thinking, she reached out and snatched the amber eye of the Hallowe'en King from where it lay on the table.

The King was taken unawares. He saw the ruse—a moment too late—but the Barefoot Princess had already fled, taking the Engine Driver by the hand, and together, they ran as fast as they could, out of the bone-white citadel and onto the dusty plains of Hel.

The King called after them in rage, but without his all-seeing amber eye, he could not tell where they had gone. Hel is dark, and clouded with the sand and dust and smoke of the dead. But through the eye of the Hallowe'en King, the Barefoot Princess could see her way, and together, she and the Engine Driver ran for the railway station, where the Night Train was waiting to take them.

But as they reached the station, they found the Night Train abandoned. No driver sat at the controls; there were no passengers aboard. The Driver's cap lay on the platform, already gathering dust. Next to it, the hour-glass gave up its last few luminous grains of sand.

The Barefoot Princess and the Engine Driver looked at each other, bewildered.

"What's happened?" said the Princess. "Where is the Driver? The passengers?"

Then the Princess understood. The Hallowe'en King had made two promises to her—promises he had sworn to keep. One was to send her back to the station in time to catch the Night Train. The other was to release the Driver and his passengers from their perpetual journey. And now she realized why the King had not pursued them further. With no Driver, the Night Train could never leave the station.

Their way out of Hel was cut off for good.

86

THE WATCHMAN

The Clockwork Princess and the watchmaker's boy had travelled far across the Worlds. They had repaid their debt to the Lacewing King—banished by the Spider Queen to an unknown, unreachable place—and yet, they never gave up hope of finding him again one day.

The watchmaker's boy became a man. He took on the trade of his master. A skilled watchmaker can earn his trade almost anywhere, and the craftsman and his strange bride became known throughout the land. But nowhere on their travels did they hear any more news of the Lacewing King. It was as if he had been erased completely from the face of that World—erased, and then forgotten. But they did not forget him, or the Barefoot Princess, who had followed him so bravely through the funnel web of the Spider Queen.

One day, in a city of many clocks, they met a fellow-traveller. A woman—not beautiful, no longer young, but vivid, bright, and fearless—who travelled with a mechanical horse and a clockwork tiger with amber eyes. She noticed the Clockwork Princess at once, and was struck, both by her marvellous craftsmanship, and by the ingenious way in which her face and her broken arm had been repaired in mother-of-pearl.

"How did this come to happen?" she said.

The Watchmaker told her the story of how the Lacewing King had saved them, and of how the riverbed creatures had mended her as best they could. But the Princess was not as once she had been. Scars of livid mother-of-pearl disfigured the porcelain features. One eye was still crazed and sunken; one arm was bent and unable to flex; and although this did not affect the Watchmaker's love for her, he was sorry that he did not have sufficient skill to make her whole.

The rider of the mechanical horse had only once seen such craftsmanship as that of the Clockwork Princess. Long ago and far away, and yet she remembered enough of her skills to understand what needed to be done.

"I can mend her," she told the pair. And so she did, in porcelain, and also restored the Princess's hair with strands of hand-spun golden thread, and took out and reset her eye, so that she was once more as beautiful as she had been in the days of her reign.

But the Princess and the Watchmaker soon found that this beauty was dangerous. Folk who had never noticed the Clockwork Princess in her headscarf and rags now gazed at her with covetous eyes. Twice she was kidnapped by pirates, hoping to sell her across the Sea, and only the perseverance and courage of the Watchmaker and his new friend were able to secure her release.

The Clockwork Princess once more took to veiling her face, like the Sand People. But that, too, attracted attention. The Sand People were not greatly loved in that part of the Worlds, and many folk flung insults at the pair—insults, and sometimes even stones. They even considered crossing the Sea and going to join the Sand People—but clockwork and sand are enemies, and the Watchmaker feared for his Princess's life. The woman with the mechanical horse travelled with them awhile, and while she was there, she kept them safe. But she grew increasingly restless; and soon the Watchmaker understood that she was eager to move on.

"If only we could find a place where folk would leave us in peace," he said. "Surely there must be *somewhere*."

"Somewhere," said the Clockwork Princess in her wistful, rusty voice. And she slipped her porcelain hand into the hand of the Watchmaker and laid her head on his shoulder. "*Somewhere*," said the Princess again, and from the depths of her mechanism, there came a sound like weeping.

The rider of the mechanical horse, who had never cared about acceptance or community, did not understand their desire to flee. Her way was to fight, not hide. But her two friends were not fighters. Outcasts from their own world; their love unrecognized by the Folk, they needed to find a place of their own; a place where they could be happy.

"There is a place," said the woman at last to her two companions. "A place of which I've sometimes heard, where people go to escape the world."

And so the woman told the pair about the Labyrinth of Forgotten Things. A place where the lost and forgotten could find shelter from the world outside. Rumours of it abounded, but the rider of the mechanical horse had never met anyone who claimed to have actually seen the Labyrinth, or knew where they could find it. And yet it was real, she was sure of it; not least because she'd heard of it so many times in stories.

And so the Watchmaker and the Clockwork Princess set off in search of the Labyrinth. They began by scouring the city streets and following the beggars that no one saw; they went into asylums; hospitals for the old and confused; they searched prisons and leper colonies and refuse tips and disused mines. They spoke to the poor and the lonely, the displaced and the homeless, until at last, after many years, they found their way into the Labyrinth of Forgotten Things. And there, among the broken things, the lovers found their sanctuary; and lived together in peace and joy for many uneventful years.

But they never forgot the Lacewing King, or gave up hope of finding him. And because the folk of the Labyrinth had no need of watches or clocks, the Watchmaker gave up his trade and simply became the Watchman; watching the Labyrinth day by day for any sign of the Lacewing King—a broken button, a bee's wing, even a cloud of fireflies—

87

THE EMPRESS'S NEW DRESS

An Empress once commissioned a dress from a famous cou-
turier. It was made of the finest silks, and trimmed with the
most exquisite lace, and embroidered all over with seed-pearls and
rosettes of grosgrain ribbon.

The first time the Empress wore it, her courtiers all fell over
themselves to express their admiration. One said, "Its blue is like
the azure of the tropical oceans."

Another said, "Its gold is like the hair upon the heads of the
very angels on high."

A third said, "Gold and azure are mere words. This dress is the
colour of lost dreams; of stardust; of eternity."

The court Poet, who found himself in danger of being eclipsed,
said, "*This. Dress. Is . . .*" and assumed an Enigmatic Gaze, as if at
an unusual smell that he was trying to identify.

But the Empress's Fool, who usually had plenty to say, said
nothing.

Finally, the Empress asked him what *he* thought of her beautiful dress. But the Fool was strangely reluctant to speak. Instead, he
capered, and juggled, and danced, and made hilarious work of a
pig's bladder, which he carried on a stick on his shoulder.

The Empress became intrigued, then concerned. "Don't you *like* my dress?" she said.

"Oh, yes," said the Fool. "It's very nice."

The Empress was not appeased by this. "Could it be," she suggested, "that *you* believe that this dress, with its many embellishments, represents the kind of expense that a compassionate ruler such as I should eschew, in favour of helping the poor, or offering aid to the needy?"

The Fool merely shrugged and once more deployed the pig's bladder, to hilarious effect.

"Could it be," said the Empress, "that this dress, in its magnificence, represents the kind of decadence that you, a simple Fool, feel the need to condemn, lampoon, and satirize?"

The Fool shook his head. "Your Majesty, no."

"Then, could it be that you consider this dress inappropriate for a woman of my age and build, and fear that my subjects will whisper at me behind my back, and call me Mutton-dressed-as-Lamb?"

Once more, the Fool shook his head.

"Then what is it?" exclaimed the Empress. "I command you to speak your mind!"

The Fool paused for a long, long time. Then he whispered in her ear, "Your Majesty, the dress is fine—but—*there's a hole in your stocking.*"

88

THE MASTER CHEF

In a far-off land, there was a royal chef of exceptional skill. In the tradition of master chefs, he worked unpaid for His Majesty, except for the scraps and leftovers that he would eat when the day's work was done. As a result, the chef was as lean as the King and his courtiers were fat, and every day he vowed to himself to find better employment.

But the chef loved cooking: it was his life. The royal kitchens were all he knew. They had seen his whole career, from pot-boy to sauce-boy to turnspit, then on to apprentice chef and finally, to his current post as Master of the Kitchens. And his skill with food was unparalleled. His palate was so sensitive that the most subtle of sauces revealed itself to him at once; he knew every aromatic spice; every herb; every seasoning. He could tell the difference between rosemary that had been picked at night and rosemary picked at noontime; he knew every colour of salt, from the pink of the Eastern Isles to the black of the Southern Seas.

His memory was phenomenal: blindfold, he could distinguish between ten thousand different cheeses; and his knowledge of wines extended to every different kind of grape in every vineyard in the Nine Worlds. His skills were a combination of natural talent and training, refined by years of experience and honed to such perfection that newcomers to the King's table would sometimes weep with emotion at the lightness of a soufflé, or swoon at the sight of an iced *pièce montée*, topped with crystallized meadow flowers and bound with spun-sugar spun as fine as a frosted spider's web. And the King himself praised him lavishly, calling him a Nonpareil, and heaping him with compliments.

Of course, the chef was very pleased at this appreciation. But praise did not fill his stomach or pay for his day-to-day living. One night, when his supper of leftover meringues, larks' tongues, and slightly lukewarm vintage champagne had proved even less satisfactory than usual, he dared approach the Royal Treasurer, a very superior personage, and request an increase of his salary.

The Treasurer graciously agreed to meet, over a late supper of tea and *petits fours*, hastily prepared by the chef. She sat at the kitchen table, ate two strawberry tartlets glazed with persimmon jelly, and listened to the chef's complaint.

"But everybody *loves* you here," she said, pouring a cup of pink pepper tea. "I can't think of any place you could go where your services would be more greatly appreciated."

The chef explained that, although he was very grateful, he rather hoped the King might offer some form of financial recompense.

The Royal Treasurer would have laughed, but she had just taken a bite from a chocolate marchpane truffle, and her mouth was rather full.

"Money?" she said, as soon as she could. "But chefs have always worked for love! And you must know how we love you. You've always been so generous. I really don't know what we'd do without you to feed and care for us."

"Well, you *could* pay me," said the chef.

The Treasurer considered this for just long enough to pour another cup of the pink-pepper tea. "I suppose that's one idea," she said. "But really, why does it matter? After all, you sleep here. You have the kitchen to yourself when the pot-boys have gone to bed. You eat the leftovers from the King's own table—"

At this point the chef pointed out that firstly, there was never all that much left over, and that secondly, they were *his* leftovers.

The Royal Treasurer crossed her arms over her generous belly. "I should have expected more gratitude," she told the chef reproachfully. "After all, being the King's Head Chef is a significant honour."

"Yes, but ma'am—" began the chef.

"You are known throughout the land," went on the Royal Treasurer. "We have made you famous; we have given you this chance to rise above the other chefs. *This* was your payment from the King, an honour worth far more than money. Don't you think it's just a little *selfish* of you to ask for more?"

The chef was abashed, but the sign of the Treasurer reaching for yet another *petit four* was enough to stiffen his resolve.

"His Majesty honours me greatly," he said. "But if he were to pay me a modest salary every week, then I could have a house of my own, and food of my own on the table. I could even maybe afford to marry and start a family. I have a little put aside—not half enough, but if only the King—"

"I tell you this in the strictest confidence," said the Treasurer in a whisper. "His Majesty the King is in debt. A man in your humble position may not fully appreciate how much expense a monarch incurs, but the overheads are tremendous. He has to pay for his courtiers; his staff; his pages; his royal retinue. His horses need to be stabled and fed; his aviaries tended; his gardens upkept. If the King were to pay his *chef* as well as paying everyone else, he would most likely go bankrupt, and there wouldn't be a monarchy at all." There were tears in the Treasurer's eyes as she said all this to the chef, and only the prospect of finishing the last of the strawberry tartlets stopped her from breaking down entirely.

"You say you have money set aside?" she said, when the last cake was finished.

"Yes, a little—" said the chef.

"Then would you consider," the Treasurer said, "offering His Majesty a loan?" She finished the dregs of the jasmine tea and dabbed at her lips with a napkin. "After all he has done for you, I think it only fair that you should show him a little gratitude."

The chef was unable to reply. Put this way, it seemed to him that he would indeed be ungrateful if he refused to pay the King. And so he handed his savings to the Royal Treasurer, who thanked him with becoming grace, and praised his generosity.

"I'm sure His Majesty will find a way to show his gratitude."

"Do know when he might—" said the chef.

"But of course, generosity is its own reward," went on the Treasurer, and swept away in a cloud of perfume, leaving the chef still glowing with pride and satisfaction. But lying on his mattress that night, watching the kitchen fire and eating the crumbs from the *petits fours* that the Treasurer had left on her plate, he could not help but think that somehow, the meeting could have gone better.

89

FLIGHT OF THE
BAREFOOT PRINCESS

Meanwhile, on a platform in Hel, the Engine Driver and the Barefoot Princess were standing before the deserted train. No sign of its passengers remained, except perhaps for a shimmer of dust that troubled the air around them. The dead were close; they were everywhere; a million deep in the shifting sands. All around her, the bees, who had followed her during her flight from the Hallowe'en King, buzzed an urgent warning. And from the desert, she could hear the sound of something that shook the ground. It was the voice of the Hallowe'en King, raised in dreadful laughter.

For a moment, the Barefoot Princess looked at the Engine Driver. They did not need the amber eye to know the King was on his way. There was only one chance of escape. The Night Train stood, black and enormous, by the side of the platform, its armour-plated flank as cold as that of some monster of the Deeps, its single headlight dark as Death. If they could only drive the Train as far as the boundaries of Hel . . .

"Why not? It's only a train," said the Engine Driver with a smile.

The Barefoot Princess looked at her. "Then let's try," she told her. "Quick, before he finds us!"

And so they boarded the Night Train and ran towards the engine room. Vacated by its occupant, the place looked more like an animal's lair than the home of an engineer. The Engine Driver took the controls, which looked both primitive and forbidding. But, it was only a train, after all; and as she took her seat and placed her hands on the dashboard and levers, the Engine Driver seemed to feel a strange and vital connection.

"I can make it work," she said. "But the engine needs fuel."

"Fuel?" said the Barefoot Princess. She looked around the engine-room. She had a vague memory of the coals the Night Train burnt; coals that were made from the compressed lives of those who had died unsatisfied; the stories of those who had died unfulfilled. But there was no fuel there; not a single shining coal. The Hallowe'en King had kept his word: every soul aboard the Train had been released into Hel's domain.

"There must be something," said the Princess. Around her, the bees buzzed more urgently. The Hallowe'en King was coming. She looked around wildly, and saw, outside in the passageway, the snack trolley from which the boy from the Night Train had offered them refreshments. A compartment in the side was stuffed with pieces of paper.

"It isn't much," said the Barefoot Princess. "But maybe if we burnt these in the engine's furnace—?"

The Engine Driver shook her head. "A handful of paper isn't enough—" she began, and then she stopped. For every scrap of paper was filled with tiny, painstaking writing. They were the stories written by the boy from the Night Train, stories that he would scatter as they passed through the Worlds of the living.

"*Stories*," said the Engine Driver. "You said the train ran on stories."

"Yes, but—" said the Barefoot Princess.

"So maybe we don't need the souls of the dead. Maybe their stories would be enough."

The Princess's eyes widened. "Perhaps. After all, stories brought us here. Why couldn't stories take us home?"

And so she began to read aloud from the papers in her hand: "*There is a story the bees used to tell . . .*" and slowly, very slowly, the Night Train's engines began to hum and cycle once more into life.

90

THE MAN WHO HAD
EVERYTHING BUT TIME

In another land, far away, there lived a man who had every-thing. He had a great, palatial home; a large and beautiful gar-den; a lovely wife who adored him; and a couple of lively children. He had a wardrobe full of fine clothes, and many pairs of expensive shoes. He had a stable of horses and a hangar filled with sports cars. He had servants; he had wealth. In fact, the man had *everything*—everything but *one* thing. Time.

Some rich men are lazy and soft. But this man was industrious. He owned a great many factories, and ran a great many businesses, and every day, he worked to build up his ever-increasing fortune. But he never seemed to have the time to enjoy his money. Even *counting* it was a chore, and so he employed an accountant to count out the coins in his treasury, and because he was a cautious man, two guards to watch the accountant, in case the man was tempted to steal. But still, he found he had no time. His business took up everything.

"Time is money," he told himself. "How hard can it be to pur-chase more?"

And so he employed more servants, to do all the things that he could not. He found a cook to prepare his meals, and nannies for each of his children. He paid an army of gardeners to care for his beautiful garden, and servants to clean and care for his house. There was a housekeeper to make all the domestic arrangements, a butler to oversee the staff, and even a special sommelier, whose only duty was to look after the wine in his cellar; to turn the bottles and to make sure none of the staff helped themselves. But still there was no time, and the man was forced to hire even more servants.

There were servants to walk his dogs and servants to ride his horses. There were servants to drive his cars and to keep the engines in perfect condition. There were servants to wind his watches; to choose his clothes; and to break in his shoes. But still, for all his money, the man never seemed to have any time.

And so he went to his butler and told him to hire more servants. Now there were servants to manage his days; servants to play with his children; a paid companion for his wife, who was lonely in his absence; and finally, an army of servants to watch over the servants.

One day, on the way home from work, the rich man's car broke down on the road. He immediately sacked his mechanic—the man was clearly incompetent—and sent his driver to fetch help. And while he waited for help to arrive, the man sat by the side of the road, and felt the sunshine on his face, and caught the fleeting scent from the fields and meadows in the distance. It was a strange sensation to be doing nothing; and the man smiled to himself, and shook his head in disbelief, and listened to the sounds of the bees and crickets in the long grass.

After a while, he realized that he was not alone there; a stranger was lying on the grass in the field beside him. The stranger was not a wealthy man; his boots were worn at the soles and his clothes were those of a labourer. And yet he was lying there in the field as if he had all the time in the world.

"What are you doing?" asked the man who had everything but time.

The stranger opened his eyes and sat up. "Nothing," he said. "It's a holiday."

"A holiday?" repeated the man. "And what do you do on a holiday?"

The stranger shrugged. "I do nothing," he said. "I walk my dog; tend my garden. I play with my children. I talk to my wife. And sometimes I just lie in the sun, quietly counting my blessings."

The man who had everything was confused. "I have servants to count things," he said. "And yet, I never have any time." He looked more closely at the stranger, who seemed somewhat familiar. "For whom do you work?" he said at last.

"Sir, I work for *you*," he said. "I'm a worker in one of your factories."

"I see," said the man who had everything.

For a few minutes longer, the two men talked. They spoke of their houses; their families; their gardens; and their working lives. The rich man learnt that the poor man had not a single servant— and yet, he seemed to have the time to do all their jobs as well as his own. He dug his own garden; helped cook his meals; shared the housework with his wife; played with his own children. He even broke in his own boots—although, to be fair, he did not keep horses, or motor-cars, or a wine cellar. Nevertheless, the rich man felt that this was all very suspicious.

Then, the driver re-appeared, bringing with him a second car and a team of mechanics to deal with the broken-down vehicle.

The man who had everything turned to them. "Have this man arrested," he said, pointing at the stranger.

The stranger protested. "Why?" he said.

"Because you are a thief, of course," said the man who had everything. "For years I have employed an army of servants to watch over my business; to look after my house and affairs; to guard my possessions; and manage my time. For years, I have suspected that *someone* was taking advantage of me. And here you are; a man with time—more time than even *my* money could buy—and you expect me to believe that it *isn't* stolen?"

91

APPLES

There once was a famous painter who only painted apples. He painted apples so beautifully that they made the mouth water. He painted them so perfectly that folk could almost smell the scent. Even the birds were taken in, so that he had to work with his windows closed, in case they flew in to peck at the fruit. Everyone wanted a painting by the famous artist; and he was happy to oblige. He painted apples in the spring, small and bursting from the bud. He painted apples in summertime, crisp and green in the sunshine. He painted apples in autumn, rosy and heavy with sweetness. And he painted apples in wintertime; waxy, shrivelled and freckled with dark spots, but bursting at the heart with taste. Every apple was unique; every painting was different; and the artist was proud of his work; respected, happy, and fulfilled.

But the people around him soon became dissatisfied. Why paint nothing but apples, they said, and let his talent go unused? Why not paint pears, or apricots, or cherries, or melons, or peaches, or grapes?

The artist protested that he knew only apples. But so many people demanded a change that he promised to try something new. And so he tried his hand at painting other kinds of fruit:

pomegranates; purple plums; ripe mangoes; pineapples. And all of these things were so perfectly represented on canvas that people came from all over the land, and returned once again hungry for more.

Time passed; and soon folk began to ask for other changes. Surely such a fine painter, they said, should not restrict his art to still-life. They wanted pictures of living things: animals, birds, and butterflies. And so, with some reluctance, the artist set to painting living things: horses caught mid-gallop with the sweat still cooling on their flanks; birds that seemed ready to burst into song; hunting dogs with lolling tongues; cats that almost seemed to purr.

And seeing his work, the people agreed that he was a wonderful artist. "But why do you not paint *people*?" they said. "Surely, the art of portraiture is the noblest art of all!"

And so, once more, after much hesitation, the artist set about painting a great canvas. It was to be the culmination of his life's work; a vast portrait of all his friends, family, and neighbours. He brought all his expertise to the task; lingered over details; fretted over the bloom of a cheek; the waxy gleam of an eyelid. For months he laboured in secret, allowing no one to enter his studio. And when the work was finished, he opened his doors to the eager crowds, and stood by as they came to watch, proudly awaiting their applause.

For a long time, the onlookers stared at the enormous canvas. Here they were, all of them: the artist's friends and family, his neighbours and his countrymen, looking out from the picture-frame like reflections in a mirror. All were stunned into silence as they saw themselves immortalized.

Then a fat woman spoke up, "Your painting gives me a double chin!"

A man who never changed his clothes said, "You've made me look like a beggar!"

A faded beauty stamped her foot. "How dare you make me look so old!"

And a bald man touched the three long hairs pasted over his forehead and said, "You've made me into a laughing-stock! I look nothing like this caricature!"

One by one, the people came to vent their displeasure at the work. The artist protested, filled with dismay: "But all I did was paint what I saw!"

"Well, you saw wrong!" the people replied, and, flinging themselves at the canvas, tore it into a thousand pieces and scattered them to the four winds. The man himself withdrew in haste, lest he suffer the same fate. And when the people had dispersed, he looked out at the carnage, and shrugged.

"Well, *that* went well," he said to himself, and, gathering what was left of his things, went back to painting apples.

92

THE EDITOR

There was a man whose life was dull, and who was very lonely. Every day he awoke to the same drab and repetitive routine. He would get out of bed in his dull house, put on one of his dull grey suits, and take the bus through the dull grey streets to his place of work.

The man was an editor of scientific manuals, and he worked in a dull little office, reading other people's writing. Occasionally he would take his pen and change a bad word to a better one. He would work there all day, stopping only once for lunch, where he always had the same rather dull meal—a single cheese sandwich, a cup of tea, an apple, and a piece of cake—then he would take the bus back home, heat up a frozen dinner, and watch dull television shows for exactly three hours before going to bed.

He had a secretary at work, whose life was as dull and lonely as his own, but it never occurred to him to talk to her. Instead, he dreamed of changing his life and leaving town, and falling in love and seeing the world and having wild adventures. But he had no idea where to start. The daily routine was all he knew.

And then one day, he had an idea. "I will correct my life," he said, "just as I correct my work. I will rename everything dull to something far more interesting."

He looked around for something to change. The first thing he saw was his bed.

"What a dull word is *bed*," he said. "Instead of saying *bed*, I will henceforth say *rocket ship*." And he smiled to himself at the thought of sleeping in a rocket ship, and thought how much more exciting it would sound.

The next day, he decided that, instead of "taking the bus to work," he would "take the space shuttle" to "explore an alien planet." It sounded so much better that way that he smiled to himself all day.

The next day, he decided that instead of "editing," he would "fight aliens," and that his "secretary" would henceforth be known (albeit secretly) as a "beautiful alien temptress." Instead of a cheese sandwich, a cup of tea, an apple, and a slice of cake, his lunch would now consist of "roast suckling-pig with truffles, wine, sugar-frosted Muscat grapes, and Queen of Puddings." These were all the man's favourite things (except for the Queen of Puddings, which was a dessert he had always longed to try but had never quite had the courage to make). Eating his lunch now became a totally new experience, and the beautiful alien temptress was surprised to hear him actually *humming* between mouthfuls of cake.

On the third day, he decided that "watching TV" would henceforth be called "making love." It made things much more exciting.

Time passed. The man was very pleased at all this. His life had changed completely. Every morning he would take the space shuttle to explore an alien planet. He would fight aliens, and sometimes give orders to the alien temptress. He would dine on the most exotic foods. Then he would go home, make love for a few hours, and return to his rocket ship to sleep. It was all very exciting indeed.

"What an adventurous fellow I am!" thought the man. "How others will envy my exciting life!"

And yet, at certain times, alone in his rocket ship at night, he would feel a certain restlessness, a certain darkness of the soul; almost as if, in spite of it all, there might be *something* still missing.

93

DISHES

A couple were happy in marriage; except for one source of contention. The husband refused to let his wife do any of the housework. Unlike so many men who seemed content to sit down to home-cooked meals and leave all the domestic chores to their wives, this man did the washing-up; and mopped the floors, and cleaned the drains, and even made his own food, for he and his wife had different tastes, and her cooking did not appeal to him.

For a time, his wife believed that this was a proof of his devotion to her, and although she sometimes secretly regretted not being able to sweep her own floor, or tidy her cupboards the way she liked, or even weed her own flower-beds, she accepted her husband's demands, believing no harm would come of it.

The other women on her street envied her this easy life. "How lucky you are," they told her, "to have such a caring husband! He treats you like a princess—no, he cherishes you like a Queen!"

But as the years went by, the wife started to doubt her good fortune. Every morning, when she awoke, she would go down to the kitchen to find her husband already there, washing his breakfast dishes. Every night, when she went to bed, she would hear him cleaning the floors.

"Perhaps I could help," she would suggest, but her husband always refused.

"You do it so *badly*," he would say. "Better that I do it myself."

"Then let me cook you a meal," she would say. "Is there something you would like?"

"I'm far too busy to sit down and eat," the husband would reply. "Now be still and stop wasting my time."

And so the wife would stand and watch her husband doing the housework, feeling a little sad, and more than a little helpless. And as the years went by, she began to understand that his insistence on doing the chores was born not of devotion, but from something altogether different. But the more she offered to share in the work, the more bad-tempered he became, complaining if his wife as much as rinsed a teacup in the sink, or washed a pair of socks in the tub, or put away a shirt in his neatly ordered wardrobe.

Time passed, and the husband's attention to detail grew ever more particular. He scrubbed the sinks with a toothbrush. He oiled the floorboards every day, and dusted the shelves, and washed the clothes, and polished all the furniture. He dusted every surface, and banished every speck of dust. He watched his wife with an eagle eye, always alert for the moment when she might drop a crumb on the floor, or spill tea on the carpet. He grew ever more impatient if she tried to intervene, or even to clean up after herself. He often complained of her clumsiness and waved aside her offers of help. And still, all the women on the street continued to envy the woman, and to tell her how lucky she was to have such a hardworking husband.

Time passed. The couple grew old. The husband's ways did not alter. Every time the wife suggested they do something together, the husband would frown and say:

"What time is there for frivolities, when there is work to be done here?"

And so in the spring, when the birds sang, the husband would be scrubbing floors; and when, in autumn, the apples were ripe, he would be sweeping leaves from the porch; and in winter, when the snowdrops grew, he would be shovelling snow from the path, complaining of the work to be done. And as always, the wife stood by and watched, which was all he seemed to want her to do, and stayed out of the way, which was the only way she could please him.

One day, there was a thunderstorm, which tore down the leaves from the neighbouring trees. The husband went out with his sweeping-brush, still angrily complaining. There he was hit by lightning and died. The widow was sincerely heartbroken. But on the day of the funeral, she came home to her empty house and stood in her sunlit kitchen and smiled, and made herself a cup of tea, and started to wash the dishes.

94

THE LACEWING KING
IN THE LABYRINTH

Meanwhile, in another World, the Watchman and the Clockwork Princess had followed the cloud of fireflies to the heart of the Labyrinth, and there they found the Lacewing King, blind and with a broken heart, in the lanes of Forgotten Things. He was not difficult to find. The Labyrinth, like all dark places, was a haven for insects, and all manner of cockroaches, beetles, and moths had been drawn to his presence. His cloak was made of fireflies; his crown, of living centipedes. His throne was a massive termite hill, sculpted into fantastic shapes to incorporate the Forgotten Things that were piled all around him. In fact, he was as regal as once he had been in the days of his former reign—except that he was dying.

Not all those who seek the labyrinth are glad to be forgotten. Some thrive, away from the eyes of the world; some fade into the darkness. The Lacewing King was one of these. Grief had vanquished him at last, and in the glow of the fireflies, his features were already blurred; his fingers almost translucent as he raised them in the dim green light.

A scarlet crow with a jet-black beak was perched upon his shoulder. It was this bird that gave the alarm as the Watchman and the Princess approached.

"*Crawk,*" it said, and the Watchman realized that it spoke in a human voice, harsh and oddly contemptuous. "Your Majesty, we have visitors."

The Lacewing King turned his bandaged face towards the red-and-black bird. "Who?" he said, in a voice that was as faded as the rest of him.

"A clockwork woman," said the bird. "And an old watchmaker."

An air of puzzlement came across the features of the Lacewing King. "A clockwork woman," he repeated. "Yes, I think I remember. But that was all so long ago—"

"*Long ago,*" repeated the bird. "*Long ago, and far away.* These people aren't real, Your Majesty. They only exist in stories and dreams."

The Watchman frowned at the scarlet bird. Something about it seemed familiar. Perhaps the harsh contempt in its voice; perhaps the way in which its eyes seemed to reflect another world. And it was always hungry. As the Watchman approached, he saw the scarlet bird snap up a dozen of the fireflies that hovered around the Lacewing King. The Watchman noticed how the King waned a little more at the loss, as if the creatures were part of him. And maybe they were: his fingertips were fading more than ever now; bleeding luminescence into the semi-darkness.

"I'm no dream," said the Watchman. "I've been waiting all this time. And I would speak with the Lacewing King alone, without interference."

The bird made a clicking sound with its beak. "What do you want? An audience? Look into my eyes, old man. I can show you marvels."

The Watchman kept his distance. At his side, the Clockwork Princess ticked and ground her restless gears. The scarlet crow saw their unease and gave a *crawk* of laughter.

"Seen enough?" it taunted.

"Enough," said the Watchman mildly, "to know that you're the Harlequin."

The bird snapped up another firefly. "Who cares what I *used* to be? Now I am the Eater of Kings. Look into my eyes, old man, and let me take you to the stars."

The Watchman averted his gaze.

"Very wise," said the Harlequin. "Now leave us. His Majesty is fatigued. And I, old man, am *hungry*."

The Watchman hesitated but did not turn. He knew of the Harlequin only through stories; but he knew of its hatred of the King, and its desire for vengeance. Its deadly gaze was powerless now that the Lacewing King was blind, but its appetite remained, endless and insatiable. It had already fed on his life. Soon it would consume him.

"Your Majesty, run," said the Watchman. "The Harlequin will eat you alive."

The Lacewing King gave an absent smile. "The Harlequin's only a story," he said. "Long ago, and far away."

"No, this is *real*," said the Watchman.

"Nothing's real," said the Lacewing King. "The honeycomb is empty."

"Not *quite* empty," said the bird, devouring another firefly. "But vengeance is like honey, my King. So sweet: so rare; so precious." And at that, it turned its scarlet head and began to feed again, as the Watchman and the Clockwork Princess looked on in consternation.

95

DESCENT OF THE NIGHT TRAIN

Meanwhile, the Night Train had started to roll, fired by the power of stories. The Engine Driver was at the controls, while the Barefoot Princess read tale after tale, all the while watching their progress through the eye of the Hallowe'en King.

Their journey was painfully slow at first; but as the train gathered momentum, they soon began to see the desert landscape around them shifting. Sand gave way to scrubland; scrub gave way to forest. For a time they travelled through caverns of ice, then mountains rising out of the sea. Then they were travelling through the sky, moving at the speed of Dream, with the stars shooting all around them and the sound of the engine in their ears.

"More stories!" said the Engine Driver, as the train began to slow down. But the Princess was still watching through the amber eye of the Hallowe'en King.

"I think I see the Lacewing King," she said. "But he looks so far away."

"We're losing speed," said the Driver. "We need more fuel, and quickly, or the Train will fall right out of the sky."

The bees that were clustered around the Princess joined in the Driver's warning.

"*Falling, falling,*" sang the bees. "*Falling into emptiness.*
Lost, forgotten, broken, blind
Dwindling to nothingness."

The Barefoot Princess looked closer into the stolen amber eye.
"That bird, that bird on this shoulder," she said. "Where have I seen
that bird before? A scarlet bird with eyes like knives. In a story, in
a dream?"

"*In a story, in a dream,*"
sang the bees.

The Princess frowned.
"It looks like a cave. Like a
labyrinth. If only I could see
the way, then maybe we could
reach him—"

"More stories!" said the
Engine Driver. "The engines
are failing. We're starting to
fall!"

It was true; the Night
Train was falling from its track
in the sky, its engines grating
and stuttering, fighting the pull
of the ground below. Around
them, the stars wheeled like
acrobats. The ground was still
in darkness.

"Quickly, please!" said the
Driver. "A story—*any* story—"

And so, once more, the
Barefoot Princess began, with
the words: "*There is a story the*
bees used to tell . . ." But she
had read out the last of the
stories left by the Night Train

boy, and somehow, she couldn't seem to remember a single tale that she had read in the Lacewing King's library, or heard from the bees, or gathered from the Sightless Folk.

"I can't *remember!*" she said. "I can't!"

"You must," said the Engine Driver. "How can you run out of stories?"

Wildly, the Princess shook her head. "I can't," she said. "I've forgotten them all!" And then, at the word *forgotten*, she stopped. Her features lit. She started to laugh.

"*Forgotten.* Forgotten! That's it!" she said. "The Labyrinth of Forgotten Things. I've heard the story so many times. *That's* where we'll find the Lacewing King!" She held up the amber eye to hers. "This will show us the way," she said. "And now, for all our sakes, just *drive!*"

By now the Night Train was gathering speed, eerily silent as it began to plummet, unchecked, towards the ground. Vainly, the Engine Driver tried to correct their downward course, and steer towards the Labyrinth. But the controls were dead; and now they could see the ground below, rushing towards them like Death itself.

"What about the bees?" she said. "Can't you ask *them* for a tale?"

But the Barefoot Princess was staring once more into the eye of the Hallowe'en King, seemingly oblivious to the fate that awaited them. And the bees were still humming their little song, louder now, and more urgently.

"*Falling, falling,*" sang the bees. "*Falling into emptiness.*
Lost, forgotten, broken, blind,
Dwindling to nothingness."

The Engine Driver closed her eyes and reached for the hand of the Barefoot Princess. "Know that whatever happens," she said, "I would not give up a moment of the time I spent in your company."

The Barefoot Princess smiled at her. "It isn't over yet," she said. "At last, I know where we have to go."

And, gathering all her courage, she began another story.

96

THE REAPER OF CLOUDS
AND THE SPINNER OF STARS

In a land above the sky, there lived a simple reaper of clouds. Every morning he would go out and harvest great bundles of clouds from the sky-fields. The spinners would then wash them in snow, and comb them free of tangles and curls, ready for the dyers. Finally, the dyers would dip the spun thread in pink and gold and scarlet light, and hang them out in the evening to dry, ready for the sunset.

But the reaper's heart was not in his work. Above him lay a field of stars, cold and sharp and luminous.

He loved to watch the spinners of stars, fixing the constellations in place and setting them on their courses.

"If only I could reach them," he said. "If only I could see their world and live with them among the stars."

But the world of the Star-Folk lay far away, above an icy mountain range which none of his people had ever reached. All the reaper of clouds could do was to observe them from afar, and dream of a life by starlight.

Meanwhile, above him, a spinner of stars was looking down from her lonely peak. Her world was all snow and ice, frozen into fabulous shapes. Giant mechanisms of ice kept the stars moving through the sky; and the snow that ran from the darkened peaks was used to wash the harvested clouds that she could see from her cold, bright perch.

The spinner's job was to fix the stars and to keep them spinning on their course. She found this enormously tedious. The stars were placed so far apart that she never met another soul. She never heard the voices of the other Star-Folk, for even sound was frozen there. But she often looked with longing at the sunny cloud-fields below, and in her cold and frozen heart, wished that she could be there.

And so one day she deserted her post and followed the path of the melting snow down from the high peaks and glaciers, and finally onto the plain of clouds, on which the sun was rising.

For a moment she forgot herself in the joy of that sunrise. Sunrise in the star-fields was nothing much to exclaim about: another star in the galaxy, and not even in her sector. But there in the cloud-lands, the sun was huge; and now came the reapers of clouds with their scythes, laughing and singing as they worked.

But one of the reapers was different. He did not sing, or laugh, or smile.

The spinner of stars approached him. "Why do you look so sad?" she said.

The reaper looked up and saw her there. She was unlike any woman that he'd ever seen before. A woman like the far side of the Moon; a woman dark as the midnight sky. The reaper was half in love with her before he could even ask her name.

"Because I dream of stars," he said. "But who are you, and why are you here?"

The spinner of stars looked back at him. She saw a man like the face of the Moon, with hair as bright as starlight. Her heart—her frozen, icy heart—began to beat like never before. And right there, she, too, fell in love, and took the hand of the reaper of clouds in her frozen fingers.

"I have dreamed of clouds all my life," she said, and told him of her lifelong dream to see the clouds at sunset. "If we could live here together," she said, "then my joy would be endless."

"If I could see the stars with you," he said, "my joy would be complete."

But as the sun reached its zenith and the midday clouds began to rise, the spinner of stars began to feel strange. The sun's warmth was unbearable: its light was suddenly far too bright. Alarmed, she realized the truth. Her frozen heart was melting.

The reaper of clouds saw her collapse and understood what was happening. "You cannot survive in my world," he said. "I must take you back to the star-lands."

And so he carried the spinner of stars back towards the snow-fields. He passed the skirt of a glacier, he laboured up the glassy slopes. By the time they had reached the mountains, he was close to collapsing, although the spinner's strength had returned as she went up the mountainside.

After a while, however, the reaper could go no further. The sun was setting, and now the clouds were pink and gold and scarlet. It was the most magical thing that the spinner of stars had ever seen, and her heart melted a little more, as she watched her first ever sunset.

But soon night fell; the stars came out. So close to the star-fields, their light was so bright that the reaper of clouds could scarcely breathe for joy. But the night had grown colder. The reaper's vision began to fail. His heart beat ever more slowly, and the spinner of stars knew he would die if they went any further.

"Let me take you home," she said, "to the golden cloud-fields."

But the reaper of clouds shook his head. "You'll die if you go back there," he said. "The sun will melt you into rain."

And so they sat there, hand-in-hand, under the brilliant, starry sky. All the stars were spinning now—except for a single square of sky, abandoned by its custodian. The spinner knew that if she did not regain her post, then the stars in her care would fall. But she could not leave the reaper of clouds to die alone in the mountains.

"If you can't reach the stars," she said, "then the stars must come to you."

And together they watched, as one by one, a thousand stars in that sector of sky began to wobble, then to fall.

"How beautiful," said the reaper of clouds, and died, with a wistful smile on his face.

The spinner of stars bowed her head and wept. The heat of her falling tears melted what was left of her frozen heart. She lay beside the reaper, and, smiling a little, closed her eyes. And then she dissolved into fragments of ice that tumbled softly through the clouds, to land as rain on the earth below.

And in another World, a boy waiting for his night-time kiss looked up to the sky and said, "Look, Mother. It's raining stars."

97

THE CAT WHO LOOKED
OUT TO SEA

There once was a cat who looked out to sea. Every day, in all weather, he would sit on a rock by the water's edge and contemplate the ocean. He watched the waves unfurling onto the pebble beach; he felt the salt wind in his fur, and in silence, he observed the mystic movements of the tide.

By night he watched the progress of moonlight on the water and heard the songs of mermaids from his vantage point on the rock. In stormy weather the Cat admired the plumes of spray that clawed the air, and marvelled at the catspaws of wind upon the brindled water. And little by little, the Cat understood that the tides were his personal mystery, and subject to his pleasure.

When he lifted a paw, the sea rose. When he twitched his tail, the tide gracefully subsided. The sirens sang for him alone; and the fish that he glimpsed from his place on the rock were his alone, to rule and command. Every morning, he would walk along the pebble beach and inspect the offerings left for him by the receding water: driftwood; shells and seaweed; shining stones and fallen stars. The royal Cat was magnanimous, viewing the sea's humble offerings with dignified approval.

The other cats all laughed at him, but the Cat who looked out to sea did not dignify their ribaldry with a response. He knew that a mere twitch of his whiskers could summon a storm that would sweep the land and consign those lesser cats to the deep. And so he endured them in silence, certain of his mastery.

One day, the Cat looked out to sea as a terrible storm prepared to break. The mackerel sky grew heavy and dark; the green waves rose like mountains. Rain lashed the pebble beach, and the monsters of the darkest Deeps rose out of the water, livid bellies to the sky.

The Cat who looked out to sea blamed himself. What thoughtless raising of the paw, or ill-considered swish of the tail had caused the ocean to rise in this way? He stood in silence on his rock, hardly daring to move, for fear of bringing disaster onto the world. And as he watched, the terrible storm gradually began to calm. The sea veered from rust-green to blue. The sun returned to its place in the sky.

The Cat was relieved beyond measure. "That was close," he told himself. "My secret power and magnificence almost ended the world."

And then he went back home to dream in his basket by a fire, while above, the Moon smiled down, unseen and unsuspecting.

98

DEAD MAN WALKING

As the Night Train fell like a shooting star towards the Labyrinth of Forgotten Things, the Lacewing King and the Harlequin were once more locked in battle. But this time, the King was fading. The bandage where his eyes had been was the brightest thing about him; and to the Watchman and the Clockwork Princess, he looked like a dead man walking.

"Fight it!" cried the Watchman. "Surely, you won't let the monster win!"

The Lacewing King gave an absent smile. "I lost a long, long time ago."

The Harlequin crowed with approval. "That's right, Your Majesty," it said. "Long ago, and far away. Long ago and far away, like in those lying stories."

The Clockwork Princess, who rarely spoke, said, "*Long. Ago. Far. Away.*"

The King turned his head towards her. "You're the clockwork woman," he said. "I thought you were a dream I had."

"*Long ago,*" said the Clockwork Princess, with a touch more insistence. "*Long ago, and far away.*"

The Harlequin *crawk*-ed. "*There's* wisdom," it said. "Wisdom, from a thing made up of cogs and wires and porcelain." It pecked at another firefly. For a moment its beak was alight with green flame, and the Watchman saw its mandibles. The Harlequin's Aspect might be that of a common bird, but inside, it was all monster—diminished, perhaps, by its fall through the Worlds, but nevertheless, still deadly.

Its dark eyes reflected the Clockwork Princess. "Do you think she loves you?" it said. "Is that the tale you tell yourself?"

"I know it," said the Watchman.

"You foolish old man," the Harlequin said. "When you go into the dark, do you think she'll follow you? She has no soul. Death shuns her. And you have only years, old man. Her time will span the centuries."

"I know that too," said the Watchman. "But that won't change my love. Or hers."

"More stories!" mocked the Harlequin. "You Sightless Folk do love them so. But what power do they really have? Death is the only power here. Death holds all the cards in the game. Death wins every war, every day, steals every moment of happiness. Death's kingdom is everywhere. What need does it have of stories?"

"Long ago and far away," said the Lacewing King in a distant voice, "*you* were a fool for stories."

"What?" said the Harlequin, surprised. Crowing, sure of its victory, it had forgotten for a time that the King was still conscious. Now he smiled again and said:

"I know you now, bird of malchance. You were once the Hallowe'en Queen. You lost your crown to a teller of tales, and your mind for a taste of honeycomb." His voice was still faint, but to the Watchman and the Clockwork Princess, he seemed more lucid than before.

The Harlequin gave an angry *crawk*. "More stories. Who told you that? The bees?"

"Ah, the bees," said the Lacewing King. "The little builders of honeycomb. A million stories; a million worlds all pressed against each other. And the bees are always making more, taking them from World to World, in spite of predators and thieves."

"Then where are they now? These tellers of tales?" The Harlequin's voice was silky with hate. "Do you hear them now, my Lord? Do you see into their worlds of honeycomb?"

The Lacewing King shook his head. "I see nothing. And yet—"

"What's that sound?" said the Watchman. "A sound like that of a swarm of bees—or a river, or a train—"

The sound he could hear was the Night Train, of course. Rushing headlong at the ground faster than the speed of Dream, its engines roaring, its brakes locked fast, the tortured metal shooting showers of sparks into the air. Aboard, the Engine Driver's hands were locked in place at the controls; steam rose from the stacks; and in the air the Barefoot Princess could smell her own hair burning.

And then, with a screeching and howling of brakes, they came to the city of towers and spires, smashing into the ground like a maul and leaving a crater half a mile wide. They tore through the realm of the Moth Queen and into the Labyrinth of Forgotten Things. There, the Train ploughed through half a mile of passageways and corridors, demolishing walls, collapsing ceilings, and then finally stopped, in a choking cloud of smoke and steam and debris.

For a time there was nothing to see but smoke, and dust, and scalding steam, and tumbling piles of Forgotten Things scattered about the Labyrinth. Then finally, as the noise subsided, and the air began to clear, the Watchman and the Clockwork Princess saw the Night Train lying on its side in the rubble amid a giant wreath of scorch-marks. Blowback from the engines had thrown the two occupants clear of the wreck, and the Driver and the Barefoot Princess were lying half-buried under plaster and dust. For a moment they lay without moving. Then the Princess began to stir. Struggling, she managed to clear the choking dust from her nose and eyes, then pulled herself clear of the rubble and reached for the Engine Driver's hand.

The Driver was still motionless. The Princess started to stand up but found that someone was standing in her way. Someone was looking down on her; someone who was dressed in black and crowned in dead man's ivory.

"You've led me a merry dance," said a quiet voice that the Princess knew well. "But now it's time for you to pay your debt to me. In full. In blood."

The Hallowe'en King had found them.

99

DEAD MEN'S SHOES

The Ruler of Hel never leaves his realm. It is one of the oldest laws of the Worlds. Life and Death are a balance so fine that if even, for a second, the gates of Hel are left open, then Death itself has no power, and Pandaemonium beckons. And yet, this is just what had happened. The Hallowe'en King had forsaken his oath in pursuit of the Night Train.

The Barefoot Princess looked up at him. His butterfly-blue, living eye looked back almost with sympathy. The empty socket of his dead eye was as dark as an open grave.

"I suppose you'll be wanting your eye back now," said the Princess, getting up.

"That would be nice," said the Hallowe'en King.

The Princess sighed and looked around for the amber eye in the dust. But it was nowhere to be seen. She must have dropped it during the crash, and now it was lost in the debris. But from the rubble and settling dust, she could see shadows emerging: the Watchman and the Clockwork Princess, both of them dusty but unharmed; and from behind the wreck of the Train as it lay like a dragon on its side, the figure of the Lacewing King, eyes bandaged, ghostly with dust, but regal still in his tattered cloak and with his crown of centipedes.

For a moment the Princess looked at him, unable to speak for the joy in her heart. But the bees, which had accompanied her on her breakneck journey, knew him at once, and swarmed to him, humming:

"Home comes the fisherman
Home comes the bee
Home from the islands
Home from the sea."

Then they settled onto his shoulders, so that soon he was wearing a coat of bees; a coat that was soft as thistledown and as golden as honeycomb.

"Father," said the Barefoot Princess, running to embrace him.

The Lacewing King put his arms around her. "The Harlequin told me you were dead."

"She *is* dead," said the Hallowe'en King with a trace of impatience. "Strictly speaking, you're *all* dead. *You* never survived the train crash, and the Driver was dead already. As for the others—" He paused to pick up something that lay in the dust at his feet. "All of you would have been dead by now, but for a technicality." The Princess looked at the Driver, who was climbing to her feet. The Watchman was frowning in puzzlement. Only the Lacewing King seemed unmoved. Arms around the Barefoot Princess, he felt a strange sensation. He had never felt anything like it before. He guessed it must be happiness.

Then came a voice from the rubble; a voice that was harsh and contemptuous.

"You left your realm. You fool." It was the scarlet bird; the bird that once had been the Harlequin. Now it was almost unrecognizable; its feathers broken and blanched with dust. But its eyes were still as sharp as tacks, and dark: darker than despair. Now it fluttered, awkward and hateful, around the feet of the Hallowe'en King, crowing and scolding angrily:

"The Ruler of Hel never leaves his realm. Didn't I teach you anything?" If Death leaves his post, then Death has no power. The dead and the living walk the Worlds. We're one step away from the End of All Things. And for what? For the sake of a Sightless girl—"

"She stole my train," said the Hallowe'en King.

The Harlequin began to laugh. It was not a pleasant laughter, and it went on for a long, long time. "Your *train?*" it croaked. "She stole your train? *You* stole my crown, my sanity. You're as ridiculous as your son. In fact, you belong together."

"My son?" Until that moment, the Hallowe'en King had failed to notice the blind man. But now, as he looked at the Lacewing King, hand-in-hand with the Barefoot Princess, he saw his own features mirrored there, and was filled with a great curiosity.

Around the Lacewing King's shoulders, the coat of bees still hummed their song:

"Dream is a river that runs to the Sea
To the Sea, to the Sea
Death is a country that longs for the Sun
For the Sun, for the Sun."

"My son," repeated the Hallowe'en King, and took a step towards him. With his one remaining eye, the eye that looked into the hearts of men, he could see all that his son had been, and everything he had become. He had been cruel; heartless; proud. Now he was something different. The Hallowe'en King was inclined to believe that this change was for the better. He took another step forward and smiled, holding out his living hand. In the palm, his amber eye gleamed with a baleful light. "Take it," said the Hallowe'en King. "Take it now. You know what to do."

The Lacewing King took the amber eye, and pulled the bandage from his face. Then, he carefully fitted the eye into his empty right socket. For a moment they saw him, one eye as empty as an open grave, the other as fiercely bright as an owl's, fixed upon the Hallowe'en King.

"I remember you now," he said. "I remember you, Father."

The Hallowe'en King nodded. "Yes. I know."

"You were the Clearwing Prince," went on the Lacewing King in a quiet voice. "You came to our World long ago, through the anger of the Moth King; the fickleness of the Butterfly Queen. You travelled the Worlds; you fell in love; you became the Hallowe'en King, and now you have come full circle; finally, back to your people."

"You can see all that through his eye?" said the Barefoot Princess.

"The Hallowe'en King's amber eye sees into all of the known Worlds. Past and present; great and small. The Kingdom of Death is a honeycomb filled to the brim with stories."

The Hallowe'en King smiled. Side-by-side, they looked very alike. "My son improves with acquaintance," he said. And from his pocket he brought out something that looked like a marble. It was small, and round, and blue, and the Lacewing King and the Barefoot Princess recognized it as an eye.

"This should be yours," he told him. "It is the eye of the midwife who brought you into the world. She stole the nectar of dreams for herself, and so I took her eye away. But it still sees the world of the Silken Folk, and it will serve you well, I think."

The Lacewing King took the blue eye and placed it into his left socket. Now he could see clearly again, and his eyes shone blue and golden as they went from the Barefoot Princess to the King, then back to the Barefoot Princess again. Then, from his pocket, the Hallowe'en King brought out a tiny vial, no larger than the ball of his thumb.

"This, too, should have been yours," he said. "It is the very last of the nectar of dreams, brought from the shores of Dream by the bees, long ago and far away. When you reach your journey's end, take it, my son, and think of us."

The Barefoot Princess was puzzled at this, but the Lacewing King nodded.

The single blue eye of the Hallowe'en King seemed to gleam with unshed tears. "I'm glad you understand," he said. "It was the only way, you know." And then he embraced the Lacewing King, gently touching the face of his son with his skeletal fingers.

For a moment, nothing happened. Then the bees began to sing:

"Death is a country that longs for the past,
Long past, long past.
Dream is a flower that blooms with the Sun
Long gone, long gone."

And at that, both they and the King vanished into the dusty air, leaving no trace of themselves behind, except for the scent of honey.

The Barefoot Princess cried out in dismay. "*No!* What did you *do?*" she said.

"Nothing," said the Hallowe'en King. "My son accepted this willingly."

"Accepted what?" said the Barefoot Princess.

"The crown, of course," said the Hallowe'en King. "The Kingdom of Death needs a ruler. It was the only way, you see."

"What do you mean?" said the Barefoot Princess. "What do you mean, the only way?"

The King—who was now no longer the Hallowe'en King, but something else entirely—looked at her with a smile and said:

"I left my domain as Ruler of Hel to pursue the Night Train. During that time, Hel was open, and Death was at a standstill. That's why you survived the crash: that is why your friends survived. But Death's domain should not be left unguarded. To do so, even for a second, is to risk disastrous consequences, not just to this world, but to *all* Worlds. The only way to avert collapse was for him to take the throne in my place."

"Your place?"

"That's right," said the King. "The Sightless Folk have a term for this. I believe they call it *dead men's shoes*."

And at that, he too melted away into the air of the Labyrinth, becoming a swarm of golden bees that rose like a ribbon of bright smoke, and hummed a song of joy and release, and love, and hate, and stories.

100

HONEYCOMB

And that was how the Lacewing King became Ruler of the Kingdom of Death. Tales of him continued to grow and spread across the Nine Worlds, which of course number as many as there are stories to be told. And the bees stayed with him, always— even in the deserts of Hel—taking their nourishment from Dream; passing from one World to the next as they did from flower to flower. For bees have eyes like honeycomb; made up of thousands of facets; each one reflecting a different world; a different Aspect of story. Or at least, so claimed the bees, in a voice which was that of the Hallowe'en King, which made it hard to disbelieve.

The Lacewing King had not forgotten the words of his royal father. Arriving in the Kingdom of Death, he took out the crystal vial, containing the last of the nectar of dreams, took out the tiny glass stopper and raised the vial to his lips.

It was only a tiny drop of the dreamflower's nectar. But the taste was like sunlight, and true love, and forgiveness, and hope. And, tasting it, the Lacewing King suddenly found that he could see into every World, every dream, every cell of the honeycomb. His blue eye saw the present, the Worlds; the souls and secret hearts of Men; his amber eye, the past, the dead, the river Dream and

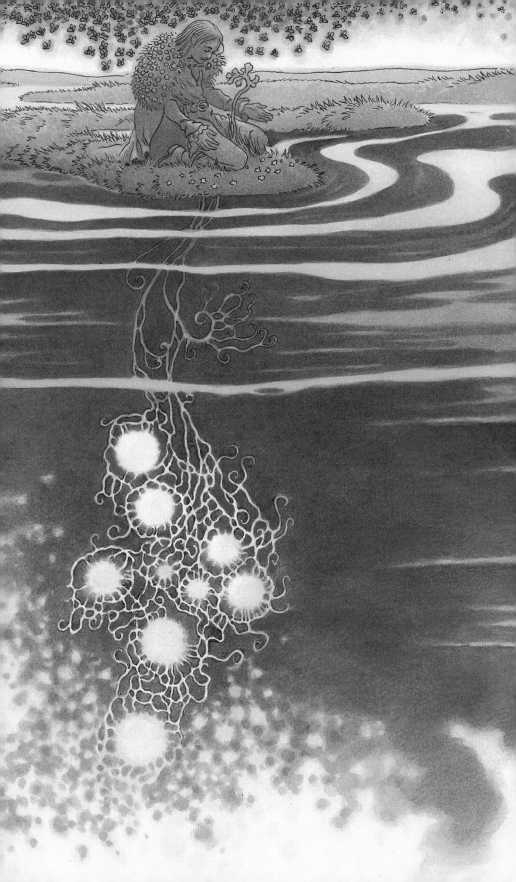

the Kingdom of Hel, infinite in its complexity. And just as he was about to discard the crystal vial, he noticed something left inside—a tiny, luminous, golden speck, no larger than a grain of pollen.

It was a seed, set in honey like an insect in amber. The King knew at once from what flower it came; and he carried it, very carefully, to the shore of the River Dream, and planted the seed in the hard, dry soil, using only his living hand—for the Ruler of Hel has a dreadful gift—and gently patted the soil into place, and silently hoped that something would grow.

And so, in time, the dreamflower bloomed once more on the shores of that river. Its petals were pale as young love; its leaves were like the starry sky; its roots were drenched with the dreams of the Folk; and its scent was like honey and heartbreak. And the bees that had followed the Lacewing King took nourishment from the flower, and carried the pollen home to where *two* Queens of the Silken Folk now ruled the Kingdom together—the Queen that had been the Barefoot Princess, and the brave Engine Driver, who had followed her back from the gates of Hel, and whose loyalty had never failed, not in the darkest of places.

As for the Harlequin, it crawled into the wreck of the Night Train, where it slept, and waking, found that the Train was once more in motion, journeying between the Worlds, ferrying the souls of the dead as yet unready to enter Hel. The Watchman and the Clockwork Princess had seen their opportunity never to be parted again, for Death had no power over her—except as a threat to the man she loved. And so they had boarded the Night Train, and the man who had been a watchmaker's boy repaired and oiled its machineries, and set it on its way again, fuelled by the dying cries of those who have lived their lives in regret, although neither he nor the Clockwork Princess felt any reason to grieve for a world that had never accepted them.

Now the Train had reached cruising speed, flashing between the Worlds like a blade, and all the Harlequin could do was watch, and gnash its mandibles. The creature howled, and threatened, and screamed, and pounded against the engine-room door. But the Night Train ran on such fuel as this, and little by little, the Harlequin, diminished by its rage and by its failure to ruin the Lacewing King, found itself shrinking, first to the size of a blackbird, then that of a hornet, until finally, it had become a single red-and-black spotted ladybird, crawling up the carriage window, bright against the cloudy glass.

The window was open a tiny crack. The Harlequin crept through it. And in time, or so say the bees, it found its way to the shores of Dream and onto the leaves of the dreamflower, where, having come full circle, it died, finally at peace with the Worlds.

The Lacewing—now the Hallowe'en—King watched all this from his royal throne of velvet and dead man's ivory. Then, using only his living hand, he drew his mantle of honeybees a little more closely around his shoulders, and smiled a little to himself as he listened to their old, old song:

"Long ago, and far away,
Far away and long ago.
The Worlds are honeycomb, we know;
The World's our honeycomb."

The End

ACKNOWLEDGMENTS

Ten years ago, I started writing little stories on Twitter. I don't know why I did this, except that Twitter seemed to me to be a place for stories, and because I felt those stories were for *telling*, not for writing. Some stories take life from the fact that they have an audience right there, ready to comment and react, and Twitter gave me that audience. It also gave a context to some of my stories – which seemed at first to be fairy-tales, but which were often also drawn from the world of current events and politics. And as time went by, people began to request more news of their favourite characters, and I began to realize that I was creating something like a new oral tradition: a new medium for folklore. An interlinked series of stories, all set in the same honeycomb multiverse as *The Gospel of Loki* and *Orfeia*, with an overarching storyline about love, magic, the power of story and the quest for redemption.

I would never have done all this without all my friends on Twitter. I know people say things like this all the time, but in this case it is literally true: without my Twitter audience; without their reactions and comments; without Twitter's character limit; without the current events and snippets of information scrolling alongside my narrative, *Honeycomb* could never have happened. In this case, the form and content and feel of the work was shaped by the medium and the audience. Even the idea of collecting these tales, rather than simply sending them out like all the other Twitter ephemera, came from you. Thanks to you, these stories have found their way into print; into illustration; into music, via the Storytime Band. They have their own life now, a life they owe at least in part to you. So thank you, little bluebirds. You make me very happy.

Thank you too to the fabulous Charles Vess, who agreed to be part of this project right at the start, and who has brought his own magic to the table. Thank you to Paul Marshall, Kevin Harris and Matt Cundy, for helping me bring these tales to the stage. Thank you to my wonderful translator, Laura Grandi, who always goes the extra mile; to my editors, Gillian Redfearn and Brendan Durkin; my agent Jon Wood; to Leanne Oliver, Alex Layt and Jennifer Hope; to Nicole Abel; to Joe Monti at Simon & Schuster, and to jacket designer Sue Gent. And of course, as always, to the booksellers, bloggers, Instagrammers and YouTubers who bring so much enthusiasm to these projects, and to whom we owe so much.

And lastly, to you, the reader, thank you for following me this far. We're going on another ride. I hope you enjoy the journey.

CREDITS

Joanne M. Harris and Gollancz would like to thank everyone at Orion who worked on the publication of *Honeycomb* in the UK.

Editorial
Gillian Redfearn
Brendan Durkin

Audio
Paul Stark
Amber Bates

Contracts
Anne Goddard
Paul Bulos
Jake Alderson

Design
Lucie Stericker
Joanna Ridley
Nick May

Editorial Management
Charlie Panayiotou
Jane Hughes

Finance
Jennifer Muchan
Jasdip Nandra
Afeera Ahmed
Elizabeth Beaumont
Sue Baker

Marketing
Jennifer Hope

Production
Nicole Abel
Fiona McIntosh

Publicity
Leanne Oliver
Alex Layt

Sales
Jen Wilson

Esther Waters
Victoria Laws
Rachael Hum
Ellie Kyrke-Smith
Frances Doyle
Georgina Cutler

Operations
Jo Jacobs
Sharon Willis
Lisa Pryde
Lucy Brem